St Gregory

Charles Harlan Boehler

Explore the World of St Gregory

Visit charlesharlanboehler.com for
Advance Copy, Newsletter and Promo.

Kilnsnake Press

Kilnsnakepress.com

Cover designs by Sumiyo.

ISBN 979-8-9879707-1-3

DEDICATION

To my lovely wife ~ for her many years of love and support. And most of all, for putting up with my many years of bullshit.

✠

PART I

Abbey of the Holy Ghost

PART I

Abbey of the Holy Ghost

✠

CHAPTER 1

Far From Home

August 20, 1859

Black waters roiled and churned. Father Ambrose Odenwald stood at the bow of the SS *Teutonia,* gazing into the gloom of the Atlantic. Storm clouds threatened on the horizon as distant thunder rolled, and his robe was wet with salty spray. The Old World of his German homeland lay weeks behind, the New World somewhere ahead. It was a long journey, far from home; one he had never wanted to make.

Everywhere was the smell of grease and coal and smoke, mixed in the briny air. Children ran across deck, their mothers calling them from below, while men smoked idly, passing the time. They stared silently into the abyss of black waters as the smoke pipes bellowed black and the engine thrummed below deck. Who could imagine something so vast? The enormity of it overwhelmed, echoing Ambrose's task. While others had chatted nervously on the long voyage, he had kept to himself—a brooding man in a black cassock, with dark eyes and stubbled cheeks beneath a head of tousled brown hair.

In the graying light, he read the letter from Cardinal Eberhard once more:

It is much to ask, but I form this commission with you in mind. I cannot bear that Bishop Stephan is missing, and I hold myself personally responsible that I could not dissuade him from his desire to save that mad fool Father Valentine. I know of your closeness to Stephan in your youth and his friendship with Christof, your late father. Indeed, how he must have served as a father to you in his own right, after your own passed when you were so young. It is therefore only right that I send you to find him, knowing you would never rest had you not personally exhausted every effort. Find whatever news you can of Stephan, whether he be alive and stranded, missing, or worse. But be cautious— Valentine is quite mad, and I fear what corruption he may seek to sow now that he has fled Mudau under threat of excommunication. Calling for the death of the pope and his own establishment in his stead reflects a frightening and troubled mind...

"Where are you headed, Father?"

Ambrose looked up from the letter. A young man leaned on the gunwale, an ashy cigarette in his yellowed fingers. Heavy air, thick with spray, curled the smoke about his gaunt and haggard face, and his eyes were listless, as dreary as the day.

"I'm seeing about a town," Ambrose replied. "Or rather, a congregation." The priest's voice was soothing. Yet his eyes were guarded.

The man flicked his cigarette into the sea, the red ember snuffed in the waves. "Does this town have a name?"

Ambrose hesitated. What could he tell other than stories written between the lines in letters sent home? A doomsday prophet, a cult, townsfolk dead and missing and his dear friend among them… It all centered around a tiny town in the wilds of the American frontier: St. Gregory.

Ambrose pursed his lips and shook his head. "You wouldn't have heard of it."

The man eyed him, studying Ambrose's narrow cheeks and hawkish nose. He nodded slowly, sniffing in disinterest, and rubbed his greasy head. It was clear the priest was not in the mood to talk. "Probably not," he said and walked away.

Ambrose turned back to the horizon, his thoughts on that distant town. His skin crawled—he had seen the blank faces of those true believers before, in the chapels that dotted the Rothaar Mountains. He had heard Valentine's prophecies of the reckoning to come. The deanery had finally rid itself of the mad priest's perverse influence. Why did Stephan have to leave on some mad quest to save him?

The gray clouds finally parted the morning the American coast rose into view. What at first was a dull green haze on the horizon grew into the outline of masts and ships, followed by a sprawling city on the hill above. A jumble of boats and ramshackle warehouses lined the docks, and everywhere a mix of people massed, such as he had never seen in one place. Ambrose blinked, unbelieving, at the dirty throng. Irish and English and French and Dutch swarmed on ships laden with sugar and spices and coffee, while black- and brown-skinned men from the West Indies—the sugar plantations of the Caribbean—hauled crates of rum. And everywhere, among such wealth, were the poor. A line of men toiled, their burned backs bowed under heavy loads of crates and boxes, while others lay drunk in alleys. Washerwomen and prostitutes swept in and out of the sprawl of squalid, nameless buildings, while everywhere homeless children ran in gangs underfoot.

As the ship neared the wharf, the smell of the harbor rose rank from the churn of the brackish water below, and Ambrose turned and covered his nose. Old crates and barrels bobbed in the black-green waves amid a filth of bottles and sewage and rotting fish. So this is the famous Boston Harbor? It was hard to believe Concord lay so near and just eighty-four years before came the "Shot Heard Round the World"—the start of the American War for Independence, which so shook the European continent with frightening and exhilarating new ideas.

A milieu of wealth and squalor lay before his eyes, and his belly trembled in nervous anticipation. His heart went out to those on board; hope and fear glimmered in the eyes of young and old alike. How must it feel to leave all that one once knew? To set foot on this land, in the press of the horde of so many others like them, knowing they would never return home? Yet their world was not the one he was about to enter. His journey would take him far into the wilds: the distant West, where the great forests blanketed the land and people were few and far between; where natives still roamed free and outlaws terrorized. Would it be like the tales he'd heard in the newspapers and letters from abroad?

The next morning saw him, ticket in hand, at the platform for a train to Buffalo. The smell of coal fire was thick in the air and soot clung to the iron scaffolding as he waited to board. Soon the chug chug of the locomotive pulled the long snaking line of cars out of the bustling downtown and into the outskirts, past the squalor of camps that lined the tracks. The great whistle blasted a mighty bellow of steam as the train roared down the line, threatening all to move, and move quickly. Suddenly Boston fell away, revealing an expanse of green fields and dark forests, where tiny houses and homesteads dotted the land, clustering in small villages. It reminded Ambrose of the hamlets in the hills of Konstanz, and he smiled at the sad nostalgia of his boyhood home.

Two long days had passed. The moon had long since set and Orion crept across the pre-dawn sky, when they arrived in Buffalo. Gas lamps glowed softly, flickering, as moths circled in the warm summer night. Few souls stirred. The city had not yet woken, and none save the unsavory characters of night roamed the black streets. Clutching his money in his pocket, he held fast his bags and waited in the station until the red rays of dawn lit the morning sky. He must have cut a queer figure, a solitary man in black cassock; a priest out at odd hours.

The wharf was but a block away and the honk of geese filled the air as he lugged his bags to the waiting steamer. The tiny shops that lined the street in old red brick gave way to the rough-cut and weathered gray of the warehouses at the docks, and finally the blue immensity of Lake Eerie opened into view. Oil shimmered on the water, purples and blues and reds in the waves, as the steamer the *Plymouth Rock* idled in the bay, its furnace bellowing a black smoke as the engine roared.

Ambrose boarded and sat above deck, looking at the shore and the mass of people that had come to bid farewell to loved ones. Men stood on the docks to watch the rumble and shake of the massive ship, while women in fashionable American dress, gayly colored in bright reds and blues, waved handkerchiefs. They reminded him of his sister, Monika, who had stood on the shore in Le Havre just three weeks ago to see him off on his journey. Her golden hair had sparkled in the sun above cheeks of rosy red; it already seemed a lifetime ago.

Suddenly the deafening horn blasted in the harbor, shattering his reminiscence, and the engines sprang to life, the ship shuddering as it gathered speed, leaving the land behind. With piercing cries, gulls alighted in the air, following the churn and gobbling the dead fish in the ship's wake. Soon they were in open waters.

"Another boat," Ambrose grumbled. The thought of being held captive on the water once again filled him with dread.

Toledo came and went, iron everywhere, spanning the Maumee River and jutting into the bay. Tracks ran like webs from the train station, extending every direction, and Ambrose found himself on a passenger car of the Great Western Railway. The land sped by in a blur of green, while plumes of blue cigar smoke turned lazily in the air, the acrid haze mixing with the musky smell of unwashed bodies in the summer heat. The rhythmic click of the wheels on the tracks lulled Ambrose to sleep as he sat sweating in the hot sun that poured through the window.

"Are you going west, too, Father?" a crackly voice said in a thick Irish accent.

Ambrose opened his eyes to see the pimply face of a boy barely into his teens, sitting across from him. Greasy red hair fell in a mop against his oily forehead as he flashed a yellow smile.

"Yes, to the new State of Wisconsin," Ambrose folded his hands, politely. "Church business. How about you?"

The boy nodded. "Everyone is going west! I'm gonna find me a farm! I just have to save up enough. I might even head to California and see if that gold rush really is played out. There's a fortune for me somewhere and I'm going to find it."

Ambrose looked at the boy's clothes in concern. His old trousers and shirt were torn and patched many times over, and his toes stuck out from holes in his shoes. "How old are you?"

"Thirteen last month!"

"What about your parents?"

The boy shrugged. "Don't know anymore. Told myself that's the last time I'd get a drunken whooping 'cross the backside. My brother Sam left when he was twelve too. It's a big country, but maybe I'll find him someday."

Ambrose frowned. "Do you have any money?"

"Don't reckon I need much. And I'll work, besides. I can hunt and trap. And I can sleep outdoors. There's plenty of places to camp, if you know the signs. Lots of folk hitch a ride on the rails, I heard. I just told the conductor my pa was on the train and if I didn't get aboard, I'd catch hell."

Ambrose dug into his pocket, fishing for change. The silver dollar was worn and smooth in his palm as he extended his hand. He only wished he could do more. The homeless and poor were everywhere. Was it really too much to hope this land would be any different?

The boy's eyes grew wide and his hand trembled. He stared in awe at the silver coin, then pocketed it nervously, lest anyone see. "Thanks, mister!"

A week later, the train from Milwaukee plunged into black woods. The open soil of worked fields ended before a tangle of trees and brambles: the mighty forest of the frontier and the end of Western expansion, so far. Shades of green lay one on top of the other as the untamed wilderness swallowed the rail line that led farther and farther away. Only the occasional station showed any evidence that men lived so far in the middle of nowhere—or at least had lived—for many times Ambrose saw not another living soul, and had it not been for the car filled with dirty and disheveled immigrants, he might have thought himself the last man in all the world.

On and on the journey continued, by train to Fond du Lac and by carriage to Brothertown, until finally a bright and sunny morning found him on an oxcart bound for St. Gregory. It lumbered down a rutted two-track as it plunged deep into virgin forest. Elms and ash and beech and maple blotted out the sun as their thick arms reached to the sky, casting the forest floor in perpetual night. The farther they went, the more uncertain Ambrose felt. How would he find Stephan in a land so vast and dark? Worse, would he become lost like him, unable to find his own way back? His thoughts troubled him, and the strange driver beside made him feel no better. The old fellow spoke little, only laughing at Ambrose's questions or muttering to himself behind a long white beard. But what he said, Ambrose could never tell.

Finally, the sun drew long shadows in the west, trickling in golds and reds through the flittering leaves as they came upon the town. Dirt roads were lined with wattle and daub homes, yellow before the coming dusk. It seemed a proper town, at first glance; they passed the stables, the HOTEL ST. GREGOR, the Post Office—all the normal businesses one would expect. But the town appeared deserted, the clop and creak of the ox and cart the only sounds on the empty road.

"Where is everyone?" Ambrose said.

"Eh?" The man turned and spoke for the first time. "Praying."

Ambrose's skin crawled and he looked about. Here and there, the flicker of drawn curtains revealed pale faces, staring. Somber eyes squinted and followed, making it plain he didn't belong.

When they finally crept to the south of the town, night settled in a sky of reds and purples. The road meandered on, into a shadowed wood that opened into a meadow beyond, where a graveyard lay in the distance. Ambrose looked nervously at the white tops of gravestones; in the dim light, the meadow seemed dead, as if conjured from old children's stories, and he couldn't help but feel he had entered a bewitched land. He swore he felt eyes upon him, as if shadows in the trees followed his passage, and in his mind, he pictured figures with ill intent: the townsfolk, the brothers in the abbey, or the ghosts of the dead in the graveyard nearby. Laughing nervously, he rubbed his eyes. *My mind is getting the better of me!*

The road turned and Valentine's creation came into view. Rough and weathered buildings sat in the long shadow of the wood: the dormitory and rectory and the various outbuildings. And above all, rising from the shadow into the

night sky, was the chapel, its black steeple and cross clear against the gray clouds beyond: the Abbey of the Holy Ghost.

A man in his fifties stood waiting by the door to the rectory, balding and plump, with a jolly smile. His simple brown robes stretched tight across his fat belly and his voice was a rumbling baritone. "Father Ambrose?"

Ambrose hesitated. "Yes."

"Of course!" the man said, extending his hand. "Who else would it be? I'm Father Meinhard. We've been expecting you. But…we were expecting three."

"Father Tobias Schenk and Father Killian Plank. Yes, they were unfortunately delayed. They won't be arriving for another month."

"So you'll be staying with us that long?" Meinhard said. "Wonderful! That will give you plenty of time to become acquainted with our fair town. I understand this is your first time in the Americas. You'll be shocked at all we've accomplished in just five short years. You may even find this place suits you and you'll wish to stay, especially after you've heard the words of Father Valentine."

Ambrose smiled doubtfully. "Tell me, when can I meet with him? I'd like to express my thanks for his hospitality— and of course there are some questions."

"He's on private retreat in the forest," Meinhard said. "I'm afraid you'll have to wait."

"A retreat? Alone?"

"Certainly. He goes when the mood strikes. Sometimes he's gone for weeks. The Lord takes care of him; never you worry. Of course, in his absence, the town and people are at your disposal and you're free to go where you will. But so as long as you stay at the abbey, you'll be expected to adhere to the schedule."

"Of course."

"Ah, one more thing," Meinhard said. "Father Valentine has also graciously asked Dr. Albrecht that you be made aware if anything strange or noteworthy occurs. As nothing ever does occur in our quiet town, this should dispel any of the awful rumors that reach the old country."

Ambrose nodded and looked uneasily at the looming building. "Are you sure there is nothing peculiar about this town?" It was an awkward question and he immediately regretted asking it.

"Are you an investigator?" Meinhard asked, raising one bushy brow. "Or are you rather an inquisitor?"

"Neither. I'm simply looking for someone. Someone dear to me, who's gotten himself lost."

"Your Bishop Stephan. I hope you find him. And as to your question, you should know there are strange things in every town. Now, you've had a very long journey and must be exhausted. Let's get you inside and get you settled."

Meinhard grasped the wooden doors, opening them to the black hall beyond, then motioned for Ambrose to enter. His face was a cheery smile, but in the shadowed light of the lantern it appeared as a grimace. Fear knotted Ambrose's heart as he peered inside. There was no turning back. The door closed with a thud and the darkness swallowed.

☩

CHAPTER 2

Post-Mortem

September 18, 1859

The wooden cart groaned and creaked in the settling dusk. Shadows fell across empty streets, the dark edges of squat buildings growing long in the light of the waning moon. Two figures—the gravedigger and his son—huddled under cloak and hat. While in the back, a white bundle rocked and shook.

The cart stopped before the doctor's office, a weathered building on the edge of St. Gregory, whose shingle creaked in the late-summer breeze, its carved words above read: DR. HERMAN ALBRECHT: ARZTPRAXIS.

The doctor poked his graying head through a crack in the door. "Quickly now, on the table, boys!" he hissed, staring warily down the dark streets.

They struggled under the awkward weight of the bundle, sweat beading their brows in the muggy night as they panted and pulled, dragging it into the tiny clinic. The room was cluttered with odd books on the shelves, and medical implements—saws and knives—lay about on every surface, mixed with the odd bottle of pills or tinctures. Diagrams adorned the walls: pen and ink drawings of anatomy and botanical sketchings of medicinal herbs, and long the far wall, past the exam table, stood a narrow and well-used hutch. Dirty glasses lined its counter beside a half-empty bottle of brown whiskey and various digestifs.

"Ho! Lift now, Poldie!" the grave digger, Sepp, said.

Poldie hefted as his balding father grunted at the other end. With a final heave the bundle crashed upon the table, sending dirty plates clattering to the floor, and the two stepped back, panting and wiping oily sweat from their necks. The men stood in silence, staring at the bundle: Sepp and Poldie on one side and Albrecht and Dr. Vieth, the Manitowoc County medical examiner, on the other.

"My good Dr. Vieth," Albrecht said. "would you be so kind?"

The examiner stirred in the corner before stepping into the light to look at his pocket watch. The distinguished man looked out of place as he smoothed his tweed vest and brushed the white ends of his curled mustache. "I trust you're taking notes, Dr. Albrecht. The time is nine twenty-four in the evening and the date is September eighteenth, eighteen fifty-nine."

"Very good." Albrecht sighed. "Let's begin."

The doctor drew a knife across the rope binding of the bundle. It frayed and snapped and a bare leg flopped into view. He drew the sheet back, revealing a torn and mangled body.

"It's the miller's boy." He rubbed his weary eyes. "Ah, poor Augustin, what happened to you?"

A grimace lay on the dead boy's face. Blood splattered his cold lips and clung in his sandy-red hair. His once pink cheeks were now dull white and stiff across his high cheekbones.

"Merciful Lord above!" Poldie cried. "Da, this ain't right!"

Albrecht leaned forward, lifting the bloodied shirt away to peer below. A gaping hole pierced the belly, diving deep into the chest, and black blood, thick and tacky, pulled at the

✠

PART II

Gregorstadt

✠

PART III

Wasuskeqsinoh

cloth as he stripped it away. Sepp cleared his throat and shuffled his feet, quietly making the sign of the cross, while Poldie looked with anxious eyes to the doctor.

"Please, sir," Poldie shook his round head and raised his hands in protest. "I'll bury them right, so they don't come back. But I don't want no part of this! Please…call me when he's all wrapped up again!"

Albrecht crossed his arms, considering. He stroked his mutton chops with yellowed fingers as the light of the lantern cast long shadows across his wrinkled face.

"I don't envy you telling his father, Otto, tomorrow," Dr. Vieth said. "These woods are filled with innumerable wild creatures. Tis a pity."

"Hm?" Albrecht said. "Wild creatures indeed."

"Doctor, please!" said Poldie.

"You'll be all right there, Poldie, my boy," said Albrecht, thumbing the cuffs of his linen shirt. "Just take breath. Why don't you head on home? Your pa will be along shortly. There's naught for you to do here tonight. But breathe not a word of this to another soul! And Poldie, best you fetch Father Ambrose."

Dr. Vieth cleared his throat. Lamplight glinted from the metal tip of his cane as he lifted the dead boy's shirt to examine the wound. "Come now, Dr. Albrecht," he said. "It is plain to see this is the work of an animal. Not everything is a phantom of the night. Maybe it's best you don't bring an outside observer, especially one with no medical training, to what is only an unfortunate accident. There are enough stories about your backwards little town to embarrass the county already. No need to invite more."

"Hm?" Albrecht looked up from the cuts and gashes. He considered Dr. Vieth for a moment before turning to Poldie. "Best fetch him."

Ambrose stared at the blank paper, pen in hand. The warm glow of an old lamp flickered, its tiny flame not reaching the dark corners of the room, and his face danced in shadows, flickering across his high cheekbones. Though he had but just reached his thirty-first year, the wan light made his hawkish nose and brown eyes seem far older.

His cell in the abbey was sparse, little more than a closet of rough board and hard plaster. The only furnishings were a bed and the table at which he sat, the only adornment the cross on the wall. The evening bells had long since tolled and the brothers in their nearby cells sat in their nightly reflections. He should have done the same. But the page before him lay empty, waiting to be filled with his report and letter of update to Cardinal Eberhard in Karlsruhe.

He sighed and rubbed his eyes. *There is nothing to tell.* He had been here almost two weeks, and Father Valentine still hadn't returned from his retreat. Without the town's leader, the people avoided him; few ventured to speak and none of them would tell of the missing Stephan or the unsavory events of the past few years. Only a stray word or suspicious glance hinted that something lay hidden beneath their polite smiles.

A soft knock came from the door.

"Father Ambrose?" a voice whispered. "Please pardon the intrusion."

Startled, Ambrose opened the door to Brother Meinhard's chubby smile. He had met the old Brother only briefly on his arrival. He couldn't imagine what he could possibly want at this hour, as he stood before him, hands on his fat belly and ruby cheeks flush from too much wine.

But before he could ask, the creak of wooden floors rose nearby and light flickered beneath closed doors, as the brothers in their cells pressed their ears to the walls, listening for gossip.

"Father Valentine said to help as we can, as an act of good faith, and to keep you abreast of any 'strangeness.'"

Meinhard stepped close to whisper. "Dr. Albrecht has sent for you."

Ambrose stared, puzzled. *What could the doctor want from me that a priest of the town can't provide?* He grabbed his Bible and cross for last rites.

Frowning, Meinhard shook his head. "You'll not be needing those, I think."

The street was empty and dark. Only scant light flickered here and there, dim in the passing windows, and Ambrose drew his hood against the feeling of watchful eyes. The old priest shuffled, leading them through narrow alleys and back roads, out of sight and out of view of the main street. The hotel passed in the distance. The horses snorted and stomped in the stable and a lone fiddle rose over the din of dishes and laughter, a woman's voice beside it. But soon, they passed and the night grew quiet again.

The doctor's office stood dark at the edge of town. Yellow light peaked through the curtains as they neared, and muffled voices rose within, sharp and heated. Meinhard hesitated, hand against the rough door, before finally knocking. The house fell still as the door slowly opened and the doctor peered cautiously into the night.

"Come in! Come in!" Albrecht waved.

Ambrose covered his mouth as a rank air struck them. The room was cluttered with odds and ends. All about lay papers and books. Saws and knives lay spread on a bureau and above was a cabinet of tinctures and powders.

The room was an odd collection of people. The old doctor tugged at his white mutton chops, lost in thought, as he paced. Meanwhile, a dapper man with slick gray hair and woolen suit bent forward, his back turned as he examined something on the table. A young man in ratty clothes and unkempt hair held his hand over his mouth, as though ill, and beside him, an old and wiry man stood, head bowed and cap in hand. Ambrose recognized the last two. *The undertaker and his son!*

"Father Ambrose, this is Dr. Albrecht." Meinhard gestured to the old doctor. "Doctor, I've brought Father Ambrose, as you asked. Father Valentine asks our good charity in the matters concerning the Catholic commission. Now, it's not my place to stick my nose where it doesn't belong, so I'd best take my leave. *Make sure none of you suffers as a murderer, a thief, an evildoer, or a troublesome meddler."*

"Peter 4:15," Albrecht said. "And I trust you to keep to such prudence on your way back to the abbey. No troublesome meddlers here!"

"I have not seen or heard a thing." Meinhard bowed then closed the door.

"Ah, Father Ambrose," Albrecht said, turning to him. "It is nice to finally make your acquaintance. You no doubt wonder why I sent for you at this late hour. It's no bother, I hope. Father Valentine asked that you be privy to anything notable."

Ambrose nodded and shook his hand, noting the callouses of his palm and the whiskey on his breath. "And I take it that bundle is something notable?"

"That remains to be seen." The doctor lifted the torn sheet to reveal the body. Dead limbs shone gray in the dim light, streaked with blood, dry and black. In the center was a deep hole, lost in the darkness of the chest. The boy looked to be sixteen or seventeen and would have been handsome in life, but now wore a gruesome countenance he would carry to the grave. Ambrose turned in horror, looking away to the dark corners of the room, anywhere but the table in front of him. He had seen death before; consumption had swept the Alsace and Baden. But he had rarely seen a body so disemboweled. Not up close. Now he was face to face with more than he could have imagined. The awful rumors seemed true.

Albrecht poured him a glass of brown liquor. Eyes watering from the fumes, Ambrose coughed and politely declined. No matter how horrid the scene, he would not lose himself to drink. Not like his father.

"Suit yourself." Albrecht downed Ambrose's glass and set it on the table next to the body with a thud.

"So," the examiner said, "now that we're all here, we can get on with it and maybe let poor Sepp leave for the night."

"Father, this is Dr. Thomas Vieth, our esteemed county medical examiner. He was in the area on business and I asked that he observe," Albrecht said. "And this is Joseph 'Sepp' Liška, the church groundsman and gravedigger, as needed."

"Somewhat oft needed of late, I'm afraid," Sepp said and hung his balding head. His thin frame was bent in sadness and his thick fingers fidgeted with the coarse rim of his dingy, frayed hat.

Ambrose extended his hand, but Dr. Vieth ignored and, grunting, turned back to the corpse. "Dr. Albrecht is an overly cautious man, Father," he said. "You'll soon appreciate that. But you'll curse his caution when he rouses you from bed at all hours of the night. Even now, he can't rest until he knows what wild creature did this to poor Augustin, the miller's boy."

"If it was a wild creature," Albrecht said. "Look here… See the breaks in the flesh along the wound? How clean they are? I would say they look more from a knife than a tooth." He prodded the flesh with a scalpel, but to Ambrose it was just a gruesome wound.

Dr. Vieth drew a pipe and took a long, slow puff. Much to Ambrose's relief, whirls of white woodsy smoke chased away the sourness for a moment.

"If it's a knife, it is the dullest one to be found," Dr. Vieth said. "This was nothing but a beast."

"Begging your pardons, sirs." Sepp looked down, embarrassed. "I think it not a man. But if a beast, it is a foul and wicked one, to be sure."

Dr. Vieth raised an eyebrow. "Oh? And what do you mean by that?"

"Forgive me, it's not my place. Only does the boy have his heart?"

Albrecht felt into the chest with his bare hand. "By Jove! He does not!"

"Wolves eat first the organs. There is nothing strange about that," Dr. Vieth said. "Come, let's wrap this up."

Albrecht ignored him, holding a lantern to the wound. "Sepp, what suspicions caused you to look there?"

Sepp stroked his chin. "I can't rightly say. Or rather I shouldn't say. You'd think me even more a fool than I am."

Albrecht turned to Ambrose. His wrinkled hand pulled at his mutton chops and his bushy eyebrows scrunched, considered. "And what are your thoughts, Father? Is this man or beast?"

Ambrose flushed in surprise as the others turned, expectantly. Why would he know? "I'm not sure how should I have an idea. I know nothing of this foreign land or its wild beasts. And less, even, of medicine. Perhaps one should search the area? Where was the poor boy found?"

"In the woods south of town," Sepp ventured. "By the small lake. 'Pigeon Lake' they call it. Young loves go there in the moonlight against their parents' wishes. Doubtless Augustin was meant to see Issa, the cobbler's daughter. But we could do no search of the grounds at night, not without waking the town."

"In that case, I'd suggest searching the grounds at first light," Ambrose said. "And perhaps this Issa may know something."

"You see?" Dr. Vieth shook his head dismissively. "The Catholic commission already hard at work investigating."

He donned his hat and rapped his cane on the wooden floor as he left. "Gentlemen, I've had enough. Good night."

Long moments passed in silence.

"Perhaps it would be in the spirit of Father Valentine's hospitality," Albrecht said, "for Father Ambrose to accompanying good Master Sepp in searching the grounds in the morning? Assuming, of course, neither of you is indisposed?"

"I cannot miss Lauds," Ambrose said. "But I suppose could come after."

Sepp nodded. "I shall have breakfast and tea waiting."

"It's settled then," said Albrecht. "Now if you gentlemen will leave me to my autopsy, I have a long night ahead of me. And I must break the news to poor Otto. That shan't be easy."

☩

CHAPTER 3

Flora and Fauna of the American Frontier

September 19, 1859

The morning bell tolled in the darkness, its deep bong ringing through the forest. Ambrose wandered in soft dreams: sunlit squares and the flicker of gold and red through glass, like dappled forests on cathedral stone. He startled awake, bewildered and confused, then rubbed the sleep from his eyes and felt the rough-cut boards beneath his feet. He was no longer in Heidelberg. Memory of the days and weeks before flooded back and his heart sank as he thought of the coming day.

Lauds came early. Priests in green chasuble stood at the altar for Mass while brothers in brown habits gathered in the nave. Their voices rose in hymn, filling the wooden chapel as Father Anselm led the Canticle of Zechariah: *"Benedictus Dominus… Visitavit et fecit redemptionem plebis suae."*

Ambrose's thoughts were elsewhere. He saw images of the miller's boy, the memories of the night before fresh in his mind, and his voice faltered, halfhearted. With so many unwelcome eyes upon him, the church felt like a prison and he wished to be away; he blushed, embarrassed that others might guess his mind. When Mass finally ended, he breathed a sigh of relief to step back into the dim morning light and feel the chilly air upon his face. Sepp would be waiting at Pigeon Lake; he should hurry.

The southern road left the town, wandering lazily along the eastern shore of the lake and the morning sun sparkled, bright and cheery, as it danced on the waves. Sepp gazed across the water, tipping his frayed hat as Ambrose approached. "It's a fine morning to view the Lord's splendor, sir." He handed him a cup of tea. "I've not much fare, but at least it's fresh."

A skillet sizzled with blood sausage, gamy and oily and black at the edges, and Ambrose's stomach turned: Sepp was poor and Ambrose couldn't refuse the man's hospitality. He accepted the plate with a wan smile.

"Hot *balten brei* on hard toast is fit for the Lord himself," Sepp said, smiling a toothless grin. "Or at least Father Valentine."

"Did you come with the first boats, Joseph?" said Ambrose, making small talk. "Or did you find your way here later?"

"Oh, don't bother with Joseph. Call me Sepp. I came with the first, sir. Sailed out from Strasbourg then Le Havre. I've been with Father Valentine for years and I think I would follow him anywhere. He's the only living saint I know."

Ambrose frowned uncomfortably at Sepp's devotion.

"I know I'm not supposed to say such things," he continued. "But I'm true in my conviction. I've seen too many causes. Too many fellows dead in the mud. At the end of the day, a man needs to find something to place his faith in…" He paused as Ambrose looked at him in confusion. "It was the battle of Leipzig. That's where I got this limp. You know they gathered up those boys' bones for fertilizer? Shipped them to Schottland, I heard."

He looked away, his old derby cap to his heart, and the look in his eye was of one given to wandering in a painful past.

*Fifty thousand sturdy souls on those trampled
plains and knolls,
who met the dawn hopefully,
and were looted their shares in quarrel not theirs,
dropt in agony.*

He heaved a sigh. "That's when I heard of Father Valentine, a man who could heal the soul. I found him in the middle of nowhere, in the Black Forest. That's where I found my Gerti too! And she and I and Poldie make three."

"I didn't know you read English poetry!" Ambrose said, smiling in surprise. "Education is a rare find amongst men.

"It's a habit I picked up to pass the time when so long away from home—hen I was a far younger man than now. We're not supposed to read such things that don't glorify the Lord. So I keep it to myself."

Sepp grew self-conscious and stared at his feet, dark eyes reluctant to meet Ambrose's gaze. Sparse gray hair blew in the brisk wind as he idly knocked at clumps of mud with his boot.

Ambrose studied him: an old man wiry and thin in pauper's clothes, standing in the mud of a logging trail. Dark shadow extended in the underbrush on either side, but in the small clearing of the trail where they stood, the light shimmered brightly on his balding head. In that moment, he seemed like a gnome from an old fairy tale and Ambrose half expected him to disappear inside a log, or beneath a stump, and leave him alone in the forest.

"Thank you for trusting me, Sepp." Ambrose said. "But tell me, why is it you'll speak so openly to me when no one else will?"

"Oh, the town?" he said. "They are only being cautious. They're used to pillory, you know." He opened his mouth to say more but clearly thought better of it and grew quiet once again.

"Liška," Ambrose said, hoping to keep him talking. "That name is from the east, isn't it?"

"*Ya.* My father hailed from Bohemia."

"Bohemia, to Leipzig, to Freiberg, to the Americas," Ambrose said. "That's quite the journey."

"*Ya,* and finally to the scene of a death," he said. "Speaking of, let's have a look around. It's not good to tarry in such places." He walked ahead, suddenly, as if uncomfortable. It seemed he already had said more than he was willing to share.

They searched the ground. The road led south, ending in a trail where the logging stopped and the trees grew thick. Warblers and wrens twittered above, flitting about in the morning sun, as bees buzzed lazily in the warm air. As they walked, the trail grew soft and water squished from the black earth around their feet. Bizarre plants Ambrose had never seen dotted the ground: the fuzzy fronds of exotic ferns mixed with fluttering, oblate leaves.

"There." Sepp pointed to where the body had been found.

A pair of footprints—Augustin's undoubtedly—came from the path along the lake but stopped suddenly in the middle of the trail. The ground was torn and impossible to read; Sepp and Poldie's tracks mixed with those of the oxen and the furrows of the cart, confusing the scene, and all about, red blood mixed in pools with muddy water. Puzzling tracks appeared and circled the site, but none led to or from, and they were so badly disturbed; it was impossible to say what had caused them. Ambrose circled, looking here and there, but could make no sense of what he saw. No tracks led to or from. No grasses were trampled leading into the forest. It was only the mucky, muddy ground that lay torn before him.

"I'm no hunter. I wouldn't know how to read these signs, even if they were clear," Ambrose said. "Are they man or beast? I cannot tell. They are spaced like a man's but too narrow. If only they weren't so trampled." He looked to Sepp, but the man stared into the distance.

"What could they be?" he said again.

But Sepp remained silent. Whatever suspicions he had hinted at the night before he now wouldn't say.

This old man is no help at all.

"Well, I appreciate the good doctor informing me of events," Ambrose said, finally. "But I don't know what more I can do."

Shaking his head, he turned to leave when suddenly a shimmer in the weedy brush caught his eye. It was long and black, glistening iridescent purples and blues, and he reached down to pick it up. It was a feather, freshly fallen and shiny, but as long as his arm and the quill as big as his thumb.

"What monstrous rooks are in this wild land!" he said. "Is this some carrion crow come to feed on the body. What do you make of this, Joseph?"

The man pulled a flask from his pocket and held it to his ear, listening as he shook it. "Carrion feathers are bad luck. At least that's what they say in the old country. You should leave it where it lay. But"—he winked and took a swallow—"they are the Lord's sign for a little nip! I think we've looked as much as we can. Maybe we should be heading on. It's not good to linger."

A howl shook the mill. Heavy sacks of grain crashed and spilled on the floor as Otto's hulking form heaved and panted. Lines of rage and sorrow crossed his broad face, as his thick hands tossed and battered about anything they could find. Lukas, the mill hand, fled through the back, as ropes and hooks and shovels smashed against the walls, gauging the rough-cut wood and chipped the grinding stone.

"Let me see him! Let me see my son!" Otto cried, spittle and snot hanging from his beard.

"I have to dress the body," Albrecht pleaded. "It's not right to be seen."

The doctor's smock was smeared a faint reddish brown. Otto fought to look away, but his eyes lingered at the sight of old blood—his son's blood. He grew dizzy and collapsed in a chair, his head heavy in his hands.

"That boy. I told him not to wander the woods at night. How many times did I tell him? Following the doe eyes of a girl. I warned him the flesh would lead him astray! But a father's words are useless against the passions of youth."

He turned to the wall in silence, tears on his ashen face. Dust settled on his wet cheeks and in his black beard, and he held his head as he moaned. In the shock of the moment, his eyes fell on things seldom noticed: dust motes dancing in the rays of the sun, the many whorls of knots and grain of timber.

"Augustin and I put up those beams and trusses not but five summers past," he said. "It helped to take our mind off things. But a child will never forget. He was by Elsa's side when she died on the boat here, and we laid her to rest in that damn abysmal sea. Now"—he waved his arm—"what use is all this?"

"Father Valentine will return soon," Albrecht said, fidgeting. "Then we will have a fitting service."

"I'll have no Voss there!" Otto roared, his eyes red with wrath. "That damn cobbler and his whore daughter, I told him to keep her away! If that Jezebel hadn't lured my Augustin out, he'd still be here."

"Now, you can't blame the girl for the acts of some night creature," Albrecht opened his hands, pleading. "She'll blame herself enough. Forgive as the Lord forgave you."

But Otto's face grew hard and he dried his eyes with a dirty handkerchief. "Keep your morals to yourself, Doctor. You're not my priest." He stood up and grabbed his staff and axe. "What manner of creature did this? Was it a man or some beast?"

The doctor sighed. "I cannot say. I've never seen such a wound."

"Show me the body."

"It's not right to see. Not yet."

"Show me!"

✠

CHAPTER 4

Meddling in the Affairs of Others

September 19, 1859

The events of the day before troubled Ambrose and he sat at his tiny desk in heavy thought. In the distance, the brothers milled about in the orchards and fields, busy at their work. A slight chill was in the air. Autumn was the season that most spoke to Ambrose's heart; It beckoned a silent reflection: the coming stillness of winter held in a moment of life's full bloom. Yet he found in this distant land his mind unsettled and ill at ease, and where once was God reflected in the passing of all things, was here a strange emptiness.

He couldn't shake it: a death, a beast, and the awkward evasions of a town who wished him gone. In spite of Fr. Valentine's overtures, the brothers in the abbey sneered in silence and townsfolk on the street looked askance. Only Meinhard, and now strangely the good Dr. Albrecht and the gravedigger Joseph, had spoken to him at all in the past two weeks. It filled him with foreboding and made raw an ache of loneliness he knew far too well.

"Thoughts of home will ease my soul," he said softly to the empty room.

Thin fingers opened the coarse folds of a letter and he looked down to words written in his own hand: a letter to his sister, unfinished:

My dearest Monika,

I am fast upon my journey across this enormous country. After weeks in perpetual storm, I arrived in Boston but three days past. The city is naught but a fleeting memory, so little time did I spend there. In truth, I am not sad that I left that place, famous though it is. You and Mother would have enjoyed taking in the sights and exploring the exotic atmosphere. In truth, I have never seen such a mix of people. It strains belief! I should have liked to talk to them all. Yet my temperament is not as yours, and for however much I may yearn to know others, I yearn for the quiet places of the world even more.

Now I find myself on a ship, in the middle of a lake of unfathomable size. "Eerie," they call it, which in our native German means "unheimlich"– though I've heard they named it for the Indians who once lived here. In two short days I have crossed the distance from Paris to Munich. When I have finally reached Gregorstadt, I will have gone the distance from Paris to Rome—all in one country! It is simply astounding!

I know you miss Stephan. Our lives would have been much altered had it not been for his generosity after father's death. I cannot believe he has been missing already for two years. But worry not, dear sister, that I write such words from my own troubled heart. Know that it is never as dire as it seems, no matter what your worrisome brother may say, only please indulge me in writing my anxious thoughts. It has ever been a challenge to divulge my heart to others. And in this land of unknown faces, all the more so…

Brothers in brown habits sat at long tables for the evening meal, their heads bowed and hands raised in prayer. The refectory was bare, and like all the other rooms of the abbey, only minimally adorned: a plaster cross hung on the far wall, and here and there, were words of embroidered scripture, but there was little else to absorb, the ting and clink of ladles in thick clay bowls that echoed off the otherwise bare walls. A gentle breeze wafted through the open window, floating sweet notes of fresh-cut hay, and before them, steaming bowls of stew filled the air with the scent of rabbit and thyme.

"Ad cenam vitae aeternae perducat nos, Rex aeternae gloriae. Amen."

Ambrose passed the basket. The bread was hard and stale in his hand, and cracked as he buttered it.

"You are not having wine?" Meinhard appeared quizzical as Ambrose held his hand over his mug.

"I haven't the taste for it." He smiled. "But I've known enough who have. *Wine makes even the wise fall away.*"

Meinhard nodded. "Ecclesiastes 19:2."

A snigger rose from somewhere beside Ambrose; he blushed, feeling the brothers' eyes upon him, then quickly changed the subject. "Father Meinhard, what kind of monstrous rooks are there here? Today I chanced upon a feather as large as my arm. I've never seen the like in the forests back home."

Meinhard frowned and the table grew suddenly quiet. Just then, a shadow fell upon the floor, dark against the evening sun; Anselm entered the hall, tall and imposing. He often dined on his own, and Ambrose had not yet seen him so close. He seemed somehow taller, and his white head of thinning hair was imperious he as scanned the room. Harsh lines crossed the old man's stern face and his piercing blue eyes narrowed in anger at the echoes in the hall.

"Meals are for silent reflection," he said. "Not idle gossip or imaginings. I hope the church in the old country has not so quickly forgotten such simple things."

Ambrose bowed his head in apology as the brothers stared at their bowls. Meinhard was right. Anselm sorely lacked for humor and it seemed Ambrose was already on the menacing priest's bad side. He had little chance of getting through this amicably.

The meal ended in silence, the brothers cringing under Anselm's relentless scowl. And after the tables were cleared and wiped, they quickly left in file for evening prayers. Meinhard grasped Ambrose's arm in the hall and pulled him close. "Let such things lie!" he whispered.

Later that night, in the dark of his small cell, Ambrose sat at his report. The silence from Meinhard had only added to the disquiet of the day, and he felt like an unwelcome intruder. The giant feather lay across his table, shimmering in the dim candlelight. Why would no one speak about it? Sepp clearly knew something. The brothers had grown quiet at the table, at its mere mention. Even Meinhard, perennially jovial, had seemed uncomfortable. He rubbed his tired eyes and turned to his report, black ink flowing across gray paper:

September 19, 1859

Your Eminence Cardinal Eberhard,

I regret that I am no closer to learning the fate or whereabouts of Bishop Stephan von Draheim.
Father Valentine has yet to break his retreat in the forest, although I have been assured he will soon.
However, it is with a heavy heart that I write early

to report of unfortunate occurrences, similar in nature to past rumors. I cannot believe they should be unrelated.

The good miller's son was found on the wooded road outside of town disemboweled, his very heart removed. Never have I seen such violence outside of war, and I shudder to recall the memory of it, for I have seen the wounds with my own eyes. They appear too vile to be an act of man, and no footprints lead to or from the scene, nor does any other evidence suggest such involvement. Yet I can think also of no beast that would act in such manner, although I confess that my knowledge of the fauna of this continent is sorely lacking.

Even today, while searching the abbey's wooded grounds, I chanced upon the feather of an enormous rook. You must think me dim or given to fancy, but I swear it is as long as my arm. Yet, when I inquired, none would speak freely of the strange creature, though clearly all knew.

I fear the town views me with suspicion on account of the commission and tolerates me only at Father Valentine's insistence. The townsfolk look askance in the street, or draw their curtains as I pass their homes. They stare in silence and are immune to any pleasant overture. It is only by the good faith of Dr. Albrecht that I am made aware of any events at all—

A wail rose from the town, shattering the night. Ambrose looked up with a start, his hair on end. What could possibly have made such a horrible noise? His thoughts crept back to Augustin's body on the doctor's table: the grimace frozen on his face, cold flesh now white, and the sickening hole where his heart had once been. Was it happening again? He crept to the door and looked down the hall. No lamps shone under the brothers' cells and their doors remained closed. *Surely, they must have heard?* He waited in silence, listening. Ordained were forbidden from leaving their cells at night, but cries of alarm must certainly be an exception? Why wasn't anyone doing anything?

The cry rose again, a deep bellowing. It was a man—two men. Although Ambrose couldn't hear what they were saying, their wails were of hurt or anger. *Damn it, why does no one help?* He peaked into the hall again. It was still silent and dark, but he couldn't risk the creak of floorboards or rusty hinges. Father Anselm would surely expel him if he were caught breaking abbey rules. He would have to go through the window.

Fortunately, the fall was not far, only several feet, and he landed with a soft thud in tall grass. In the night, in his black cassock, Ambrose looked as no more than a shadow under the half moon, and he ran toward the cries under the cover of darkness. Thistles scraped his side as he plunged through stands of sumac and brush before finally meeting the dusty road. Ahead, the lanterns and fires of the southernmost homes twinkled through the trees.

The voices grew louder. It was clear now a quarrel had broken out. *Surely the whole town must hear!* He knew it wasn't his place to meddle in their affairs and he hesitated. He shouldn't have snuck out. It certainly didn't sound like some wild and feral beast attacking. *But why isn't anyone stopping it? In a God-fearing community such as this?* Should he help and be found out, or stick to his duty and sneak back to the abbey? He looked down at his bare hands, empty of even a stick to defend himself, and felt completely ill-prepared. *Damn it!*

Through the trees ahead, a hulking man raged and hollered by lamplight before the shuttered windows of a sleepy house on the very edge of town. It was Otto, the miller, stumbling and yelling in the middle of the road, waving his fists at a panicked figure who stood guarding the door.

As he crept closer, Ambrose could see it was Bernd, the cobbler, in his nightgown. His sandy blond hair fell in once-sleepy eyes that were now suddenly white in fear, and his flabby cheeks were flushed red. A heavy staff was in his hands that he waved threateningly and smacked against the porch beams to ward the miller away, even as Otto circled slowly closer and closer.

Behind Bernd, Ambrose saw a pale girl peek through the shuttered glass. She was startlingly familiar and Ambrose almost cried out in surprise. She looked just like his sister when they were young, running in fear from the street gangs of gutter children in Konstanz. Her eyes were tearful as her trembling hand clutched the curtain.

"Otto, you know not what you say!" Bernd waved his staff. "My Issa hadn't a hand in this!"

"Your hussy of a daughter called my only son from his bed to wander the woods at night!" Otto shrieked. "I told you to keep her from him!"

"You can't account for the passions of youth. I'm sorry for your boy, but he let his heart rule him too. It was not Issa's sole fault!" Bernd poked the air with his staff threateningly, as Otto knocked it away.

"Your daughter cast a spell upon my boy!" Otto pointed at the man. "She is a Jezebel. Nay, your daughter is a whore!"

A wail rose from the house, and the poor girl fled the window into the darkness within. Bernd's face grew red as his grip tightened around the thick wood. "You best get ye gone, Otto," he said, "before I take this stick to your head!"

The miller scoffed, his chest puffed as he kicked the dirt in the road. "I will make a shoe out of you to beat your own ass, you good for nothing cobbler!"

With that, Otto lurched forward, fists raised and towering. His lips trembled in anger as hot sweat beaded in his black hair. Bernd charged into the road, circled in his thin night gown, waving his staff and striking the air here and there. It looked as though it would come to blows any minute.

Before he could think, Ambrose stepped between them, hands raised. "Please! Stop!" he pleaded. "Don't make this tragedy worse! Don't sin against your neighbor!"

"Who the hell are you?" Otto said, dark eyes narrowed as he stared down at the priest. "A man can't sin against a man. He can only sin against God. You're that one from the commission, sticking your nose where it doesn't belong! Meddling in affairs of the church isn't enough? Now you have to bother a simple man in his grief?"

"It's a terrible tragedy, but it's not a young girl's fault," Ambrose raised his hands, pleading. "No one can be blamed for something like this."

"Except the one who did it!"

"But it wasn't her," said Ambrose.

"Of course, my girl didn't have a hand in it!" Bernd shouted.

"Bernd, that's enough from you!" Otto snapped. He turned to Ambrose, glaring, his fists balled as he stepped forward. "Why couldn't she have done it? Say it! Say what you mean!"

"Well... I mean to say..." Ambrose faltered. "...is that whatever ungodly creature did it, no man is safe, day or night. I've...seen the wound."

"Oh, have you now? You've seen the wound?" Otto wrapped his thick hands around Ambrose's cassock and yanked him up to his toes in the middle of the road. "Gawking at my boy like you're seeing the sights, are you? Did you get a look at his open belly? Enough to chat about back home? Damn you to hell!"

Otto struck his fist hard into Ambrose's stomach. Hot air hissed with a sickening humph and he collapsed on the ground, gasping.

"He's a man of the cloth!" Bernd shouted in horror.

Otto loomed above, his jaw tense and quivering as he raised his fist to strike Ambrose again.

Suddenly a flash in the dark caught the miller's arm, pulling and twisting and the giant crashed to the ground, cursing. He rolled, angry and ready to pounce, but his eyes grew wide as he stared down the barrel of a rifle. A wiry man with red hair in a nightgown stared down at him.

"Cool your head, Otto!" the man yelled.

"Goddamn it, this doesn't concern you, Jacob!"

"No. But I've had enough! You would have woken half the town, acting like…this. Shame on you! You think you honor your son in such a way? Get home afore I show you some wrath of my own. Let's just see how touchy this here trigger is." He cocked the gun.

Otto stammered in his rage, his lower lip trembling as the spittle ran down his beard. He rose, kicking the ground and fuming, as he stared down the barrel of the gun. "To hell with all of you!" he finally cried, shaking his fists above his head. With a backward glance of malice, he stormed away into the night.

Bernd smiled apologetically before backing meekly into his house, and Jacob Durst turned to Ambrose lying bruised and winded in the dirt. All was dark again. The curtains fell across the windows of the Voss house and the night forest lay still, just yards beyond. If any of the other townsfolk had heard, they made no sign of it.

"Thank you for that," Ambrose wheezed. "I don't know what he would have done.

Jacob spat in disgust. "A meddling father out after evening prayer," he snarled. "Get ye gone!"

☦

CHAPTER 5

Killian and Tobias

October 4, 1859

It was late afternoon, when, two weeks later, the mule cart slowly approached the outskirts of town. The road from Sheboygan was twenty miles, and the trip had taken the entire day. Now the shadows grew long as the sun set, purple and red in the billowy clouds. The cart creaked and thumped as the wheels slipped in dried tracks or met potholes in the road, and the two priests sitting in the bed—one young and thin, the other old and fat—were thrown to and fro against the sides, nursing their sore backs against piles of dirty burlap. A wizened, old man cracked the reins when the roads were rough, laughing as the mule pulled hard and launched the cart over the ruts. The fat priest glared with a ruby face, flush with annoyance, but the younger one beside him laughed along with the driver.

Yellow fields of oats waved in the warm breeze, and the young priest, bright-eyed and rosy-cheeked, breathed deeply the fresh-cut hay in its stooked bundles. Brown hair fell across his fair skin and he smiled with boyish enthusiasm as he pointed at orchards, speckled red. "Tobias, such apples!"

Tobias, the old and stocky priest beside him, held fast the rough sides of the cart with a fat hand as he was knocked about. His balding head was flush in annoyance. "Damn it, Killian. I'll care when I'm off this blasted cart! I can hardly bare another jolt. I'll be lucky if I can sit again in a week."

"Ah, it's just as well." Killian laughed gleefully. "You'll see dandy red, swollen apples when you see your ass in the mirror."

"You and your damn uncle!" Tobias muttered. "I don't know why I ever agreed to be your chaperone."

"Because I remind you of your youth?"

Tobias sighed and shook his head.

The cart rolled slowly through the southern end of St. Gregory, then through the thick trees, along Pigeon Lake, before opening to a meadow, a wooden steeple and cross poking over the treeline in the distance. Lumbering, it finally drew to a stop at the Abbey of the Holy Ghost, where a jolly priest stood waiting, a smile on his ruby face and plump hands on his fat belly.

"Ah, the last two have finally made it," Father Meinhard greeted them as they stepped down from the cart, stiff and sore. With a deep groan, Tobias rubbed his aching back.

"Pleased to meet you. I'm Father Meinhard," the man said, extending his hand.

"Father Tobias Schenk. And this"—Meinhard gestured— "is Father Killian Plank."

"Plank? As in Bishop Walter Plank?"

"The very same! He is my uncle in Stuttgart. Do you know him?" said Killian.

"Only by name. Father Valentine has spoken of him. They were in seminary together. As you were as well, Father Tobias?" asked Meinhard.

"Quite right. We all knew each other upon a time, though it's been many years," Tobias said. He looked with misgivings to the meadow: the graveyard in the distance and the brooding trees of the forest that surrounded. Finally he turned to the rough boards of the abbey and the black cross above. "Tell me, how is Valentine and when may I greet him?"

"The good father is in silent retreat. He will be back when he's back. As for reminiscing, you should know Father Valentine spends all his time engaged with the Lord," Meinhard crossed his arms. "Now come. Let me show you to your rooms and you can settle in. But"—he turned and stepped close, then lowered his voice—"when Father Valentine is away, Father Anselm leads in his stead. Best not to be noticed!"

The old driver cackled to himself as the mule cart pulled away, creaking down the path and out of sight. Tobias and Killian exchanged uneasy glances as they looked to the abbey looming ominously above. There was no easy way back now.

"Well, come on!" Meinhard said. "You must be hungry from the journey. I remember that all too well! From New York to Boston by train, then on to Toledo by way of Lake Erie. And then another train to Milwaukee! How long did it take?"

Sighing, Tobias rubbed his back again. "Too long."

"Indeed!" Meinhard laughed, deep and throaty. "Let's get you something to eat!"

They were struck by the abbey's spartan interior. It would have felt impoverished if it had not been well-crafted. The walls were plain white plaster with little adornment aside from a cross in every room. The wooden floors were unfinished and worn with grooves from use. The chapel itself had the barest of ornaments. A pair of brass candelabras sat on the vesperal cloth of the altar, a carving of Christ on the cross above.

"Vespers is at four," said Meinhard. "I'll leave you to get settled in."

When they retired to their separate rooms, they found them to be as spartan as the rest of the abbey. A worn trunk held their linens and cassock, while a desk and chair sat beside a narrow window, where they were expected to study scripture. Tobias looked at the rope bed and frowned, poking at the corn husk mattress in disappointment.

Before long, the chapel bell, deep and rolling, tolled the call to prayer. Brothers in brown robes led the way in silence filling the chapel before the altar. Tobias and Killian could not help but notice the sidelong glances and murmurs, and when they turned to look, they were met by suspicious eyes staring back at them.

In the chapel, Father Anselm stood before the altar, tall and thin and severe as he led them in prayer. His voice rose and fell as the candles burned low. *"Gloria Patri, et Filio, et Spiritui Sancto, sicut erat in principio, et nunc, et semper: et in Saecula saeculorum. Amen."*

Ambrose found Tobias and Killian wandering the halls after service. Tobias brooded as usual, his face drawn in chubby frown, while Killian followed closely, his gray eyes wide in bewilderment. In the darkening gloom, they looked like floating ghosts.

Ambrose tiptoed behind, waiting for the perfect moment to poke his thumb into Tobias's belly. The man turned with a gasp and a start. A look of laughter flashed across Ambrose's face as he pressed his finger to his lips. "Meet me in the orchard," he whispered.

Under the trees, the cheerful sun of afternoon gave way to the steel clouds of early autumn. A chill wind rustled the leaves above, and Tobias plucked a red apple, polishing it on his cassock. Sweet juice rolled off his round chin. "Doesn't quite make up for the paltry supper," he said. "But it helps."

"Well, I'm just happy to see the both of you!" Ambrose exclaimed. "I've been here without a friendly face for almost a month now. Tell me, how was the boat ride across the sea?"

"The ship was pleasant!" Killian said. "Although the cities and trains were challenging. I'm glad Tobias was with me; his English is much better than mine. Some of those people are so hard to understand!"

"Ever the exuberant youth." Tobias shook his head in disagreement. "It was two weeks of endless blue I'd rather not remember."

"Ah, it wasn't so bad!" Killian chimed in, laughing. "It was peaceful seas this time of year, they said, although the meals were rationed a bit lighter than the good Father Tobias's preference. We should have stayed longer; he could stand to lose a bit more."

Tobias rolled his eyes, ignoring him and glanced at the Abbey on the far side of the meadow. "Tell us of this quaint, little town. What have you learned? Have you met Father Valentine or learned anything of Bishop Stephan?"

"Father Valentine is in the woods, they tell me," Ambrose said. "He's been there since before I arrived. That would be almost four weeks ago. They say he takes silent retreat in the forest, but I can't imagine any man, let alone an aged priest—no offense to you, Tobias—living as an ascetic in the wilds, with so many savage beasts and inclement weather. It was dreadfully hot and humid before you arrived, and the mosquitos are enough to drive a man insane. As for Stephan, no one will say. This town is closed to me and the people grow silent when I near. The brothers will have nothing to do with me. I fear I am shunned."

"Valentine was always an eccentric," Tobias offered. "He wanted to 'live as the apostles,' meaning a life of poverty, of course." He waved to the buildings. "That explains the abbey at least.

"As for Stephan, I know that must be hard," he continued. "I know what he meant to you and the influence he had upon your youth, even if you haven't seen him for many years."

"He's the reason I joined the seminary." Ambrose looked away, pained. "And it's also why they let me in. Had it not been for him and his closeness to my father, I would have stayed in the Catholic Boys' Home, or worse, on the streets of Konstanz."

Tobias clasped his shoulder. "If anyone can find him, you can."

In the distance, brothers in brown robes went about their duties, hoeing in the garden and hauling wood and water. A lone crow cawed from the steeple, its black head bobbing as it watched them intently. Killian shuddered and turned his back. "Who leads while Valentine is away?"

"There are two: Anselm and Meinhard. The latter seems to be ordained by Father Valentine. Of course, Valentine hasn't the authority, so I'm not sure what exactly to think of him. As for Anselm, he's Valentine's trusted confidant. He is a severe man. It's best to stay on his good side, which means staying away from him. But what his actual story is, I have no idea."

Tobias folded his arms, his brow furrowed and considering. "Well, we must be delicate, as you know," he said. "Cardinal Eberhard still presses for Valentine's excommunication. The rumor of this undoubtedly has reached here. If I know Valentine, he'll want to court our favor in the hopes we make a good report to convince the Grand Ducal Council in Karlsruhe that this affair should be put to bed. We must tread carefully or risk being driven out before our investigation is complete. It won't help our cause if he himself decides he no longer needs the church."

Ambrose nodded. "What has the cardinal said since I've been away?"

"Well, you can only imagine. But more damning is the most recent letter from the deanery in Sasbach." Tobias drew a folded paper from within his robes and read aloud:

Regarding the prophecies of Father Valentine von Eschen...these deplorable writings are a rambling of self-indulgent nonsense, deceptions and banal imaginings, entirely without substance or basis... There can be no doubt the scheming author chose such visions of doom as the apocalypse for his obsessive prophecy in order to take full advantage of the fear, loathing, and trepidation of our modern times. He preys upon the superstitious and uneducated, who would rather believe in demons and miracles than what scripture says is right and true.

"If that weren't bad enough, all deaneries instructed their priests to denounce Valentine from the pulpit, saying his works…

…are the delusions of a madman, filled with errors long condemned by the church as heresy, and meant to confuse simple hearts and minds.

"Let me see!" Ambrose grabbed the paper, shaking his head. "They certainly don't mince words! It is good that he left. But this letter will anger many people here. We must walk lightly, though that will be even more of a challenge given recent events."

Killian raised an eyebrow. "What recent events?"

"Unfortunate and odd occurrences, like the rumors of the Black Forest," Ambrose looked over his shoulder as if someone might hear. Turning back, he frowned and told of the miller's boy and his fruitless search of the grounds. "The doctor cannot say whether it is man or beast or something else entirely."

"What terrible timing," Tobias said. "And terrible news to arrive to." Suddenly he lost his appetite and tossed the apple aside. "Let's pray it doesn't happen again."

The deep toll of the bell rang clear across the meadow. The day had grown eerily shadowed and chill.

Evening prayer called.

☩

CHAPTER 6

A Body in the Stream

October 7, 1859

The body of the woman lay against the soft bank. From her coarse gray hair, Ambrose guessed she might have been in her midfifties. Her dress was plain and modest, of a faded blue and threadbare, and on her face were the lines of many years of sorrow. Blood was mixed with mud in unusual tracks, like the ones where Augustin's body had been found, and the bubbling brook at her feet splashed on the rocks like tiny bells, painting the scene in a macabre cheerfulness. He covered his mouth with his hand and turned away.

"I thought it best you see the site undisturbed," Albrecht said. "Although I don't think this is what Father Valentine envisioned when he asked me to inform you of any strange or unusual happenings."

Joseph and Poldie stood by the dead cart, hats in hand, and Ambrose noted the boy's trembling lip. "Who was this poor woman?" he asked.

"Rosa, sir," said Joseph, cap in hand. "Rosa Schurr. She always came here before sunrise to get an early start on washing. Didn't like to be around people. Poor thing never had it easy. She came with the first boats. The church wouldn't annul her marriage to a beast of a man, so she fled here with her brother Bernd."

"Bernd Voss? Young Issa's Father?" asked Ambrose.

Joseph nodded. *"Ya,* the same."

"She kept her married name?"

"No, she remarried. Father Valentine allowed it. It seemed only right. It's a pity, though. He died from Paris Green not long after."

"Paris Green?" A dark cloud passed over Ambrose's face. "Did he take his own life?"

"Now, we're here because of Rosa, not Will," Albrecht said. "Besides, it's not right to gossip, least of all about the dead."

They stood in silence. The babbling brook sparkled in their eyes as it danced in the early-morning sun. The mule snorted and stomped in annoyance, its tail swishing away the flies. Soon the townsfolk would be up and would hear the news.

"I should like to call the other fathers," Ambrose said. "I haven't a head for such things—nor do they—but I should like their observations all the same. At the least, I should like not to carry the burden of observation on my own."

"Nay, that I cannot allow," said Albrecht. "I don't know those fellows. I'll talk to you alone." He turned back to the body. Strands of uncombed hair waved in the wind and dark circles ringed his tired eyes. "Let's get her up before the town comes to gawk."

Kneeling, Ambrose examined the site. The tracks were long—perhaps as long as a foot—but thin, except for what could have been a footpad. They were broken and seemed to slice into the earth, in the same way as at the muddy trail where Augustin had been found, and as before, they were too smudged to be clear and nothing led to or from the area. "Is there anything that leaves such marks?" he asked.

"None that I know of, sir," replied Joseph.

"But it cannot be a man?"

"Not unless he has the narrowest feet in all the land," said Albrecht.

As they stared, the bonnets of washerwomen bounced in the distance, cresting the hillock in blues and grays and reds as they hauled their linens to the brook. Their voices rose, chattering across the glen.

"Quick now, up we go!" Albrecht ordered. "Before the town goes a stir!"

Joseph and Poldie struggled to get the body into the cart. "Time to get your hands dirty, Father!" Albrecht said, slapping Ambrose hard on the back.

Ambrose grimaced as he grabbed a limp arm and pulled. Memories of his father's clinic raced through his head: the smell of old death and embalming alcohol mixed with the bloody coughs of consumption in the next room; bodies hidden beneath sheets as his mother shuttled him out, scolding; his father's ghostly countenance before he died. Shuddering, he pushed them away.

Straining and struggling, they heaved on slippery ground. The earth gave way under Ambrose's feet and he slipped and fell, his fingers spreading wide as he sank into the muck, the must of dark earth and old leaves rising to meet him. Quickly he got to his feet. Mud clung to his boots and cassock as the men finally hoisted the body onto the cart and stood panting, covered in mud. Albrecht tossed a sheet over the corpse, and Joseph and Poldie hurried down the trail.

"Best we meet tonight when fewer folk are about," Albrecht told Ambrose. "I'll talk to Father Meinhard again and ask him for your assistance. Oh, and best clean yourself up. You look a mess!"

That morning, Killian and Tobias walked the town's main street. A group of women pointed and whispered in front of Köppen's General Store, and Killian blushed, his face bright red. Up the street, others glanced and quickly turned away. The blacksmith studied them coolly from his grindstone, his gaze lingering uncomfortably long.

"We're not wanted here," Tobias said. "We are what Valentine's prophecies speak against." He stared stubbornly ahead, refusing to notice them. Killian nodded, yet it seemed he couldn't look away.

The small town was a backwater Killian hadn't imagined. He knew the new world would be filled with excitement and danger, and the sweat and tears of breaking in the untamed land. But he hadn't anticipated the harsh solemnity and lack of revelry and art. The houses were all of fresh hewn timber and plaster, but there was not a stone wall or foundation to be found. The streets were plain dirt, dusty in the sun and muddy in the rain. St. Gregory had the feel of an outpost town built quickly and with no time for beauty. There were, of course, no lofty cathedrals like in Köln or Heidelberg. In fact, there was very little art at all, save for the wooden crosses or macabre shrines chanced upon on empty country trails. Such starkness seemed mirrored in the eyes of the passing townsfolk.

"Ah, the baker!" Tobias nodded. A wooden shingle hung across the street with the image of a carved pretzel and a stalk of wheat; below it were the words STOLZ BÄKEREI. "Finally a real meal. And it looks like a café, besides."

The door creaked open and the nutty aroma of freshly baked bread wafted over them. Two women stood at the counter, whispering, "…no good will come of her. First Augustin, now Rosa. That Voss girl has cursed them! Mark my words, there's more to come." The door rattled shut and they glared at the intrusion. Their noses turned, they left, leaving Killian to stare after them, confused.

The café now empty, they sat in comfortable silence, warm rye bread and coffee on the table before them. Tobias cut a small loaf, smiling at its satisfying crunch. Soon, soft butter and cheese melted over the steaming doughiness.

Killian sat quietly, feeling the warmth of the mug in his hands, doing his best to ignore the baker, who, with slitted eyes, looked on from the counter in disapproval.

"My good sir, pray tell, who is the man of the Voss family?" Tobias rubbed his chubby chin and raised his bushy brows. "Inquiries from family back home and all."

Frowning, the baker turned his back and busied himself. "The cobbler," he grunted.

"I see," said Tobias. "And if I needed the cobbler to fix my boots, where would I find him? I saw a cobbler shop that was closed on the way."

The baker shook his head, annoyed. "That's Hartman's. Voss is down the street toward the stables. If you can't find him there, his house is on the south side by Jacob Durst the carpenter. Claudia or his daughter Issa would know where he is. But leave him in peace; his sister died today."

"I'm terribly sorry to hear that!" said Tobias. "In that case, I shan't bother him. It's a shame how these things tend to happen."

The baker scowled and turned away once more.

Meinhard's face beamed a jolly smile, his cheeks red as an apple. "Off to go exploring? It's a fine day for it and a fine country as well!" He stood in the abbey's kitchen, stuffing a cloth bag full of cheese and sour apples and old bread for Tobias and Killian. "Ah! For your consideration." He winked and stashed a flask of wine inside. "There's a footpath around Pigeon Lake and a meadow on the south side. Not much used by the folk and you'll likely not see another soul. But stay on the trail. You're liable to get lost if you wander, and the forests are thick and dark. Now, off you go, before Father Anselm spies you!"

It had turned into a glorious autumn afternoon. The sun peaked its head around the scattered clouds and lit the forest in soft golds. The cart trail ended where the logging had stopped, and the wood quickly grew dark and shaded. The narrow path wound among cedars and birch as it followed the eastern edge of the lake, dipping around the squishy sinks and shallow bogs.

"Damn it!" Tobias exclaimed. His foot had slipped off the path and into thick mud. His chubby face turned red and Killian choked down a laugh. As soon as they entered, the forest became alive with the hum of mosquitos. They batted and slapped them away but were soon covered with bites. "Fine day, my ass! Damn fool."

Soon the path turned east and led up a hillock, where a rocky outcropping looked over the lake. From its top, they could see the southern edge of the town with the abbey's steeple in the distance. To the west, the black cross of the town's abbey poked above the trees.

"Ambrose said Augustin's body was found somewhere along the trail. But I think we've passed it. He didn't mention a hill or a view of the lake," Killian turned and tugged his narrow ears in puzzlement.

"It seems this traipsing through the marsh wasn't worth it," Tobias grumbled as he rubbed the mud from his boot and scrunched his wet toes. He pointed to a glade in the distance. "Let's head to that meadow at least and have a bite to eat."

The path led on gradually away from the lake, and the marshlands rose to a thick underbrush of maple and beech forest. The croak of frogs slowly fell away, and the twitter and call of birds grew clear overhead. A sudden burst exploded from the underbrush, and the flap of frenzied wings thundered by. A large bird alighted to the branches above, gazing down at them accusingly as the wood erupted in the chatter of angry squirrels.

Killian pointed. "Turkey!"

As the path climbed ever higher, the trees thinned and the underbrush gave way to grass and soon a meadow opened before them, hedged by the red spikes of sumac. A herd of dear grazing in the distance caught wind and with a flash of white tail bounded into the forest.

"I think it's time for some supper!" Tobias said.

Their hearts were light in the golden sun. Happy to be under the open sky, they sat on a large rock in the middle of the meadow, chewing on hard bread and aged cheese. The wine was poor, but the sun was warm on their backs and the afternoon glow made them cheerful.

"It's a harsh land," said Killian. "The people seem hard here. No one smiles. Of course, they don't in Augsburg or Stuttgart, either. But this much worse."

"It must be difficult." Tobias shook his head, considering. "I can't imagine sailing that sea knowing I would never go back. Then to give everything you own to the Association. But then I wouldn't have left to begin with."

"Was it really so bad for them back home?" Killian asked, gnawing on hard crusts.

"I think some people are never happy no matter where they are. When a charismatic man claims to offer salvation and miracles, they become blinded to their own good sense."

Killian sat in thoughtful silence and stared at the wispy, autumn clouds. "What was he like?" he said finally and passed the wine.

"Father Valentine?" said Tobias. "I haven't seen him in twenty years, since long before he left. We didn't hear rumors of his condition until well after seminary. But even then, he was always a little unsettled. He was silent and mostly kept to himself, but he had a fervor in his eye, and when he got on a topic, he was like a man possessed. Mostly, he railed against the decline of our times. It was only later he started to write his 'prophetic visions.' It's a shame Bishop Stephan followed him here to try to bring him back to the fold. Now, we've lost him too."

"I'll never understand why the bishop left," said Killian.

Tobias gazed at the trees in the distance, past the waving autumn grasses, and his thoughts turned to the past. "He thought he could save him. They were close once, I heard."

They sat in silence for some time as the warm glow of afternoon turned to dusk. Shadows lengthened and the sky grew cloudy as a chill wind began to blow. "We'd best head back," said Tobias.

"What is carved on that tree?" Killian pointed suddenly.

At the far edge of the meadow stood a tall beech. Drawing close, they saw the tree marked the entrance to a narrow, hidden path that ran into the dark hemlock. On its bark was an unusual symbol: a circle with sharp petals within. It was rough under Killian's fingers and the hair stood up on his neck.

"That's a daisy wheel," Tobias whispered. "An old witchy symbol."

Killian squinted, confused. "For what?"

"I don't know. Let's just take a quick look."

Tobias made the sign of the cross, and they entered down the path. Darkness enveloped, like plunging into night. The path wound around the gnarled roots of old hemlock and moss-covered rocks. As they went, the air grew still and the chatter of birds from the meadow seemed distant. Streams crossed the way, and here and there planks were laid. Slowly the trail rose and the trees broke and opened into a shadowy glen, gray from the clouded sky.

An immense ash grew in the center, its giant trunk wrinkled and green from moss. The boughs reached high and spread over the glen so only pockets of dim light shone through. At its feet they saw an altar as tall as a man. Rough-split planks formed a sloping roof and the sides were of twisted branches. In its center stood a wooden carving of a woman with long flowing hair, at her feet an old offering that was now dried flowers and scattered bones.

"Who is that?" asked Killian. The glen was empty, yet he peered into the dark wood a sudden fear of eyes upon him.

"Well, it certainly can't be the Virgin Mary. Her dress and pose are all wrong. This figure seems less a virgin and rather more suggestive." Tobias frowned and studied the long, flowing features. "This place does not feel right. I think we should go."

"Best not to be out in the woods at night!" a husky voice called.

Killian jumped. A man approached where no one had been just moments before. He set down his bundle of sticks before them and stretched his back as he looked at the sky, curly red hair falling across his freckled face.

"I think we're lost!" said Tobias.

"I should say you are! And you'll only get more so going this way. Best turn around and get a move on, or you're liable to get 'et come nightfall." He gave a curious wink and Killian shifted uncomfortably.

"I am Father Tobias and this is Father Killian. We're from—"

"St. Gregory, I know," the man said. "That's why you shouldn't dawdle. You're lucky I was passing through, to let you know night comes quickly here."

"Are you going to town? Perhaps you could accompany and make sure we don't take a false way," suggested Killian.

The man shook his head. "No. I don't live in the village. Too many people, if you take my meaning."

"I think do." Tobias smiled faintly. "We're not wanting to intrude. We'll be on our way." They turned to leave. The dark path loomed ahead, but before they entered, Tobias turned back. "Who do we have to thank for reminding us of the time?"

"Nicolaus," the man called back.

"Nicolaus, who is that shrine to?"

"The lady! Can't you see?"

✠

CHAPTER 7

Cold Coffee

October 7, 1859

T he body rested on the table. Yellow flame flickered and danced across the dirty sheet as darkness swallowed the rest of the room. Albrecht puffed his pipe, his cheeks lit red as the nutty tobacco smoke filled the room. Ambrose sighed, his chest heavy and tight. He had hoped to see a look of peace on the woman's face, but by a trick of the light there was a grimace.

"Well, let me show you what I found," Albrecht said. He drew back the stained sheet, revealing a hole of thickened blood. A white rib, broken and snapped, pierced the alabaster skin, and the air smelled of iron and raw flesh. Ambrose grew dizzy and every fiber in his body urged him to leave, yet could not look away.

"I'd put the time of death at around five," Albrecht said. "The cause seems quite obvious. Notice the same deep cuts. Just the heart is missing, as with the miller's boy. But look here on the forearm…" He pointed to the jagged lacerations "She was defending herself."

"What would have caused that?" asked Ambrose. "Was it the same as whatever attacked Augustin?"

"That's the riddle. It's too jagged for a blade but too deep and clean for an animal," Albrecht said. "As for whether it's the same, it would certainly appear so."

"Does any animal take only the heart? There were no tracks to or from either site. Surely a man must leave tracks?" Ambrose shook his head, confused. "Does this happen often?"

Albrecht turned away and didn't answer. He took a bottle from the shelf and his hands trembled as he poured, brown liquor swirling in a dirty glass. He swallowed in a gulp and sighed before pouring another. He handed a glass to Ambrose, who politely declined. *"Kümmel,"* he said sheepishly. "For my belly. Seeing all this…gets to a man."

The doctor turned away again, staring into the blackness beyond the window. Long moments passed, still but for the rattle of the window and the rustle of leaves in the sudden gusts of wind. A candle wavered in a chill draft as thunder rolled somewhere in the distance. To Ambrose, the world suddenly felt dark and small, and he and the doctor and the body were the only ones in it.

"Doctor, I'm not sure what to do," he said finally.

Albrecht turned. "Well, why are you here?"

"For the commission, to look into the disappearance of Bishop Stephan. And, well, to report on rumors. To see if there's any truth.

"Oh, what rumors are these?" Albrecht said.

"Do you not know? Did you not come with Father Valentine on the boats?"

"Of course," Albrecht said. "I've heard it all. I have been with Father Valentine a long time. Maybe almost as long as you've been alive. But I'm curious what you have to say about it."

The old doctor stared at him, calm and oddly resigned. Ambrose couldn't guess the man's mind. No furrowed brow or squinted eyes hinted at his thoughts, and he felt a sudden twinge of fear that whatever trust he had would be lost if he said the wrong thing now. Now wasn't the time for church politics or judgement.

"Strange things seem to follow him," Ambrose said. "We'd all heard of his claimed miracles in Urach and Mudau. Everyone looked the other way. But as you can imagine, the deanery took issue with his mystic writings and prophecies. How could they not? Valentine wrote of coming war and the destruction of the state. He administered sacraments against the prescriptions of the Council of Trent. Of course, he was suspended: *'ab omni officio parochiali et sacerdotali.'* He didn't leave the deanery much choice in the matter."

Albrecht sighed. "That was all in a different world."

"Yes. No one expected his 'spiritual recollection' at St. Peter's to make him change his ways. And he's transplanted to the new world now, so none of this really matters." Ambrose paused for a long moment. "But back home there are still rumors from the families of those who left. Loved ones have stopped writing or gone missing. There have been bizarre accidents reported. Some letters suggest their writers have slowly gone mad. And always there are Father Valentine's prophecies of the end of the world, and the spiritual sickness of our times. The Church has strictly spoken out against such interpretations of the teachings, of course. At any rate, it is too similar to what happened before. There's nothing an unofficial Catholic Commission can do about it here. There's no religious authority in this land. But we should know nonetheless, if not for the sake of the families back home, then for those who might follow."

The doctor drew the sheet back over the body and stared into the darkness, his brow wrinkled in the flickering lamplight. Rain tapped against the window, the room lonely and dark as the long moments stretched on in silence. Ambrose couldn't tell whether his answer had angered the old man or whether he was lost in thought.

"Why are you aiding me?" Ambrose said, finally. "Father Valentine asked that you share with me any peculiar events, yet I doubt he meant this. Certainly he must not have expected any of this to happen. You could have kept all this from me and kept it all hidden from my report. Others would have done so."

"Because I want it to stop," Albrecht said. "And I cannot do it by myself. Father Valentine is a good man but misunderstood. Some of the other fathers at Hofsgrund may have described him as 'simple' and 'innocent,' but in truth, he has an earnestness others find threatening. And he also isn't the man he was back home. He is softer now. I think this land has changed him for the better. But I can no longer deny there's is a strangeness at work, as well. Dark things seem to follow him and I don't know why. I fear I'm too close to see it."

"Then what should I do?" Ambrose said.

Albrecht filled his glass with more *kümmel* and downed it in a swirl and a gulp, letting the glass clatter on the table. "Help an old man make sense of things," he said.

The next morning, the sun bathed the white chapel walls in patches of warm light. A solitary voice rose to the heavens and the congregation bowed, silent before the brother's hymn. After the horrors of the night before, Ambrose felt his spirit lift, as if his very heart would burst, and a tear ran softly down his cheek. The town was such a conflict of ugliness and beauty. Such song could have filled the cathedrals at Köln or Vienna. *How could such a voice be in this backwards place?*

Mass slowly drew to a close. Father Anselm bowed before the altar as the carving of Christ looked down, sadness and pity immortalized on his wooden face. Breaking form, the priest turned suddenly and held up his hands. All faces looked to him, expectant.

"Our town has seen its share of loss," he began. "The Lord has called both friends and family back to His kingdom above but not always in the manner we would wish. It is not our place to say what is right and what is wrong. Now, two more have been taken from us. In such times, there are some who would curse or question God's ways. You must admit such weakness in your heart. Only by admitting can you become more steadfast in your faith!

"Know that everything that is visited upon you, every heartache and loss, is just in the eyes of the Lord. That is the penance for our original sin, and that suffering is the price to enter the kingdom of heaven. Let no man take your rightful suffering away from you!" He leveled his gaze at Ambrose and Tobias and Killian, seated in the back. "Let no false prophets claiming forgiveness corrupt your hearts."

He raised the chalice with its white veil to the cross above before turning to the congregation. *"Hic est enim calix sanguinis mei…"*

The townsfolk smiled, serene, as a line led to receive the host. Anselm's face was placid as he set the dry wafer on their tongues. Ambrose and Tobias and Killian exchanged worried glances. "False prophets claiming forgiveness," Tobias muttered. "A self-serving corruption of the Lord's message that will surely keep them in line."

With Mass finally ended, they stood on the steps of the church as the cheery autumn morning greeted them; the leaves of maples and poplars, touched with the first change of color, fluttered in the nearby forest. The hum of happy talk surrounded them as folk met and laughed before the open doors and friends gathered nearby. An old man grinned, cap in hand. "Mass is over. Time for a drink! *I mean, tea.*" Another, nearby, winked under a head of pure white. "I could do for a cup of tea myself!" he said, laughing.

"Don't tell Father Anselm!" Together they ambled down the road.

"Despite it all, they seem happy," Ambrose said.

"It would seem," Tobias grumbled. "But I don't trust this religious ecstasy one bit,"

The townsfolk milled about the steps, laughing. Girls giggled and blushed while boys smiled for their attention. Their mothers shooed them away and their fathers ignored them, talking to one another in nods and handshakes. It could have been a normal Sunday in any small town.

Suddenly a shout, angry and slurred, rose above the happy talk. "Damn you, Voss!" it roared. "The nerve of showing your face in church!"

Everyone turned. An enormous man staggered into their midst, his Sunday jacket torn and pants muddy. He glared with red, swollen eyes. "Voss!"

The crowd parted. Whispers rose as men stood before their wives, their arms outstretched. "The miller's drunk!" they said. "Poor man lost his boy! I can't imagine the pain."

Otto reeled, bleary eyed and searching, as Bernd stood fast, Claudia and Issa behind him.

"How could you!" Otto yelled. "How could you, Bernd? Go to church? After my boy!"

"Otto, you should go home now," Bernd said. "This isn't right. You'll have a clear head tomorrow and you'll regret it."

"I've a clear head now! How could you let her in the church?" he sputtered. "I told you to keep her away from him. Away from my boy!"

"Otto, it's no one fault!"

"It's *her* fault!" He pointed his finger at Issa. "She killed my boy! Your whore daughter took him from me. Seduced him into the night! And now he's dead, cold. How could you? And Rosa now too, your own family!"

The townsfolk whispered and pointed as Issa stifled a cry and buried her head in her mother's sheltering arms.

"Damn it, you old drunk fool!" Bernd yelled. "Get out of here! There's no cause for this!"

"She'll get you too!" Otto waved his finger at the townsfolk. "She'll take your loved ones away! All of them!" Otto glared at Ambrose. "And you, damn priest! I told you to git!"

The townsfolk shifted uncomfortably, whispering to one another, smiles and happiness forgotten. The women shook their heads and walked away as the men cursed under their breath. The congregation dispersed under a cloud of heaviness, and soon the dusty street was empty.

"Otto!" Anselm shouted from the church steps. "You make a mockery of the Lord's Mass and a fool of yourself. You should beg God's forgiveness for such selfishness."

"But she killed my boy!" he protested.

"She did no such thing. The Lord has a purpose. Nothing is wasted, not even in death. Now get home and get to bed. I expect to see you tomorrow for penance, after you've slept it off."

Ambrose sat with Tobias and Killian, silently stirring cold coffee. The bakery was filled with the bustle of townsfolk. The baker busied himself behind the counter, filling baskets and bags with loaves of nutty wheat, dark rye, and pumpernickel. Some had loaves tucked under their arms, while others sat at tables with steaming cups in hand. Most, though, had simply come to gossip. No one glanced at the three priests in the corner, and for the moment they appeared forgotten.

Blue and gray bonnets bobbed as women spoke in hushed tones and the long brown beards of the men wagged with ahs and ums. The occasional whisper floated to the priests' table. "…always knew she was trouble." A man nodded, hat in hand. "Such a good lad was that Augustin, and Otto's only one. Now he's alone after Elsa passed." A wrinkled face scowled beneath wiry hair. "...shame he was led astray by that good-for-nothing waif."

Killian absently tore at a crust of bread, a frown of disbelief on his face. "This is not what I expected the new world to be," he said. "It doesn't seem big and open. I heard this was a land of equality and brotherliness, but it seems smaller and meaner than anything back home."

"Best to get it out of your system now, my boy," Tobias said. He sipped the bitter, cold coffee and set it down in disgust.

"We're no closer to finding Stephan, even after I've been here for more than a month," said Ambrose. "I'll have to write another update for Cardinal Eberhard soon, and I have nothing new to say, save for more death and the insular ways of this place."

"Be sure to mention that shrine in the woods," Tobias muttered.

"Why does everyone think this girl Issa had something to do with the deaths?" asked Killian.

Ambrose rapped his fingers on the table. The grain was rough and jagged where it had split from age, and he picked at a splinter and frowned. "I think people make sense of things any way they can, even if they know it's absurd. It's undeniable now that the rumors were all true. Everything we heard from Mudau and Urach. The good Doctor Albrecht has shared with me his own fears. He said as much when he showed me the body. He admits a dark cloud of misfortune follows Father Valentine's 'spiritual magnetic Association,' though he claims not to know the cause."

"Joseph," Killian called, as the man passed.

"My good Fathers." Sepp said, turning with a nod, his hat in hand.

"Joseph, why do people blame Issa for the recent deaths?" Killian said.

The old man fidgeted uncomfortably, rubbing the coarse brim of his wool hat. He looked to the room out of the corner of his eye, but the townsfolks' backs were turned to him. "Well, Augustin had gone to see her that night," he whispered. "He'd gone nights before too."

"But how can one blame a child for the actions of a beast?" Killian asked.

"Children should obey their parents," said Sepp. "At least they say that here. God decrees it. They both met, even though Otto forbade it. And what's more, they met at night, in secret. Judgment follows indiscretion."

"But you can't believe the girl had anything to do with the death of the old woman, her own aunt?" Ambrose said.

"Bad luck comes in threes," the old man replied, shaking his head.

Killian opened his mouth in protest. But Ambrose shook his head. *There's no convincing some people, Killian. You'll learn that soon enough.*

"Issa had nothing to do with any of this," a soft voice said.

Ambrose turned. A young woman stood beside him. Raven black hair fell in waves upon her shoulders and beneath her bonnet was a face of smooth porcelain and hazel eyes. Her pursed lips quivered, but whether from fear or anger, he couldn't tell.

"Issa is my friend," she said. "I watched her as a girl. She is a pure heart who could never do anything to hurt another. Anyone who blames her should be ashamed. Everything she does she does for love. And now she suffers for love too. While the rest of you gossip."

Joseph frowned, embarrassed as she chastised. But Ambrose found he couldn't look away. Something about her held him, something alluring and oddly familiar. Hints of memory, long dormant, stirred in his heart, though he couldn't say why.

"Please, miss, what is your name?" he said.

"Annaliese Fährmann."

"Annaliese," Ambrose repeated. "I apologize. I don't believe Issa is to blame. I want to find out what is. I inquire not to gossip, only to help."

A smile of disbelief passed her lips. She placed a soft hand on his shoulder and he felt his heart quicken. "Issa is a good girl—"

"Annaliese!" a man called. "It's time we head home."

She smiled then nodded as she left to meet her step-father at the door. The man stood stern and disapproving, sharp eyes glaring at Ambrose. The door slammed behind them and she was suddenly gone.

"If you'll excuse me, sirs," Joseph said, "I'll leave you to your business."

The old man left to meet Poldie at the counter. A round woman in a gray dress stacked bread into the boy's hands, her thick fingers squeezing tough crust as she searched for the right loaf. *That must be Gerti.* Satisfied, she filled her basket and led her husband and son out the door.

"We have to find what did this," Ambrose said, suddenly serious.

Tobias looked up with a start. His spoon clattered as it fell into the cold cup, and he looked at his hand in surprise.

"I promised the doctor," Ambrose said.

"I don't know what three priests can do against a murderer or some wild beast in the woods," said Tobias.

"I have to try."

"I'll not go into those woods again," Killian said, his eyes wide in alarm. "I don't want to see the lady of the shrine."

"I agree," said Tobias. "It's not our call to meddle in the affairs of this backwards town. We're here for Bishop Stephan."

"I understand," said Ambrose. "I can't ask you to help. But this is something I must do."

Tobias's eyes narrowed. "You're not on another crusade, are you?"

☩

CHAPTER 8

All the Stars in the Night Sky

October 4, 1859

In the cold darkness, the wind blew against his naked body. No moon or star shone from the heavens. Soft tickling brushed his legs, moving with the wind, and his hair stood on end. Dried grasses. A meadow. All was still, no nightly noises broke the deathly silence. The edge of the forest lay near. He could not see it, but he felt it. It threatened, looming and secret. He knew must enter.

The trees grew closer. A path plunged into the heart of the wood, blacker than the blackness surrounding it. He stood at the entrance, his hand reached out to steady, finding a tree. The bark was rough and scarred as he slid his hand across: a circle with petals. A symbol of some kind. Like icy fingers, the wind caressed his neck.

I have to enter.

The darkness pressed upon him. He fought to leave but found himself deeper within. Something watched. He felt the eyes upon him, all around and staring from the black. The dark path stretched on and on, and the must of the nighttime forest hung heavily. His bare feet touched dried leaves and cold waters. All was silent, but for the pounding of his heart.

The path opened, revealing a small meadow, macabre and green, swathed in dim light. No moon or stars lit the glade, but he saw nonetheless. An ancient ash towered in the center, gnarled and knotted like an old woman, a shrine at her feet. A fair maiden with long hair carved in wood looked at him from within, her face sweet and sultry, and her head wreathed in a garland of birch and elder. White bones lay at her feet. A child's bones. His bones.

His hand rose. Her wooden cheek was smooth under his fingers. He hated to touch it but couldn't resist. Her eyes opened to stare at him, and on her face was a consuming smile.

Something wound and grasped his ankle, rough and strong. More, like hands, reached out to him. A hole opened in the ground. Roots pulled him down, gripping and encircling. Cold, wet earth fell, covering and pressing upon him. Dirt filled his open mouth and he struggled to breathe, his chest weak against the pressure. His heart pounded as he clawed in the darkness and he struggled to scream but could not fight the awful weight on his chest.

With a desperate gasp, he pulled himself away from the terrible dream. He forced his eyes open, only to see a face staring down at him. Large yellow eyes laughed above a bulbous nose and sharp teeth. A creature squatted on Ambrose's chest. Fetid breath, hot and rank, fell on his face as it grinned balefully. A creak came from down the hall and the creature turned, its pointed ears quivering. Ambrose screamed with all his might, but all that came out was a croak. He flailed, crashing on the floor and trembling in cold sweat. Fists balled he leapt up, circling and striking the empty air in panic.

There was nothing there. His heart raced as he stood naked in the darkness. The pale light of the moon lit the tiny room. He turned. Nothing. He feverishly struck a match, the yellow glow of the lamp filling the room. Nothing was under the bed. Nothing in any corners. The room was empty. The flame danced in his shaking hand. *What horrible nightmares! The* horrors *of the day have followed me into my dreams!* He sat and feverishly began to write.

October 4, 1859

What fearful visions find a man in the blackest hours of night... Such dark thoughts of mine...

The night grew long and morning Mass could not come soon enough.

The autumn breeze in the graveyard carried a morning chill, a hint of the winter to come. A crow cawed on the steeple, black against the blue sky as it stared. Poldie dug in the hole below, while Sepp stood above, wrinkled hands grimy with dirt. The old man shook his head as he waved his hands.

"Nay, sir. I shan't go with you," he said.

"But I don't know this queer land," said Ambrose. "I can't tell the paths from the deer trails. I'm liable to lose myself within. I could surely use your help as a guide."

"If you don't know it, you best not enter." Sepp leaned against a headstone and wiped the sweat from his brow; Ambrose frowned at the irreverence. "Ah, Agnes doesn't mind!" Sepp patted the gravestone. "And I don't mind if she minds neither. Funny bird, she was. I miss her. Made the best apple pie. But it always gave her wind! Made for quite the All Hallows' Eve." He chuckled.

"Sepp, you said what's done the killing wasn't a man. But you also said it wasn't a beast," Ambrose said, scowling. "I don't know what you're about with your secrets, but surely someone has to find whatever it is, either way."

"I'll not say more about what I don't rightly know. You'd think me dim. But I won't enter the forest," he said stubbornly. "I can't, anyway. I have this here hole to dig, and one more for Rosa, besides."

Ambrose crossed his arms and looked away. Lines of gravestones stretched to the edge of the wood, mossy and shadowed, with briars overtaking. So many for such a young town. He rubbed his tired face, surprised by the scratchy stubble. *How long since I slept?* After so many wakeful nights, the days were starting to blur.

"Good morning, Sepp!" a voice called.

Sepp jumped up from the gravestone and turned. Father Meinhard approached, gray eyes twinkling as he flashed the old man a wry smile.

"Ah, Father, yes, good morning," Sepp stammered.

"How's the digging?"

"Slow going. It's all clay, you know."

The chubby priest nodded and inspected the hole. The thunk and plop of Poldie's spade measured the silence; the boy's face was dirty and streaked in lines of sweat as he heaved and grunted inside the hole.

"Well, don't break your back. But see it gets done in time for the funeral." Meinhard said.

"Father Ambrose!" Meinhard said, turning. "You look positively haunted."

"I find it hard to sleep these nights, what with all that has happened," Ambrose said. "It gives a man bad dreams."

"Well, we have a prayer here," Meinhard said, smiling. "Maybe a trifle to some, but we take it to heart. I'm sure your mother told it to you when you were a boy, but it works for the wee hours of the night.

Now I lay me down to sleep,
No Night-mare shall find from the deep
But through all of the seas instead shall fly
and count all the stars in the night sky

In the name of the Father, Son and Holy Ghost, amen!"

Ambrose smiled through gritted teeth, his eyes glaring. "Thank you, Father. It surely has been years since I've heard that. How could I not remember such an efficacious rhyme. Old childhood memories… I won't forget again soon."

"I'm sure! The old ways are the best," Meinhard said, slapping Ambrose on the back with a fat hand. He stopped and scratched his head. "Now why am I here? Oh, yes, Father Anselm has said you may have the day for your commission matters. But be back by vespers. And Ambrose"—he leaned close to whisper—"Anselm doesn't like this night business with the doctor. Best be mindful. Well, I'll leave you gentlemen to your day. *Auf wiedersehen.*"

Meinhard's black shape shuffled through the tall grass, hands outstretched and brushing the headstones as he passed, his hands lingering on the graves of old friends. He grew smaller in the distance until finally the door rattled shut and he disappeared inside the abbey.

"Begging your pardon, sir," Sepp said. "There's a woodsman lives to the south of the lake. Nicolaus is his name. You might try him."

Killian stood outside the hotel, his hand hesitant upon the brass knob. The white siding was bright and fresh in the noon sun, and the wooden stoop had been swept clean that morning. The shingle above looked promising: a carved image of a barrel and a mug and, below, the name HOTEL ST. GREGOR. Yet hotels were rumored to be houses of ill repute in the lawless, frontier lands. Or worse, in a town like this, a hotel might be a place for Valentine's followers to congregate. He looked at Tobias doubtfully. "Do you think anyone is likely to talk to us in here?"

"Nope. But a nice break is good for thinking. And I, for one, need a break from this town."

Killian nodded and opened the door.

The polished oak bar glistened in warm yellows, a shelf of brown bottles behind it. A table of laborers turned from their lunch to stare, mud and dirt clinging to their pants, Nearby, a trapper picked his few teeth with a giant knife, eyeing them curiously. The bar back caught their reflections, and for a moment they looked absurd: two priests in black cassocks walk into a bar, one fat and balding, one young and skinny. But all shame was forgotten with the smell of warm bread and roasted pork floating from the kitchen.

The barman turned, eyebrows raised as he held a glass to the light, his thick Hungarian mustache painting a perpetual frown. "No spitting," he said.

They stopped, confused.

"Even if you're both Fathers, I'll have no tobacco in here."

"We don't chew," said Tobias.

"Hm…" The barman squinted. "You're priests in a tavern. Who knows what you do? What would you have?"

"How's today's lunch?"

"Hocks and kraut."

"Hocks it is. And two beers!"

They sat in a corner away from the others. The hall emptied as the lunch crowd left. The trapper left to smoke on the stoop, and the laborers returned to work, leaving piles of dirt where they'd sat, while a buxom maid bussed dishes and swept the floor, sandy blond hair falling in her youthful face.

"Salt of the earth, Killian." Tobias laughed heartily. "This is what you came to see, so take it in."

The young priest stared curiously, as he sipped his ale. The hotel didn't seem to be a meeting place for the religious townsfolk but a wayside for wanderers and laborers and opportunists who had followed the westward expansion.

Voices rose from the table beside them. A thin man in a fine suit argued prices with a salesman, tapping at pictures in a catalog. "This is ten percent higher than two months ago!" he slurred.

The salesman fidgeted uncomfortably. "Mr. Gatterman, transport costs are up. The new rail lines to St. Louis and Kansas City are expensive."

The man in the suit downed his beer and slammed the glass on the table. "Bah! Wool import is down fifty percent. You're a cheat!"

The barmaid came with their lunch, interrupting the priests' eavesdropping. Hot plates of hocks and kraut steamed scents of sweet and sour. A smile spread on Tobias's chubby face as he raised his beer. *"Prost!"* He breathed deeply, a smile on his face as he chewed. "Much needed after that bland abbey fare! Now, if only we could get some peace and quiet to enjoy it." He paused then added, "That man is half in the bag." He eyed the nearby table in annoyance, then turned his back toward the two men with a loud thump. But the man in the suit was oblivious, pounding his fist in anger.

"Mr. Gatterman, I don't set the price, sir!" the salesman protested.

"Damn Brit, always taking off the top," Mr. Gatterman said, spilling beer on his wrinkled suit pants. "Every month different! Amalia!" He held up an empty glass, and the barmaid shook her head knowingly and returned with a fresh one.

"What do you think of this Association?" Killian said.

"You mean the town's governing body?" asked Tobias. "They claim it's a 'spiritual utopian society.' This country seems to be full of them, it would seem. Funny, I don't remember any utopian societies back home."

"Is it true all their earnings are held in common? No man earns a wage but is given only what they need? Dinner and a roof over their head, I mean."

"Except for Mr. Fessler behind the bar," Tobias said. "He owns the hotel. And a few more who provide other 'unclean' services. Father Valentine brought his flock here to practice some type of 'love communism,' or whatever he called it. He's always had romantic ideas of the past. Everything is held in common, and the people pray and work and watch over one another."

"Communism? You mean like everything held in common? Like what Marx and Engel preach? Isn't that what caused the revolutions?" asked Killian.

"The failed revolutions, yes. At least it partly did." Tobias sighed and folded his arms, thinking of the past. "1848 was a trying year. Their notions are still the issue of debate in the universities and there's said to be an undercurrent of resentment among the common folk still. We've likely not seen the last of it."

"But what is 'love communism?'" Killian squinted in puzzlement. He looked around at the bar—at Mr. Fessler wiping his bar glasses, and Mr. Gatterman arguing with the salesman next to them. He couldn't imagine them at all as communist.

Tobias tapped the coins in his pocket; they clinked beneath his black robes. "I haven't the vaguest idea, seeing as I will certainly have to pay for this meal," he said. "I suppose it's the money philosophy behind Valentine's particular brand of religion. If you're going to build a town around the values of Christian Universalism, it helps to have the wages reflect that. As in, no wages. You can't have a communal asceticism of the spirit and still get paid. Things would get confusing quickly. To that end, 'love communism' has a palatable sound to it, I suppose."

"Do you think that works?" Killian said. "Or...could work?"

"You youth are so romantic." Tobias rolled his eyes. "There's a reason we've traipsed all this way. So I would say no, it doesn't. But it also doesn't help there's all these 'mystic writings' and talk of the end of the world. Just nonsense to rile people up and make them fear."

Killian finished off his beer and nodded, considering. Voices barked from the nearby table, loud and heated, interrupting them. The man in the suit was scarlet with anger, while the salesman pointed firmly at a circled price in his catalog.

Tobias shook his head in annoyance. "Salt of the earth, Killian."

Dishes jumped and clattered as Mr. Gatterman slammed the table once more and turned to sulk. The salesman stood abruptly, stuffing papers and catalogs under his arm. "Mr. Gatterman, alcohol and business do not mix. And you, sir, are three sheets."

"I'm a sheet and a half at most!" the man said.

"You have a brick in your hat. You're positively corned. I've a mind to suggest that Mr. Finley suspend your account. Good day!"

The door slammed shut and the room fell to awkward silence. The man picked at his meal, his fork scraping idly against the plate. The barkeep clucked to himself, his mustache waging, and shook his head as he held a glass to the light. No spots. He turned to leave, apparently more interested in the back of the house.

Tobias drained his glass and rubbed his tired eyes. "Not the lunch company I'd hoped for."

"Do you think it's possible Stephan never made it here?" Killian asked. "No one has said a word about him or seems to have any knowledge of him whatsoever."

"Stephan!" They turned in surprise. "*Ya,* that bastard was here! You can tell your damn people back home he can go to hell."

Mr. Gatterman glared blearily at them, his fists balled, as he sat suddenly on the edge of his seat. A quiver of anger passed his jaw, and he looked as though he might leave or stop talking or worse.

"He *is* a bastard!" Tobias laughed, playing along. "What did he do to you?"

Mr. Gatterman stared in suspicion before cautiously peering over his shoulder. "He and that damn Anselm. I told them I couldn't do it! I told them it wasn't enough time."

Tobias leaned forward. "Enough time for what?"

"To sew their vestments," he said. "And the cost went up on account of that damn Finley, the wholesaler. But Anselm and Stephan said I was taking off the top…trying to keep a little for myself. So I said I wouldn't do it. Then they came up with damn stories and lies! Put me on probation and threatened to kick me out of St. Gregory! Now the whole town thinks I skimmed. Bastards! It's all lies!"

"I take it you're the tailor," Tobias said. "What's your name, my good sir?"

"Eh? Edmund. Edmund Gatterman."

"Well, Mr. Gatterman, how would you like to get your good name back? If I can find that damn bishop, maybe we can get him to tell the real story. Any idea where he is?"

Mr. Gatterman grew silent and brooding. He slumped with eyes closed, breathing heavily, as they waited. Tobias clanged his glass on his plate in case he had fallen asleep. Finally he opened his eyes and drew close.

"I'm not supposed to say," he whispered. "Anselm and the others…Winfried and Florian. They started talking about 'paths to purity.' Mortification, subduing one's desires, or some such. Only whispered, you see. But I can hear…"—he tapped his ears— "I don't want no part of that. They've met at times, it's said, at night after vespers. Late. I don't know where. There's a room. A room in the abbey… Then Stephan was just gone! Just gone and no one said anything. And Father Valentine said he was on personal retreat and we should say nothing about him to any soul. But I don't care. I don't care anymore… Make their damn vestments. All I do."

He slumped in his chair, his head heavy on his chest. Tobias gave Edmund's chair a gentle shake, and the tailor's head rolled slightly as he snored.

He turned to Killian. "It's time to go."

☩

CHAPTER 9

Games in the Dark

October 10, 1859

Dried grasses waved in the midday sun as Ambrose walked south. The road grew thick with thistle, and bumblebees buzzed lazily at purple flowers. Houses grew thin on the southern edge of town as the black forest encroached, threatening with deep and extending shadow. The cobbler's house lay shuttered, closed against the morning light, the Voss family hidden somewhere within.

The woodsman Nicolaus lived south of the lake. Joseph had said his house was a small cabin at the end of a deer trail. The only way was through the dark woods and the hike would take several hours on the twisting, turning path. "If you hit Endries Bog, you've gone too far," he had said. "And if you hit Cedar Lake, you're plumb lost!"

The dirt road plunged into the gloom of the forest, and the air beneath his feet rose moist and cold, heavy with the smell of wet earth. Giant trees, dark and mossy, towered high into the sky, a shadowed canopy of maple and ash and beech touched red and yellow with the first hint of autumn.

Ambrose pulled his collar against the unseasonable chill. White fog clung to the bushes and weeds and lingered on the trail. All around, the patter of chill drops fell pale and shimmering to the ground and toadstools glistened red and orange, poking from rotted logs. In the gray mist, there was no sight or sound of any other soul. All was silent.

The road seemed to stretch on for miles when suddenly a movement caught his eye. The underbrush shook and a figure emerged, old and bent: a woman with long white hair. Her ancient face was cut with deep wrinkles and grooves, and long white hairs hung from her chin. She seemed not to see him but sniffed the air, her crooked nose poking from beneath her shawl. In her wrinkled and bony hands was a basket of mushrooms, and the air grew thick with their mustiness. As she neared, Ambrose saw her unseeing eyes, milky and wet, wandering.

She must be lost!

He opened his mouth to speak when she turned and grasped his hand, her blind, white eyes staring into his. "Out to find the *nachtkrapp?*" she said.

Ambrose blinked, uncertain of what she could possibly mean. "Wh-what?"

But the woman cackled and stepped into the trees, swallowed by the darkness.

Icy shivers raced down Ambrose's spine, images of dark fairy tales in his mind. He had barely entered the forest and already he was surrounded by sorcery. *What kind of a place is this?* He looked after her, but she was gone. No sound or movement came from the underbrush. It was like she had never been there at all.

The road narrowed to a trail that wound its way among the marshlands. Maple and ash gave way to thick stands of cedar. Muddy earth squished under Ambrose's boots, and they were soon soaked. All around, the wood was still but for the rustle of leaves in the tops of the trees. No birds called in the thickets. No squirrels chattered in the boughs. A strange silence hung in the air, and the sound of his breath was loud and set him ill at ease.

So deep in the forest, he imagined hidden eyes upon him. He looked behind as he went, but there was nothing. Nothing to the side. Nothing above or below. Even so, he couldn't shake the feeling that something followed. He froze, the back of his neck covered in cold sweat. A soft laugh rose muffled in the distance. Or was it the wind? Ambrose held his breath, listening, his heart pounding in his ears. But there was nothing. Only stillness and the awful watchfulness upon him. He picked up a stout branch and gripped it tightly, as rough bark dug into his palm, heavy and comforting. Looking over his shoulder, he hurried down the trail.

Finally the path climbed slightly and the air grew lighter as he left the boggy marsh. Ahead he spotted the rocky outcropping the townsfolk called *Aschenputtelfels,* the Cinderella Rock. The name sounded pleasant, but Killian had described it as a dark and craggy thing, filled with cobwebs and deep holes. Nevertheless, as he climbed his heart grew lighter. The sun peaked through the trees and the uncomfortable feeling seemed finally left below. Maybe it was the wind after all.

But he hadn't gone far before the faint laugh rose again.

Ambrose whirled. Peering into the dark wood, he clutched the branch overhead. Silence. The eyes were upon him again; something watched. He spun, turning back and forth. In the shadows, strange shapes appeared, faces in old stumps and logs, gnarled bodies in the trees.

Something caught his heel. *A root! Damn it!* He fell backward with a humph and lay blinking at the sky. The light seemed suddenly dim and the heavens were gray where they had been clear moments before.

Ambrose rose to his feet, dried leaves clinging to his robe, crinkly and brittle as he brushed them away. He peered and listened, but there was nothing in the shadows. The feeling was gone. Dappled light flickered in the placid flutter of leaves, and a chickadee called in the branches above: *chickadee-dee-dee!* The wood was calm.

The old fairy tales of the dark woods of Konstanz and the wooded foothills of the Alps above came back to him—stories he hadn't thought about since childhood. His heart jumped with the same eerie feelings of youth, when he'd wander the old wooded mountain trails, far from the grime of the city. He had felt the watchful eyes then too. He rubbed his head and laughed at himself. *A grown man letting his mind get the better of him. This town is making me see things!*

The meadow must be close, he thought and, before it, the deer trail that led to Nicolaus's cabin in the woods. Hopefully the man would be there and would be willing to help. He turned to set foot down the path but stopped. The trail that had been straight moments before had suddenly forked. No one had mentioned a branch in the path! Ambrose stared, wondering what to do. Both paths looked the same. *Damn it, Joseph, why didn't you come with me?* He sighed. *Left it is.*

The trail plunged into thickets of pine on either side. After several hours, a large flat boulder jutted into the path, taller than his head. Thick and springy moss was soft under his hand as he climbed up to rest and the heady scent of pine wafted on a light breeze. The moss soothed his aching back, and he gazed at white clouds poking through the trees.

His thoughts drifted to family and friends. His sister Monika's twenty-sixth birthday had come and gone. He had never missed it before. But now he couldn't even be sure his letter had reached her at all. All Saint's Day was approaching soon and he wouldn't be at his mother's side to light candles at his father's grave. At this rate, he had no hope of being back by December, as promised. He closed his eyes for a moment and wandered in memories of home: the smile on Monika's face on Christmas morning; a crackling fire cozy against frosted windows; the cinnamon spice of streusel and coffee.

Thunder rolled in the distance. Ambrose jumped, startled. The sky was dark, and gray clouds rolled above. Blackness crept across the forest floor. *Did I sleep just now?* It would be dark soon, and he wouldn't be able to find his way back. His chest tightened. *It must be close to vespers! Anselm will be furious!*

He raced down the path, past the thickets of pine and mossy rocks. Somewhere ahead would be the path back. It had to be close. The Cinderella Rock would be just ahead in the distance and then the way straight back to town. He ran against the setting sun, flush against the cool air, sweat beading on his brow and chest. *Just ahead! That must be it!* But he stopped dead in his tracks. It was the same mossy rock he had just sat on. He whirled about, looking in all directions. How could this be? Footprints were clear on the soft ground. One track leading to towards him, another leading away. The thunder boomed again, closer now, and his sweat turned chill as he stood in shock. There was nothing else to do: he ran on.

The path wound up. *That must be it!* But he stopped again. It was the same mossy rock, again! Now two sets of tracks led away. *How could I be going in circles? It's a straight path!* The wood grew darker, and he ran, panicked, as fast as he could. Again the same mossy rock. Three sets of tracks led away. *What the Devil is this!* The light was failing and his heart sank. Slow realization crept in. He was stuck in the woods at night, while somewhere in the darkness a murderous thing roamed.

Ambrose struggled to remain calm, forcing his breath to slow. There was nothing he could do. *Fire. I need fire.* Dead branches littered the floor like dried bones, rough and sticky with sap. Soon a pile grew as he hurried against the dark curtain of night. *Hopefully it's enough to last!*

The brushes rustled. It was close, but he didn't see it. Something ran past him. *That wasn't a deer!*

His hands shook as he fumbled with a match. A yellow flame burst forth, a tiny point against the darkness, and the warm smell of sulfur filled the air. The flame took and grew, hot yellow tongues twisting around sticks and branches. The running stopped. The thing, whatever it was, was still. Ambrose couldn't see it, but he felt it watching him. He fed the fire, stoking it ever higher.

An eerie wind sighed in the trees, its icy hands caressing his neck as fat drops of cold, autumn rain fell, pattering on the forest floor. Ambrose stood guarding the fire, as smoke wreathed around him and his eyes watered. The thing hadn't moved. It made no sound, but he knew it was there.

Night crept slowly onward. The pile of branches dwindled, and Ambrose watched the flames burn slowly down. As the light dimmed, the footsteps rustled again. A laugh pierced the air, high and cackling, like a man's, but not. *It's coming!* Ambrose reached frantically for more wood. Again, the footsteps stopped as the fire grew. But all too soon, it burned low and they approached once more.

Ambrose threw more branches on as quickly as he could, but the pile was dwindling. His heart sank. *There's not enough!* He felt the eyes upon him, watching, waiting for him to stray from the light. He spun around, desperately searching, but there was no more wood! Mocking laughter pierced the night as the rustling grew closer.

I have to move the fire! A dead pine stood nearby. Ambrose grabbed the blackened end of a burning log. Hot embers seared his hand and he cried in pain as the thing laughed, again. Ignoring, he ran.

Footsteps followed. He turned and they stopped, but he saw nothing. Slowly he backed away until he felt rough bark against his back. The branch in his hand was nothing more than embers, dull and red, and the black night threatened to swallow.

The footsteps came again, quicker now. Ambrose grabbed a branch above, thick and sappy in his hand. Desperate, he held the flame aloft. Little tongues of fire caught in the dry twigs, their light chasing away the darkness, and quickly the flame grew, angry and hot, rising into the boughs. The pine tree erupted in a blaze of light and heat, and the footsteps ran away into the night. Ambrose stood facing the darkness, brandishing his stick above his head, a dark shape framed against the raging light.

"So he was there in the abbey all along!" Killian peered from inside the woodshed, watchful for anyone who might stumble upon their hiding spot.

Tobias leaned against a stack of wood, rubbing his fat hands as he thought. "Seems like it. Now the question is 'Where did he go and why?' What happened to him? Was there some accident? Is he being held against his will? Is he still here, or is he somewhere else? And what of this 'mortification' business? I don't like the sound of that."

Killian fidgeted nervously, dusty cobwebs sticking to his fingers as he picked them from the wall. The beams and rafters fluttered with their soft silk, waving in the cool breeze, and somewhere overhead, a flock of geese honked on their long way south.

"What's this about there being a room in the abbey? Did they keep him there?" he asked. "What are they hiding and what do they plan on doing with us?"

"Is this the adventure you hoped for?" Tobias laughed, slapping him hard on the back. "I don't think it's anything as sinister as that. At least I hope not! Still, it's strange. Why are there so many secrets here?" Frowning, he scratched his balding head.

The vesper bell tolled from the steeple, deep and melancholy. Solemn notes called the priests to prayer, as thunder grumbled in a sky that had suddenly turned dark. The wind picked up and the sweet smell of overripe apples rotting in the orchard filled the air.

"We should lay a trap for Florian and Winfried," Tobias said. "Let's pretend we're sympathizers. If they take the bait, we'll know the tailor was right and we'll know Stephan actually was in the abbey, and we still have hope of finding him. If not, we'll look no more foolish than we already do. Now which one do you think is easiest to fool?"

"Winfried is a real tyrant in the kitchen, I've heard," Killian rubbed his narrow nose, considering. "I think he'd be too cautious to fall for something. Florian, on the other hand, is clever. But maybe he also thinks he's too clever to be fooled."

"Good thinking!" Tobias said. "The chamberlain it is. We'd best hurry. It wouldn't look good to be late!"

The chapel quickly filled with the brothers coming in from the rain. The smell of wet earth poured through the open door as candles flickered yellow against the plaster walls. Tobias and Killian looked to one another. Where was Ambrose? They stood in a sea of brown. Only Anselm and Meinhard wore black priest's robes. They turned, expectantly, with every sound at the door, but as Anselm began the liturgy, there still was no sign of him.

He was missing from dinner as well. Tobias and Killian exchanged worried glances in silence. Anselm stewed in anger at his absence, scowling at the head of the table, the rapping of his fingernails on the table blending with the thrum of rain against the windows.

When evening prayers ended, Killian hurried to Tobias's side and they walked through the yard. "Where is Ambrose?" he said, his voice high and tight. "We should have gone with him! What if something has happened?"

"Ahem!" A monk cleared his throat, chastising them for breaking the silence.

Tobias hushed Killian and pulled him behind a tree. "Maybe he was only delayed," he said. "Ambrose is a shrewd man. He may seem overly affected by the world, but beneath it all, he has a sharp mind and good instincts. He knows how to take care of himself, more so than you'd guess. Don't stir yourself up just yet. Besides, we have our own job to do here. While he's away, we need to find out what this chamberlain Florian knows. Hopefully, we'll be able to surprise Ambrose with some good news when he makes it back."

The following morning, after breakfast, the brothers busied themselves with their various duties. Tobias and Killian wandered the grounds, searching for Florian, mindful not to appear suspicious. They finally found him in the linen closet, a sheet of inventory paper in his hand.

An elderly brother, bent and hobbling, struggled with a basket of linens in the doorway, his wrinkled hands feebly grasping the awkward load. Florian cast a sidelong glance of annoyance as the basket caught the doorframe and the man crashed to the floor with a cry. The wicker creaked as he fell and linens spilled and unfolded on the ground.

Florian seethed, his thin frame coiled, as if ready to strike, and his narrowed eyes dripped venom. His thin face was drawn in a tight sneer of wicked enjoyment. "Peter!" he yelled. "The Lord does not waste! Nor does he tarry. Nor is he sloth. Look at this extra work you've created. And almost ruining the basket, besides. Pay attention!"

The old brother cowered, trembling. White hair fell in his eyes as he hurried to gather the fallen sheets. Florian stood over him, delicate fingers balled in a tight fist and raised to strike. But he stopped short as Tobias and Killian approached, stepping back and smoothing his brown robes.

"However Father Valentine preaches love," he said, reluctantly helping the old brother to his feet. "Now hurry along. 'Go to the ant, O sluggard; consider her ways, and be wise.'"

"Yes, sir." The old man bowed and hurried down the hall as Florian glared after him, arms crossed.

Tobias winked at Killian and turned to the chamberlain. "In these sinful times, we grow ever more estranged," he said. "We've lost the original piety our faith was founded on. If only the desert Fathers could see us now. What would Saint Gregory say?"

Florian smoothed a wrinkle in his robe in feigned disinterest. "That seems not in keeping with the church."

"In keeping with which church?" Tobias inquired. "We must be on constant guard against false teachings. It is the will of the flesh to grow soft and decadent and so weaken the spirit."

Uncomfortable, Killian squirmed, but Florian didn't seem to notice.

"Is this the position of your Catholic commission?" asked Florian.

"Now, my good brother, I don't know you well enough to say what's in my heart," Tobias said. "That trust has yet to be earned. I will only say that Luther, for the protestants, did not do enough. But unlike him, we do our work from the inside."

Florian smiled faintly. "That's not at all what I expected to hear. What of your compatriot here? Is he mute? Or does he think the same?"

"Killian? It's not his place to speak in front of his elders; love is to walk in obedience. And, I might add, silence. But yes, the truth is easily obscured and looks can deceive. Hence, our prudence. But we must also act in haste if we are to be a guide in these dark times of sin and so usher in the

New Jerusalem." Tobias looked around him then lowered his voice. "You see, our purpose is disguised. You think we're here to find our dear lost bishop, but we have in fact come to show solidarity. So tell me, how shall I appease the church back home. Have you seen Stephan?"

Florian looked over his shoulder; the hall was empty and quiet. All the brothers were attending to their duties, in the kitchen and gardens and the laundry. He considered them for a moment, lips pursed and dark eyes narrowed, before smiling and leaning close to whisper in a velvety voice, "I cannot say where he may be. I am sworn to secrecy. But I will tell you this: your bishop is alive. Come, there's someone you should meet."

✠

CHAPTER 10

Damn You, Joseph!

October 11, 1859

The dark shadows slowly receded. A dim light woke across the forest, chasing the blackness into holes and hollows. Somewhere beyond the curtain of trees, the sun must have poked its head above the eastern horizon, and in the dawn's light, the phantom faces of the night revealed themselves as twisted, gnarled boughs and stumps. Dew hung heavy on the pine needles above, and the air was chilly with fog. Ambrose's robe was damp from mist, and his collar was drenched in cold sweat from the night before. All around, the earth was scorched. Behind, the remnants of the dead pine lay in a heap of broken branches and smoldering embers. There was no sign of the monster. No creature stirred in the underbrush.

Overcome with exhaustion, Ambrose slumped against the mossy rock. Every part of him ached. He still clutched the branch, painted red from his blistered and bloody hand. As the sun broke through the trees, he finally rose and stumbled down the path. The trail back had but one set of footprints. The others, from when he had raced in panic, had disappeared. Or perhaps they had never been there?

The path wasn't as he remembered. It wound lazily back to the main trail as it had when he had first set foot on it. The Cinderella Rock loomed in the distance, and the morning was still and peaceful. Wrens and jays called in the branches above, and a deer bounded away in a flash of white tail.

Soon Ambrose stood at the fork in the road, stumbling wearily on the long walk to town. He was too tired and hungry to look for Nicolaus the woodsman any further. Besides, Anselm would be even more furious, should he be away any longer. They might not let him back into the abbey.

The path dipped as it headed to the marsh, and he found himself looking over his shoulder at the slightest noise. When the brush rustled ahead, his heart stopped. He dove behind a tree as a sound, like singing, rose far off in the distance. As he hid, it grew closer and soon was almost upon him. Suddenly he recognized a popular tune from home: *"Lied des Uhrmachers"*; the voice broke into song:

Die Uhr schlägt elf.
Die Zeit ist stumm,
wie einsam ist's um mich herum,
nichts will zurück mir kehren.
Genug, genug.
Bald schlägt es zwölf,
den letzten Schlag, Gott helf, Gott helf,
werd ich ihn endlich hören?

Overjoyed to hear the gloomy yet familiar lyrics, Ambrose stumbled onto the trail, and collapsed on the ground. A thin and wiry man with a mop of red hair jumped back. His yellowed and sweaty shirt, clinging to his chest, beneath old suspenders that held up felted, woolen pants. His eyes grew wide as the crazed-looking priest burst from the underbrush. *"Hoi!* What are you a doing sneaking out of the brush?" he yelled, fists raised.

"Oh, praise the Lord! I had no hope of seeing another soul in this godforsaken wilderness!"

"How would you, hiding away like that? You're liable to give a man a heart attack. Or yourself a hard knock on the head from my staff."

"Are you Nicolaus?" he gasped.

"*Ya,* what's it to you? Who the hell are you?"

It was some time before Ambrose could tell of the horror of the night before, and his voice shook when he spoke of the laughter in the woods and the creature that had stalked him. Nicolaus eyed him suspiciously, listening intently to the wild tale. Suddenly he burst out in a hearty chuckle clutching his belly.

"Ah, Lord, what've ya done to yerself? You would be such a one to go and get yerself lost and conjure all sorts of phantoms in the dark." He clapped Ambrose's back. "You, sir, played with a fox all night."

"No…" Ambrose said, shaking his head. "I know a fox and that wasn't one!"

"Ah, yer mind's gotten the best of ya. A fox may sound like a man at night and they'll play with you just for sport. You'd best be off to town afore you lose yourself again."

"It can't be!" Ambrose said. "There's something in the woods. It took Augustin and Rosa and who knows who in the years before. Joseph Liška told me to find you. He said you're a woodsman who knows these parts. You live in the forest; you must have heard or seen something."

Nicolaus scowled. His eyes gleamed bright and his red beard was snarled and snagged; he looked like a wild man. "Only thing in these woods is what you yerself bring in."

Ambrose squinted, perplexed. "What do you mean by that?"

"Evil takes to evil. Nothing mysterious about it. Keep your heart pure and no harm can come to ya. A priest should know that. Are ya sure you're as strong in your faith as you think?"

Confused, Ambrose shook his head. None of this made sense. Why was this man saying these things? This wasn't a crisis of faith or doubt; people were actually dying.

"You don't understand," said Ambrose. "Something is after those who stray out of doors at night. You know the lands—won't you help those in need?"

"There's nothing here," Nicolaus growled.

"Why're you saying that? You know that's not true. Is this about money? I can pay you. I have coin."

"I don't want your coin!" Nicolaus snapped. "Don't waste your time on a wild goose chase. Damn it, if you're so worried, take this. Ironwood will serve you better than that pine branch." He handed Ambrose a stick as big as a staff before easily breaking Ambrose's bloodied pine branch over his knee.

"But—"

"There's nothing in these woods!'

Nicolaus hoisted his bundle and set off down the trail, red hair flopping and blowing in the breeze.

What am I doing out here?

Ambrose sat on the damp ground and rubbed his eyes. The trees stretched on endlessly. The sloping trail before him was several hours trek through soggy marsh, over roots and under boughs. Even the thought of it was exhausting. Yet he couldn't remain in this black forest, filled with treacherous laughter and evil spirits. The morning sun had chased them away for now, but who knew when they might return?

Why am I out here, and not a hunter or a woodsman? What did those brothers in the abbey know? Damn it! Am I a fool? We're going to get ourselves killed on this ridiculous crusade. Valentine has a hold over this place. A darkness follows that man!

There was no soul to be seen on the trail, and the dark shadows of the wood held an eerie loneliness he couldn't shake. Gray fog rolled into the marsh below, seeming to rise out of the very black earth itself. The ground beneath him was wet and cold, and his robe clung uncomfortably, growing damp even as he sat there. There was nothing to suggest the town was nearby; the path back could have been an animal trail for how big it was.

He stared miserably, considering. No one wanted him here. He was an outsider. Even as a man of God, he was unwelcome. Although Ambrose couldn't tell what these people believed, he was beginning to feel it wasn't the same thing as him, at all. The townsfolk were dark and suspicious and fearful. Who knew what lurked in their hearts?

To hell with you Albrecht! To hell with this place! I should go back to Heidelberg. If I leave tomorrow, I can be back by Christmas. I can make Christmas Mass at St. Peter's. I can sit by the crackling fire with my mother and Monika, eating stöllen *and* lebkuchen *and drinking coffee with cream. Cardinal Eberhard can't say we didn't try. I didn't come all this way for spirits to chase me in the woods at night!*

Suddenly memories of Stephan rose in his mind: his father drinking with his childhood friend until the early hours. The house was filled with music, his mother with her zither and father with his Waldhorn. Stephan played mandolin, and the click of Monika's shoes kept time. Stephan's giddy laugh was infectious and filled the house, and soon they all laughed along with him. In the mornings, they'd hike in the hills above Lake Konstanz. When his father died of consumption and drink, and Ambrose's world crashed down, it was Stephan who saw to it he would enter the seminary. And it was Stephan who had helped his mother with the little spare money he had. Ambrose couldn't abandon him to this place! And what would Stephan say if he gave up on this town now? He always had fought for the destitute, against those who would take advantage. Was this town not the very thing he so decried?

To see Issa so scorned and blamed filled him agony; she was so much like his sister. The old guilt rose inside him again. Why did Monika have to suffer in poverty and sickness and abuse on the streets and in the factories when he was saved? Her sacrifice must mean something, and he knew he could never look her in the eye again if he should leave another so like her to the same fate. He blushed in shame and dried his eyes, stumbling to his feet, sore and stiff. The ironwood staff was heavy and comforting in his hand, and he forged on.

Despite the sun, the fog grew thicker, and he hurried forward, hoping to get through the marsh before the trail was overcome. Soon, though, it was lost in white and the going grew slow and treacherous. Many times, he stepped off the trail by accident and sank into the black muck. The path wound back and forth, this way and that, and never in a straight line, and it was only by feeling his way with his staff that he was able to stay on it at all.

After what felt like hours, the fog started to break. The wall of gray grew thin and the ground opened in patches. Wisps of white, like ghostly arms, gave way to let him pass and the ground grew firm. The trees thinned and the sun poked through the leaves. Finally Ambrose rose to a hillock, leaving the last remains of mist behind.

He peered around. A meadow stretched on all sides, ringed by the forest in the distance. Coarse grasses swayed in the breeze, painted in spottled yellows and grays under patchy clouds. He turned about. There was no trail! He had lost it in the fog! He must have somehow walked off it completely, even in the midst of a marsh. The way back was still shrouded in fog, and he could no longer see where he had come from. Under the clouded sky, he couldn't even tell which way was north.

Ambrose's chest grew tight and his heart dropped. There was nothing familiar; no rock or tree or hill in the distance. He was lost! Freezing cold and wet and lost! Every step he took in this place only lead him farther astray. His face flushing in anger, and he brought the staff down hard on the ground, beating over and over. The rough bark tore his blistered hand, but he didn't notice.

"What do you want from me?" he cried. But his voice was small and powerless against the vastness.

Cold and famished and spent, he cast himself on the ground in despair and stared bleakly at the sea of grass. He had no idea how far he had walked. Miles? His water skin was almost empty, and his crusts of bread were eaten long ago. Realization slowly sank in that he might not make it back. If he didn't starve out here, he would die of exposure, or the beast would find him and kill him in the night.

"Damn you, Joseph!" he yelled.

The abbey kitchen smelled of fish as Tobias and Killian entered. A bland stew of perch and bluegill bubbled on the cast iron stove as wisps of blue smoke coiled in the dim light, seeping from holes in the stovepipe. Brothers in brown robes busied themselves cutting bread and chopping carrots and turnips while Winfried stirred the pot, tasting. Thin broth trailed down his brown beard as he looked up, dark eyes suspicious. Florian nodded to the door, and the four men stepped down the creaking stairs into a cold earthen cellar filled with barrels of potatoes and sauerkraut and onions and carrots laid in crates of sand.

"These two claim to be followers of the true gospel," Florian said.

Winfried eyed them up and down. His bulk filled the cellar and the goat smell of his sweat rose rank in the tiny space. His dull eyes shone dark with malice in his wide face and poor Killian squirmed under the man's brutish gaze. "I find it impossible to believe that anyone who serves Cardinal Eberhard could know the false from the true," he said.

Tobias nodded, unperturbed, his ruddy face placid. "We may serve his will at times, but we are hardly servants of his heart and mind."

"They say they work in secret to change things from within." Florian nodded at Tobias and Killian.

"Within what?" Winfried said.

Tobias chose his words with care; he knew nothing with certainty. He must be vague yet believable. "We have our own goals," he offered. "They're similar to yours. You have friends in the Old Word. We have the ability to ease the church's worries with our report."

Winfried glared; the giant man towered above, and the threat of violence loomed. "Your church doesn't concern us," he said.

"Of course not!" said Tobias. "But it would concern those back home who may need but a nudge of encouragement to join their families here."

"What do *you* know of the true gospel?" Winfried asked. The big man clenched his meaty fists and knocked on the wooden barrels in agitation, the sound of the thump struck their chests and rattled in their ears.

"That the New Jerusalem awaits and we must prepare for it," Tobias soothed.

Florian pranced eagerly, almost jumping up and down and stumbling over bags of flour in his eagerness. "Do you believe St. John spoke true? Or was he the victim of his own fanciful visions?"

"I believe the true revelations of a holy man are the fanciful visions of the common fool who doesn't understand them," Tobias replied.

"Then have you heard of this revelation?" Winfried said. "Father Valentine says the decadence of this age is the movement against the very kingdom of God itself and will end when the will of the state no longer heeds the will of God. Rongeanism shall be the blast of the trumpet that opens the gates of hell and the very manner and way of this world's death. *The name of the star is Wormwood; and a third of the water became wormwood, and men died from the waters because they were made bitter.*"

"Revelations 8:11," said Tobias.

Winfried's brow pinched. "Don't lie of your intention. You are here now. If you speak the truth, you have nothing more to seek. Cast off your black cassocks for simple brown robes."

"But we must work from within," Tobias pressed. "We must maintain appearances, to reform until the time is right. We also can't trust and act in aid until we are certain of your intentions, and that can only come after we know of the bishop's fate."

"Your church is beyond reform." Winfried crossed his arms and a dark shadow crossed his face. "You clearly aren't ready. I shall tell you nothing. Not until you forsake your false ways completely. New Jerusalem is not to be found between two worlds."

"If you don't believe our intentions, at least believe our concern is true," Tobias said. "Can you tell us nothing of Stephan's fate and where he might be?"

"No," said Florian. "His room is empty. Until you're dressed in brown, we'll say no more."

☩

CHAPTER 11

Our Missing Brother

October 12, 1859

Tobias and Killian walked in the shadow of the wood. The path that skirted the forest was chill as they wandered past the mossy gravestones, the southern end dipping out of sight and lost in a tangle of wild raspberry. The sky was gray, like so many lately, and autumn storms threatened on the horizon. Anxious, Killian fretted with his hands, unsure where to put them. Finally he crossed his arms, holding himself tightly.

"I'm concerned about Ambrose," he said. "We haven't seen him since yesterday morning. Something must have happened!"

Tobias walked slowly, arms behind his back, gazing at the steely clouds; he was worried too. A frown spread across his face, but he kept his thoughts to himself, lest he worry Killian further.

"Do you remember the trial of Franz Schmidt?" he said finally. "You would have been young. Maybe ten or twelve."

"Barely," said Killian. "I heard about it when I was a boy, but my parents always kept the story from me. Later I heard more at seminary—mostly rumors and gossip, though."

The deep bong of the church bell rang, echoing in the forest as it tolled the hour, and birds alighted from the trees in a panicked flurry of feathers. They priests eyes shot to the abbey, half expecting Anselm or Florian or Winfried upon the trail. They ducked behind the thorny bramble and raspberry that covered the trail and peered past the chalky white gravestones. No matter where they went, it seemed, the haunting feeling of the abbey followed.

"Franz Schmidt was an evil man." Tobias said, looking over his shoulder. "He never should have been allowed into the priesthood. It was only his father's money and influence that swayed opinions. He was never right in the head. They say he had a mean streak and liked to watch things suffer. As a boy, he spent his days at the butcher, watching the slaughter of cows and sheep and swine. It's said he had a morbid fascination with the grizzly business and would stare at the animals strung up, as they were skinned and sliced."

Killian nodded. These parts he remembered.

"Schmidt took a secret lover, an Italian maid by the name of Gianna," Tobias continued. "It was less that she had a fancy for him and more that he was persistent and held sway in the community. He insisted she work for him. When she became pregnant, he slit her throat and chopped her body up to dispose of her, just as he'd seen the butcher do when he was a child. Her family was in Piedmont, too far away to raise an inquiry. No one much cared when her body was fished from a canal. So her case languished, untouched in the courts, and she became just another poor, forgotten, missing working girl.

Tobias rubbed his bulbous nose and took a deep breath as he thought back to those days, pausing to lean against a scrubby boxelder that drooped over the gravestones.

"Somehow Gianna's father got in touch with Ambrose. When no one else would listen—neither the police nor the church—Ambrose investigated the case. He was the one who found the bloodied clothes and uncovered the affair.

And who was he? Not the police. Not an investigator in any way. Just a concerned man."

They stopped at the edge of the graveyard, hidden behind the bramble. Killian shivered, the hair on the back of his neck stood on end as he waited for the rest of the story.

"The police finally opened a case and it went to trial. The church elders at the time wanted to dismiss it. Police action against clergy would question the church's own disciplinary powers. Schmidt pleaded insanity, claiming a long history of family instability. He claimed to hear voices that demanded he sacrifice in the name of the Lord. The judge was a friend of Schmidt's father, and the case seemed like it would be tossed out. But Ambrose wouldn't have it. He dug further into that heinous crime than anyone else would have. Eventually he found a diary planning the crime, proving it was premeditated, and a receipt for a life insurance policy in Giana's name. But not her signature! That signature was no Italian's. I don't know how, but Ambrose found Schmidt's second lover—the secret, secret lover. The one who forged the signature. When he presented this, the judge was forced to convict Schmidt. Cardinal Eberhard, who was a bishop at the time, was so impressed that he took young Ambrose under his wing.

"So, listen…" Tobias squeezed Killian's shoulder. "If there's anyone capable of taking care of himself and getting to the bottom of things, it's Ambrose, even if he's too humble to admit it. I'm here because of my past acquaintance with Valentine, whatever good that may do. Still, I may be able to understand him in the end. You're here because your uncle Walter thought it might cure your wanderlust and give your overly romantic heart some rest upon your return. And he also had the influence to get you here. But it's Ambrose who has been entrusted to see this affair through. He may falter, but he will never give up, especially not on one so dear to him as Stephan, though he hasn't seen him in seven years."

Killian sighed in relief. "I had no idea he was involved in that case! Or that the murder was so gruesome!" he said. "I suppose you're right. I don't know Ambrose all that well. But Uncle Walter speaks highly of him! It's just a shame that we've come up on a dead end ourselves. Winfried and Florian certainly don't trust us now. I don't know how we'll ever find Stephan under their suspicious watch. I fear we must give up."

"Now, Killian, didn't you hear?" Tobias grinned, as they walked again along the brambled path. "Dear Florian slipped us a vital clue on accident. There's an empty room where Stephan stayed—or was kept. I'm guessing it's the locked one at the end of the hall. There's no other locked room in the, abbey save for Valentine's own. All we have to do is break in."

Ambrose stood wearily. The dead grass of the desolate meadow waved softly in the chill breeze, and above, the clouds rolled in the October sky. The fog that had carried him here had vanished, slinking back to the fens and marsh, exposing thick forest and underbrush on all sides. A break in the clouds cast a dim ray of sun, and faint shadow fell on the ground. This certainly wasn't the meadow Tobias and Killian had mentioned. Somehow Ambrose had wandered southwest through the forest, far away from town. *That way looks north to me. At least it's as good a direction as any.* With a sigh, he picked up his staff and walked on.

The woods swallowed him, with no path or trail leading through the underbrush. Brambles and briars scratched and tore, and his arms were a thatch work of bloody lines. Mosquitos buzzed at his ears and bit his arms and neck, and gnats flew at his eyes and blinded until he lost track and could no longer tell his way. He swatted at them furiously, cursing, but it was no use.

As the hours passed, the gnarled trees looked suspiciously familiar. The same faces in knobbly bark peered from their twisted trunks, and twigs hung where he had snapped them earlier. Ambrose stopped in dismay: he was going in circles.

He collapsed, slumping against a log and staring blearily into the distance. His head was heavy in his hands as hot tears ran down his cheeks. His lips dry and cracked, he swallowed the last drops from his water skin. The ground before him blurred and he looked up, dizzy; endless green stretched in every direction and he could no longer tell where he had come from.

Slowly the shadows lengthened. He had no idea how long he had been there, maybe an hour, maybe the whole day. Soon it would be night, and darkness would descend on the forest. The gloom and shadow would creep from the holes and the furrows until the land was sunk again in the black of night. He had no matches to light a fire; he had used the last the night before. He would be defenseless against the monster that surely followed him. Clutching his staff in dismay, he waited long moments for the day to end.

Boom! A crack, like thunder, echoed through the beech and ash. A musket! Someone's out here! Ambrose leapt to his feet, ears pricked up. The forest was still, shocked at the blast. Long silent moments passed. Where did the gunshot come from? He opened his mouth to cry out, but heard the thunk of an axe in the distance. *Thunk.* Pause. *Thunk.* It sounded close!

"Hallo!" he called.

Silence.

Thunk.

Pause.

Thunk.

He raced toward the sound. A root caught his foot and he crashed to the ground. Up again, stumbling, running headlong toward the sound. *Thunk. Thunk.* A tangle of wild raspberry rose up, blocking the way. Ambrose crashed into the brambles, desperately forcing his way through. Thorns scratched and tore at his flesh and robe, leaving blood and frayed cloth.

Thunk.

Closer now. Just ahead, through a patch of pine! He smelled a fire. Wood smoke wafted, heavy with burned pitch, wreathing white around branches and boughs.

Thunk.

He burst into a small clearing. A lanky man in deerskin pants and jacket stood with his back to him, axe in hand as he split a small pile at his feet.

"Hallo!"

The man turned in surprise, a puzzled look in his eyes as he scratched a long beard streaked with gray.

"Hello?"

Ambrose stumbled into the clearing and collapsed by the fire. The man looked curiously at the odd figure before him. Every inch of the priest's bare skin was bloodied and scratched, and his cassock was torn.

"Gott und Himmel, sei Dank! Ich bin verloren!"

Smiling, the man rubbed his chin and tossed the axe against a log. "I'm sorry, Father, but my German is rusty. We can try French if you prefer."

"Oh, my apologies! You're an Englishman?"

"Indeed, I am. Silvanus Messam at your service. But Silas will do just fine."

"Well, Silas," Ambrose said. "I'm Father Ambrose Odenwald, and I fear I'm completely lost. I thought I would die in these woods until I heard your musket shot!"

"I should say so! You look half dead already," he said, handing him a skin of water. Ambrose took it thankfully and drank a long drought. Sighing loudly, he stretched out his hands to the fire, feeling the blessed warmth.

Silas cut down a grouse that had been hanging then handed Ambrose a hunk of bread. "Eat this. I'll cook this bird, and you can tell me how you found yourself out here."

Ambrose sat quietly for some time, chewing on hard crust, as Silas's horse sniffed at his dirty robes. The grouse turned brown on the spit, juices sizzling as they dripped into the fire, and the air was sweet with the smell of roast bird. Finally he sat back and told the man his tale—most of it, anyway.

"So you're here to investigate the little town of St. Gregory?" asked Silas. "It's good that someone does."

Ambrose's eyes shone bright with interest. "You've heard stories then?"

"Ah, who hasn't? Nothing noteworthy, though. But cultish towns have a way of creating tales around them."

Silas tossed a log onto the fire, the flames licking and curling as embers popped. Dusk settled on the land, and a pale sliver of moon poked through the trees.

"You did well to chase the creature away with fire," he said. "If you hadn't, we wouldn't be talking right now. It's not wise to be alone and unprotected in these woods at night."

Ambrose nodded. "Do you know the woodsman Nicolaus? The one who lives by the meadow south of town and collects ironwood? He scoffed and said it was a fox."

Silas rolled his eyes. "Nicolaus is a fool, but more than likely he was trying to fool you."

"Then what was it? Nobody admits that anything exists!

"I can't rightly say," Silas said. "The folks in nearby Altona claim a beast is in the area. Something they call the Steinthal monster. But the true story is lost in gossip and conjecture. The thing is said to live in the Kilnsnake marsh, north of the stony valley. Steinthal, as it's more properly named, though it's not much more than a rocky gully."

"Why would the folks in Altona talk of a beast when the folks of St. Gregory deny it?"

Silas took a seat on the ground across from Ambrose. "Small towns like to keep their secrets, you know? Especially the 'Godly' ones. Secrets and shame and blind devotion are the glue that hold them together."

He tossed another log onto the fire. It crashed and settled, and the flames grew high and bright. The sweet smell of roast bird filled their tiny camp, and hot juices bubbled and sizzled as Silas cut the meet with his long, Sheffield knife. There were no plates, so the woodsman cut the bird on a stump and Ambrose skewered it with a sharp stick.

Ambrose's eyes lit with glee and he greedily tore into it. His stomach clamored as if he hadn't eaten in years, and though the grouse was unseasoned, it was the most succulent bird that he had ever eaten. Steam wafted and the juices burned his fingers as he scarfed it down. Hot oil dripped down his chin, but he didn't care, and he grew heady from warm food, after so long being hungry in the cold.

He stuffed the last bits into his mouth, even sopping up the juices from the log with hard crusts of bread and licking his fingers. Finally, he laid back, hands behind his head and stared at the boughs above, flickering in red and yellows. "So, are you from Altona?" he asked.

"I usually stay there in the fall, when herb roots are best to harvest. Goldenseal and bloodroot, mostly. Ginseng too, if I can get it. But that's usually farther north. If I'm in these parts, I'll stay in Altona well before I stay in St. Gregory. Altona is at least educated, which is hard to find in these parts."

"Oh," Ambrose said. "Are you a doctor?"

"Of a sort. More of an herbalist. Or alchemist." He winked. "Have you ever heard of Constantine Rafinesque? I studied with him in Philadelphia."

Ambrose shook his head. "I'm sorry; I haven't."

"No. I suppose not. He was one of the eclectics. The first actually. Quite the polymath. A brilliant man, but with a mercurial heart, who died in obscurity."

Ambrose rubbed his chin in thought. "You came to the New World to study with him? "Why?"

"Because everything is known in Europe and it's all locked and hidden away. But enough about me. Tomorrow we'll see about getting you back. Do you know where you lost your way?"

"South of St. Gregory," Ambrose said. "In the marsh just east of *Aschenputtelfels*—what you would call the Cinderella Rock. A strange fog rolled in, in the middle of the day, and I lost my way."

"Hm, well, you're a good three miles south of where you started. Best get some sleep, now that you can. And mind you don't wander of in the middle of the night."

Silas handed him a wool blanket, coarse and oily, and stoked the fire high and bright. He lay down on the forest floor, cradling his musket in his arms, and pulled his wide-brimmed hat over his face, leaving Ambrose to silently stare at the black night above.

"You know what its real name is?" Silas said suddenly. "It's not Aschenputtelfels. The Menominee called it *Osepaqamowaw*. Its full name is *Anamakiu Osepaqamowaw*. Or something like it. I don't speak the language, so it's probably all mangled in the retelling. The townsfolk must have thought *Osepaqamowaw* sounded like *Aschenputtel*. Hence, your Cinderella Rock."

"Anamaki Osopamawa." Ambrose said, struggling with the phrase. "What does it mean?"

"Rock of the demons that dwell in the earth."

☩

CHAPTER 12

Ero Mors Tua

October 13, 1859

T he waning moon bathed the abbey in pale light. Stars twinkled in the night sky, and crickets chirped merrily in the distance, unaware of the coming winter. Dark shadows stretched from junipers in the courtyard as Killian quietly slid the window open and landed lightly on the soft grass. He crept to the large pine at the edge of the graveyard and waited. Soon a black shape darted from shadow to shadow, hurrying to meet him. Tobias dashed under the pine boughs onto a bed of soft needles, hands on knees.

"You're pretty quick for an old fat man!" Killian whispered.

"Oh, to hell with you!" he gasped.

They studied the abbey. No lights shone in the windows; no shadows moved on the grounds. All was still.

"The room is at the northwest corner, away from all the others," Killian said.

Tobias nodded. "I wish we could've just swiped the keys from the linen closet. "But that damn floor is so creaky, I couldn't step foot out of my room without waking the whole place. I'm not looking forward to climbing through another window."

"It doesn't look like anyone saw us sneak out. Let's go!"

"That excitement is exactly what your uncle Walter hopes to temper," Tobias said, then smiled suddenly. "Hold on to it a bit longer."

They stood and made ready to go. It was a short run between and behind nearby trees. Tobias squeezed the young priest's shoulder and nodded, but before they could move, a lonely call rose from the deep forest: *whip-poor-will, whip-poor-will!* It was an eerie, otherworldly sound.

"Peitscherwille!" Killian said and peered into the night.

"I didn't know they had them here," Tobias said. "They say hearing a *peitscherwille* is bad luck. Let's hope that's an old wives' tale."

They crept from tree to tree. The abbey grew near, its dark steeple looming above, black against the pale moon, until finally they crouched against its side. The rough-hewn boards were coarse beneath their hands, and the grass was cold and wet with dew. Tobias peered around the corner, breathing heavily. The field was empty; no one had followed them.

They crept in silence, darting glances at the windows of the brothers' cells above, fearful of any face that might appear there. Finally, where the shadow of the abbey was darkest, they stopped and crouched. The room lay on the other side.

Tobias felt the frame. Old paint, curled and peeled, cracked under his fingers. The window was stuck. "Damn it!" he hissed, then drew a long thin knife. The blade glinted as he struggled to work it behind the sash. It barely fit, but finally the sharp edge clicked where it hit the lock; with a slight scrape of metal on metal, the latch creaked open. "I hope no one is in this room!"

"Where did you learn to do that?" asked Killian.

"Never mind!"

The window slid up with a squeaky scrape of wood on wood. "Hop in and get me a chair," Tobias said. "I'm too old to be climbing in and out of windows at night."

Killian climbed and found a chair in the dark room. It creaked under the old priest's weight as he hoisted himself up, and Killian stood at the open window, bracing Tobias against a fall. The process was painfully slow as they struggled to remain silent, until finally the old priest stood panting inside. The floor creaked and shifted under their feet, and they paused for long moments, listening, but there was no movement in the darkness. No sound of slumber came from the bed. No floorboard creaked in the hall.

"Come. Let's have some light." Tobias drew a match, and a flame sparked, sulphury and bright. The kerosene lamp sputtered bitter smoke as the fire took, and the space grew in soft yellow as the shadows were chased to the corners. They turned, eyes wide. The room was a chaos of rubbish. Small amber bottles lined the wall. Wax dripped from old candles, covering the desk and floor, and linens lay in piles in a corner.

"What happened here?" asked Killian. His voice shook in the darkness, and he held his nose against the must and foulness that lay thick about them.

All around were signs of frantic, fevered writing. White chalk was scratched on the floor and wall at odd places, and the room was strewn with papers. Strange objects lay scattered on the desk; a dark handled blade, next to one of white, lay in a chalice of dark liquid. Gray ash spilled from a brass censer. All about was a disarray of smudge and scribbled paper, covered in a thick layer of dust. Clearly no one had been here in some time.

"What is that?" Killian pointed. Above the bed, in large, dark letters, were the words, ERO MORS TUA, O MORS.

"I shall be your death, oh, death," said Tobias. The flame cast haunting shadows and his visage appeared ghastly;

sallow light colored his cheeks in sickly yellow, his eyes framed in sunken shadow.

Killian shuddered to see Tobias so transfigured and looked away. "What is the death of death?"

"The overturning of all things," said Tobias. *"The end that will be revealed."* He touched the dark letters. "This is dried blood."

"Look at this!" Killian stepped back, afraid. "A scrying mirror. I've read of it. But what does it say?"

In a corner, a black mirror stood in a wooden frame. Around it, strange letters in white chalk were scribbled on the floor.

Tobias bent down. "I can barely read this English! This must be old. Let's see if I can make it out… It says, *'Now brother,' quod the devel, 'be noght wroth; thy body and this panne been myne by right. Thow shalt with me to helle yet tonight. Were thow shalt knowen of our privetee moore than a maister of dyvynytee.'"*

He stared at the scribbles for some time, working them over in his mind as he scratched his head. "Now what does this mean? I think it says, 'Now, brother,'" spoke the Devil, 'don't be angry. Your body and this pan' pan…maybe mirror? are mine by right. You shall with me go to hell yet tonight, where you shall know of our privetee.' What's privetee? Secrets? That must be it. 'Where you shall know of our secrets more than a master of divinity.'" This is Chaucer, I believe. I just barely remember this from Fr. Von Ammon's class in the classics at the university in Göttingen. Well before your time!" He paused and stepped back. "What kind of madness is this?"

"Did they really keep Bishop Stephan here?" Killian hissed. "What were they doing to him?"

"Lord, I hope not! But whatever they were doing to whoever was here, it was surely ungodly! What a hellish mind. Look!" Tobias picked up an unopened letter from the desk. The script was bold and florid, and thin long lines were traced elegantly over the white paper. They immediately knew it was from Cardinal Eberhard.

"It is addressed to Bishop Stephan." Sighing, Tobias looked to Killian in dismay.

"They kept him prisoner here!" Killian cried.

Tobias's finger shot up to his lips. "Hush! If we're caught, it won't end well for us. We're heretics to them and heretics burn, no matter the country! Let's not be two of those who never come back!"

Killian grew quiet and folded his arms tight against his chest. The yellow flame flickered in an unseen draft, wafting kerosene smoke, black and acrid, and the room pressed against him like a twisted dream from which he couldn't awaken. He grew dizzy as the foulness surrounded them, and he slumped with his hands on his knees, waiting for it to pass.

The floor blurred in and out of focus as he stared at the papers at his feet. There, among them, was a small old book. An inexplicable curiosity compelled him, and he reached to touch its worn leather cover. The book fell open in his hands as he picked it up. Old type cluttered the pages, running to the very edges, and every empty space was filled with a scrawling hand written in the margins. Loose paper stuck out here and there, filled with notes from different hands. The cover was bare, but as they looked inside, it seemed several different books and notes were bound together. Flipping through, Killian saw strange titles within: '*Dissertations sur les apparitions des anges, des démons et des esprits... et vampires de Bohême... Grand Grimoire... et Pape Honorius...* He didn't know why, but something compelled him to take it. Without thinking, he put the book in his pocket.

"Whose hand is this?" Tobias said, picking up a scrap from the floor and studying its spidery scrawl. "Let's see what it says..."

Augustus was wrong! Proclaim this to the heavens above and the hells below, for we are those who pave the way for the coming judgment. That original sin must be cleansed in the fires of repentance. Through death will we be restored. As Satan is the true agent of the Lord, so do we make ourselves devils...so that such good may work through us. Only as righteous evil are we the tool of the Lord, to act in the face of the timid and corrupt. So fire burns fire. Burns away the impure, that we may usher in the New Kingdom. That evil, our necessary evil, shall be transformed to good, as Lucifer himself is redeemed. Thus, do we know we are chosen. For the New Jerusalem, there must be first pangs of death before pangs of birth...

"It goes on like this!" Tobias cried. "Look, here's Revelations: *Et cum aperuisset quintum sigillum... And when the fifth seal he had opened, under the altar did I see the souls of them that were slain for the word of God and for the testimony which they held. And they cried with a loud voice, saying: How long, O Lord, Holy and True, dost thou not judge and revenge our blood on them that dwell on the earth?*

The hairs on the back of their necks rose. Killian's hands trembled in the growing unease, and he felt like an intruder, as if something resented their presence and wanted them out. Dark hands seemed to reach from the shadows and claw with icy fingers, and the room was suddenly chill.

They looked up. Something wasn't right. Something stirred. They couldn't see it, but they felt it. The yellow flame grew dull, as if all color had drained away, and flickered, though there was no wind or draft. Killian pointed, his face white. A faint light reflected in the black mirror. Two figures stared back at them, dim and hazy: the thin frame of Killian next to the portly Tobias. But behind was a wispy shape. Perhaps a trick of the light played with their fears, but it seemed a hazy figure stared back.

Tobias spun, holding the lamp high. There was nothing behind, yet the feeling remained. The tiny flame flickered again, threatening to go out, and a fear of the darkness suddenly fell upon them. "The window!" Tobias pointed. "Let's get out of here!"

Ambrose woke to the warm smell of coffee, the pot hissing and bubbling. For a moment he was awash in memories of home. Bacon sizzled on a pan with eggs crackling in the fat, the sweet aroma filling the little camp. He sat up and winced, every muscle stiff and sore.

"Thought you'd sleep the whole day away. It's almost ten!" Silas winked. "But I suppose you've earned a little rest."

"My Lord, is that coffee?"

"A priest taking the Lord's name in vain?" He laughed.

"Oh, my good man, I assure you, it is not in vain!" Ambrose said. He held the cup with joy, breathing deeply as white steam danced on rich blackness. "What kind of man packs coffee—and a pot to make it—out in this wilderness?"

"Why, a civilized one, of course!" Silas grinned, cheerfully. He handed him a plate of eggs and bacon and hard bread. "Take your time. I've already eaten."

A short while later, Ambrose dabbed the last bit of yolk and sighed. The fears of the previous day had washed away and seemed like a lifetime ago. Bright sun streamed through the leaves and lit the forest floor in dappled gold and a warm breeze brushed his cheek. It held the faintest chill of autumn, a hint at the winter to come, and he smiled. The fall always filled him with a happy nostalgia, and for a moment, he forgot where he was.

Silas busied himself rolling blankets and packing bags, while the horse snorted and shifted, eager to be on its way. "We should see about getting you back to town," he said.

The moment was broken. A weight fell upon Ambrose's chest, and he suddenly was very weary from the days before. "In truth, I came searching for whatever creature lies hidden in these woods," he said. "I was looking for Nicolaus. I was told he was skilled enough to help, but he refused. I'm indebted to you for saving me. I surely would have died. So, perhaps this is too much to ask, but you seem to know your way around this land and you can clearly shoot a musket. Will you help me find this thing?"

Silas leaned back on his palms. "Find it and do what?"

"Put an end to it, of course."

"You're a priest. What help do you need from me?"

Confused, Ambrose shook his head. *What could a priest do against a wild animal?* Silas clearly had spent too much time in the wilderness. Being so far away from civilization, he must have grown superstitious. Ambrose looked up to see the man studying him. In his leather coat and hat, he looked like a wild man from some forgotten mountain.

"What do they teach you in seminary? Anything useful?" Silas said, chuckling to himself. "I can look after myself well enough in the wilderlands. But to traipse after some beast and hunt it at its own lair is another matter entirely."

"How *do* you stay safe out here?" asked Ambrose .

"Oh, I've learned some things along the way." He reached into his shirt and pulled forth a silver talisman that hung around his neck; it glittered and sparkled in the sun. He took it off and handed it to Ambrose. It was a curious round of rough-worked silver, hammer blows still visible on the surface. On its face was etched a triangle, in the center of which was the sun, with the face of a man. A flame was carved at the top point and a star each on the other two. Below was a croix pattée and the words **"NE CRAIGNEZ SERVANT DU SEIGNEUR."**

"'Do not fear, servant of the Lord,'" Ambrose read. "What is this?"

"That's my secret. It's not the words that are important; it's their power, how they bind."

Ambrose moved closer to the fire. "Don't you think that's a little superstitious?"

"I guess they really *don't* teach you anything," Silas said. "How do you think I'm still alive? Because of superstition."

"Well, you are a strange one Silas." Ambrose handed the talisman back. "But you're all I have in this wilderness, and I need your help. *Innocent people* need your help. I'd like to think the Lord brought us together for a reason."

"My God, and you think my beliefs are odd," he said, rolling his eyes. He turned to his horse and scratched his ear. "What do you think, old boy? What would you do?" But the horse gummed and snorted and turned away. "I don't think he likes the idea," Silas said, laughing.

"Please, I'll pay you. I have the coin and I can write for more."

"Why is this so important to you?" Silas said.

"I've seen two deaths in one month's time," Ambrose said. "These poor folk have been led astray by coming here and are now further lost in some foul enchantment that keeps them witless. But if we can end the beast and show them it was real, and not some perverse, divine judgment, perhaps this bewitchment will end."

"You're hoping to save their souls? I should have known." Silas spat into the fire and crossed his arms and the horse shook himself in annoyance.

"Maybe I am." Ambrose sighed. "But what would I be if I didn't try? If I should leave now, I should never be able to look my sister in the eye again. The cobbler's daughter, Issa, reminds me of her. And there is the matter of my father's friend, to whom I am indebted."

Silas frowned. "You would want to risk your neck hunting some rumor, for a town that would rather view these deaths as a form of divine judgement? You could hitch a ride on a mule cart to Altona or Sheboygan and be on a train to Milwaukee in two days. You could be back home in six weeks, in time for Christmas."

Ambrose held his head in his hands as images rose unbidden: Issa's face in the window, dark with grief and guilt; Annaliese chiding him, her hazel eyes mournful. The memory of her haunted him: her porcelain skin and the shiny waves of her raven-black hair, the feel of her touch on his shoulder.

"I just have to," he said. "I made a promise."

"And you'll plow headlong into fate, having not the faintest idea what you're running toward." Sighing, Silas stroked his beard in silence for some time. "All right, Father Odenwald," he finally said. "I'll accompany you as your guide—for the right coin, that is. It seems my principal charge in life has become to see that you don't get yourself killed."

✛

CHAPTER 13

They Won't Find Her Alive

October 14, 1859

Your Eminence Cardinal Eberhard,

I must write you in earnest, alone and without the counsel of Father Ambrose. The good father has taken leave to go on investigations of his own into the forest, and his whereabouts are unknown. He sought a woodsman in the forest to help him find the beast responsible for the recent killings in St. Gregory. Killian is concerned for his safe return. I had to inform him of Ambrose's role in the Schmidt investigation. The good father can surely take care of himself—or at least that it is what I implied.

The true purpose of my writing is to inform you of the news regarding Bishop Stephan. He was here; of that I am most certain. Furthermore, he was here for some time. It seems he was held, most certainly against his will, in a cell in the abbey. Certain "brothers" claim he yet lives, though they will not divulge where. Killian and I have yet to gain their trust, and in truth I worry what such trust might cost us.

Father Valentine's notions of the end times and the coming revelation are most certainly at work in impressionable minds, and these aberrant and confused views—this heresy—appear only to have grown. He always seemed, to my mind, to be rather simple and naïve, if not entirely harmless. I could never imagine him as the instigator of anything truly evil. Rather, his danger has always lain in his inspiration of others, who may misintend or misunderstand the purpose of his words.

But now, his chiliasm seems channeled—his naïve musings are set into dark arts and evil intentions. What we saw this night strikes a chill in my heart, for we have found the very room where Stephan was kept in. While he was not there, there were letters from you, unopened and piled on the floor. But what else was in that room I can only describe as horrible and unholy.

The appearance of the room is of one gone mad. If "cleanliness is next to Godliness," then the occupier of this hovel stands a universe apart, for filth is strewn about in every corner. Soiled linens lay in piles; used and dirty cups and plates line the walls. But it is the content of the filth that is the worst, for I can say with certainty that within are to be found tools for the practice of the black arts. Scripture adorns the walls, the choice of which suggests a beseeching or appeasing of some power. Strange instruments clutter the desk—a chalice and blades, even a scrying mirror in the corner. That horrid room worked such an affect upon me that I could have sworn some evil watched from dark corners, though as I write, such notions seem childish.

The writings within, which Stephan was undoubtedly forced to read, suggest the captors view themselves as a necessary evil that will hasten the arrival of the New Kingdom—an evil for which they will be ultimately redeemed, as Lucifer is himself (or so they claim). I have taken key scraps as evidence, though I dare not send them by post; I can never be sure if my letters reach you unmolested.

What this means for our time here, I cannot say, only that Stephan has not gone missing. All evidence points to the fact that he is a prisoner. I will attempt to mail this posthaste, but I must wait for the letter carrier to Eaton and deliver this to him myself. I don't know who we can trust here. Not Florian or Winfried, and certainly not Anselm. Perhaps many more.

I'm not sure what more we can do. I suspect our time here is coming to an end, but I shall await your reply.

Yours in Christ,
Tobias Schenk

p.s. I think Killian has gotten more than he bargained for on this trip.

The underbrush rose thick around them, a wall of green leaves marking the border of their sunny glade. Silas hacked with a large blade, at times huffing and panting, and the horse grunted, stumbling among the fallen branches and stumps and glaring at Ambrose in annoyance. Hidden roots caught Ambrose's toes and twisted at his ankles, as young branches slapped and scratched. Nettles growing in the marshlands stung their hands and brought tears to the priest's eyes as he silently cursed. How he had ever managed to push his way through and find Silas the day before he couldn't imagine.

"Are you sure you have enough money to pay me for this wild goose chase?" Silas grumbled.

The day wore on as they trudged through the thick forest. With luck they found the occasional deer trail, but these they couldn't follow for long. It was only a short way before they plunged into the understory again. Little light reached the floor from the thick leaves above, and Ambrose wondered how Silas knew at all which direction they were headed. Yet the man never turned or deviated and seemed always to know the way. Ambrose guessed they must have passed the west side of St. Gregory, but he had no way of knowing for sure. There was nothing in the forest to show any signs of people that had come before.

As they pushed north, the trees thinned and patches of clear sky opened above them. Ambrose was surprised to see fallow fields below, forgotten and overgrown. In the distance, the square frames of a cabin jutted from the trees and as they approached, they saw that the house stood empty and deserted. Clay chinking lay fallen on the ground amid a bed of ferns, and the door hung on half a hinge. Rough claw marks were gouged deep across its wooden panels.

"What do you suppose did that?" asked Ambrose. "Was it a bear?"

Silas shook his head. "Bears have four claws, not three."

"Well, what was it?"

"I don't know. But hold tight to your staff!"

A break in the trees showed a clearing ahead. Wooden crosses poked through a sea of dead grass and the forest pressed from all sides, slowly overtaking. Ambrose walked through the family graveyard, and bent to pick moss from a cross. Deep lines were carved underneath. They read:

𝔥𝔞𝔯𝔬𝔩𝔡 𝔊𝔲𝔢𝔫𝔱𝔥𝔢𝔯,
geb. 1797 𝔎𝔬𝔟𝔩𝔢𝔫𝔷
ges. 1854 𝔈𝔞𝔱𝔬𝔫

"Where's Eaton?" he said.

"That's the old name for Walders, before all the Norwegians settled there."

Ambrose shook his head in sadness. "I wonder what they were doing all the way out here?"

"Dying, evidently," Silas remarked, scratching the horse's ear. "Isn't that right, King Henry? Isn't that just the way of people?"

"Your horse is named King Henry? Why?"

Silas leaned close to the fuzzy ear, whispering, and the horse snorted in laughter. "Some other time," he said. "We should go."

The land slowly sloped down. It wasn't more than a mile before they came upon a small lake. Sparkling waves glittered in the noonday sun, and a cool breeze blew off the water. They sat on a log eating cold grouse and bread. Silas took a swig from his flask and passed it to Ambrose, but he politely declined. "Suit yourself." He took another swallow and thumped the cork into the flask with a squeak.

"We should go," he said. "There's a hermit that lives around these parts. Old Man Wilke. I've never talked to him, but I've seen him. Best we keep out of his sight."

"You've never tried to say hello?"

"No. He talks with his musket. But you're welcome to try, once we're done with this little jaunt."

They left the lake quickly, moving away from the woodsmoke in the distance. Beyond, the land sunk in potholes and gullies. Limestone rock lay in great piles on the forest floor and in the bed of the creak, and the slopes of the valley were littered in white that poked beneath the green leaves and patches of moss.

"This is Steinthal, the stony valley," Silas explained. "The folk at Altona say a beast lives at the marsh at the end of the Kilnsnake River. But I guess they saw it here first. At least that's how the story goes."

"What do they say it looks like?"

Silas laughed and scratched his beard. "Well, my dear Father Odenwald, that's just the thing, isn't it? No one really knows. Oh, plenty say they do. And they all repeat the same stories. But no one's seen anything proper. They say the creature is as large as a man. Or larger. Or smaller. It has one eye. Or two. Or three. Or five. It's hairy. Or feathered. You know how stories go."

Ambrose scowled. "I thought you believed in stories, Silas. Isn't this why you're wearing that necklace?"

"Oh, don't get me wrong," Silas waved a hand. "I believe in stories, just not the ones they tell."

The creek meandered north, twisting and turning for several miles, its babbling waters dancing and playing across the sandy bottom. The land rose slowly as they left the rocky Steinthal below, and they walked along banks lined with ancient cedars, their gnarled and knotted branches a tangled mass of green above.

As the sun set, Venus gleamed on the horizon, bright against clouds of purple and red. Shadows lengthened in the forest below, and the floor was dark when the creak finally merged with the Kilnsnake River. On either side, the wood gave way to a large swale, empty of trees, where tall grasses and cattails swayed and rustled in the evening breeze, chill as it rolled in from the lowlands. The last mosquitos of the season buzzed at their ears and neck, biting in hot pinpricks. Ambrose swatted them miserably and lost his footing, slipping and sinking into the bank, his feet squishing in a black muck that smelled of rotten eggs.

Silas laughed at him as he led King Henry to the river. The horse sniffed and stomped and pulled at the reins, refusing to go near. "You can lead a horse to water, but you can't make him drink, eh?"

"What is that?" Ambrose asked, pointing. Long, narrow tracks were cut into the mud all around the shore. "Those look like the tracks I saw around one of the bodies!"

Silas turned to his horse. "Ah, maybe that's what's bothering you. What do you smell, boy?" King Henry snorted and shook his head; Silas turned back to Ambrose. "Let's get off this cold bank and find some higher ground. We'll need a fire tonight. A bright one."

They took turns keeping watch. Ambrose sat bundled, listening to the night sounds. The wind rustled the forest floor in cold gusts, scattering brittle leaves. Night creatures stirred in the woods all around. A screech pierced the air, haunting and shrill, and coyotes laughed and chattered as some poor creature screamed. Ambrose stared into the night, searching, as his heart pounded. The coarse wool blanket scratched his neck, and he brought it up to his ears and clutched his staff tightly. He looked to the sky, but all was dark. The waning moon was hidden and with it the pale light on the water. Clouds must have rolled in under cover of darkness. *Please Lord, don't let it rain!*

The morning dawned, dark and chill, under the gray October sky. Though Ambrose hadn't slept at all, he thanked God at least it hadn't rained last night, and he rubbed the tiredness from his eyes and scratched his stubbled chin. Silas looked glum as he silently cleaned his musket by the fire. Gray water from the barrel finally rinsed out clear and he spread oil on the bore. His brow wrinkled as he focused on his task.

"We'll follow the Kilnsnake to the marsh," he finally said. "Keep your eyes open."

The river stretched north, then east, plunging again into dense forest. Stands of ash and cedar crowded the bank and the going was slow. After many hours, the trees opened to reveal a wide, flat expanse of rush and cattail. Finding the high ground, however, proved slow and difficult. King Henry struggled in the muck as the ground again grew soft, and he sank to his knees and gummed in displeasure. All about were the same odd tracks, but they were still too trampled for him to make out. "We must be right in its haunt," Silas said.

Ambrose picked a feather from the ground and held it aloft. It was as large as his forearm and jet-black. "I saw one like this before. Do you know what kind of bird this is? Is it some kind of eagle?"

Silas shook his head.

"I thought you knew the beasts of this land," Ambrose said, frustrated.

Silas laughed softly. "My good Father, how could I know all the strange things of this place? I know enough not to be dead yet, and that's saying something. The Menomonee and Winnebago tell tales of giant birds that hunted them long ago. Although they say they weren't birds but spirits in bird form. Maybe what dropped that feather inspired them. Or maybe it's actually one of those spirits. Who knows?"

"I'm sorry," Ambrose said. "This trek is wearying. How could anything so far out be responsible for the town's murderers? I suppose the foulest beasts live in such dark places."

"Hm," Silas said. "In my experience, the foulest beasts live in the light. But I guess we'll find out soon enough."

"Have you ever been to this marsh?" asked Ambrose. "How will we find this thing when we don't even know what we're looking for?"

"No. And no idea." Silas said. "This is your adventure. I'm just the one taking your coin."

Ambrose was silent for some time. Talk of wilderness spirits made him uncomfortable. It stirred old feelings from childhood, when he would walk the woods alone. Always, it seemed, a world had lain just beyond his sight, filled with unseen things, light and dark and sometimes gray. He felt them close by, though he could never see them: elves and dwarves and nymphs and darker things he dared not think of. The church had driven such things from his mind. But in the dark wilds, they grew near again.

A bend in the reed opened, and a small hillock rose above the swale. A lone mallard eyed them in the grass. The snap and crunch of their footsteps cracked in the stillness, and she raised her head, neck straight, and called in alarm: *kanc, kanc, kanc, kanc!* As Ambrose and Silas grew closer, she burst from the weeds in an explosion of brown feathers and a whistle of wings.

From the top of the hill, the great marsh stretched out before them. A sea of dead stalk waved brown in the chill wind as black water coursed in twists and turns of hidden currents and stagnant pools, rippling in the wind. The solemn bleakness might have been beautiful but for the weight of their search.

Ambrose pointed. "What's that?" A shape stuck out from the mud, thin and dull and white. It was unmistakable, though he tried to deny it. Silas yanked it from the mucky bank: a bone. "A deer bone?" Ambrose called. "A leg?"

"No."

"Then what?"

"A leg." Silas paused. "But not a deer."

The hairs on Ambrose's neck rose and he shivered. "It's too small to be a man's!" he protested.

"It's a child's."

"You're sure it's not a deer?"

"I've butchered enough deer to know a deer bone, Father," Silas said. "This poor creature didn't get here on its own. It looks like we might just find this thing after all."

"There's more." Ambrose pointed again. Ahead, leading away, deeper into the marsh, were scattered bones here and there. "We can't just leave them!"

"We most certainly can. Put them in a pile and come back for them if you must. Give them a funeral later. We're not going to go hunting in the marsh with bags of bones on our backs."

Ambrose frowned and made the sign of the cross. "Well, at least they'll lead the way."

"Where the hell is that damn postman?" Tobias drummed his fingers on the café table, staring intently out the window.

"Are you sure he's coming today?" asked Killian. His youthful face was tense and worried, lips pursed under his thin nose.

Tobias nodded. "It's Monday the tenth. He comes Monday, Wednesday and Friday. He damn well better come. I can't hold on to this letter any longer. Waiting through Sunday Mass with it tucked in my pocket was too much. I kept feeling Anselm's eyes boring though me. The sooner the cardinal hears what's going on here, the sooner we can get out of this godforsaken town."

Killian glanced nervously at the counter. The baker glared back at them, rubbing his hands on his flour-dusted apron. An old man sat in the corner eating *brötchen* and reading a worn Bible. Otherwise, the bakery was empty for the moment. "What was in that mirror?" he whispered.

"I don't know," Tobias said, tapping the edge of the envelope on the table. The clack set them both on edge, but he continued. "In the light of day, it all seems foolish. The more time goes by, it seems better explained by a trick of the light on our jittery nerves. What else do you expect, sneaking around and breaking in like a child? Now I wish I hadn't written some of what I did. It paints me as a damn fool."

Killian leaned forward. "But what about the room itself?"

The door opened. A gust of wind blew crumbs across the table. Killian whirled, fearing it might be Florian or Winfried or, worse, Anselm. But it was only Amalia, come to get bread for the hotel.

"Some illness of the mind." Tobias looked over his shoulder. "Some communal derangement or mass hysteria. Psychosis, I believe the new sciences would call it."

Killian whispered. "Is it all of them? I never heard it being so bad at home."

"Doesn't really matter. Not if we don't live to tell the tale," Tobias said. "Some things aren't worth finding out."

The bakery was filling with people. A silver-haired woman walked in, basket in hand. Two more townsfolk followed, stopping in for lunch. They all eyed the priests in the corner.

"But where is Ambrose?" asked Killian. "It's been four days!"

"I don't know." Tobias squeezed the young priest's hand. "But have faith—he'll surprise you."

Killian looked away, doubtful, and Tobias felt the emptiness of his own words.

"There is the postman!" Tobias pointed to a man in a blue-gray cap and jacket, hitching a sleek gray horse across the street. "Finally!"

"How do you know that's the postman?"

"The cap, I'm guessing," Tobias said. "I'll be right back."

As he hurried across the street, Killian sat in silence. More townsfolk entered. Some he recognized, but many he didn't. Sepp and Gerti laughed with a young woman in the corner.

"Oh, Helen, and how is your Mr. Durst? Is Mr. Fährmann's chapel keeping him busy?"

The woman nodded. "Busy and happy. The roof will be up next week." She smiled. "Speak of the Devil, there he is now." Sepp said. "Francis, how is your Annaliese doing? Any suitors yet?"

Gerti blushed and scolded him with a tap of her bonnet.

The sudden crowd made Killian nervous, and he looked anxiously to the window. Across the street, the postman had his arms folded. Tobias waved his letter in the air, a shiny silver dollar in his hand. Undoubtedly arguing about the price, Killian thought. The man's face was red, and he pointed to the post office, grabbing his reins and readying to leave. Tobias finally raised his hands in apology and entered the building, exiting a short time later with the postage. The postman grabbed the letter and shook his head before turning the horse around and trotting out of town.

Tobias strode back in and sat down. "Can you believe that? Eighty cents to mail a letter home? I should have slapped a stamp on my forehead and mailed myself."

Killian's eyes darted pensively. "At least it's on its way. The sooner we hear back, the better. I'm ready to go home."

Tobias looked at the crowd gathering, noting the disapproving glances; the drawn eyes and scowls. He tried to ignore.

"I'm sure you are," he said. "Let's leave this place. But I don't want to go back to the abbey just yet."

"Me either!"

The door burst open with a bang. Everyone in the room turned, suddenly silent. Bernd Voss stood in the doorway, his face ashen white and lips trembling

"My Issa's gone!" he cried.

The folk stared in confused silence.

"My Issa's gone!" he yelled again.

"Now Bernd, what are you saying?" asked Francis.

"My daughter's gone! She wasn't in her bed this morning. She isn't at the shop. She isn't anywhere!"

"Sometimes she has a mind to wander," Francis said. "I'm sure she's just out and about."

"No! Not at night. Not after Augustin!"

The townsfolk stared, their faces blank and perplexed, while Bernd looked as though he might burst, waving his arms frantically. "Help me, goddamn it!"

The room suddenly sprang to life. Chairs squeaked against the floor. Men bolted up and women looked to one another.

"All right Bernd, tell us everything," Joseph said.

Pacing, Bernd ran his trembling hands through his hair. "She was never right. Not after Augustin and Rosa. She wouldn't eat. Wouldn't sleep. Wouldn't leave the house. She just locked herself away. She blamed herself for everything. That damn Otto! Going around accusing defenseless girls! Now she's vanished in the night. Only left a note that said, 'I'm sorry.' We have to find her!"

"Sepp," Francis called to Joseph. "Let's round up the town and get a search going, all the able-bodied men we can find! We'll comb the woods to the south and all around the pond." Joseph nodded, hat in hand, as he squeezed Bernd's shoulder.

The men left in a rush. For a moment the bakery was quiet. The women turned to one another, eyes wide, and all at once the room broke out into a gaggle of gossip. "Poor man, he's lost his reputation, his sister, and now his daughter." A voice in the back whispered, "Where could she have gone? How could she do this to her family?" Gerti shook her head. "There was always something about her, even as a baby. Maybe she did have something to do with those deaths and she couldn't live with it." She leaned close and whispered. "Or maybe she's run off to join the evil in the woods."

An old woman gasped. "Gerti! Don't say such things."

Gerti sniffed and stuck up her nose. "You can't tell me she didn't cause trouble around here."

Tobias scowled as the din of gossip filled the room. "Let's leave," he said in disgust.

The door rattled closed behind them. But through the glass, they heard an old woman's voice. "Mark my words," she muttered. "They won't find her alive."

☩

CHAPTER 14

The Nacktkrapp

October 15, 1859

The gray sky grew dim. Dead trees stood bare and bright against the darkness in the distance. Shadows lengthened across the stretch of brown grass and black water, and a cold wind swept the open marsh, its icy claws wrapping around their necks and seeping through their clothes. Ambrose shivered, his muddy robes clinging wet to his thighs, water squishing in his worn leather boots.

"Let's camp here," Silas said. "At least the land is a little higher." King Henry grumbled and fought against his reins. "Now boy, I don't want to be here either! But remember, somehow it's become our duty." Silas scratched his ear as the horse shot Ambrose an irritated look.

"Let's have a look." Silas drew a spyglass and peered across the marsh, his gaze settling on a stand of elms ahead. "There. There is where this labyrinth is leading us. It's been bringing us ever closer all day."

He passed the glass to Ambrose. In the dim light, the stand of trees was a blot of dark leaves. In the middle, a mighty ash rose to the sky, its crown a great tangle of brown leaves and branches, like some giant nest. Shadow fell from its boughs, casting the ground in darkness, but for a pile of white at its base.

"Is that…"

"Bones," Silas muttered, shaking his head. "Like you said, they lead the way. Let's get what we need for a fire, and quickly. The more the better."

They gathered dead wood from all around, at times sinking and splashing into the water and sinking into the thick muck. Slowly the pile grew. The axe thunked, and chips and flakes fell about the makeshift camp. As Silas took a step to swing, he sank into the muck. "Damn it!" he cursed, kicking his muddy boot against a stump. "What do you think of our little quest now, Father?"

"My mind is a blur, Mr. Messam." Ambrose's breath was heavy, his muscles aching. "It's scarce been four days since I left town. Almost two months since I arrived. Yet it feels like a lifetime. A lifetime of fighting mires and brambles…and people, most of all. I can hardly recall when it wasn't a fight."

"Well, let's get a fire going and get our wits about us," Silas said. "We've got a long night ahead, with more fighting to come, undoubtedly. We'll have stale bread and the last of the grouse—cold, though. Let's not fill the land with the smell of flesh, even if there is the smell of fire."

Soon the flames crackled and grew. Red tongues licked the twigs and leaves, and Ambrose stretched his hands to the first warmth of the day. As they silently ate, steam rose from his black cassock as it dried and mud flaked under his fingers.

Silas drew his pipe. Sweet, spicy tobacco filled the air, warm and comforting, and his face glowed red as he puffed. "So, tell me your story," he said. "I know what you're doing here, but I don't know why."

"The families back home—"

Silas waved a hand. "I know all that. But *why* are you here?"

Ambrose hung his head and frowned, working his hands through his dark brown hair. *Why am I here?* He knew the question wasn't what it seemed. Strange that this wild man was the only one who had asked it. Taken aback, he struggled to think, but his mind was blank and everything seemed as though it were barred behind a stout door. He stared at his hands, looking for answers in the grimy wrinkles of his palm and the dirt under his nails—anything to keep his mind steady.

"My father was a doctor," he said finally. "He died of consumption, from bad air in the slums. No one else would go there, so he did. When he took ill, he left for the sanitarium, and we never saw him again. After his death, the hospital denied my mother's widow's pension. Although they did send a 'pretty' letter of condolence. We lost our cottage soon after. The only work my mother could find was in a mill as a comber—that is, until she lost her fingers. After that, she was a washer and stripped the dead to sell their clothes. Some nights, when times were especially lean, she... didn't come home until morning."

He grew still for some time, remembering. The fire popped and cracked as he stared, flames dancing in his eyes. He seemed in a world all his own.

"My sister Monika was a match dipper," he said after some time. "That is, until the other girls got phossy jaw. A girl's jaw one day just broke while she was talking. A rotten chunk of bone fell clean out. Monika left after that. Went to work for a canary. It wasn't much better, but at least her face didn't rot.

"My mother sent me to Konstanz Catholic Boys' Home. Bishop Stephan, the man I came here to find, was a friend of my father. He knew the director and saw to it that I was taken in. My mother couldn't afford to feed me and she knew if I was taken in, maybe I'd make the seminary. She wouldn't have to worry about me. Unfortunately they didn't take girls, so Monika had to stay. I didn't see my mother or sister for twelve years. I have no idea how they got by. When I finally got my stipend, I sent all that I could to keep them off the street. Now they have a small apartment in Konstanz overlooking the lake, while my duties took me to Karlsruhe."

"And now you're on a quest to save the souls of the damned," Silas said, "as penance for your good fortune?"

"Maybe…"

Silas puffed in silence. The red glow lit the man's weathered face as he gummed his pipe. "And if you die in this marsh, what will happen to them?"

"They'll be taken care of," Ambrose said. "The church owes me that."

"Humph. Well, we'll see…"

Grimacing, Ambrose looked away, staring into the cold black. "This isn't what I imagined, when I left the Port of Le Havre," he said. "It was sunny and bright. A gorgeous late-summer morning. I was drinking tea and watching the harbor. So many colors and people. Smells everywhere. The bakeries and cafés. And the foul harbor water, of course. But there was life everywhere. Who would have thought in two months' time I would end up sitting in the cold muck, under gray skies, surrounded by a field of bones, in the middle of nowhere?"

Silas smirked. "Well, I'm so happy I can share the journey with you."

"What about you?" Ambrose asked. "Any family back home? Or a sweetheart nearby?"

A pained look passed Silas's face and he turned away. Ambrose might have missed it in the dark and it was only by chance that he saw the man's eyes grow wet. Ambrose blushed, embarrassed and wishing he hadn't pried, while Silas simply shook his head and answered in a single word. "No."

An awkward silence lingered for some time, and in the stillness, they listened to the sounds of night: a cold wind blowing across the open marsh, dead trees swaying in an eerie whisper, like voices.

"What is that!" Ambrose pointed suddenly.

A blue light hung over the water. Perfectly round, it swayed and crept where no man could be, moving slowly back and forth. Another appeared behind it. Still another, closer. Wandering, the pale orbs filled the darkness around them.

"Is that the will-o'-the-wisp?"

"That's one name for it. It's *Ignis fatuus,*" Silas said. "Although I prefer *Ignis cadaveri.*"

"Corpse fire?"

"Corpse candle. The souls of the dead. Don't look at them. They won't come near the fire. But turn your back," Silas said. "I don't know why. It just feels right."

Ambrose moved closer to the fire, but his eyes drifted into the night. They were still there.

"You could have stayed back in Konstanz, or Karlsruhe, rather," Silas said, tapping his pipe. "Your family was taken care of. You didn't need to come here."

"I needed to find Stephan. But I've also seen what can happen to a person. This world grows harder by the day. The hopelessness and despair. Toiling in the mills, the canaries, the shipyards. Children suffocating in the coal mines or dying under the gears of some factory, belching such black smoke that it covers the very ground and buildings and even their faces.

"That's not a way to live. Where is there hope in any of that? Men give into the bleakness of it all, lamenting all is empty and meaningless. They take to drink and cast thoughtless violence at one another—and worse—at those most innocent.

"I cannot be a party to such dejection and nihilism. Men need hope and faith in dark times. Marx, for all of his good intentions, said, 'Religion is the opiate of the masses.' He was wrong. It is despair. Despair is the opiate of the masses.

There is no force like nihilism to give free rein to the intoxication of men's bassist impulses."

"I see why you're out here now," Silas said. "You're an innocent. Not naive but innocent."

Ambrose leaned back, the phantom lights disconcerting as they hovered in the corner of his eye. "Well, what would I be if I didn't try? To fight against the darkness, against the clouding evil in men's hearts. That is a fight I can feel good about."

"Well, there is no end to evil." Silas laughed. "So you'll have no shortage of opportunities to feel good."

They grew silent once again, staring thoughtfully into the fire. Sparks popped in the night, wood hissing and crackling as the waning moon crept across the night sky. King Henry grunted, nuzzling Silas for another sugar cube.

Suddenly a horrid shriek pierced the blackness, rising from all sides, bloodcurdling and shrill. King Henry reared and the men leapt to their feet. Ambrose held his staff overhead, eyes wide, while Silas grabbed his musket and poured powder into the barrel. The cloth and ball thunked from the rod as he cursed. "Forgot to load the goddamn thing!"

A rush of wind and footsteps circled the fire, just out of sight. Another scream. It split their ears. *What horror is this?* Ambrose had never heard anything so disturbing.

They cast more wood on the flames, and the logs crackled and sparked, the flames growing high into the night. The thing retreated, always out of sight, then paced and turned. A whoosh of wind rose, and now it paced from the other side.

"What the Devil is it?" cried Ambrose.

"Let's hope we don't find out in the dark!" Silas said. "King Henry, cover your ears!"

A spark and blast of flame shot from the barrel into the darkness. They waited. Long moments passed. Nothing. Then another scream, and the frantic pacing started again.

"Damn it!" Silas packed another ball.

The thing was all around them, hidden in the shadows, clawing at the ground and screaming at the fire and at them. Ambrose looked to Silas in panic. The man's eyes closed as he listened, his breathing slow and deep. The creature had stopped for a moment, pawing the earth just outside the light. He held his breath and opened his eyes.

The musket sparked and a blast burst forth. The night blazed. A flash of yellow lit a dark figure in the distance. Its scream split the night, but it was different. It was filled with pain and rage. Gunsmoke hung white in the air, thick with burned metal and sulfur. Then silence.

"Did you hit it?" Ambrose said.

"I don't know," said Silas. "But it's not here now. Unless it's tricking us. I'd better pack another."

They stoked the fire high, bright sparks dancing. Slowly the ringing in Ambrose's ears passed. They waited, but there was no sound of the beast. Only black night lay thick around them as the wind whistled eerily in the dark.

Dawn broke, dark and brooding, after another sleepless night, and the last wood smoked in piles of gray ash. Brooding clouds loomed in the west, the thunder of storm rolling in the distance. All about, the ground was torn and trampled. Deep gouges cut into the swampy earth.

"Do you see this?" Silas crouched, pointing. There, in the mud, was the first clear footprint. Long lines ran together, like fingers tipped with knives.

"It looks like some kind of bird. But…it's twice the size of my hand!" Ambrose exclaimed.

The tracks ran to the edge of the brackish water then suddenly stopped.

Ambrose pointed. "Look there!"

Dark-red splotches covered the ground. Blood was trampled into the mud, its drops and spills flowing in tracks to the water.

"You hit it!"

"And look at this." —Silas pointed—"A limp. You can see from the stride. I must have hit it in the leg. Finally some good news." He shouldered his musket and made ready to leave.

A ridge of earth snaked among the pools of the marsh, leading them ever to the center, where the stand of dark trees stood. Black water pooled and flowed on either side. All was silent but for the rustle of their steps and the sigh of chill wind in dead cattails. Ambrose stared at the clump of dark trees in the distance and touched the cross around his neck. *Surely God must prevail!* He hadn't imagined finding so horrid a beast in so desolate a land. Now that he was here, a cold fear gripped his heart. Silas had said the seminary hadn't taught him anything useful. What did he mean? *Useful for what?*

"Well, father, I do believe there is no time like the present," Silas said. "Be careful. We're entering the beast's lair now. There's no telling what it will do. But of a certainty, it won't be good."

Ambrose looked up. All too soon, they had neared the stand of trees, and dead wood poked from the waters here and there, bare of bark and leaves. Silas hitched King Henry to tree. The horse eyed him forlornly but didn't fight to follow.

As they entered, the marshy wood seemed to swallow them. All about, the earth was littered with white. The bones of deer and goat lay scattered like the leavings of a ghastly banquet, and here and there were the clear remains of some lost soul. Ambrose looked hurriedly away, only for his eyes to fall upon a skull among the weeds. Silas stooped to pick it up. A hole had been pecked or gouged into the back; the gnawing of mice and rats had whittled it away in scrapes and pocks, but the break had been caused by something larger. Sharp edges stuck forth where the mice hadn't yet chewed. The skull was small, obviously a child's.

"What is this hellish place?" Ambrose asked, grimacing. "What wild land has demons that do such as this?"

"Did you think monsters and foul beasts were only found in the old country?" Silas said. "As to what it is, I think it fairly obvious now that it is some kind of giant eagle, though this one hunts at night. Perhaps it's a lost species, like the bones of those ancient beasts they dig out of the earth, though I trust the natives' description more. I think it's a spirit in bird form. Jacques Marquette claimed to have seen one almost two hundred years ago. He said it was as large as a calf, with horns like those of a deer or elk. It had terrible, soul-piercing eyes, and a mane and a face like a man's. It was covered in scales and had a long serpent's tail. But Marquette was a Jesuit and a zealot, so not entirely trustworthy as far as sources go."

With a shudder, Ambrose looked anxiously over his shoulder. Whether Marquette was trustworthy or not, anything seemed possible. In the wilds, it wasn't so difficult to imagine bizarre, nightmarish things lurking and prowling in the shadows; *mahre* – night demons – haunted his dreams, their twisted faces snarling; witches and hags stalked the deep forests; and devils taunted from the marshlands. All the while, the priests and brothers were sinister and suspicious, covering the town with a darkness akin to those very monsters in the wilds. Why should there not be ancient demons or prehistoric creatures dwelling in the dead brown of an autumn marsh?

Ambrose let out a long breath. "If you knew this, why are you helping me?"

"I'm honestly rather curious. Aren't you?"

"For the love of God," Ambrose said, "I am not."

Silas laughed, eyeing Ambrose as he grasped his cross. "There are gods in the New World too, you know?" he chided.

Ambrose ignored him and shook his head bitterly.

They walked in silence, quiet now as they crept deeper. The beast was nowhere to be seen, but evidence of it lay all around. Among the bones were the white droppings of some immense thing. The trees around were covered in guano, and it lay thick on the ground, as if they stood beneath a giant roost. If this was a spirit or god, it had a form like any other animal, monstrous though it may be. Somehow, seeing the mess of it made it all the more terrifying and real. This wasn't a phantom that preyed on the weak of heart or mind. This was a flesh-and-blood thing. A thing that hungered— and later shat its victims in white slop upon the ground and trees, to leave the air foul with the smell of ammonia. Whatever monster had relieved itself here was very much alive and very near.

Yet they couldn't see it. There was no sound in the trees or rustle in the brush. All was still. Ambrose turned and looked all around. The feeling of eyes was upon him, yet he saw nothing. How could he not see something so big it could carry away a child? He looked to Silas, who shrugged and shook his head. *Gone?* he mouthed. They made ready to wait. Maybe the thing hunted only at night and now it slept. An unsettling thought ran through Ambrose's head: they might be waiting in the dark for some hidden thing to strike. They would be exposed and hunted like Augustin and Rosa and the owners of the bones at their feet. Silas's musket and Ambrose's staff seemed paltry and weak.

They didn't have to wait long. Suddenly, the trees above shook with a sound of wings. They turned. A flash of black fell upon them. Ambrose was thrown to the ground as a roar of wind scattered leaves and twigs. His eyes closed against the dust and dirt, and he cried out as powerful blows struck him about his head and back. But just as quickly, it was gone.

He leapt up. Nothing was there! Silas staggered to his feet. Red trickled down his face, and on his arm, a deep gash showed red flesh beneath. Blood soaked his shirt as it flowed down to his hand.

The two men turned, looking. The branches shook above. Silas raised the musket, jerking back and forth, seeking. First one, then another tree, bucked and swayed. Something leapt or flew from one to the other. Ambrose couldn't see it, but Silas trained the weapon on the swaying branches all the same. A shot rang out. *Boom!* Their ears rang and they could hear nothing, yet they saw the tree shake then grow still. Furiously Silas crammed another ball into the barrel.

Wings flapped behind. A gust of wind blinded them, and they were tossed to the ground again. Ambrose struggled to his feet. A flurry surrounded, wings beating down upon him. His chest tore in pain, blood seeping from the gash. Silas wailed at the beast with the butt of his musket, but in a blur the creature was gone into the treetops. Silas fired after, but missed again.

Ambrose spun, looking to the heavens, his ears still ringing, while Silas quickly grabbed the ramrod. A whoosh of wind and it was upon them again. Ambrose saw it for the first time as it fell on Silas with a flurry of anger. Talons slashed. Great black wings beat all around him, striking him down and battering. Ambrose struck the beast from behind with all his might, again and again, bringing the staff down. The creature wailed and took to the sky, wrenching the musket from Silas's arms and casting it deep into the woody stand.

The monster circled overhead, its monstrous red eyes glaring above a beak of jet-black. Ambrose's mind reeled. *How had it known to take the gun?* Giant wings flapped and stretched, at least ten feet wide. As the beast landed on a branch, the tree groaned and creaked under its weight. Silas drew his blade. The creature screamed and took to the air, fearless now they were unarmed. A moment later, it fell upon them in a fury of talon and feather as Silas swung his blade wildly. The monster screamed and struck with its giant beak, grabbing hold and dragging him, a taloned foot raised to strike and gouge his belly.

"Are you going to help, Ambrose!" Silas screamed.

"How?" he cried, beating the beast with his staff.

"Say a goddamn prayer! Are you not a priest?"

"This isn't a demon. This is an animal!" Ambrose cried.

The gigantic bird turned, and in that moment Ambrose was startled and taken aback. The look in its eyes was almost human. The creature grabbed his staff and tossed it into the woods, staring at him. It lifted its taloned foot and made ready to rake Silas's belly open.

"Now! Be a priest now!"

Ambrose froze, his mind blank. He had never encountered something like this. The only monsters he had ever known were human. Nothing had prepared him for what was before him now. He grabbed the cross at his neck and desperately spoke the first words that entered his mind. *"Sancte Michael Archangele defende nos in proelio, contra nequitiam et insidias diaboli esto praesidium. Imperet illi Deus, supplices deprecamur…"*

The monster turned, confused for the briefest of moments. *Was it the prayer or coincidence?* It was just long enough for Silas plunge the blade into its chest with all his strength. A bloodcurdling cry split their ears, and the thing fell writhing and wailing upon the ground. Blood gurgled in its throat as it grew still.

Ambrose collapsed to his knees, wet earth squishing beneath him. Drops of red splashed on the ground as he blinked, falling from his own forehead, while Silas lay staring at the gray sky. All around, the land was still. He held his head in his hands for long moments as the ground swirled around him. Finally he could bear it no more and bellowed at the heavens—a scream of anguish and rage. *How could*

God allow this creature to be? His muscles seized and froze, and he collapsed under the pounding pain.

Long moments passed in silence as he lay watching the wind in the leaves above. The sky grew slowly lighter and the clouds broke when he finally got to his feet. Silas grasped his hand, calloused and rough, and Ambrose winced as he pulled. The man stood, blood dripping from his arms and face, shreds of leather jacket hanging loosely.

"You look like hell," Ambrose said.

"Then I'm in good company," Silas said, pointing.

Ambrose looked down. A white rib glistened in a red gash. His chest was wet with cold blood, and as he looked, the wound began to burn.

"Took you long enough," Silas groaned.

"How did you know a prayer would work?" Ambrose said, shaking his head.

"I didn't. But the world is full of natural and unnatural. You'd do well to learn the difference."

Ambrose shook his head incredulously. "You mean some unholy thing? I can't believe that."

"You'll find that 'holy' and 'unholy' don't hold much weight in the real world—the world outside of your familiar pastures. There is belief and lack of it, and sometimes power to be found in both. Before you presume to know, look at the thing first."

Ambrose looked down. The creature on the ground looked like no bird he had ever seen. It strained the mind with its size. Its wings were easily fifteen feet wide, and each claw was as large as a finger. But as he stared, everything appeared wrong. Its feet and legs were thin like a bird, but its knees were turned. Its chest was less the barrel shape of a bird and more like the flat chest of a man's. But it was the face that drew him, and he couldn't look away. The beak was long and sharp, but the head was round, as if its visage were a mask.

"This looks like..." Ambrose began.

"Like a man…somehow."

"My God. What it is? And where the hell did it come from?"

"Sometimes these things just are," Silas said. "And sometimes they're drawn—maybe to St. Gregory. The natives say sometimes people are cursed. Either way, best we tie it up and bring it to town."

"Yes. They need to know," Ambrose said. "What strange land would breed a creature like this? Someone must know what this is. Someone will study this. This is some ancient and forgotten creature. I can't accept this is some infernal demon."

Silas shook his head. "Suit yourself."

☩

CHAPTER 15

Innocence Lost

October 17, 1859

T he memorial for Augustin and Rosa took place in the chapel. A voice rose, pure and clear, its tenor falling in soft waves. Two more met and wove together. Three brothers stood before the altar as the dappled reds and yellows of the stained glass above fell about them. *"In Paradisum...deducant Angeli,"* they sang. The hymn washed over the congregation, and Tobias looked to their faces, downcast and in sorrow.

The voices ended in a long and mournful silence. The chapel was still, the air heavy with grief. Anselm rose and turned toward the pews, his green chasuble bathed in fiery red from the glass above. The old Bible creaked open and he made the sign of the cross. "A reading from Isaiah 34, the Lord's Judgment Against the Nations:

Come near, ye nations and hear, and hearken, ye people: let the earth hear and all that is therein, the world and all that proceedeth thereof.

For the indignation of the Lord is upon all nations, and his wrath upon all their armies: he hath destroyed them and delivered them to the slaughter.

And their slain shall be cast out, and their stink shall come up out of their bodies, and the mountains shall be melted with their blood.

And all the host of heaven shall be dissolved, and the heavens shall be folded like a book: and all their hosts shall fall as the leaf falleth from the vine, and as it falleth from the fig tree.

For my sword shall be drunken in the heaven: behold, it shall come down upon Edom, even upon the people of my curse to judgment.

The sword of the Lord is filled with blood: it is made fat with the fat and with the blood of the lambs and the goats, with the fat of the kidneys of the rams: for the Lord hath a sacrifice in Bozrah, and a great slaughter in the land of Edom.

And the unicorn shall come down with them, and the heifers with the bulls, and their land shall be drunken with blood, and their dust made fat with fatness

Killian frowned in disgust as Tobias's heavy breath grew angered beside him. "The only thing not in Latin," he mumbled. "A horrible tribute to the dead."

"We know Augustin and Rosa were pure," Anselm said. "We know they were saved. We know that they weren't of these wicked nations, as we know we ourselves are not. We are not those who stand apart from the Lord through vanity and sloth and false piety." He stared accusingly at Tobias and Killian.

"But know these two souls are saved," he went on. "They are saved as we shall be. For we are the true believers who endure the insults and injury, those slings and arrows of the unrighteous, in the name of the Lord.

"On all sides we are beset with evil. That we endure in the face of such persecution is testament to our love and faith, that we may be made pure in the eyes of the Lord. And only in this purity revealed may we usher in His New Kingdom on earth.

"Augustin and Rosa knew this. They lead by example, suffering the tragedy of life at the hands of unknown evil, impossible to understand. They have made the ultimate sacrifice, and through their suffering, they have been made pure. Let us reflect upon their lives and what this sacrifice of theirs reveals of our own lack—our own inability to meet them in kind. For it is this purity in the face of the final days of corruption that brings us together. It is this purity through sacrifice that is the Kingdom itself. As the Lord Jesus died for our sins, so do we die for him."

The Bible closed with a heavy thunk, and Anselm held the chalice aloft.

"This is the most disgusting Mass I have ever heard," Killian whispered.

"Mourn, son." Tobias shook his head. "Mourn for a flock led astray."

Mass ended and the doors creaked open. The yellow of afternoon lit the old floor, fine dust dancing in the light, glinting off the worn grain of wood.

Mourners slowly collected on the lawn. The miller looked away, arms crossed. "I'm so sorry for your loss." A woman's wrinkled hand gently squeezed. "Augustin was a fine lad, taken too soon."

Bernd held Claudia's arm. The townsfolk drifted away, careful not to meet their gaze. Soon they were alone and left behind.

A voice rose from the crowd. "Come. There will be a fine meal at the opera house."

The townsfolk marched in solemn procession. The streets were empty as they walked to the hotel. Tobias and Killian walked behind, distant from the crowd, and didn't hear as Anselm approached.

"Do you not approve of a town's right to grieve?" Tobias and Killian turned to see the old priest glaring at them.

"It's not my place to approve or disapprove of one's grief," Tobias growled, "only perhaps the manner of it."

"What do you know of manners?" Anselm snapped. "You and your hypocritical Catholic commission have done nothing but spy and abuse our good will. And now Ambrose has traipsed off on his own petty adventure, mocking our good will. I've a mind to cast you out, regardless of what Father Valentine says. If he wants to speak with you when he returns, he can find you sleeping on the street, where you belong."

"Oh, don't take the trouble. We'll be gone very shortly!" Tobias snarled.

All of a sudden, a commotion rose in the town ahead. Muffled voices broke out in surprise, falling over one another in a din. "We found the beast!" a voice cried.

"That's Ambrose!" Killian blurted.

The crowd parted as they stepped forward. In the middle of the street stood two bloodied men and a dirty horse. The crowd kept their distance. Women covered their faces with their bonnets, and the men guarded them with outstretched arms. Killian's face grew bright. It was Ambrose! But on closer look, he cried in alarm; the priest was covered in bruises and bloodied. His cassock was ripped, and the skin beneath was a sickening wash of black and blue and green. A great rend tore his robe across his chest, and the bare skin beneath was cut to the bone. The other man looked no better.

"What happened?" he cried.

"We found the beast!" Ambrose said. "We found what killed poor Augustin and Rosa. We killed the Steinthal monster!"

Murmur and whisper rose around them. The folk scowled. "He's mad!" they said. "Ruining our only memorial! Can't they leave us in peace?"

Bernd stepped into the circle, tense as he pointed. "I told you! I told all of you! My Issa didn't kill anyone. She had nothing to do with it! And she's gone. Gone because of you!"

"That Jezebel seduced my boy out at night!" Otto roared. "If she didn't kill him, she still put him in harm's way with her lascivious charms!"

Cries rose from all sides. Francis Fährmann stood between them as the men raised their fists. "How can we know what you say is true?" he said. "How can we know this is the beast?"

"Listen!" Ambrose said. "I'll tell you everything."

When they quieted, he told of his search through the woods and his getting lost and finding Silas. He told of their trek through the wilds and the marsh and the horrors and death in the swampy land and how they finally managed to bring the beast down together. "That's where I've been this whole time," Ambrose said. "Hunting this thing."

They shook their heads. Men waved their hands in disbelief. "That's too much! That's naught but a tale and a tall one at that," Francis said. "How could you make up stories at a time like this?"

Silas drew his blade and cut the rope. The beast fell to the ground and unfurled. Giant wings spread out, and the unearthly head looked up, its red eyes staring at the sky. Women screamed and men gasped.

"How dare you!" Anselm cried. "How dare you bring some foul and hideous thing before us with your wild claims? Why, any man could bring a wild creature here and claim the same. And that you would do so on this day, of all days. The nerve!"

"Dr. Albrecht," Ambrose called. "Please check the talons. Check the wound on my chest. Does it not look the same as the wounds on the bodies?"

The doctor leaned forward, wire glasses perched on his broad nose. "Hm, indeed it does!" he said, measuring. "Very similar indeed!"

"Nonsense! This is merely a rotten excuse to explain your absence," said Anselm. "Four days you were gone. Four days of missed Mass and prayers. That is conduct unbecoming a man of the cloth. All for the sake of the lies of your commission. You have abused our good will and faith. Get out! I cast you out of the abbey at once! Pack your things and never set foot inside again!"

The crowd stood angry and bewildered, filled with fear and scorn. Silas shook his head, a look of knowing on his face, and as Ambrose gazed at the crowd, he saw no kindness. Only Bernd looked up, too afraid to speak.

Suddenly, a high and piercing cry came from down the street. Two boys sprinted towards them in the distance, their tiny voices shrill and panicked. Their mother grabbed and smacked one as he passed. "There you are! Missing Mass again!" But the other kept running, not even stopping to look at the monster at his feet.

"There's a body!" he said. "A body in the water!"

Bernd cried aloud and scooped up the moppy-haired boy, carrying him as he pointed the way. The town raced after them toward Pigeon Lake.

Two fishing poles lay cast aside in high grass on the wooded shore. Something lay crumpled in the water: gray fabric soaked and floating. Ripples gently washed against a leg of pale white. Bernd splashed into the water and turned her over, knowing before he saw. Golden hair clung to a face now bluish white. He wailed and collapsed, sobbing as he held Issa's body. The townsfolk stood in shocked silence, not a word passing between them. Then all at once, whispers passed between them, amongst mutters and cries of disbelief.

Finally Anselm ordered them all home. Long moments passed, and Joseph and Poldie returned with the dead cart, rattling and creaking on the trail. The doctor waded into the water and placed a hand on Bernd's shoulder. Together, they carefully lifted the poor girl from the water and set her in the cart. Ambrose turned, heartbroken and dismayed. For all his efforts, he couldn't save Issa in the end, and his thoughts returned, unbidden, to Monika. He had failed.

Annaliese watched from the bank, her eyes red and tearful. Ambrose couldn't bear to look at her, but as he left she paused, laying her hand softly on his arm. She held him in her hazel eyes, a faint smile on her lips, and leaned close to whisper gently in his ear. "There is more to this town than you know."

PART II
Gregorstadt

✠

CHAPTER 16

Ritus Dedicationis Ecclesiae

October 30, 1859

A mbrose rose late. A small square of yellow sun lit the floor in an otherwise dark and dingy room. The din and clatter of dishes rose from the hall below and, with it, the smell of fried oil. With a heavy heart, he pulled on his tattered robe, poorly stitched across the chest, and glanced at the dirty mirror. His tired, unshaven face startled him every time. *Soon I'll be on my way. Finally.*

The hall below was a roiling mass of people. The last few weeks, the HOTEL ST. GREGOR had been filled with traveling workers headed to the neighboring town of Kiel to finish the bridge before the ground froze. Ruckus shouts reverberated in the air as they crowded at tables and milled at the bar, laughing and cursing. Killian and Tobias sat in a corner at the far end, and Ambrose scowled at the thought of wading through the throng. *When did I start to loathe this town?*

"You look like hell," Tobias said.

Ambrose sat down and Amalia thumped a cup down on the table in front of him, black coffee spilling on the white tablecloth. He tried to smile but found he could not. All he managed was a glower.

"I feel like it too." He sighed. "How can you stay at the abbey after everything?"

"It's horrible!" Killian blurted. "Every time I pass that cursed room, I think of the hellishness on the other side of the door. I can't wait to get away. And Anselm barely lets us leave these days."

"We'll be leaving soon. Rest assured," Tobias said. "I don't expect to hear from Cardinal Eberhard for at least another month, but we're not waiting. We're certainly not waiting for Anselm to confiscate my mail and read the cardinal's reply. I know your mind, Ambrose, and I know you won't leave things undone, but I implore you to come with us. I know we came for Stephan, but our own lives are on the line now, and there's no cause to think he's still alive, no matter what Florian and Winfried say. Either way, there's nothing more we can do. The cardinal has all the answers he needs."

Ambrose nodded. "By the first Sunday of Advent at the latest, I will be boarding a ship back to Le Havre. There's nothing more I can do for this town and no one wants me here either. I agree, Stephan must surely be dead by now. I will contact the state authorities in Milwaukee in any event. We haven't the ability here to search where we need to. We are powerless." He glanced around at the harsh faces; Amalia scowled from across the room. Rumors about him appeared to be giving the hotel a bad name.

"What happened to that beast you brought back?" asked Tobias. "Surely that won you some favor? Anselm hasn't let us out in almost two weeks and no one has said a thing about it."

"Buried in some back forty and forgotten." Ambrose waved his arm. "It's as if it never happened. No one knows what it was and no one was sent out to document it. No one talks about it and no one asks."

Killian picked at the bits of yolk and potatoes, suddenly disinterested. "What about Issa?"

Ambrose's face grew dark and a twinge of pain settled in his chest. The gruesome image of the girl's body in the lake rose unbidden in his mind. "Laid to rest in a lonely glade, hidden away in the woods, with no family or loved ones beside. Albrecht said there were no signs of struggle, so it was declared a suicide. Thus she had no funeral, and couldn't be buried in the church graveyard."

They grew quiet for some time. The clammer of breakfast had long cleared, as the workers had left. Killian eyed Ambrose with concern. He had grown withdrawn and his mood was heavy and distant. Even now, he was lost in dark thoughts, brooding in silence.

"You need to get out," said Tobias. "When was the last time you had any sun? Or slept, for that matter? What have you even been doing for the last two weeks?"

Ambrose seemed not to hear. He traced the coarse stitching of his cassock across his chest as he stared into space. The wound below was still tender. "No one talks about Augustin or Rosa," he muttered. "But they talk about me. And they stare."

"Listen…" Tobias shook his arm. "You can't stay here all cooped up. None of this was your doing. Francis Fährmann has finished building his chapel, and the town has been invited for a dedication Mass. You should come with us. It's a good ways in the woods, but it should be a nice little country shrine. There's a caravan leaving in an hour."

"No." Ambrose shook his head. "There's nothing left for me to do. I have no more obligations to this town. I'm not going to show up just for appearances. And being cooped up in a tiny chapel with Anselm and the town sounds like a terrible idea, besides. I'm done."

Tobias leaned back in his chair. "Unfortunately there's one more thing left to do. Father Valentine has returned. He's the one delivering the Mass. We at least need to see him before we go."

"Francis Fährmann," Killian said. "Annaliese's step-father? Maybe she could use a kind word in a time like this. She must be heartbroken to have lost her friend. I'm sure she appreciated everything you did, Ambrose, even if it was too late for Issa."

Ambrose looked up. Annaliese's soft smile flashed in his mind, comforting and confusing. A strange longing to see her ached in his chest.

"The wagons leave in an hour?" he said.

The cart bumped and banged in deep ruts. The two-track was barely cut from the forest and brush, and brambles hung from the sides to grab and tear at their clothes. The clop of the horse's steps was swallowed by the heavy wood that surrounded them. All the while, Ambrose gazed in silence as the sea of autumn leaves rolled slowly by.

Father Meinhard chattered in the seat next to them, bouncing with excitement. "That farm is Franzel's. Good man. Donates heavily and always lays down a few bottles of cider for me." He winked. "And that"—he pointed to an overgrown field and a collapsed house—"is Helgeson's. Ino fell down a well he was digging and cracked his head. Most say he was drunk. But…some say it was his wife that bopped him on the head and pushed him in."

"Tell me about Father Valentine," Ambrose said, rolling his eyes as the fat priest droned on.

"Oh, he's been gone quite a stretch this last time," Meinhard said. "Our little town isn't the same without him. I'm glad you'll get to meet him! You might just decide to stay! He's sure to have his medium with him. I wonder what you'll think?"

"His medium?" Tobias said. "Who, or what, is that?"

"Jonah," he said. "He's one of those pure simpletons. The boy can't read or write, and in fact, he can scarcely speak! That's how you know he has the divine gift and not some trickery of the Devil. The Devil is too clever, and you should never trust clever people. When the time is right, he'll forget himself and give a divinely inspired sermon. The angels speak through him."

"And what do they say?" Killian asked, eyes wide.

"Mostly follow and obey Father Valentine," Meinhard said, laughing.

The forest opened abruptly to the rolling pastures of the Fährmann farm, bright in the autumn sun. A small chapel stood on a hill, painted freshly white, and below, the townsfolk milled about in their Sunday best, the men in brown woolen suits and women in blue and gray dresses, modest, yet finely sewn. Francis Fährmann pointed to the steeple as the men around nodded and wagged their beards in interest.

A small crowd had gathered, and in its center, stood a strange figure, like a man but somehow wild: Father Valentine. A mass of disheveled hair fell upon his shoulders, brown locks knotted and tangled with leaves and twigs. A thick beard hung in waves about his chest, covering a robe of undyed raw cloth. At his side stood a peculiar-looking boy of twelve or thirteen, sullen and withdrawn. Yellow hair fell unkempt over a forehead too broad, and his eyes stared blankly in the distance.

"That's Father Valentine. And that"—Meinhard nodded to the boy—"is Jonah." The cart rolled to a stop. He hopped off with a heave and thump and, puffing, straightened himself. "Right, well, I'll leave you to mingle. Be sure to catch up with Father Valentine!" With a wave, he lumbered up the hill to join the others.

The townsfolk stood in clusters here and there, laughing and smiling at old stories and jokes. Yet they scowled when they saw the three of them and turned their backs and whispered. Friendly faces were few and far between.

"I'm so glad I came," Ambrose muttered.

"The fall colors are nice at least," Killian said, doing his best to stay lighthearted.

"We're only here to talk to Valentine," Tobias said. "For whatever good it does. Then our commission will have finally done its job and we'll be on our way."

A voice rose out of nowhere, wavering and unsteady. The priests turned to look toward the pitiful sound. Otto stood pleading with Valentine, his hands awkwardly at his chest.

"Otto looks horrible!" Ambrose said.

The man's face was pale and gaunt. He must not have slept or eaten in weeks. He was a shadow of the man who had struck him in the road not a month before. Beads of cold sweat glistened in black brows, and a tremor passed over his square face. Dark circles ringed sunken eyes and painted a haunted, ghastly visage. Ambrose shuddered.

"Will I see my boy again?" Otto said, trembling and weeping. "I've failed him, him and his mother. I don't deserve to be saved."

Valentine took the miller's hand and held it to his chest, a look of pity on his face. "Hear this and know that it is truth," he said. "Any man who has love in his heart—true love—will surely enter the Lord's Kingdom. Anyone who knows a love that recognizes no other will surely not be denied, for such love is the Lord's love and to love such is to walk hand in hand with the Lord. Love the Lord as you did your Augustin, and more so, and the longings of your heart will be answered. Your sins will be washed away in that love that knows no differences."

Otto's cheeks glistened with tears and he smiled, sadly. "I just wish Issa hadn't led him astray!"

"No, no, no…" Valentine chided. "Such love is small love. That is the love of friend alone, the love of differences. That is not God's love."

"Surely one cannot love as God," Anselm protested. "How can one presume to know the depths of the Lord's love? What man would presume to know the Lord himself?"

Valentine turned. His gray eyes were piercing, the color of clouded sky, and a tangle of hair blew wild in the cold breeze. "The Kingdom of Heaven lies within. One who knows the Kingdom knows nothing else." Turning to Otto, he smiled. "Now go. Stand in God's new chapel."

Otto turned to the chapel, a newfound joy on his face as he joined the others.

"But what of my Issa?" Bernd said. "Is she damned? She wasn't in her right mind. She was stricken by shame and grief, no thanks to this town. Is there no mercy for her? Must she suffer eternally?" The man's chest heaved as he coughed and shook, dark trails of cold sweat tracing the collar of his Sunday shirt, once fine, but now damp and oily.

"He looks almost as bad as the miller," Killian whispered.

"My dear man," Valentine said. "What evil things have come to pass? Issa was a frail and pure spirit. She succumbed to her own romantic sensitivities. The black bile was too stirred after Augustin. Had I been here, perhaps things would have ended differently. I am sorry. I know your pain, but the soul you should be most concerned with is your own. Issa is out of our hands now. Is it not said that he who loves his son or daughter more than me is not worthy of me?"

"But…she received no service!" Bernd wailed.

"It is enough that we love her," said Valentine. "But can we know her mind? Can we say one driven to such torment acted of her own free will? So are we also so arrogant to presume to know the mind of God?" He held the man's face to his own. "I will do a funeral for Issa. I will go on my own.

The Lord, in his wisdom, may pass his final judgement over her, not man.”

“Thank you!” Bernd said, nearly falling to the ground. “Thank you and bless you.”

He turned, his face was soft in a daze of relief, and as he left, he wore the faintest smile. Now, only Valentine and Anselm were left.

“We cannot do a funeral to Issa!” Anselm protested. “It is sacrilege! She is a suicide. She is damned. What of divine retribution? What of the punishment of sin?”

“Anselm…” Valentine shook his head. “Someday you must die yourself and see the living God before you, not the one of your imaginings. Trust in the Lord with all your heart and lean not on your own understanding. Do not be wise in your own eyes.”

“Yes,” Anselm protested, pacing in his black cassock. “But we have still to run our town, and such a community needs order, lest it give in to man’s baser instincts. Sometimes love is best expressed through the rod.”

“And that,” Valentine said, smiling, “I leave to you.”

Anselm’s face grew dark. Wordlessly he turned and left. The pasture cleared as the townsfolk of St. Gregory walked up the hill and filed into the little chapel. Finally, when all had left, Tobias, Ambrose, and Killian approached the mad priest.

“I don’t remember you being such a fan of the New Testament while in Stuttgart,” Tobias said. “You had more fire and brimstone to you, Valentine, and not a small amount of revelations.”

“Tobias!” Valentine exclaimed. “I finally see you again!” He squeezed the chubby priest in such strong embrace that Tobias was left gasping. “It is this land! I feel within it a silence I’ve long looked for but not felt until now. Such a stillness opens the soul. Have you been out in our fair wilderlands? One cannot help but find the love of God here, or at least his own purpose here on this earth. Such simple truths are so drowned and hidden by the din and smoke of the old world."

Tobias eyed him suspiciously. "But what of the coming New Kingdom? Are you not preparing for—or, rather, beckoning—it?"

"It will come to pass," Valentine said, with a disarming smile. "Of that I am certain. But I know now that the keys to the New Kingdom are not in fear or penance. No. They are in love."

"Many grotesque and unloving things happen in this loving town," Ambrose muttered. But Valentine smiled as if he hadn't heard.

"I'm happy for your realization," Tobias said cautiously. "And for our part, I hope our presence hasn't disturbed anything. But please, before we can be on our way, I must know one thing: where is Bishop Stephan? We have heard rumors—"

"He was here and now he is gone," Valentine said. "That is all I can say."

"Please," Tobias pressed. "It would settle affairs back home and also bring some comfort to his family. It would certainly paint you in a favorable light before the Grand Ducal Council."

"I care nothing for the council." Valentine waved his hand dismissively. "They have not the power to prevent my ministry or obstruct my intercessions for the souls of my flock. I shall pray, lay hands, or exorcise as needed. They can excommunicate me as they see fit. But all they can do is estrange themselves from me. They cannot estrange me from the Lord. As for the bishop, a man finds himself in the wilds of this land and the wilds have much to show. Be content with that. Now come. Let's not be late!"

The townsfolk parted in silence as they entered the tiny chapel, making way as Valentine passed. Soon he was swallowed by the crowd. As the priests stepped foot inside, they were greeted by the nutty smell of fresh-cured paint and new plaster that glowed brightly in the autumn sun. The Virgin Mary gazed down upon the flock from her seat above the altar, the infant Christ in her arms. Her porcelain frown was one of pious severity. "The Lady of Loučim," Meinhard whispered. "Brought all the way from the Šumavan forest."

Valentine stood before the altar, his hands raised and beckoning. "Rise and be joyful, for you have witnessed the power of the Lord, who works through you, our loving Mother. Who among you still doubts his healing power? Where medicine and the modern powers of man have failed, the mystery of the divine has prevailed!"

Murmurs swept through the crowd. Heads nodded and hands rose in prayer.

"Our brother Francis Fährmann was left with no hope of recovery. Our dear Dr. Albrecht said that fever of the brain is fatal in one week. Yet here he stands, strong enough to build this roof over our very heads, where but two months before he lay at death's door. The mysterious workings of the Lord are before you, plain as day! So take heart and take faith, you who yet suffer, you who yet harbor quiet doubts and misgivings."

The people smiled. Their eyes were bright in bliss as they swayed, and the air around was heady and euphoric.

"In good brother Fährmann's recovery, we see the power of repentance and redemption through prayer," Valentine continued, his voice clear and resonant. "For it is clear that this illness, as is true with all illness, is a corruption first and principally of the soul." He laid his hands upon Francis's broad shoulders. "Now you are cleansed and made pure once more. And so we stand in this chapel, now christened as the Chapel of our Lady, built to honor our divine Mother and our Lord, who alone have power over life and death, sickness and health. So, you who suffer, look inside yourselves. Where is your faith lacking? How long will you stand outside the door to His Kingdom?"

The people bowed in silence. Bernd alone looked up, his eyes raised to the martyrs in their wooden frames. Beads of cold sweat glistened on his trembling face and Ambrose looked in pity at the turmoil of the man.

"Gloria et Patri et Filio et Spiritui sancto in saecula saeculorum." Valentine made the sign of the cross. "Psalm 86: the Lord loves his foundation upon the mountain…"

Ambrose bowed his head. Valentine's voice rose and fell like soft music as the service wore on. Memories washed over him: Issa's innocent face, fearful in the darkened window; the ghostly pale bodies of Augustin and Rosa. Thoughts of home arose unbidden: Monika would be sitting at her desk, his letter in hand, wondering when her brother would return. Ambrose's chest ached, and his heart was heavy with loneliness, as he walked in a field of memories one washing over another.

"…iudicabit orbem in iusto et populos in fide sua." Valentine kissed the altar. "This chapel is blessed."

The townsfolk clasped one another's hands as bright smiles spread wide and soft murmurs filled the room.

"Now let us hear form Jonah," Valentine said, beckoning the boy forward. "Let us be silent and see what foretellings find us on this auspicious day. Let us listen to the will that speaks through our divine young man."

Valentine motioned. A hush descended on the crowd, and the boy reluctantly stood, his gangly limbs awkward before the room. With slow, uncertain steps, he shuffled to the altar coming to stand next to Valentine. Before the crowd, the boy seemed bent and fearful, his nervous eyes flitting self-consciously. A moment's glance settled on Ambrose, filling him with disquiet.

"Go ahead, son," Valentine urged.

The boy closed his eyes. Moments passed in silent waiting before he began to sway. Finally he straightened. Hunched shoulders rose and his chest was full and proud. A tremor passed, and his boyish features suddenly seemed terrifying. His chubby youth transformed as his cheeks seemed to grow long and hollow and his eyes sunk deep. The hair stood up on Ambrose's neck, as it appeared some otherworldly creature stood before them.

The crowd waited expectantly. The boy's muscles trembled and quivered, and he swayed and rocked as if some spirit struggled to burst free and reveal itself. Brown locks shook and danced about his face until suddenly he stopped, looking like someone possessed. His eyes opened, white and rolled back in his head, and he gazed unseeing at each of the priests in turn. A low voice rose as if from the ground, deeper than any man's, as Jonah stood in a trance.

"No!" He raised his arm to point at the three of them, his voice guttural and growling. "The words are a seal that only piety and penance shall reveal. You have saved no one. The book is shut! Away!"

The boy's white eyes bore into him, and Ambrose shuddered in fear as the face held him in ghastly transfixion. The townsfolk turned, suspicious and cold, their eyes narrowed in judgment. A weight, like some unseen force, pushed against Ambrose, filling him with dread as it willed him to leave. Valentine shook his head, a smile of pity on his wild face, as he motioned them quietly away.

"We need to leave now!" Ambrose hissed. "We're not wanted here!"

The townsfolks' glaring faces followed them out the door, until finally Ambrose pressed the iron handle shut behind him, locking the chapel away and they stood dumbfounded on the steps.

Ambrose filled his lungs with cold air as the awful weight faded. A chilly wind rustled the autumn grass and was crisp on his face. In the distance, the red and yellow leaves of fall danced merrily in treetops, oblivious to that strange world just beyond the chapel door.

"That's the same feeling I had in Stephan's room!" Killian said. He looked nervously back at the door, as if it wouldn't hold. "I felt that when I looked in the mirror!"

"I think we need to go," Tobias said. "I'm not waiting. I'm walking back! I've spent my last night in that abbey. We'll be joining you in the hotel after all, Ambrose." He clapped a chubby hand on Ambrose's back and ruffled Killian's hair. "I honestly hadn't imagined seeing anything like that today!"

"What was wrong with that boy?" Killian said. "Do you think it was some kind of falling sickness? Some phlegm of the brain? Or was he…possessed?"

"I don't know and I hope to be far enough away not to care," Tobias said.

The woods drew near as they hurried on. Red leaves danced in the breeze as the soft rustle of wind scattered them on the frosted ground. Golden light flickered through the trees and the must of autumn rose to meet them. Tobias and Killian joked and laughed, the strangeness of the chapel fading as they left it behind. Yet Ambrose's heart weighed heavily in his chest. His thoughts lingered on Issa, and he turned Jonah's words over in his mind: *You saved no one.*

"You couldn't help her, you know," a voice spoke, soft and sad and sweet. "No one could."

They looked to see a pale figure behind the trees. Raven-black hair fell in waves about her porcelain face, as Annaliese stepped into the open.

"What do you mean?" Ambrose asked. His breath caught in his throat and his voice trembled. His heart ached at the memory of the poor girl.

"Issa wasn't meant for this world," she said, smiling sadly. "She had one chance to be known. It's a rare thing to truly know someone; it doesn't always happen. Many people live lives completely unknown. When Augustin died, she felt no one could know her again. There are worse things than death, you know?"

"But what of eternal damnation?" Tobias said. "She took her own life, after all."

"What does anyone know of eternity?" she said. "I feel I've lived a lifetime of eternities already."

Her smile was sweet and distant, and as the leaves fell in reds and golds, dancing and falling about her, it seemed to Ambrose that she alone existed in the whole world. An uncanny silence held him, and the heaviness in his heart was for a moment forgotten. As she turned to leave, his heart ached and he wished she would stay.

☩

CHAPTER 17

I Hope It's Not Catching

November 4, 1859

An old undershirt lay folded on the bed, its dingy cotton splotched with the brown of old blood where a rough tear across the chest had been hastily stitched together. On the floor, a carpet bag sat crumpled and, beside it, a black doctor's bag, worn and scuffed.

"Where's your trunk?" asked Killian.

"I left it at the abbey. Anselm didn't give me time to call a porter." Ambrose glowered. "Thankfully Dr. Albrecht gave me his old bag, not that any of these rags are worth taking." He traced the rough mend of his cassock, holding it to the dirty window to see the light stream through the holes and stretched stitching. "I need to talk to Mr. Gatterman and see about a proper mend."

He tossed the robe in a pile on the desk, amid a clutter of dishes and papers. The giant feather he had found those weeks before fell to the floor, and he held it to the light, slowly turning it, its black veins shimmering iridescent with oily patterns. It seemed impossibly delicate, as if it hadn't come from the wings of that monstrous beast. He wrapped it carefully in old linens.

"Why are you taking that?" Killian asked.

"It seems important," Ambrose said. "Who would have thought last July that all of this would have happened? Who would have thought there were beasts like this yet alive in this age? In this small town lost in the wilderness? This small town, run by mad prophets and sinister priests."

"Maybe you should leave it," Killian said.

"But who would ever believe?" Ambrose said bitterly. "Who back home would hear our report and think we're not half mad? Besides, someone should document this creature, if no one here will."

Killian frowned. Ambrose wasn't the same since he had come back—not since Issa's death. Something had changed in him. He even had stopped going to church. By all accounts he was rarely seen, and only ever with the doctor. He appeared ever preoccupied, and his eyes were always distant, as if his mind were in some other place. Even now, his brow was tense and furrowed, and a darkness ringed his eyes, as if he hadn't slept in weeks.

"We might make it back for Christmas!" Killian said, hoping to raise his friend's spirits.

"We might just!" said Ambrose. "I know Tobias will be happy. I don't think he's ever missed a Christmas market." He paused and added, "Or the mulled wine that comes with it."

"Or the *stöllen* or the *lebküchen* or the cookies and cakes!" Killian sniggered.

Ambrose snorted, and Killian began a fit of chuckling. Soon they broke out in laughter. Killian held his belly and lay on his side, his red face and laughing hysterically into the bed.

"You look like a beet!" Ambrose said, wiping away the tears. For a moment, it felt like old times, and Ambrose sat grinning at the ceiling. "Where is Tobias anyway?"

"At the post. Sending a letter to Cardinal Eberhard, letting him know we're leaving soon."

"I really regret it, you know. I'd hate to think we're leaving Stephan behind. But I've been kicked out of the abbey. I've worn out my welcome, and what little restraint these folk have may not last much longer. I honestly fear for my person. And I fear for yours, as well. You and Tobias should head back. I'll stay in Fond du Lac or Milwaukee and contact the state authorities there and report Stephan missing under violent circumstances and feared kidnapped. Although…I have no idea who those authorities would be. I'll send word to the cardinal to send more people and the church can enlist the official aid of the government here."

"Shouldn't we stay with you?" Killian asked.

Ambrose shook his head. "No. You're too young and Tobias is too old and fat. If anything happened to you, your uncle Walter would have my head. It's a shame we couldn't do more, but we've come up against a wall."

Tobias hurried to the post, letter in hand. The autumn morning broke pale and clear after the night's rain, and the sun lit the rooftops in sparkling droplets. The muddy street was empty, the only sound the honk of geese above as they made their journey south. The cobbler shop was shuttered; dirt and dried leaves lay in piles at the corners, and fresh cobwebs fluttered in the window. Bernd must not have been there for some time. He tried not to think of it and hurried on.

His memories turned to a world far away: the first frost would be settling on the forested hills back home, and his heart was light at the thought of seeing them again soon. The brisk wind was bright against his cheeks, and the day hinted at coming journeys and departure. But his morning reminiscence was suddenly broken by the clop and slop of heavy feet. Behind, mud sloshed in quick patter; someone was panting and wheezing behind, hurrying to catch up. Tobias gritted his teeth, pretending not to hear.

"You really should come back and spend your last few nights in the abbey." Meinhard gasped, a rare frown on his chubby face. "It would be the polite thing to do."

Tobias hurried on without turning. "Thank you kindly for the offer, Father. But I think Anselm would rather have us all leave."

"Nonsense! He may be a little cold, but I promise you he'd like nothing more than to extend our hospitality until we can all wish you a safe journey," Meinhard protested. "Well, all except Father Ambrose, I suppose."

"I appreciate the sentiment, but I fear we've overstayed our welcome. Especially after the chapel. It seemed quite clear that we were witness to things we weren't meant to be."

Meinhard looked away uncomfortably. "Ah, well, you mustn't pay that any mind. Jonah doesn't commune well when new folks are about. You have to be one of the community, as it were. One of the...chosen."

"And we're clearly not. If the angels talk through the boy, they clearly had nothing to say to us," Tobias said, looking over his shoulder.

Meinhard clasped Tobias's arm, insistent. "But what of Father Valentine? Don't you want to spend your last days with him and say farewell?"

"I know Father Valentine," Tobias said, his face growing dark. "Remember, I've known him quite a long time. Father Valentine will be the same whether or not I say farewell. He is perennial in his conviction. We're just passing momentarily in his light."

Meinhard stared at the muddy ground, his shoulders sunk and a frown appeared on his face. "There's no convincing you?"

"You'll come to know this is for the best."

Meinhard opened his mouth in protest when an eerie wail rose suddenly in the distance. It was a pitiful howl that stood their hair on end, but just as quickly it was gone.

"What in God's name was that?" Tobias said. They stood still, listening, but all was still but for the whistle of the wind in the eaves of shops nearby.

"At least let me walk with you," Meinhard said, turning back to Tobias. "It's been days since we've spoken. Where are you off to on this cloudy, windy day?"

"To the post," Tobias said reluctantly.

"Good! Then on to the post!"

They trudged on. Tobias did his best to ignore Meinhard, who chattered beside him. The going was slow and soon their feet grew heavy with wet clay. Clumps of mud stuck to their boots, and they stretched out their arms to balance, taking careful steps around piles of fresh manure. Tobias's foot slipped and his hand sunk into the muck as he caught himself. His face grew red as he brushed mud from the envelope.

"Doesn't it just figure?" he grumbled.

"You're lucky!" Meinhard laughed. "Look!"

At his feet, steam rose off a pile of fresh manure. A rider on his horse turned in the distance—a merchant, by the looks of him—and smiled and tipped his hat.

The wail rose again, closer now—a mournful cry echoing in the alleys. This time there were words. "I see her!" it cried. Yet they could not see where it came from.

"Who is that?" asked Tobias.

Meinhard turned in surprise, looking here and there, but the slick clay gave way under his heavy feet. Mud squished under him and he slipped. In a crash he fell chest first into the pile of manure.

"Oh, for the love of God!" he exclaimed, struggling to his feet.

Tobias held his belly amid peals of laughter. "Don't take the Lord's name in vain!"

Meinhard's face was red as he picked off bits of mud and manure.

The wail rose again, this time closer, and they stopped, looking here and there. A gaunt figure stumbled into view. Pale flesh hung thin off his hollow cht eeks, and his gray hair blew wildly in the wind. The man staggered, lumbering and unsteady, like some ghost fresh from the graveyard.

"I see her!" he cried.

"Is that Otto?" asked Tobias. "Is that the miller?"

"Otto!" Meinhard cried. "My God, what happened to you?"

"I see her!" he cried again, and pointed. His vacant eyes stared past them, fixed on something they couldn't see, and he fell to the ground, mud splashing as he dropped to his knees. Tobias and Meinhard rushed to his side, struggling and slipping, and the door of the bakery flew open as the townsfolk rushed into the street.

Tobias held the miller's head. Otto's pale skin was cold against his hand, and beads of chill sweat ran down to soak his wet collar. Meinhard stood in shock, mouth agape, as Poldie and Jacob rushed past.

"Call Dr. Albrecht!" Tobias yelled.

"Yes!" Meinhard said, blinking. "Yes, call the doctor! Poldie, get Sepp and fetch the cart!"

The horse clopped and the cart creaked and shook as it raced toward them. Jacob strained against the miller's weight as Poldie lifted his legs and Tobias struggled from behind. Finally, with a heave, Otto crashed into the cart. The whip cracked, and with a "Ha!" Joseph raced to the doctor's as fast as the horse could go.

Silence settled once more. Wide eyes looked to one another, bewildered, no one daring to speak.

Tobias shook his head. "I need a drink."

The townsfolk gathered at the stoop of the HOTEL ST. GREGOR. Meinhard downed a mug of beer on the porch and reached for the door, the townsfolk following, but

Harold Fessler stood guard with a broom in hand. "You'll not be tracking mud in here," he growled. "Just tell Amalia what you need."

"What's wrong with Otto?" Gerti cried.

The crowd shouted over one another. "Is it cholera?" a boy asked.

"No, it's not coming out of that end. His trousers looked clean but for the mud," a man said, as others nodded in agreement.

"It's consumption!" a woman whispered in panic.

"Now, now," said Jacob. "We need no such dire proclamations. It's too quick for that, and besides, Dr. Albrecht will have to cut him open to be sure." Shocked cries rose in protest.

"Come, people, come!" Meinhard said, raising his voice above the crowd. "Trust in the Lord and trust in Father Valentine! Illness is but sin of the soul, purged in the fire of bodily penance. One needs but have faith!"

Tobias shook his head. "Faith healers!" he muttered. "Of all the dumb…" Clutching his letter, he hurried to the post.

"This is quite a tear, Father," Edmund Gatterman said, looking casually at Ambrose's poorly patched robe. The monstrous talon had sliced clean across the chest, and bits of spare string held the rip together, pulling and threatening to tear.

"How soon can you mend it?" Ambrose asked. He sat in the hotel's dining hall in old and ill-fitting shirt and pants, rented from Mr. Fessler. The tailor was behind in his work, or likely just didn't care, and the hotel was the only place he could find a new set of clothes.

"Well"—Mr. Gatterman set his glasses beside his beer—"not for a week at least. I've got other orders, you know."

Ambrose rapped his knuckles on the table in annoyance. "You know I plan to leave in a little more than week, yes? I thought you hadn't much work since falling out of favor with the town."

"Well, people still need new dresses and suits from time to time. And now that Valentine is back, the abbey seems to have forgotten their grievances. Speaking of"—he smirked—"it's strange to see a man of the cloth in common shirt and trousers. It's a…amusing."

Ambrose shifted uncomfortably in the unfamiliar clothes; a shirt and pants, two sizes too big, rented from the hotel owner. The starched collar dug stiffly into his neck as he pulled and tugged, a toothy grin spreading on Mr. Gatterman's face.

"Are you sure you're not occupied with other things?" Ambrose asked, unbuttoning his collar in frustration. "You seem to have certain proclivities." He gestured to the beer.

"What are you suggesting?" the tailor said. He glared and carefully straightened the wrinkles of woolen suite as he looked down his nose at Ambrose. "And what business is it of yours? You can mend your own damn clothes, for all I care."

"I apologize." Ambrose held up his hands. "It's not my place to say. Or care. This has been a very taxing few weeks, if you hadn't guessed. And you're not the only one to have fallen out of favor with Anselm and the abbey. He kicked me out after all. And now Otto is sick with some strange ague that we can only hope isn't catching."

"He's not long for this world, they say." Mr. Gatterman shook his head. "Leastways that's what the doctor says. Mind you, he says not to say so! But we've a right to know, haven't we? Aren't we all in the same town? What happens to one likely happens to another."

The kitchen door creaked open, and Amalia bustled out, plates in hand, her blue dress swishing around empty tables.

Steam rose off a plate of pork and potatoes set down in front of the tailor.

"And nothing for you, as usual, I suppose," she said, glancing dismissively at Ambrose.

"Just coffee, thank you."

"Amalia, dear, have you heard anything of Otto?" Mr. Gatterman whispered. "They say he's not going to make it."

She glanced at the empty room and plopped down in a chair beside him. A mischievous smile dimpled her youthful cheeks as she relished in the gossip, and leaned close, to hiss, "Not just Otto! Claudia is sick too!"

"You don't say!" Edmund said. "Well, she must have gotten it from Bernd. I heard he was quite pale at the chapel. His shop has been closed for days. I thought he was in mourning, but perhaps there's more to the story."

"And that's not all. Jacob has been looking pale of late." She touched a finger to her red lips. "Now, you didn't hear that from me."

The two leaned close, ignoring Ambrose. The room was silent but for their hushed whispers, and Ambrose looked away, momentarily forgotten. He cleared his throat uncomfortably. "Poor Claudia. It's a shame to lose a child and have a husband take ill, and now she's ill besides. It's a poor stroke of luck."

"Luck?" Amalia said, her eyes narrowing. "Some say it was because of her daughter. The family suffers for that crazed girl's sin."

Ambrose shook his head, "Now that's not—"

"Amalia!" Harold called from the back. "Come get this down to the root cellar."

She stood quickly and straightened her hair, glancing nervously around the room as the hall echoed with the bangs and bumps of her father stacking heavy barrels and crates.

She motioned to Edmund's empty glass. "Another one?"

The tailor scowled as he looked at Ambrose. "No. I'm fine for now."

"Suite yourself," she said, and hurried to the back.

"Otto, Bernd, Claudia, and Jacob are all sick," Ambrose said. "Did they come down with something at the chapel?"

Mr. Gatterman shook his head. "They couldn't have. Jacob didn't go. We were toasting one another's health. Seemed better than spending time with that Francis Fährmann. Speaking of which"—he pointed—"I've heard strange stories about you three. Seems Jonah didn't take well to you."

"What is with that boy?" Ambrose shook his head. "The poor soul looked possessed or seemed to suffer from some disease of the mind, what these new philosophers might call 'dissociation.'"

"Eh?" Edmund said, scowling. "I haven't a clue what you're talking about or any strangeness you've been reading. The boy is a medium, plain as day. Simpletons are pure, you know, too simple to be corrupted.

"Why does someone like Father Valentine need a medium?"

"My good man"—Edmund laughed—"even a priest such as he needs confirmation."

☩

CHAPTER 18

Small Town Gossip

November 7, 1859

Tobias knocked softly on the door, listening. A week had passed since they'd left the abbey and joined Ambrose to stay at HOTEL ST. GREGOR. In the early morning, a narrow window lit the hall in dim, dusty light that faded to darkness at the far end. The upstairs was still but for the occasional creak of loose floorboards from a guest room down the hall.

The old priest rapped again, louder. Killian's bleary face peered through the crack, his wild hair standing in a tangle over his half-opened eyes.

"Tobias? It's barely dawn."

"Morgenstund hat Gold im Mund," Tobias said matter-of-factly.

"What?" Killian said, squinting.

"The early bird gets the worm?"

"Yes, but…the second mouse gets the cheese."

"Quite right." Tobias laughed. "But I need to stretch my legs. I can't keep cooped up in here. Let's check on train tickets. I want to make sure they don't try and raise the price on us. Then we'll have a bite at the bakery."

Killian sighed and looked forlornly at the warm bed. Frost clung to the edges of the thin glass window, and chill air swirled at his naked feet. It was a cold day, and he would rather have stayed inside. "What about Ambrose?"

"Best to not bother him. I don't think he's slept in days. Now hurry up and get dressed! Let's go see Mr. Baumgartner."

Outside, the bitter wind chased the last warm sleepiness away. The sky was gray with dark clouds that threatened snow, and the few people on the street were bundled against the unseasonable cold. White frost etched yesterday's boot prints and cart tracks, and ice formed in the hollows and divots of the road. The whole ground crunched and cracked as Tobias and Killian walked the uneven ground and their feet were sore by the time they reached the post.

"They say the winter will be early this year," Tobias said, stumbling. "Lucky us. Of course this will all thaw and be mud again by noon."

They stumbled into the post, shaking off the cold. The sun had barely broken the horizon, yet already an old and wrinkled woman stood at the counter, gossiping. From the pained look on the postmaster's face, it seemed she had been there some time.

"…I told him no good would come of it. But that man will never listen." She paused as the priests entered, just long enough to show her disapproval, before turning back. "Have you heard? Ottilia Clemens is cavorting with a man from Walders. Some half-breed French. Eloi Grignon. Some say he's not even Christian. A family of fur traders when there was New France that turned native. He's a trapper and a porter and whiskey runner and a ne'er-do-well. Works at the Central Hotel."

"I thought all the old French families were Jesuits and all Jesuits were Catholic," Mr. Baumgartner said, taking off his blue postman's cap to scratch his balding head.

"No. Not this man. He's some half-French, half-Indian heathen. Claudia says Ottilia calls him *'Wakosha.'* She is driven mad by the whole affair. They'll have a red-man bastard child. Mark my words!"

"Hm," said Mr. Baumgartner. "What does her mother say about it?"

"Ah, that old biddy! I don't talk to her."

"Well," he said, fidgeting. "Walders is a strange place. They do things differently there."

"And they should stay there!" She scowled.

The man nodded and smiled thinly. "Can't argue with that, Gilli. Anyway, this is all I have for you this week." He handed her a letter. "Now you take good care Mrs. Platten."

Gilli scowled as she took the envelope. "Now what does *she* want?"

The old woman left and the tiny office grew quiet. The postmaster cleared his throat, ears red in embarrassment. "What can I do for you fathers?"

"Tickets!" Tobias said. "What's the price of tickets lately? Thought I'd better check. I don't like surprises."

"Of course." He thumped a large book on the counter. "Where to?"

"Well, we'll need a stagecoach to Fond du Lac from Kiel if we're to get anywhere. But our final destination is Toledo."

The man turned the pages of the dusty book, jotting down quick figures.

"$13.46 by second-class for one person," he said, frowning and scratching his head. "But I suppose you'll be needing to go through Johnson Creek to get to Chicago."

Tobias shook his head impatiently. "I don't know what that place is, but if it's on the way, we need to go through it."

"Well, that's just the thing." Mr. Baumgartner unfolded a letter. "See? There's been an accident on the line there."

He handed the letter to Tobias apologetically. The old priest's eyes glared as he handed it back without looking.

"See? An ox hopped onto the track. Somehow the cow catcher didn't knock it loose and it got tangled underneath. Says here"—the man put on his spectacles—"the engine was tossed into the ditch; the baggage car ended up in a pond; five passenger cars were destroyed, and fourteen persons died and more than thirty injured."

"You're kidding!" Tobias shook his head.

"Terribly sorry, but it'll take at least ten days to reopen the line."

"Well, I can't rightly be mad about it, with such loss of life. What rotten luck on all sides," Tobias muttered. "Does this happen often?"

"Why, no sir!" the man said, brightening. "This is the very first time!"

"Of course it is." Tobias turned to Killian, who stared dismally at the floor. "Well, my boy, we're stuck here another week and a half, and that just figures. Might as well get some coffee. We have nothing but time."

"Will you be wanting tickets then?" Mr. Baumgartner asked.

"For the line that's broken? No."

The bakery was a chatter of troubled voices. The air hung heavy and brooding, spilling into the street beyond. Glass panes rattled as Ambrose shut the door and faces turned, drawn and dour, staring at his borrowed clothes. He tried to ignore them, but he heard their hushed whispers. His strange appearance only added to the townsfolks' confusion. He looked for Tobias and Killian in annoyance, finally finding them huddled in the back.

"There you are!" Killian said. "Coffee? Streusel?"

Ambrose sat down and sighed. He could feel Tobias and Killian smirking. He felt like a fool—a clown in borrowed pants and shirt that hung far too large. His cassock was with Mr. Gatterman to be mended, and in the meantime, he sat in ratty laborers clothes. Billows of loose fabric hung about the arms and chest, worn and patched here and there, with squares of reds and blues in odd patterns. As Tobias and Killian laughed, memories of the orphanage flooded back: a child in hand-me-downs lost in a faceless sea.

Tobias eyed Ambrose with a wry smile. "What happened to your clothes?"

"Being mended by the tailor." Ambrose shook his head. "I had to rent these from Harold Fessler. They're tacked on to the room and board."

"How kind!" Killian chuckled.

Scowling, Ambrose turned away, looking at the crowd. It seemed half the town had gathered to talk and gossip about Otto and the mysterious illness that had befallen him.

The door creaked open. Francis Fährmann stood tall and lean in the doorway, his wife just behind him. "Ho! Francis! Barbara! Come have a seat," a man called form the table nearby. Chairs squeaked and dishes clattered as space was made. Gerti and Poldie and the butcher and many more welcomed them in, and soon they were chatting away.

The baker thunked plates and cups on the table in front of them and hurried away. The carafe steamed, and nutty coffee warmed Ambrose's hands and he smiled. *Thank God for small favors!* Streusel steamed sweet spices, in striking contrast to the bitter mood of the room, and he savored every bite, doing his best to ignore.

"Well, what do you think?" Tobias said.

"At least the streusel is good," Ambrose said. "Otherwise, this situation would be unbearable. But I suppose I can put up with another week. At least we can enjoy some autumn colors before we leave."

"You'll be enjoying more than that, I'm afraid," Tobias said. "Apparently there's been an accident on the line. We'll be delayed a good ten days, at least."

"Christ!" Ambrose said, and blushed immediately. He sighed and rubbed his eyes. "This whole place seems bent against us."

He opened his mouth to speak, but voices from the table beside rose in earnest.

"Bernd, Claudia, Jacob…" Barbara Fährman sighed.

The butcher sat beside her, his thick fingers rapping on the worn table, clicking under stubby nails. "Have you seen Otto?" he said. "Pale as a sheet and thin as one, too. He must have lost near twenty pounds in sweat." More worried voices rose, whispering of sickness and doubt.

Sighing, Ambrose turned back to the table. He tried to forget and enjoy the morning, but the streusel seemed flat, like it had lost all flavor. Tobias stirred cold coffee, a sour expression on his face, as metal scraped on white porcelain, grating against Ambrose's ears. *Why didn't I stay in bed? There's simply no point to getting up early.*

"Well," he said, forcing a smile, "Mr. Fessler can't even get to mending my cassock until next week, so maybe it's meant to be."

"By then you'll own those baggy clothes outright," Killian said.

"I should be so lucky."

The room fell into gloomy silence. Even the townsfolk were sullen and withdrawn, yet no one left. No one dared leave the meager comfort of the warm bakery for the cold loneliness outside. Ambrose's heart sank at the thought of spending another ten days in the town. Maybe it would be safer in Walders, though he had heard it was a lawless place, filled with brawling and boozing and gambling.

In the stillness, a percolator bubbled and roared, and Ambrose found his mind wandering to the comfort of such meaningless noise. He didn't notice the voices from the table beside them until Tobias nudged him. Looking over his shoulder, he saw their dour faces, drawn and frowning amidst whispers.

"It has to be some kind of ague but from where?" asked Barbara.

"Those woods along the marsh are heavy with foul mist and miasma," said Max the butcher. "I've always cautioned that. And Otto's place is right on that foggy stream. My da always said you stay outta the woods when the damp's arising."

Mumbles and groans rose from the table and Gerti shook her head.

"What, Gertrude?" Max snapped. "What've you got to say?"

She scowled and ignored him, as the man grew red in the face.

"Was anyone sick at the chapel?" Barbara asked. "I'm not saying they got it there or in the woods on the way. But maybe someone had the ague there and didn't know."

"Nay!" Francis thumped the table. "Only Otto looked a trifle out of sorts, but he's grieving. Who wouldn't look as he? Claudia and Bernd too. But they looked healthy given the circumstances. Jacob didn't even come, as usual. But he's sick too! He didn't get it there."

"Now, I meant no offense," Gerti said, tapping his hand.

"No, it's not the chapel," Max said. "It makes no sense. I can't rightly say. But some things seem…unnatural."

"Oh, you!" Gerti rolled her eyes. "Maximillian, you always see demons and devils in the shadows!"

"Don't take it so light, Gertrude!" He scowled and crossed his arms. "There's angry souls and troubled spirits and worse hiding under your fat nose!"

"Oh, hush!" she said, smacking him with her bonnet.

The table grew quiet as the townsfolk sulked in anger, and after all they had been through, the three priests couldn't help but find their bickering hilarious. Killian broke into a toothy grin and Tobias stared at the ceiling, chubby hand over his mouth, desperately trying to cover his smile. Ambrose struggled to hold in a laugh but suddenly snorted and chuckled.

"Ahem!" he coughed, pretending to clear his throat, as he was met by silent glares.

"You know," the butcher said, looking at the three of them, "none of this happened before that Catholic commission came to town."

The priests squirmed uncomfortably and looked away.

Out of the corner of his eye, Ambrose caught a flash of blue. It passed the window and his breath caught in his throat. "Um," he said. "There's something I need to do."

"Where are you going?" asked Tobias.

"Don't eat all the streusel!" he said, and hurried from the table.

Annaliese's dress swished and swayed from her slender waist—tiny yellow flowers dancing in a field of azure ruffles and white lace. The street was empty but for her graceful figure.

"Miss Fährmann!" Ambrose puffed, out of breath.

She turned to him, pale in the sun. "Father Odenwald?"

"I wanted to wish you farewell," Ambrose said. "We'll be departing soon. Given all that's happened, I hoped to see that you are well and managing."

"So soon?" she said, and it seemed her spirit dropped.

"Well, our commission's work has come to an end," he stammered. "And, I've come to feel in no uncertain terms that this town wants us gone."

"Some would be sad to see you go... But I don't blame you for going. I'm sorry you haven't found your bishop."

"Why would anyone be sad?" Ambrose said, blushing.

She turned away, as if she hadn't heard. A sad smile lay on her lips as she gazed at the forest in the distance.

"I envy you," she said, finally. "We left Loučim when I was fourteen, my parents and my brother and sister. I never wanted to come here. My heart still walks in that old place, in the dells and glens and hollows that only I knew."

"I'm sorry. I didn't know," Ambrose said. "Loučim is in Bohemia, in the dark Šumava Forest. That must have been hard. But you can't fault your parents for wanting a better life. There's not much opportunity in the old places anymore."

"I wish they'd left me," Annaliese whispered. As her hazel eyes gazed into the distance, she seemed lost in a world of memories, fair and forgotten. "I knew the spirits there. I heard their laughter in the valleys and streams. I called them by secret names." She blushed and looked away. "You must think me silly; some romantic girl given to flights of fancy. It's not so. The voices of the forest are strange here. I cannot talk to them."

Ambrose frowned. "I'm sorry you can't go back."

They stared at the sky in heavy silence. A lone crane called, gray against the pale clouds, only to fly away unanswered, its mate lost or far away.

Annaliese's red lips broke into a fragile smile. "Do you ever remember your dreams? " she said. "Some nights I dream I'm standing on a rocky shore. The waves crash all around and the air is thick with salt. My cheeks are cold and moist, and my dress is wet from the spray. The waves crash endlessly under a steely sky. And I'm far, far away. Far away from here." She squeezed his hand and his heart quickened. "Someday I'll buy a ticket, as far as the line goes."

✠

CHAPTER 19

Who Do You See?

November 9, 1859

As the three priests walked in silence, the pale sun of afternoon trickled through the gnarled boughs and knuckled twigs of the old orchard. Brown leaves still clung here and there, occasionally falling softly to join the dry drifts of the ones before. Ambrose found his gaze drawn to the wood and, beyond, the cross and steeple, black against the gray sky. The distant bell tolled, solemn and grave, four times to mark the hour. The light had grown already dim as the short autumn day passed toward evening. As they walked, the rustle of leaves shattered the silence and seemed terribly out of place in the wild stillness that crept from the forest. Finally they could stand the sound no more and stopped among the trees.

"What will your report say?" Tobias asked, resting against an old trunk.

Ambrose drew a crumpled scrap from his pocket and read:

The town is yet under the sway of this would-be prophet. He certainly enjoys the roll of the charismatic and eccentric faith healer he took such pains to cultivate back home, although he would wish to present himself to us here as a man reformed. He claims not to care for his status in the church and believes himself to be beyond the papal reach. This may, in fact, be true. Few laws govern this land, and he may be acting entirely outside of doctrinal authority.

He would have us believe the influence of this land has tempered his millennialism. To be sure, such views are most certainly still held, but their rancor and damnation are less, at least in outward appearance. Even so, I thoroughly doubt his sincerity.

More damning, however, is the matter of Bishop Stephan, of which he refuses to give any account, saying that he is here of his own free will. He claims the bishop is on 'private retreat' and is safe and unmolested. However, given the state of Stephan's cell and the perversions found there, I can hardly believe this to be the case. I believe that the bishop, if he is still alive, is being held captive and is in mortal danger. In fact, we ourselves are in much the same state, though we see not yet the bars of our cell. For this reason, we shall depart at the earliest opportunity. I fear what would happen to us, should we stay. Tobias shall accompany Killian back home, while I remain behind in Milwaukee to seek whatever authorities may govern this infernal land.

They were silent for some time. Hearing his letter aloud, they could no longer deny how dangerous their position was.

"Valentine is taken by madness. Whatever decency he once had is gone," Tobias said. "That spectacle in the chapel exposed his smoke and mirrors. Something is going on and

I don't trust it. I don't agree with this decision that I should leave you here. You should come with us."

"My heart is torn," Ambrose said. "It pains me to leave. I feel I am abandoning Stephan, if he's even still alive."

"Is it possible that the bishop is here willingly?" asked Killian, as he peered past the old apple trees nervously. "Could he possibly be under Valentine's sway?"

Tobias put up a hand. "Certainly not! They have no love for each other. It is only that they had a peculiar kinship long ago that sent Stephan on this his wild path to redeem him. But whatever actual fondness they had for each other has long since withered. Remember that eleven years ago he and Johannes Ronge were foremost in criticism of Valentine's damn fool pilgrimage to the Holy Coat of Trier. His association with Ronge was long before Ronge lost all good sense and formed his 'New Catholic' community and published his rebuke of King Fredrick William. That damn fool had to flee this very summer to England to save his own head. Stephan had nothing to do with any of that, of course, but his past connection would have made Valentine loathe him. It's hard to believe Stephan could have been welcomed here, stayed for any length of time, or changed his own views on the matter."

"But could this actual place change someone?" asked Killian. "Valentine said it changed him. And everyone in the town seems so different from the people back home. They couldn't have been this way when they left, could they? I feel strange here. There's a strangeness in the land."

"Nah, son, don't let him into your head," said Tobias. "That's how he gets to you. It's all nonsense."

"Silas said something to me when we were deep in the forest," Ambrose said suddenly. "At the time, I dismissed it as local superstition, but now I'm not so sure. You know the city on the great lake? The one called Manitowoc? The name comes from the native tribes. They called it Manidoowag. Silas said it meant the land of evil spirits. He said the spirits weren't always evil, just now." He paused as an eerie whistle of cold wind howled in the dark and distant wood. The land seemed to be listening. "Maybe this place has its own spirits. What dwells here that we cannot see?"

"Valentine said you bring the spirits with you when you enter the woods," Killian said. Maybe the spirits are us."

"Ambrose, this isn't like you." Tobias scowled. "You know there are no such things as spirits. There is only the fanciful imaginings of the naïve, easily led astray."

Ambrose gazed out at the meadow and the white teeth of the gravestones in the graveyard. How different the land must have looked before all the settlers came. Where were the graves of the natives they took the land from?

"Maybe so, but what horrors did these lands see, I wonder?" Ambrose said. "What blood is soaked in this soil? If there ever were spirits, how could they not be angry?"

They looked up. A thin whistling broke the silence. A leaden tune, haunting and out of key, wound among the old apple trees. A metal spade crested the hill, followed by a head of white hair. Joseph hummed the lines of some forgotten song, a shovel on his shoulder and lamp in hand.

"Father Ambrose! It's good I've found you!" he puffed. "Dr. Albrecht would like to see you posthaste!"

"What for?"

"Couldn't say! Not my business!"

"Well, thank you for your discretion," Ambrose said. "Although it'd be nice to know what's so urgent. Where are you going anyway?"

"Going to dig a hole, Father."

"But it's almost dark."

"Yes, sir. But this hole must be dug before the frost and it's unseasonably cold of late. I expect to be at it all night."

"A hole for what, Joseph? You're speaking in riddles."

"Oh, begging your pardon! Have you not heard? Otto's dead."

Albrecht stood before the shuttered house in his old woolen suit as the hours lengthened and the shadows grew. The old man's wrinkled hands fidgeted, his doctor's bag held tightly in their grasp, as he peered down the road. Finally Ambrose emerged on the trail, a thin man in ill-fitted clothes two sizes too big. Weeks of rough stubble darkened his face below eyes that had grown pensive and wary.

"Ambrose! You're finally here! I hadn't wanted to enter alone," the doctor whispered. "I need another set of eyes. And someone to talk things through. This business with Bernd has got me rattled. I don't want to see him alone. Would you mind?" He stopped suddenly and lifted his glasses. "You look dragged out and run ragged."

"You're too kind," Ambrose said. "I feel as well as I look, I might add. But what could I possibly help you with? I'm no doctor and our commission is over."

Albrecht paced on the stoop, floorboards creaking. "Never mind that! This is actually important. I can't explain it. I can't rightly wrap my own head around it yet. But I need an impartial witness. Someone to observe the same things and see if they actually…are…if you take my meaning."

"I don't," he said.

"See if they actually are the same things?" He waved his hand. "Oh, never mind. But will you come? Just to help an old man? Nothing's catching, I'm quite sure of it. This is unlike any communal ague I've heard of."

Ambrose frowned at the shuttered windows, dark against the pale sun. "What of Bernd and Claudia? What would they think of me gawking with my unprofessional opinion?"

"Oh. Let me do the explaining. Just follow my lead."

"All right." Ambrose sighed. "If it helps."

"Wonderful! It does!" he said. "Now keep your eyes peeled."

The door creaked open to a scene of disarray. Pots and dishes lay dirty on the table, dry and molded. The air was heavy and rank, as if no breeze or draft had swept the house in some time. A labored breath gasped somewhere in the next room. All about, a young woman's dresses lay strewn, their hems frayed as if gnawed—Issa's dresses, Ambrose guessed. He coughed and held his breath as Albrecht thrust his head into the dark room.

"Claudia?" the doctor called. "Claudia?"

A chair creaked. A harsh cough filled the tiny house as Claudia peered from behind the door, pale and sweaty.

"My God, you've lost at least ten pounds!" Albrecht cried.

She pointed at Ambrose. "What's he doing here?"

"Oh, you know Father Ambrose. He's here to help with Bernd."

Claudia's bleary green eyes stared, blinking. "If Father Valentine can't help, then what's a nonbeliever to do?"

"Father Ambrose is here to consult medically. He trained in Munich at the Ludwig-Maximillian University with Professor Ringseis," he lied. "The same as Father Valentine. He will surely be a help."

"Fine." She hung her head. "This will take us all anyway. He's this way."

She led them to the bedroom. A blanket lay on the floor in spite of the chill, crumpled on a pile of soiled linens. Everywhere, dust and dirt lay thick on the sills and in the corners, and dirty plates from days before were stacked, cluttering the tiny room and seemingly forgotten. Bernd lay wrapped in a thin sheet, soaked and yellowed. His pale skin hung sallow and gaunt off empty cheeks, and his sunken eyes gazed unseeing at a ceiling swathed in cobwebs. Ambrose turned and quickly covered his mouth against the sour smell. What sickness plagued these poor people? Ambrose stood at a distance, worried he might catch whatever illness was in the air.

Albrecht eyed her closely. "What's happened here, Claudia?"

"What's happened where?"

Albrecht frowned, ignoring her as he tended to Bernd. Clammy skin met his fingers. "His pulse is slow, barely forty-three beats per minute. Bernd? Bernd? Wake up!" He waved his hand in front of the cobbler's eyes and snapped his fingers. "Claudia, would you give us a moment?"

She nodded. "I'll put the kettle on."

Ambrose stepped gingerly around piles of soiled linens and refuse. Try as he might, he couldn't look away from the poor man's withered frame, and in his mind was seared the man's haunting expression. The walls pressed upon him and he longed to flee.

"What's happening here?" he asked.

"Claudia seems sick too," Albrecht said. "And she's getting worse."

"I thought you said this wasn't catching!"

"It's not, I assure you. Now help me move him."

They stooped to hoist the man up. He was light under their arms as they set him up in the bed.

"He must weigh barely a hundred pounds!" Ambrose said.

"Muscle wasting. Look how the skins sags. There's nothing to fill it." Albrecht placed his hand on the cobbler's head. "A cold fever. There's scarce any warmth in this man."

Bernd's head lolled to the side. Crazed eyes, bleary and delirious, rolled up and stared. "I see her," he whispered, his trembling hand reaching for the doctor. "I see her there."

"Who?" asked Albrecht. "Who do you see?"

"Right there! She's looking at me!"

They turned to the empty room. A haze of dust floated in the dim light of drawn curtains. Save for dresser drawers turned out on the floor, there was nothing there.

"She's there! Can't you hear? Can't you hear that awful chewing?"

Albrecht shook his head, placing a hand on the man's head to comfort. "Otto said the same thing before he died," he said. "Some kind of shared delusion, with shared ailments. The progression looks the same. But what could cause it? The only thing close is St. Anthony's Fire: *ignis sacer*. But no one else in the town has it and Bernd never ate rye—it wasn't good for his humors."

"Claudia!" Bernd wailed. "I see her, Claudia!"

"We should go," Ambrose whispered. "We're making him worse."

Bernd's eyes filled with panic, and his mouth uttered a silent scream. Ambrose jumped back, tripping over a torn dress, and fell crashing into a pile of filth.

"I know! I know!" Claudia rushed into the room and cradled his head. "There are shadows everywhere."

"Do you see her too, Claudia?" Albrecht said. "What do you see?"

The woman held Bernd's head in her lap, rocking back and forth. "Shadows," she said.

"Claudia, dear, pay attention now. You need to see Bernd takes these regularly, and you too!" The doctor drew vials from his bag. "The ingredients are clear. Tincture of aconite and belladonna in the one, bryonia and ipecac in the other. Take one spoon of the first on the hour. Take one spoon of the second on the half. Take it until it's gone. Do you understand? This is important. Say it back to me."

"One on the hour, one on the half," she said. "Doctor, I feel fine. Just a little tired from looking after Bernd. There's nothing wrong with me. I can certainly follow simple directions."

"Good. And this one is just for Bernd. The one marked, 'camphor monobromate.' Every two hours. Say it back to me!"

"Every two hours!" Claudia rolled her eyes. "Good Lord."

"I'll check on you tomorrow," Albrecht said. "Now be good and take your medicine. And open the windows and get some air in here!"

The walk back was gloomy and silent. Ambrose couldn't get the sour smell of sickness out of his nose, and he coughed and spat. Albrecht, meanwhile, shuffled on, his head bowed and lost in thought. The wary eyes of the townsfolk followed them on the main road, whispering and pointing before hurrying away, giving the doctor a wide berth.

Albrecht's wrinkled hand unlocked the door. Another wave of foul air washed over them, this time different. It was not so much the smell of sickness but of death. *Does it smell like this everywhere the doctor goes?* Ambrose was starting to deeply regret volunteering to help.

Albrecht held a match to the lamp; yellow flame danced and grew and the shadows crept to the corners. Otto's body lay on the exam table. A stained and bloodied sheet covered what must have been a hole in his torso, and the miller's pale face lay before them, a coin on either eye.

"It matches no known disease," said Albrecht. "If it was spreading, why would both Otto and Bernd have gotten it? They have no love for one another and certainly spent no time together. But if it's not spreading, then why have some people come down with the same sickness? I've checked Otto's insides. Nothing is amiss. Look."

Albrecht drew the sheet. A metal plate sat on the table, holding the dull reddish purple of a heart and liver and kidneys. The man's lungs had been drawn from his chest and the branches and pockets of bronchi and air sacs lay sliced open. A wave of nausea washed over Ambrose as tight pains gripped his belly. He rushed outside as bitter acid rose in his throat, and vomited in the dirt beside the door. Slowly, he stumbled back, legs shaky.

"Oh. Forgive me," Albrecht said, barely paying attention. "But look here! The lungs are clean. There's no consumption. There's no lung pathology at all. Same is true for the liver. There's no sign of infection or illness anywhere."

"I'll take your word for it, Doctor!" Ambrose said, quickly turning away. "But believe it or not, I didn't actually study medicine at the University in Munich, as you claim. I have no idea what I'm looking at."

"Yes, I suppose." He covered the body. "Well, it's all clean. There's no sign of poison either. No arsenic. No digitalis. The progression doesn't match aconite or nightshade or hemlock or any other thing I can think of. The only thing they shared in common was the well, but no one else is sick and the well has been safe ever since it was dug. Why would it be tainted now? And why do they all have the same feverish dreams? They all claim to have seen 'her,' whoever 'she' is."

He tapped his pipe, ash spilling onto the dirty table. Soon a new ember glowed red and sweet nuttiness filled the air. The pipe clicked between the doctor's teeth as he sat lost in thought, white smoke wreathing his frosted whiskers.

"Look here," he finally said, handing Ambrose a letter. "It's from Dr. Vieth, the medical examiner. Wants to know if there's an outbreak. How do these rumors reach him so quickly?"

Ambrose shook his head. "I don't know what to say, Doctor."

"I know. Thank you for indulging me. I need someone with whom I can talk this through. There's no other doctor about that I can confer with who doesn't first think of laying on hands."

He grabbed a bottle from the shelf. Brown liquor splashed in a dirty glass, glints of yellow flickering in lamplight. He handed it to Ambrose, but he politely refused.

"Hm, that's right. Tastes like turpentine anyway."

"You know," Ambrose said, "there may be someone you could consult with. That Englishman, Silvanus, who killed that monstrous bird. He has had some training. Part of some new school of thought called 'Eclectic,' some budding American theory. Maybe he has some ideas."

"What could it hurt?" The doctor snorted. "Only my reputation, I suppose. Still, if everyone dies, my reputation is hurt anyway. So what the hell?"

"What do you mean you're going to Altona?" asked Killian.

Ambrose shouldered Dr. Albrecht's old satchel; it hung heavy on his shoulder, filled with odds and ends for the journey. An old skin glugged and splashed; beside it the hard edge of a long knife, borrowed from the autopsy table.

"Strange circumstances, as always," said Ambrose.

"What circumstances?" Tobias replied. "Sit down and have a bite at least."

Ambrose sat and leaned forward, looking over his shoulder. The chair creaked as he sat, but otherwise the only other sound was the clatter of the kitchen, muffled behind closed doors. The hall outside was filled with empty tables.

"Listen," he whispered. "I can't say for certain, but you ought to stay away from the townsfolk as much as you can. There are sick people about. Dr. Albrecht says it's not catching, but who knows? It doesn't follow any pattern or have any rhyme or reason, at least not what's seen in the Old World. Maybe this is some new American disease. In any case, I suggest you stay away from questionable people, bad food and drink, and foul air. I plan on doing the same."

"And leave us here while you go off to the big city?" Tobias scoffed. "I don't feel rightly safe here, but I suppose if we stick to the public areas and stay away from the abbey, we should be fine for a few days. Besides, as much as I don't like this place, I can't stand rough cart rides over fallow fields anyway. My backside is still sore just from getting here. But if you're not back in time"—he pointed with his fork—"we're leaving without you."

"It's only twelve miles," Ambrose said. "Shouldn't take more than a couple of days, there and back, if I can find a carriage or a cart. If not, I guess I'll walk."

Killian's eyes grew wide in disbelief. "You'd walk alone on those forest roads after what you've seen?"

Ambrose nodded. "I guess I would."

"Like I told you, Killian. He's on another crusade," Tobias said. "Well, best be off then."

"All right," Ambrose said, shouldering his pack, "I'll be back in three or four days. Let's see if I can find a carriage. Although I don't know how I'll find Silas when I get there."

"Silas? That crazy Englishman?" They turned in surprise. Harold Fessler stood behind the bar, wiping smudges from a glass with a dingy rag. He plunked it on the counter and grabbed another. "Rumor has it he's not in Altona. He headed to Walders. Least that's what a passing Pollock told me."

Ambrose sighed. "How long have you been standing there, Harold?"

"Long enough, I suppose." He held the glass casually to the light.

"Nothing's safe from your ears," Ambrose said. "Well, you know where I'm going and probably why, so how about finding me a carriage?"

"Should be old Louis Baumgartner off to take the mail, I would expect," he said. "Usually leaves around noon. He's a quiet man but could do with the company."

"All right then. I'm off."

He opened the door and chill wind gusted against the dingy lamps, flickering oily smoke against the walls. Reluctant to leave, he turned one last time and called, "Stay away from foul air, foul food, and foul company. That goes for you as well, Harold."

☩

CHAPTER 20

Walders

November 10, 1859

The muddy trail had dried in the deep ruts and furrows of cart wheels and horse hooves, and the rickety cart creaked and bounced on the rough ground. Trees loomed, gnarled and bent like old men, their bony arms stretched to the cloudy sky, as the road north snaked around their giant trunks as it crept through the dark wood.

Louis Baumgartner cracked the reins when the old gray mare slowed. "C'mon, Bess," he clucked. "C'mon now." His white hair fluttered across a wizened face and he sighed. "She ain't what she used to be."

Dark shade grew in the distant copses and hollows as the steely sky glowered in threatening storm. Below, the crackle of dried leaves underfoot filled the air, musky and sweet, and Ambrose peered into the shadowed depths—so much like the black forests of home. The deep woods always had the sense of watchfulness, and he pulled his coat tightly around him against the oppressive silence. As the miles stretched on, he could take it no more.

"Mr. Baumgartner, where are you from?" he said finally.

"Hm?" The old man turned and smiled, several teeth missing. "Sentheim. In the Alsace. Do you know it?"

"Afraid not. But not because it's not important, I'm sure."

"Oh, it's not." He laughed. "I didn't stay there long. I left from Hamburg on the *Hammonia* in 1849. No work to be had as a weaver in the north. Least not with all the new mills. 'Course there's no work to be had as a weaver here neither."

"Then why did you come?"

"Well," he said, frowning, "Father Valentine..."

Ambrose grew quiet again. The last thing he wanted to talk about was Valentine, and soon the rhythmic creak of the cart was all that marked the slow passing of the hours. As they drew deeper into the wood, strange paths left the trail, like deer paths, but small piles of white stone lay placed here and there as if to mark and, above, a pagan symbol carved in the trees: a cross with a circle above.

Ambrose craned his neck to look, but the paths twisted and turned out of sight. "What is at the end of the trails?"

"I couldn't say," Mr. Baumgartner said, frowning.

"You've never been to look?"

"It's best to keep to the trail. Lest you lose your way."

"Well, who made them?"

Mr. Baumgartner shrugged. "I don't know. They were here before me."

"But I thought Gregorstadt was the first town in the area. Who would have been here before to make them?"

"Don't know. Never met them to ask."

Ambrose shook his head and sighed. *Typical.* "What is Walders like?" he said finally.

"Oh...Walders," Louis said, grimacing. "It's rough and strange. Loose morals. Given to drunkenness and brawling. You'll likely find plenty of souls there in need of saving."

A pale sliver of moon gleamed in the evening sky as yellow lights twinkled through the darkened trees. The forest opened to the town, the sharp smell of smoke rising from distant chimneys. A hound bayed in the distance as a fiddle took up a jaunty tune and a din of merriment filled the dark streets somewhere beyond. Laughter rose amid the banging of pots and pans and occasional gunfire. The city seemed in a mad uproar.

"What's going on here?" Ambrose looked around bewildered.

"Who knows what goes on in this town? There is always some devilish revelry, and the less I concern myself with it, the better." The cart slowed at the stable and Mr. Baumgartner nodded. "Here we are. The Central Hotel is just up the street. If anyone can point you to what you're looking for, it's Jim Sipper, the owner. Big, burly brawler behind the bar with a picador under his nose. You can't miss him. I'm leaving tomorrow at first light. If you're not at the stable, you'll be walking back."

Nodding, Ambrose shouldered his bag. Long shadows of black buildings stretched in the pale moonlight. Homes gave way to dark storefronts closed for the night, the silver light of the moon glinting off etched lettering and leaded glass: EVENSON, ATTORNEY AT LAW; BERGE, UNDERTAKER. In the distance, yellow light spilled from the hotel, illuminating the dark road in a patch of pleasant color. "Where is Silas in all this?" he said to himself.

The ruckus grew louder. Lanterns crested the hill past the hotel, swaying and bouncing with the wild steps of dancing revelers. The quick taps of a drum joined a lively fiddle, and pots and pans and claps and shouts kept time with an old folk ditty. Dogs barked and frolicked in the light, wrestling and playing.

The wild parade swayed in drunkenness. Bleary eyes glinted in the light above broad grins of laughter. Men staggered forward, shirts untucked and unbuttoned, sloshing bottles of beer and cider in their hands, as figures streamed from the hotel, joining the revelry.

Brash voices took up an impromptu song, brazen and lurid:

Oh, Miss Maria has got a man, has got a man, has got a man.

Oh, Miss Maria has got a man and Miss is Mrs. come morning.

And what of the one who gave her hand? Who gave her hand? Who gave her hand?

A father will do what a father can and hang his head in mourning.

The crowd cheered at the end, firing revolvers into the air and clanging pots and pans. In a moment they were upon Ambrose as they passed, weaving and swaying. Quickly he ducked into the shadows as the party slowly made its way down the street, the last stragglers stumbling behind.

"What's happening here?" Ambrose called.

"A wedding!" a man said. "You never seen a wedding?" 'Not like this!"

"Maria Delebek got hitched!" another chimed in. "Come join the fun!"

Ambrose stared after them, blinking. Who would invite a priest? Just then, a yellow torch passed as a man hurried to catch up. The red flame flickered for a moment in the darkened glass of a closed storefront, and a motley figure flashed in the corner of his eye, mirrored below the etched letters of the word UNDERTAKER. It gazed back, pale and unshaven, ragged clothes hanging loosely and far too big. He looked at himself in shock. *They didn't invite a priest. They invited a bum!*

The doppelgänger in the glass stared back as memories flashed, unbidden, in his mind; his boyhood years in

Konstanz; dark alleys filled with beggars and vagrants and the slums of the docks. For a moment he saw an image of what might have been. Just as quickly, the flame passed and he was left in shadow again. Unknown and unrecognized, he felt a strange curiosity well inside him: a desire to know a different life. *I'm probably going to regret this.*

The parade wound through the streets, never making a straight line. Ambrose was soon turned about and at the mercy of following the throng. Cries reached a fever pitch and the crowd stopped before a house; they must have reached their destination. "Gudmund! Ho, Gudmund, where you hiding?" The fiddle played on and hands clapped. "Show us that pretty Maria!" A light flickered in a window as a curtain was drawn. "Goodie Gudmund, get your ass out here!" they called.

The door creaked open to a chorus of cheers and a lantern lit an old man's wrinkled face. "Maria and Martin are indisposed," he said. "Thank you for the well-wishes and congratulations. But they won't be coming out." The fiddle stopped and hands waved. "Boo!" they cried.

"Now, if you wish to wish us all well," the old man went on, "you can do your wishing on your own. And here's a bit of liquor to help you on your way." Bottles clinked and clanked as he hefted a crate down the stoop. A chorus of cheers rose again. "Now good night!"

The fiddle started again and the crowd took up a jig. Pots banged and shots rang into the night air in bursts of flame. The old man turned to leave when suddenly his head popped in a burst of red. Drops of blood splattered the faces of those around, thick and black, and Gudmund Delebek fell dead on the ground. The fiddle stopped and the crowd stood in stunned silence. Red blood soaked into the dirt, spilling into the street from a gaping hole in the back of the man's head.

They stared in drunken confusion. "He's been shot!" a voice cried. Whispers and mutters rose. Men looked to one another, bleary eyed and swaying. A wail rose from the house, and the bride ran frantically down the steps to cradle her father's head. "Was an accident!" someone shouted. "Surely it must've been an accident!"

The groom burst from the house, rifle in one hand, revolver in the other. "Who did it?" he screamed. "Who killed him?" The crowd scattered and ran. Dry clay and gravel crunched under their fleeing feet, and pots and pans clattered to the ground.

"Get the sheriff!" the groom screamed.

Ambrose looked in wide-eyed horror as the crowd pushed him back, jostling him down the street. His feet carried him on their own as he ran in a daze into the darkness.

Ambrose stumbled into the Central Hotel. A blur of color washed before him: yellows and browns and reds. Harsh shouts filled the room, beating against his ears. "Killed him!" a voice bellowed. "They shot Delebek!" A thunder of boots stomped and shook, floorboards creaking as they clomped across. "Find him! Find the bastard!"

Ambrose turned, dizzy. A brown fuzz of angry faces raced toward the door. A rough hand clamped his shoulder, thick fingers digging into his flesh. His heart pounded in panic, and he raised his hands to defend himself. But the man cast him out of the way, and he tumbled across the room as they barreled out the door.

Dishes crashed and shattered, falling all around as a sharp edge of pain smacked Ambrose's ribs. The table skittered and tumbled, chairs creaking and clattering on the floor, and Ambrose lay gasping for air, broken glass and shards of pottery beneath him.

"Hey! If you're drunk, get the hell out!" a voice barked. "I've had enough shit tonight." Thick hands lifted him by the collar, dark eyes squinting, inches from his face. The burly man with the picador breathed heavy with anger, smoke and whiskey on his sour breath. "You're not drunk," he grunted. "What's wrong with you?"

"They shot him," Ambrose muttered. "Right in front of me."

The man plopped Ambrose into a chair. It creaked and settled and his head fell limply to the side.

"Ah, you were at Delebek's. That damn *charivari!* Every time. Hey!" He slapped Ambrose hard across the cheek. "Wake up! Get yourself together."

"I've never seen a man shot before…"

The man folded his thick arms across his chest. "Oh, it's your first time here? What are you, another drifter come to the asshole of the world to die?"

Ambrose squinted. Nothing made sense. Yellow lamplight flickered at the bar, staining the walls with smoke and dancing dizzyingly across a row of bottles. The burly man loomed over him, thick neck and shoulders straining against a red pinstripe shirt. It was like a carnival gone mad.

"No," he said. "I'm a priest. Father Ambrose Odenwald. From Gregorstadt. My robes are in to be mended. These are borrowed."

"A priest! From St. Gregory!" the man said, laughing. "How do you like that? Well, then here you go, Father." He plopped a mug of beer onto the table. "A drink on the house, for seeing your first murder."

Ambrose waved his hand. "No, thank you."

"Drink!" the man barked. "I'd not refuse a sacrament in your holy house. You'll not refuse one in mine. You best take the night slow. The shock won't hit you all at once."

Ambrose raised the glass. Bitter liquid, thick and malty, filled his belly, but he felt no different. The man eyed him, as if knowing his mind. "That's how it is now," he said. "You're not going to feel right ever again."

Ambrose stared numbly at the empty room. A dingy cloth spread dirty water across the bar as the man scrubbed, watching the priest stare out the window into the night. With a sigh, he sat beside him and lit a cigar. His thick fingers struck a match, sulphury and pungent, and a red ember glowed.

"So, Father," the man said, taking a long puff. "Why are you here anyway?"

"Are you Joseph Sipper?" asked Ambrose.

"Yeah, Joe. Why?"

"Have you seen an eccentric Englishman? Long hair and tangled beard? He looks like a crazed wild man."

"Crazed men we have aplenty," the barman said, "but Englishmen not so much. I expect you're looking for Silas. He's at the Crystal Buffet down the street, wasting my porter's time and money." Joseph leaned forward, thick smoke curling his yellowed his fingers as he pointed. "You tell that son of a bitch to pay up before he leaves. If he skips out on his debt again, I'll take it out of his ass."

The door creaked open. A man entered, hat in hand, his pale face lined with frown. Joseph looked up, questioning. "It's not good," he said, shaking his head.

"Damn it," Joseph swore.

"I should be on my way." Ambrose staggered to his feet. The room spun and he grabbed the wall. "Thank you for the beer. I'll give Silas your regards."

Blackness shrouded the back streets and alleys. A bitter silence lay heavy on the town, broken only by the hiss of chill wind. Night had descended long ago, lanterns snuffed and curtains drawn; only the glint of empty bottles hinted at the mad parade just hours before.

Ambrose staggered and tripped in the darkness, his legs weak and shaky. He wandered aimlessly, with no real idea where he was going. Walders was a sprawl of darkness, and he was dark within it. *Why, God? Why did this happen?* He knew the horrors in men's hearts. Had he not given last rites to all manner of them? Even rapists and murders? Had he not seen dead soldiers bundled in white sheets after the failed revolts? Yet, this was somehow different. He knew of human cruelty, but a foolish accident seemed somehow worse, on this day of all days: a wedding day. *What am I even doing here anymore?* His search for Silas seemed meaningless after everything he'd seen, but it was all he had in the moment to hold onto.

He stumbled on in a daze of shock, the dim light in the distance creeping closer. He must at least be headed in the right direction. Ahead, leaded glass came into view, twinkly with the warm glow of light from within, and below, the name CRYSTAL BUFFET was etched in the window. He stumbled on the stoop. Reaching for the horse hitch and missing, he tumbled into a horse that grunted in annoyance. His faced mashed against a muscled side of coarse hair thick with the smell of hay and manure.

"King Henry! Oh, good boy," he said. "Thank God I've found you. You're smart to mind your own business. Now where is Silas in all this?"

He labored up the steps. Cold brass met his hand as he turned the knob and stumbled into the room, squinting and coughing as the sour and smoky air rushed past his face. A table of dark faces turned from their card game, eyeing him suspiciously. A thin man looked overlong from beneath a battered bowler, while another peered above his hand of cards. Ambrose asked after Silas and the barman nodded to the back.

Stumbling his way down the hall, he came across a dingy sheet drawn across a darkened room. Low voices came from within. He could not make out the words, but he heard an English accent. *Please let this be Silas!* He peered within.

"Father!" Silas said in surprise. "What are you doing here? Never mind…you look like hell. Have a seat."

Ambrose collapsed in a chair, as Silas glanced with laughing eyes, bemused at seeing the disheveled priest, in

Walders of all places. Beside him sat a dark-skinned man, lean and with long black hair. The face was striking: proud eyes sat above broad cheeks. As the man calmly took him in, Ambrose found he could not look away and stared like an uncouth child. He had never expected to be sitting at the same table as an Indian, and his head swam with a mix of hearsay and conjecture, gleaned in the papers and overheard in the streets, and in his dazed state he couldn't make sense of any of it.

"Ambrose, this is Eloi. Eloi, Ambrose," Silas said. "Ambrose is a priest, although you'd never tell by looking at him right now. Looks like he's trying his hand at being a hobo."

Eloi nodded, smirking. "I hope you didn't bring your God with you. A man can't get away with anything anymore."

"Not to worry," said Silas. "The good Lord can't see through this haze of smoke and stink. Eloi here"—he turned to Ambrose—"red-French bastard that he is, is at the moment trying to cheat at cards. Good thing the Lord can't see that either."

"Ha!" the man snorted. "You play so badly I don't need to cheat."

"Wait a minute." Silas paused and pointed at Ambrose with his pipe. "You're not here on another crusade, are you? Why *are* you here?"

Silas eyed him closely. Ambrose had lost weight and his clothes hung loosely off his bony frame. He scarcely seemed the same man. The priest opened his mouth to speak but couldn't find the words. He sat in numb silence and stared at the table.

"Anyway…" Silas said, "this is that damn fool priest who talked me into walking into the nest of an *inamekwak*,"

"It's pronounced *inaemehkiwak*," Eloi said.

"Eh…" Silas waved his hand.

"Are you…native?" asked Ambrose.

"Half. My mother was Menomonee, my father French. But I never met him. He was gone before I could walk."

"I've never met a native," Ambrose said.

"Oh, well, lucky day. Congratulations," Eloi sneered.

"Sorry," Ambrose muttered.

"Well, you look to be still a little shaken, Father," Eloi said. "You're lucky to be alive."

"Yes," Ambrose said. "I also just saw a man shot in the head."

"Agh!" Silas thumped the table with his fist. "Terrible business. Gudmund gone just like that. I'm sorry you had to see that. This damn town has no sense."

"Joe Sipper says I'll never be the same."

"I'm sorry," Silas said. "He's right about that, I'm afraid."

"He said something about a debt," Ambrose added. "Told me to remind you."

"Ah, just a misunderstanding. Don't worry." The cork squeaked as Silas filled his glass. "Never repay a debt to a drunk man; he'll never remember you did. Old Joe has some pretty big britches, having helped found this 'fair town.'"

"If he had a purse to match those britches, I'd like him far more," Eloi said.

"What does 'Walders' mean, anyway?" Ambrose said, "That's a strange name."

"It's named for 'Walders' in Norway," Silas explained.

"But this looks nothing like Norway."

"Of course not. Norwegians can't be trusted."

Ambrose sighed. The weight of the day was unbearable and his mind felt swathed in a thick cloud. Idle chatter, after what he'd seen, seemed crass and made his heart ache. Without thinking, he reached for Silas's glass and filled it, coughing as he drank in a gulp. Silas shook his head and poured him another.

"Have you found your bishop?" he asked after some time.

Ambrose shook his head. "He's gone, held captive somewhere. Tobias and Killian found his room, where he was held against his will, but he was no longer there. They said it was filled with all manner of dark and twisted writings, like the imaginings of a madman. Everywhere were the signs of black arts—demonology and necromancy. Killian thought to grab this." He drew the book from his bag and set it on the table. "I don't know what it means."

Silas picked it up, tracing the name as he translated. "Dissertations on angels and dæmons and ghosts and vampires from Bohemia and Moravia and Silesia and all those dark Eastern countries." He flipped through the pages, stopping here and there to read. "Collections of Grimoires of Honorius and others. Random spells for finding and protecting and making someone fall in love. Terrible spells to summon demons. Jesus! This is quite the collection. It seems like you stumbled across someone's personal study. From the look of it, this is hundreds of years old. It's amazing it survived the fires of the witch trials."

He set the book on the table, and Ambrose looked at it with a feeling of dread and awe. In the darkness, it seemed to call to him, and he looked away, wondering what to do with such a horrible thing.

Eloi shook his head in disgust. "The land changed since St. Gregory was built and those crazy people came. I wasn't much older than a boy, but I felt it and I knew. There was always a darkness on those woods. Maybe that's why they chose that place. *Qui se ressemble s'assemble*. I don't go to there anymore. Only this fool Englishman does." He waved his hand at Silas. "You say you don't know where they keep this bishop? You know that town Chilton, to the west? Do you know its real name, before the empty white names were put on top? It's called *Wasuskeqsinoh*: Old Graves in the Marsh. There are caves in that marsh with graves inside, from long, long ago, before my people were here. Your crazy

Valentine might have found his way there. People like that are always drawn to such places."

They grew silent for some time. Silas puffed his pipe, lost in thought. Gray smoke filled the room, whirling and turning about his head like the image of an old magician. Talk of St. Gregory put Eloi in a foul mood and he stared at his empty glass sullenly.

Suddenly Silas looked up. "Why are you here, Father? It's not to show me this book or talk about your lost bishop."

Ambrose sighed and shook his head. "No. That's not why I came. There's some sickness spreading in St. Gregory. Something the doctor can't figure out. He says it's not catching, yet it spreads. But not to everyone. Just to certain people who seem close in tragedy but distant in every other way. A cold fever possesses them and sweat pores out and, with it, all comprehension. Soon after, the body wastes and there is death. I thought you might have an idea what it is— something you learned from the new American Eclectic School. Maybe it's some New World sickness."

Silas leaned forward, chin in hands. "Who's getting sick?"

"A miller, whose son was killed by that bird monster. And the parents of the girl who drowned herself as a result. They're now sick as well."

Silas stroked his wavy beard, lost in thought. "Ambrose," he said. "Tell me everything."

Ambrose spoke late into the night as Silas and Eloi sat listening. The table was silent but for his tale and the squeak of cork and the glug of whiskey. Finally he ended and they sat in silence.

"I don't think that's a sickness," Silas said. "At least not a normal one. If there's a link between the victims—and I think there is—it's not physical. I can't say for certain, but I think the answers might well be found within that book."

"The book?" Ambrose recoiled.

"The book," Silas repeated. "It would be quite a thing that your bishop is lost; the town is overrun with dark priests trying their hands at necromancy; and now a strange illness is spreading. I don't believe in coincidence. And I don't believe it's a coincidence that you have that book now. It's up to you to figure this out."

"This can't be your answer!" Ambrose said. "After all this, I hoped there was a chance you might know of some exotic disease. But this? This can't be your answer!"

"This is my answer. Now you've had a long day—the first of many long days for you, I think. You need to sleep on all of this. I suggest you stay here tonight. I'll talk to Mr. Berge about getting you a room."

"Berge? The same Berge as owns the undertaker?"

Silas nodded. "The same. Try not to think about it."

Ambrose sighed. "I don't know what to say. I'm completely lost and adrift. Nothing makes sense anymore. I don't know how I can survive in a place like this."

"You need to find your strength, Father," Silas said. "And that strength is not to be found where you think it is."

Silas stood to talk to the barman, leaving Ambrose alone with Eloi. The dark man stared at him uncomfortably, and Ambrose made ready to leave when a leathery hand clamped down, fast upon his arm.

Eloi stared at him, dark eyes bleary from drink. "Worms don't spoil a man's living flesh. They follow the stench of death."

"What?" said Ambrose, his hair suddenly on end.

"I've heard whispers of dark practices," Eloi went on. "Who hasn't? You can hear it on the wind. The birds chitter of it in the morning and the wolves howl of it at night. Evil circles like carrion buzzards, circling both living and dead. But you forgot a truth…or never knew it. Evil is not created. No dark arts bring it into being. It doesn't spoil or corrupt; it only follows. It follows what it is already corrupted."

✚

CHAPTER 21

Evil Follows

November 12, 1859

T he HOTEL ST. GREGOR was quiet; only the calls of distant sparrows broke the predawn stillness. The candle had long since burned out, and the dim light of early morning lit the dingy glass in cloudy gray. Ambrose sat hunched at his desk, his brow furled as he poured over the old book, tracing the titles with his finger: 𝕯𝖊𝖘 𝕰𝖘𝖕𝖗𝖎𝖙𝖘 𝕱𝖆𝖒𝖎𝖑𝖎𝖆𝖗𝖘.... 𝕬𝖕𝖕𝖆𝖗𝖎𝖙𝖎𝖔𝖓𝖘 𝖉𝖊 𝕾𝖕𝖊𝖈𝖙𝖗𝖊𝖘... 𝕾𝖕𝖊𝖈𝖙𝖗𝖊𝖘 𝖔𝖚 𝕯𝖊́𝖒𝖔𝖓𝖘... 𝕬𝖕𝖕𝖆𝖗𝖎𝖙𝖎𝖔𝖓𝖘 𝖉𝖊 𝕻𝖊𝖗𝖘𝖔𝖓𝖓𝖊𝖑 𝕹𝖔𝖊𝖗𝖙𝖊𝖘... 𝕯𝖊́𝖒𝖔𝖓𝖘, 𝕵𝖓𝖈𝖚𝖇𝖊𝖘, 𝖊𝖙 𝕾𝖚𝖈𝖈𝖚𝖇𝖊𝖘... Strange words and horrible tales swam on the page, fading in and out of his vision. He slammed the book shut with a thump that shook the desk and rattled the dirty plates and bottles.

He rubbed his tired eyes as he filled his glass from the bottle. He longed for sleep, but it wouldn't come. Instead he downed the glass, grimacing as the liquid burned his throat. He held the half-empty bottle to the light. Flickers of yellow danced and sparkled in the brown liquor. His heart was heavy with the weight of shame. How did it come to this? *I have become my father…*

A soft knock came on the door, quick and urgent.

What day is it? He stared blearily, trying to remember. It was Sunday. That day used to mean something.

He opened the door just a crack. In the darkness beyond, Tobias and Killian stood waiting, expectantly.

The old priest's eyes narrowed. "Are you coming to mass?" Tobias said.

"No. Are you?"

"Well, it is Sunday," said Tobias.

"I thought you left the abbey for good," Ambrose said. "I thought we were keeping out of sight."

"Yes, but everyone will be gathered there today," Tobias said. "It would be strange not to go. It would look rather obvious if we weren't there."

Ambrose waved his hand as he swayed, grasping the door. "I…have things to do."

"Are you talking about that damn book?" asked Tobias. "Are you drunk? My God, it's before five in the morning. What's gotten into you lately?"

Ambrose struggled to speak, but the words wouldn't come. His chest felt heavy and tight, and his thoughts swirled, none of them connecting. His eyes grew wide and he slowly pointed to his head, his hand in the shape of a gun.

"*Boom!*" he said.

"Ah, dear boy," Tobias said. "You have to let that go. You have to give that up to God. That's why you should have come today, even if it's to mass with Valentine. It's a shame, but there's nothing to it now. We can't have you showing up to the Lord's house all pigeon eyed. Come on now." He led Ambrose to the bed. "Killian, let's cover up our dear brother lest he wander the streets and make a scene."

Killian lifted Ambrose's legs and Tobias covered him with a blanket. The door clicked shut, and silence filled the hotel as the town left for Mass. In a stupor, Ambrose stared at the ceiling. Thin beams of light danced on the wall, and a cobweb, white with dust, sparkled and fluttered in an unseen draft.

When he could bear it no more, he cast the blanket aside. Sitting back down at the desk, he opened the book once more. The worn pages fell open, grimy and tattered, and black words stared back at him: *La Resurrection d'un Mort est L'ouvrage de Dieu Seul.* He read the title aloud: "The resurrection of the dead is the work of God alone."

Damn it, Silas. Why did you have me search in this horrid place?

Letters peaked out from the pages below, not printed but drawn by hand, long and thin. Valentine's hand? Or someone long before:

Nachzehrer: that which devours after. That which follows from the pagan east. What haunts the darkened churchyard. In villages beset by plague and mysterious death. Sickness but not. Unholy and violent it begins. It starts with the first. Body not stiff. Lips yet red and open.

Ambrose shook his head. *Nachzehrer?* He thumbed through the chapter: *Magia Posthuma.*

He slammed the book shut and threw it to the floor. *No! I cannot!* He paced the room, anxious and trembling. Glancing up, he saw his face in the mirror. A gaunt visage stared back, terrifying and unfamiliar. Lines of scowl crossed his darkened brow; he seemed a man utterly consumed and the room was all at once suffocating.

Hurriedly he stripped off the old shirt and trousers, feeling the cold air against his skin, and pulled on his old cassock. It was still torn and poorly patched; Mr. Gatterman, perennially drunk and in no particular hurry, had still not fixed it and Ambrose had taken it back. Its familiar feel, now, cleared his head and he hurried down the hall, anxious to be under the open sky.

Wind swept the empty streets, barren on Sunday Mass, as dark clouds blotted the sun in patches on the dull earth. Ambrose wandered aimlessly, his head down. Although he didn't realize it, he walked ever south, as if pulled by an unseen string.

Dried mud crumbled underfoot as he left the more trafficked streets. The wattle and daub of the original town gave way to the rough and raw wood buildings on the edge of the forest; the icehouse and the log yard; the garish red windows of Köppen's General Store. Jacob the carpenter's house loomed on the left, its curtains drawn fast. Beside it, the home of Bernd Voss was now boarded up and locked tight against the fears of some unknown illness.

Claudia's funeral would take place in the next few days; her plot was already dug next to Bernd's. Dr. Albrecht had found no obvious illness in either of them, yet they had wasted away as the miller before. No treatment had slowed their death or eased their minds, and Ambrose and the good doctor could only watch as their spirits passed. As he thought of the sorrow on Albrecht's face as he drew the white sheets over their cold bodies, suddenly Eloi's words came back to him: "Evil follows."

What is it following?

The road plunged south through the wood, twisting toward the abbey, its brambled edge thickened into dark forest. Gnarled trees stood guard like sentinels, their mighty arms stretching to the sky, the bony fingers of bare twigs piercing the gray above. Below, leaves crunched and crackled, and Ambrose shivered as the brisk wind wrapped its icy hands around his neck.

As the forest fell away, the meadow opened before him, rolling up to meet the abbey in the distance. The graveyard lay in the long shadow of the wood. White slabs of mossy stone poked through tangles of dead grass, and faded wood crosses leaned and bowed, their arms loose and falling. He wandered amongst the stones, his outstretched hands brushing the coarse stalks of brown dock and yellowed mullein.

Claudia's fresh grave lay before him, its open mouth dark and gaping. Beside it was a rectangle of bare covered earth and a cross above hastily carved:

𝕭𝖊𝖗𝖓𝖉 𝖁𝖔𝖘𝖘
geb. Kirchzeiten 15 Apr 1813
ges. 12 Nov 1859

Ambrose knew no stone or cross marked Issa's grave; her lonely body was laid hidden in a woodland glade.

He sat on a fallen log, gazing forlornly into the open earth. The cold ground would soon cover Claudia, hiding her deep within. As he stared, memories, old and dark, rose: his dead father's eyes, pale and sunken from consumption; long nights of cold hunger, after, when his mother didn't return; Monika in tears one pale morning, made a woman too soon. *She has blond hair, so much like Issa's.*

"Fancy seeing you here, Father," a voice said. Ambrose jumped with a start and turned to see Annaliese smiling, her cheeks blushing slightly.

"What are you doing in the graveyard?" he said.

"Skipping Mass," she replied. "No one ever notices. I haven't been in years."

He stared for a moment in shocked silence, half thrilled and half appalled and at total loss.

"I already know what they're going to say. Don't you? There's only one way to heaven and it's theirs."

A frown settled over Ambrose's face. "You don't agree?"

She sat down, her body warm beside him. Her raven hair danced in the wind and tickled his face. "I don't think fear is the same as love," she said.

"But…that's not the Lord's teaching," he stammered.

Annaliese looked away and seemed not to hear, gazing into the gray distance. "You know, every autumn is the same," she said. "The winds bring such a melancholy. The leaves burst in reds and yellows, then fall to such brilliant stillness. I don't know why, but I want to join them. I want to lose myself in that quiet and never come back."

She turned to him and in her hazel eyes was a look of sadness and longing, far older than her nineteen years. She reached out suddenly and took his hand, squeezing. It was small and warm in his own and his heart raced, and to his surprise, he didn't pull away. She smiled mischievously and blushed, leaning closely as if to whisper a deep secret.

"I can't bear to be in that church," she said. "Every time they gather in joy. But as theirs grows, my own withers and dies. I can't stand it. I can't stifle the voices of my heart as if they're the fanciful dreams of a girl. I'd rather lose myself in the dark forest, even if its voices are so strange and different from home."

She pulled away suddenly, as if remembering herself, and her cheeks blushed red hot. "I'm sorry! Please don't think me untoward."

Ambrose looked away, confused. She mustn't give up her faith, even in this town. Yet, in that moment he could not even find his own. For the first time, he felt himself a hypocrite. All he knew was that the warmth where her hand had been was now cold and it made him strangely sad.

"Well…what are *you* doing here in the graveyard?" she said.

"Skipping Mass." He sighed. "Like you, I suppose."

"Maybe you don't want to be saved either."

"I don't know. I feel very far away from salvation at the moment."

"Well," she said, "I've never skipped Mass in favor of a graveyard with anyone else. You don't feel very far away to me."

It was Ambrose's turn to blush. He stared at the ground, uncertain. There was so much he wanted to say—to tell someone. He could barely keep it in. Stephan, a man he had at one time loved so dearly, was most likely dead: the victim of heresy and ungodly teachings. Could Ambrose have saved him? If he had been in better contact, could he have kept Stephan from coming to this land at all? The wasting deaths of the town had ever filled him with uncertainty and now the horror of that night in Walders played relentlessly in his mind, haunting him. Death followed him everywhere. Or he followed it. And when he looked, he found no solace in the Church. He was entirely alone. No teaching lifted his heart, or made sense of any of it, and the horrid doubt where his faith had been only drove him further away: a shame he would rather deny. And now, to sit beside warm flesh and blood, to hear her voice like clear bells ringing, and see the light dance upon her hair and flash in her eyes. He longed for something real, to take her warm hand in his: to hold it close and bare his soul. To be absolved. But he couldn't find the words.

"Have you ever been to Walders?" he said finally.

Annaliese nodded. "Just once, but I know I don't want to go back."

"I feel like I'm losing my way," Ambrose said. "Or losing my mind. Losing something… I don't know why I'm telling you this. But I'm afraid to enter the abbey church."

"I think behind those doors is a cage," she said. "That's why I'm afraid to enter."

"That's blasphemy!"

"Oh?" she said. "Then why are you out here and not inside?"

He hung his head. She was right. His chest grew tight with the realization.

"I feel dark," he said. "Some heaviness hangs about me…or this place. It follows me, even in my thoughts and dreams. I need to get far away."

As he spoke, the deep solemn ring of the bell tolled in the distance, signaling the end of Mass. She stood quickly. "I must get back to the church before I'm missed!"

She squeezed his hand, and her soft lips brushed his ear, warm breath tickling as she leaned close. "When you're gone," she whispered, "I will miss our chance meetings."

She hurried away, leaving him confused, her elfin figure slipping among the trees. For a moment Ambrose's breath stopped.

The bell rolled over the brown meadow, echoing in the bare branches of the nearby woods. The weathered doors of the church creaked open, revealing the darkness within. Distant figures in their Sunday best lingered in the shadows before spilling onto the lawn. Men in brown suits and hats stroked their long beards, "ahing" and "umming" to one another, while women in gray dresses and red ribbons clutched their purses fast and leaned in for laughs and whispers.

Ambrose tried to ignore them. There was no place to hide, and he regretted having stepped out of the hotel at all. He longed for something solid, something real. He wandered among the white of headstones, reaching out to touch them. Brittle limestone flaked white in his hands, leaving dust on his fingers.

How many bodies in this plot of earth?

His eyes fell upon a new plot, fresh and brown and not yet grown over: the miller's grave. A simple stone, donated by the church, stood witness:

Otto Voight
geb. 2 Jan 1807 Odenwald
ges. 3 Nov 1859

His gaze wandered then suddenly fell upon an odd shape poking from under a tangle of dead grass. Lifting the stalks, he stared in puzzlement. An old enamel bowl lay hidden on the ground, dented and dinged, with black chips knocked out. In its center was filled a red liquid, like blood, with a fold of parchment within. Ambrose leaned close, smelling. It was wine—and something else. *Mugwort?* He lifted the parchment, carefully unrolling and reading the strange words within: *"Constricti et ligati in voluntate mea."*
What the hell?

The wagons headed back to town, hooves clopping on the trail. The townsfolk glared as they passed Ambrose, suspicious of the drunk and crazed priest crouching in their cemetery. Whatever he had wished to accomplish by hiding, he had utterly failed.

Tobias and Killian talked in the shadow of the church. Even from this distance, Ambrose saw Meinhard shuffle over to them. They must have seen him too, for they quickly walked away. Meinhard followed closely, struggling to keep up as they moved faster and faster, pretending not to see him. Eventually he gave up and rested with his hands on his knees, breathing heavily. They were halfway down the road when Killian pointed to Ambrose in the graveyard.

"What are you doing in the cold and in the cemetery?" Killian said as they grew close.

"A better question: are you sober?" Tobias asked. "At any rate, it's nice to see you in your robe."

"Look at this." Ambrose ignored and pointed. "What is this?"

Tobias frowned. "A bowl of blood?"

"Wine." Killian poked it with a stick. "And some weeds and resin?"

"Mugwort and myrrh, I believe," Ambrose said. "There's notes I read in the book. Herbs and spells and old pagan monsters and fairytales. Mugwort and myrrh are used in necromancy."

"That goddamn book!" Tobias spat, his round face flush with anger. "I've half a mind to burn that damn thing in your sleep. If you ever did sleep. It's taking your senses."

Ambrose grimaced. "Well, what about this?" He handed him the parchment, the ink bleeding and barely legible.

Tobias's brow furrowed. "'To my will constrained and bound,'" he translated. "What does that mean?"

"It was in the bowl."

Tobias gritted his teeth in anger and kicked at the dirt. The last of the wagons rattled down the trail and the meadow grew quiet. The three priests stared at the ground in silence. The wind rustled the meadow of dry grass and dead wildflowers. A gentle sea of brown rolled up to meet the church, and in the boughs of a lone copse, two figures stared back: Florian and Winfried.

Kilian turned to Tobias. "I think you should tell him."

"Tell me what?" said Ambrose.

Tobias sighed. "I didn't want to say anything, on account of your condition lately."

"Tell me what?!" Ambrose insisted.

"That singer at the abbey with the beautiful voice, the tenor. His name is Isidor Clement," Tobias said. "He found us right after Mass, just as we were leaving, and beckoned us into a dark corner away from prying eyes. It seems he found something he shouldn't have." He tapped his chest and papers crinkled under the folds of his robe. "There wasn't time for us to look, but he spoke of something hidden under our noses. He wouldn't say more. But maybe this bowl and writing has something to do with it."

"Ah, so maybe this isn't taking my mind," Ambrose said, scowling.

"Ambrose, it doesn't mean we can do any—"

"Shh!" he hissed. "Look! Winfried and Florian are among the trees. They've been there since you walked over. I thought they were engaged in their own conspiracy, but they haven't left. They're watching us."

"We should go!" Killian said.
Tobias nodded. "I think you're right!"

✠

CHAPTER 22

Exsurgent Mortui

November 17, 1859

Ambrose lit the oil lamp and candles. It was not yet evening, but the dim, autumn sun barely lit his hotel room, and they gathered around, hot wax sputtering and dripping on the table. Tobias reached into his robes and peered into the corners of the room, as if fearing unseen eyes in the darkness. He drew forth pages of a journal, ripped and partially burned, their black edges smudging his robe and hand. "Isidor found these. He wouldn't say where. Or maybe he didn't have time. But he works in the kitchen. My guess is they were partially burned in the stove."

"He seemed frightened," Killian added.

Tobias nodded. "Yes. He constantly looked over his shoulder. He didn't want to be seen with us and certainly not with these papers. But something bothered him enough to go against his fears. Apparently not everyone is on the side of Anselm and Valentine. Well, let's see what they have to say."

He spread the pages out on the desk. The brittle leaves cracked and broke as he laid them flat. "These are all barely legible. Someone's personal journal, or letters, looks like."

Ambrose picked up one of the pages. "Here's something," he said. "'Before the Great Work, the *karcist* must make pains to renounce, holding only to such things as are pure, for in purity there is power and will to control: the purity of abstinence, the purity of mortification, the purity that is the virtue of the sacrificed. Lacking purity, one is corrupt, and that corruption is the same as the one who is called...' Not much more is legible, except this: 'What greater purity is there than that of the Victim Soul? How else would the New Kingdom on earth be ushered? For only in suffering is there redemption and the burning away of sin.'"

"What's a *karcist?*" said Killian.

Ambrose shrugged. "I don't know. And what do they mean by a 'Victim Soul'?"

"Look." Tobias pointed. A circle, half burned and barely discernible, had been sketched on the back of the page. Letters ringed the inside, encircling a pattern of lines and smaller circles. Below it read; "Know by this seal and draw the circle as instructed, invoking the names and wards as taught."

"What the hell is this?" asked Ambrose. "Killian, what do you have?"

"I'm not sure..." he stuttered. "'By this shall we know. At Christmas Mass, as the midnight bell tolls and the host is raised, bow in secret and utter these words: *Exsurgent mortui, et ac me veniunt.* At the appointed tomb, make prayers and wait.'" Killian looked up. "My Latin is terrible. What does it say?"

"Arise, dead one, and come to me," Tobias shuddered.

"This sounds like some unholy conjuration!" Ambrose said.

"You know..." Tobias ran a hand over his face and stared out at the darkening dusk. "If an ox hadn't wandered onto the track, we'd be in New York or Boston by now. It's cruel fate really. And now we have this. What are we supposed to do with this? We're a simple commission of three: a madman, slowly losing his mind, a peach-fuzzed babyface, barely filling out his robe, and an old fat man. What are we honestly expected to do here?"

"I'm going back tonight," Ambrose said.

Tobias looked up in alarm "What? Where?"

"To the cemetery."

"Why would you do that?" Killian and Tobias cried together.

"There must be answers there." He waved the tattered book. "Disturbed earth and offerings to the dead. Dark conjurations. Florian and Winfried spying on us. Something is happening, and it must be at night. Maybe *this* night."

Tobias sat down with a thump. The chair creaked and groaned, and he rubbed his balding head with a chubby hand. "For the love of God, why?" he groaned. "Why must you try to solve every problem? This has less and less to do with us. I'm sorry for Stephan, but he came of his own foolish will and this seems little to do with him. We've done all we can. Stay here and contact the authorities in Milwaukee, but let's just leave already."

"But isn't it the right thing to do?" Ambrose said.

"For whom?" asked Tobias. "The people here seem quite fine with their fate. Maybe they like being the 'Victim Sacrifice'? Maybe it actually does bring one closer to God?"

"I'm going to do this," Ambrose said.

Tobias leaned forward, his brown yes glaring. "I'm not going with you." He jabbed a thumb at Killian. "And you're not either! If you don't make it back, your uncle Walter will kill me."

"I'm going to do this," Ambrose repeated, his eyes defiant.

"Damn you and damn your crusades!" Tobias said. Scowling, he banged a fist on the desk.

Ambrose gathered his wool coat about him and shouldered his pack. The sharp edge of the mortician's knife was hard and comforting under his arm. "Do what you must," he said. "If I'm not back by morning, get on that train to Boston, the both of you."

Cold wind struck his face as he set foot on the street. The waning crescent moon cast the ground in ghastly light, and the long shadows of the woods stretched out, beckoning to him. A biting wind blew, prying and prodding beneath his collar. He drew his coat about him and set off into the darkness.

Evil follows. What does it follow?

Ambrose stood with his back to the Abbey of the Holy Ghost, shielding the tiny lantern from spying eyes. He paced the cold ground, skirting tangles of dried grass and thistle, twisted among the white headstones. Claudia Voss's grave lay open, bare and black in the earth, still empty and waiting. Bernd's beside lay undisturbed. He stooped to look. Yellow light lit the fresh ground, but no tracks stepped upon the grave or disturbed the earth; the tufts of weeds and grass surrounding were empty and free of anything out of the ordinary. All looked as it had in the light of day.

He rose, feeling the night. The pale moon hid behind a passing cloud, and the meadow was swallowed in blacks and grays, darkness stretching into the frigid gullies and hollows of the thick forest beyond. The mournful howl of a wolf rose long and low in the heart of the wood, and was answered deep in the distance. An eerie air seemed to rise from the ground, as if watching and waiting, always just behind, and Ambrose shivered and held fast the knife. It was cold and hard in his hand and did not fill him with any comfort.

The miller's grave lay at his feet. Ambrose searched the ground, but it was undisturbed as well; the only footsteps were his own from hours before. Yet the bowl was gone! Only bare earth met his hand and a depression where it had been.

The feeling of watchfulness grew and the hair stood on the back of his neck. As he peered at the graves in the eerie darkness, the shadows grew in his mind: fleeting movement at the edge of vision; the crack and rustle of twigs and leaves, just beyond hearing. He looked at his tiny flame and quickly snuffed it out. What small comfort the light cast would be a beacon to the shadows that crept beyond.

He stood deathly still, listening as the stars slowly crossed the sky. The graveyard was empty and still but for the lonely call of a night bird in the darkness. Only the missing bowl hinted at visitors. *But who took it?*

He suddenly froze, his breath tight in his chest. *When had they taken it?* He peered slowly into the darkness, unable to shake the feeling of being watched. A shape caught his eye: a lump of shadow. *Was that always there?* It seemed to move. Or were his eyes playing tricks on him yet again?

He turned back to the trail, anxious to leave, but another lump of shadow sat nestled in the weeds he had passed moments before. *That wasn't there!* His breath quickened and he moved slowly, carefully. Maybe it hadn't seen him. But to his horror, the shape in the weeds stood. A black figure stared at him. His heart pounded in great thumps as a chill prickle dripped down his spine. A moment later, he saw the other shape in the distance stand, both of them now staring.

Ambrose turned and ran with all his might. Blurs of ground and weeds and headstone flashed underfoot. They gave chase, racing after him. The wooded trail grew near, but the thump of rushing steps gained, filling his skull with pounding and cracking. He gasped as the cold air burned his lungs and his legs ached, but he pushed himself harder. The figures were almost upon him. He could see their long shadows and hear their raspy breath in his ear.

Suddenly, an iron grip clenched his arm and yanked. The hard ground rushed to meet him, knocking the wind from his lungs. He looked up to see a dark shape, tall against the moon. The man kicked him again and again, his heavy boot crashing into his chest, as pain exploded, searing his aching ribs. Ambrose raised his hands against the blows and strikes, flashing dark on dark. A black shape rushed, blurry in the corner of his eye, and his head exploded in searing pain as the world around him turned dim and gray.

Dull shapes stirred in twilight—not seen but felt. Rough hands yanked and pulled as Ambrose was dragged across the hard ground, broken by the sudden stab of sharp branches. He felt himself heaved in the air and crashed down again, hurled against the unyielding bark of a tree. Cold dripped in drops and splatters, tracing lines down his face and neck. Something wet. The murmur and rush of blood pounded in his ears.

"He's dead," a voice hissed, silky and distant. Calloused hands poked; a sharp slap across the face, a vice grip twisting his head from side to side.

"Fetch a knife to be sure. And a shovel."

Two blurry figures came slowly into view: Florian and Winfried pale in the light of the moon. The dim light cast them in long shadow, and they loomed ghoulishly above him, pallid cheeks against dark eyes.

"That fool Valentine," Winfried spat. "That manic fool. And the people love him for it. He never should have let these outsiders in."

"They are weak," Florian said. "They don't know the path of purification."

"And the weak will never enter the Kingdom. Let's put an end to this one's spying once and for all. Let's see him try to write his report from a shallow grave."

Florian nodded and retreated into the wood, a shade floating in the darkness. Quiet settled on the forest. The trees above loomed bare and bony, and a terrible chill crept over

Ambrose. Searing pain chased away the numbness and shock as the night grew old. His muscles trembled and shook as waves of cold and sweat swept over him, and as his teeth chattered, his mouth grew bitter with the iron of his own blood. He struggled to fight or flee, but he was too broken to move.

"Ah, you're still alive." Winfried smirked. "You're stronger than I thought. No matter. You won't be for long."

Winfried paced, waiting impatiently. After some time, leaves rustled in the distance as footsteps grew closer. *Is it Florian coming to kill me?* A figure approached through the trees, too dark to see.

"Hey!" a voice bellowed.

Winfried whirled. A bulky form charged from the shadow, face dark and drawn. Frayed folds of cassock flapped as branches snapped and cracked.

"Ha! We get to get rid of two of you!" Winfried said as Tobias barreled toward him.

The man balled his fists and swung wildly in the dark, yet Tobias was surprisingly nimble. He sidestepped and charged full force into Winfried, knocking him to the ground with an "Uff!" Ambrose looked on in helpless panic, struggling to cry out against the blood in his throat.

Tobias landed on top, striking and punching, as Winfried struggled under the old priest's weight. Finally the cook's calloused fingers found soft eyes, and Tobias screamed, batting him away. In a blur, Winfried was upon him, his heavy hands tight and twisting around Tobias's throat. The old priest gasped and wheezed in panic, fighting the iron grip as his eyes bulged red. His frantic hands grew weaker and slowed, and Ambrose watched in horror as the life slowly faded from the man.

Thump!

Winfried slumped. Hot blood spilled on Tobias's face as he struggled to push the giant off him. Finally Winfried fell to the side, his glassy eyes gazing at the dark night above, unseeing.

Killian stood trembling. His knees were weak, and the bloodied branch in his hand was suddenly heavy. He tossed it aside as a wave of nausea washed over him and fell to the ground vomiting bitter bile onto his hands.

"Is he…" Killian started.

"Dead," Tobias replied, stumbling to his feet.

"I…I didn't mean to…"

"Look at me." He grabbed hold of Killian and shook him. "Look at me! You're all right, son!"

"I killed him!" Killian said, his voice shaky as his eyes widened in shock.

"You did no wrong." Tobias said.

"Thou shalt not kill?" Killian cried.

"Oh, you'd let me die? Then have him come after you? Then Ambrose?" Tobias said, holding him fast as he swayed. "What did Jesus say, Killian? Don't you remember? *If you don't have a sword, sell your cloak and buy one.*"

A wheezing gasp rose from the ground, and they looked to see Ambrose, arm raised and trembling, as he struggled to speak.

"Damn it, Ambrose, what do you get yourself into?" Tobias said, checking his body for injuries.

"Coming back," he whispered. "Florian…"

"Goddamn it!" Tobias said, "We need to get rid of the body! Killian put out that light!"

The two priests grabbed hold of the dead man's arms and strained to drag him across the rough and bumpy ground. His limp flesh hung heavy, and they heaved and pulled, sweat falling from their brows. Thorns tore at their robes and skin, biting and scraping as salty blood trickled down. "God, why is he so damn heavy?" asked Tobias. They gave a final pull and the body rolled downhill into a hollow, thumping and knocking as it went.

"We don't have a shovel," Tobias said. "Let's put him in a gully and cover him with leaves."

Quickly, Tobias and Killian gathered all the dead leaves around, scraping the wet earth and hiding the body in a musty mound.

Ambrose moaned from above the gully. "Fuck!" Tobias said as they struggled back up the hill. In the distance, a yellow flame bobbed among the trees.

"Up you go!" They hoisted him up and dragged him into the forest, finally finding the roots of massive willow to hide among. There they huddled, shaking and panting.

"Hey!" Florian yelled, moments later. "Where are you? Winfried! Winfried, where are you?" The brother circled the underbrush, stopping here and there to listen. "Where have you gone?"

The three priests huddled together, Tobias's hand over Ambrose's mouth. The minutes grew long and the shadows lengthened. Still, Florian searched in the dark. Finally, after tense and long moments, the rustling steps crept slowly away.

"Let's get back. Quick!" Tobias hissed.

Ambrose cried out as they stood, his muscles sore and stiff.

Tobias put a finger to his lips. "Quiet! Quiet! Quiet!"

✠

CHAPTER 23

Something to Take the Edge Off

November 18, 1859

Your Eminence, Cardinal Eberhard,

I must write to you again, alone and in earnest. Despite our best efforts, our return shall unfortunately be delayed. The events of this foul backwater have once again transpired against us in the most evil of ways. The whole of St. Gregory seems bent against our good intentions, the rotten roots of malevolent design branching ever deeper.

All lies beneath a facade of brotherly love that would hide any hint of malicious intent. Father Valentine would pretend to be given to his own rapture—giddiness in the Holy Spirit, he would call it. What I, myself, would rather call an ungrounded mania. It is with this giddiness that he would hide his dark designs, yet it is, in fact, this giddiness that is the surest evidence of them, for it is through this pretense to divine rapture that Valentine spreads his confused teachings and misrepresentations of gospel and scripture. (Anselm you know and have no love of. But Florian and Winfried are the muscle and tendon, what follows the impulse of this would-be prophet's mad mind.)

And it is in this that I fear the most for Ambrose. There is an evil truth here to be uncovered, to be sure; a foulness that dwells outside of gospel. It is one with which, in this new land, we are powerless to contend with. Yet I know him. I see it in his eyes; he will not stop. He will dig deeper and deeper. And I fear that in such intimate inquiry he will lose himself to it and be forever changed—his eyes opened and made part of it—and he will be unable to return. If Ambrose has a sin, it his unending need to know. For the sake of his mind, it would be better to leave such things to God.

Why, his very digging is the cause of our delay. Following the thread of strange and perverse intention—its true nature I do not rightly know—he has roused the ire and violence of those priests aforementioned. They set about him with every intention to silence his inquiry by ending his life. It is only by chance that he has been saved, though with grievous injury. Yet we are forever changed at the price of saving him—Killian most of all. More I cannot say, not in written words. That tale must wait.

For now we must bide our time in hiding, waiting for our wounds to heal, lest we arouse the townsfolks' suspicion. When Ambrose can again walk—and when our bruises have faded—we will be on the first train away, as fast as may be.

Until then I shall do my best to stymie Ambrose's native impulse to champion truth and salvation, for surely in this case it shall either get him killed or drive him mad.

God willing, you shall see us come February at the latest.

Yours in Christ,

Father Tobias Schenk

"We've gotten ourselves into a real pickle, this time," Tobias said. He stood with folded arms, his face drawn in a glum frown. Killian sat on the floor of Ambrose's room, silently staring out the filthy window.

A din rose from below: the thumps and tings of pots and pans; a deep voice, garbled and yelling. The sweet smells of the kitchen—glazed ham and autumn pies—drifted warm and lazily on the air as raucous laughter and off-key song hummed the floorboards at their feet.

"Let's have a look in the light of day," Tobias suggested, unwrapping Ambrose's bandages. He pulled back crusted strips of old linen to reveal a mess of black and purple swelling. Ambrose's eyes were dark and swollen almost shut, and his cracked lips flashed gleaming drops of fresh blood. Drawing back the covers revealed a smattering of bruising and boot marks, dark blood tracing and pooling the lines of his ribs. Ambrose held his breath in pain and feebly pushed the old priest away before finally giving up and staring at the ceiling.

"At least nothing's broken," Tobias said, trying to sound optimistic. "Nothing important anyway. Maybe a rib. Maybe your head. But that was broken anyway."

Ambrose struggled to laugh, but only managed a groan.

"What do we do now?" asked Killian. The boy had aged, Ambrose thought. Dark circles of sleeplessness hung under his eyes, and he seemed a man, decades his senior. The innocence of youth finally had been shattered.

"We do nothing," Tobias said.

"But I killed Winfried. They'll come and take me away and put me on trial. I'll hang. I deserve to."

Tobias put up a hand. "No one knows it was you. Even if Florian suspects anything, he'll have to admit their attempted murder of Ambrose."

"Which means we can't say anything, either," Ambrose wheezed.

Tobias gave a quick nod. "Quite right."

"So there's no justice for anyone," Killian said, his eyes dark.

"The young are always concerned with justice," Tobias said, smiling sadly, "I remember that. Age will burn it out of you, for better or worse. After witnessing a lifetime of endless injustice, the only sane thing to do is let it go and let God be the judge."

"They'll get theirs," Ambrose said bitterly. "Justice takes many forms."

"What do we do now?" Tobias said. "We can't be in public so bruised. It would arose suspicion. People would start asking questions. And you, I don't suppose you can travel anyway."

"Travel?" Ambrose coughed. "I can barely talk."

"We're not going to make it back for Christmas after all," Tobias said, sighing. "Damn it, I should have kept a better eye on you. That's the reason Cardinal Eberhard wanted me on this trip, you know? To deal with your inevitable obsession."

"Then you're not doing your job very well." Ambrose winced as he tried to smile. "Killian, you'll have to be our eyes and ears on the outside. Do you think you can manage?

You'll have to sneak us food and drink. Preferably drink, if you have to choose."

"How can you just sit there like nothing's happened?" Killian snapped.

"Listen to me!" said Tobias. "Some things you have to let go, no matter how much you want to hold on to them. They won't do you any good. You wanted to come along, get some experience in the world, grow up a little before accepting your new position. Well, this is what that looks like. I'm sorry, but it's not going to be easy. Life isn't."

"I can't just let it go," he said. "There's blood on my hands. Blood and sin. I need to confess."

"Confess to us! We already know all the ins and outs and actors. I accept your confession, my son. Ten Hail Marys and don't breathe a damn word to anyone."

Shaking his head, Killian turned back to the window.

Tobias turned to Ambrose. "What were you doing in the graveyard anyway?"

"I had a hunch. Notes in the book. Something about offerings at a grave and disturbed ground. I don't know what it means; nothing was clear. Just hints really."

Tobias sighed. "That damn book. Wish we'd never shown it to you."

Killian looked up suddenly. "You mean conjuring the dead? Necromancy? Are they raising spirits?"

Ambrose nodded. "I think they think they are."

"Are you going to put this in your report? Not the part about Killian. The black magic?"

"I don't know," Ambrose said. "What would I even say? We don't even know what it is or who's involved."

"We know Valentine and Anselm and Florian and Winfried are," Tobias said. "Anyway, it doesn't matter. I already wrote a letter to Cardinal Eberhard. He needs to know why we've been delayed."

"We need to get to the bottom of this," Ambrose said, "for the sake of this town.

Tobias rubbed his aching head. "You're going to be the death of me."

A drab sky loomed gray over St. Gregory, its gloom mirroring Killian's heart. He walked the muddied roads, Tobias's letter forgotten in his hand. Frost touched the edges of footprints, and thin panes of ice crunched in puddles underfoot. Soon his boots were soaked. In the drear of autumn, the tiny town lay on the edge of the world: a lonely place, forgotten by the civilized lands abroad.

His thoughts returned to Heidelberg once more: the cobbled streets and arched buildings; the sweet notes of music under grand architecture; the spice of bakeries and cafés. Here, all that greeted his eyes were the bleak frames of squat buildings, one next to the other. No joy touched his heart. No music greeted his ears. Only dour piety hung leaden in the air.

The faces of the passing townsfolk reminded him of Winfried. He wanted to run. To get far away. To not be seen or heard. But their glances followed after, always watching. The post office was just ahead, the sight of it almost causing him to run. He was so eager to be off the street that he didn't see who was standing within and rushed in without looking.

He stopped dead. Anselm towered at the counter in his black robe, his white hair stark against the shadows and his mouth was a sneer. The air was tense and twisted with the feeling of him. Annaliese was there too. He must have come in right after her. She stood far away, almost pressed to the back wall, her face bowed and obscured by a lacy hat as she tried to hide from him.

Anselm slowly turned, glaring with icy eyes that made Killian tremble.

"Father Killian," he said. "I was just bemoaning to Mr. Baumgartner that our dear Winfried seems to have gone missing. You wouldn't happen to know where he's gone, would you?"

Killian's face grew white and dread froze his veins. "I'm…sorry, Father. I don't."

Anselm's eyes narrowed in suspicion, staring too long. Killian's knees trembled and he thought he might faint or confess everything in that moment, as if the man would draw it out of him somehow. But at the last moment, Anselm turned back to the counter.

"Ask everyone," Anselm told Mr. Baumgartner. "Everyone that comes in. I want to hear from all of them. I want this town to wake up and fear that one of our own is missing. A brother, no less."

"I-I shall make a list…" the postman stammered.

Killian backed out onto the stoop, quietly closing the door behind him. His breath was tight in his chest, his heart racing. Even outside, he could here Anselm's voice rattling the glass in its frames. Hard footsteps struck the floor as the man turned to leave, and Killian fled behind the side of the post, his back flat against the wall. Sweat dripped from his chest and neck, and he silently cursed, praying to not be discovered.

The door creaked open. Soft footsteps fled across the walk: Annaliese. Close behind was the heavy thump of Anselm's steps.

"Annaliese!" Anselm called. "How are you doing after Issa's death? I know you two were close."

Killian pricked up his ears as he peered around the corner.

"I'm fine, Father. Thank you," she said as politely as she could.

Anselm frowned, studying her in disapproval as she recoiled from him. The street grew quiet and what few townsfolk there were shrank from the priest, finding excuses to enter the bakery, the hotel, the saddle shop, anything but the post office.

"Your mother has told me you've not been yourself lately. Have you been given again to your romantic flights of fancy?"

"No!" she said. "I'm just focused on my work at the farm, and there's much to do. There's sewing and cooking and my aunt Gilli needs looking after. It helps keep me from thinking of things."

"I worry about you. You'll never find a husband or fulfill God's plan for you with your head in the clouds. Are you still hearing voices? The voices of the wild places are evil spirits that lead one astray. There is only one true voice and that is God's."

"I haven't been hearing voices! I know now not to listen to them." Annaliese hung her head, tears in her eyes as her lips trembled. Killian's face grew hot in anger, yet he dared not confront the man.

"I haven't seen you at Mass," Anselm said. "Have you been backsliding? It would pain me to have to correct you again. Your father is such a pious man. He worries so about your soul, as do I. You're at an age when your youthful flesh will start speaking its own passions, leading your heart to temptation. We have ways of tempering that, if you've forgotten."

Annaliese fell back as he stepped towards her. Her letter crumpled, a slight crinkle in the air, as she held her fists tight to her chest. He grabbed her wrists and drew her near, touching her side, a far too familiar gesture.

"Please!" she protested. "I have to go. My father is waiting for me and if I'm late he'll come looking. I haven't listened to any voices. And I'll be sure to see you in Mass this Sunday."

"Hm. We'll see," he said, letting her go. "I have my eye on you. Now best hurry to your father."

Anselm turned and left, cracking and sloshing through the ice and puddles as he strode to meet Florian in the street. The two talked quietly. Although Killian couldn't hear what was said, he saw Florian shake his head and Anselm scowl. The older priest pointed in the direction of the Hotel St. Gregor, and they set off down the street.

Killian circled the post office, ducking from sight, as Annalise hid behind old barrels and crates. Her head was buried in her hands and her chest heaved in soft sobs. Killian blushed, unsure what to do. As if sensing his presence, she finally looked up, eyes red and tearful.

"I'm… sorry, Miss Fährmann. I didn't mean to sneak up on you," he said. "I was… Are you all right?"

"You were hiding from Anselm," she sniffed, drying her eyes.

"Well…yes."

"Just like everyone else."

Killian looked away, ashamed.

"I suppose you heard everything?" she asked, getting to her feet.

"I'm… sorry…" he said.

"Oh, Killian, it's not your fault. What could you do?" She squeezed his arm.

"I just wish I could've done something," he said. "Something good for once."

"Killian," she said, shaking him gently, "you look terrible! What happened? Why are you shaking? Is everything all right?"

"I'm afraid I can't say." Tears fell from his eyes and his breath hitched. He looked away, embarrassed. "I'm sorry. This place isn't what I thought it would be. I wasn't ready for this kind of adventure after all."

"Oh, Killian," She sighed. "Nobody is."

She suddenly hugged him. Killian fumbled as he hugged her back, uncomfortable at her closeness and unsure of what to do.

"What about you?" he said. "Are you all right? I don't understand what's going on here."

"You mean with Anselm?" she said, her eyes hard. "You never had such people back home?"

"Well…I mean…" He blushed. "I never dealt with them personally. I guess because of my uncle, I was… off limits. But my brothers in seminary told stories sometimes."

"How could you stay in a place like that?"

"Leaving wasn't an option."

They grew silent. A gust of wind blew across their cheeks, prickly and shivering, and tiny flakes of white snow danced on the wind, settling on wooden shingles and blown into corners. Annaliese looked away, staring at the gray sky. "Sometimes staying isn't either."

A soft, quick knock thumped the door. Ambrose stirred awake, confused. A square of yellow sun fell on the heavy quilt and warmed his face, and above, bright motes of dust danced and sparkled in the rays like tiny worlds, kicked up as he shifted under the covers. He coughed and winced in pain as hot tears gathered in his eyes.

The knock came again, softer but more urgent. "Ambrose!" a voice whispered. "Ambrose, it's me, Albrecht."

"Doctor…" He winced.

The air was biting and cold as he pushed the blanket aside and struggled to stand, prickles of hair rising in goose bumps in the chill. He strained and grasped at the bedpost, laboring to pull himself up, his ribs screaming in protest. Finally he slid from the bed and fell to the floor with a thump and a cry.

"Ambrose?" Dr. Albrecht said.

"Damn it!" he gasped, forcing himself upright. His bruised, aching muscles spasmed as reached the desk, his hand shaky as it searched for the whiskey bottle. Finally finding it, he took a large gulp that burned and made him cough and jolted him in pain again. He clenched his fist, his face flush with anger as he tasted the bitter iron of his own blood on his tongue. Florian and Anselm and Valentine, all "men of the cloth," walked carefree, while he endured such pain, hidden in a dark room.

"Ambrose?"

"Hold on, damn it!"

The lock clicked, and he peered out into the drafty hall. Albrecht stood anxiously, looking toward the other rooms, his mutton chops waving with the bob of his head.

"Can I come in?"

Ambrose ushered him in. "Make sure you lock it. I don't know who's spying out there."

The doctor nodded. "Of course."

Ambrose fell into the chair, bottle in hand. Brilliant purple and deep black stood out in giant puffs and swellings about his eyes and cheeks, their edges not yet fading, while drops of dried blood clung in clots about his lips and fallen on his chin.

"Killian said you got a walloping," Albrecht said, examining his face.

"I'm hoping you're the only one he told."

"Now don't blame him. I pushed. Besides, he knows who it's safe to talk to," said Albrecht. "If I didn't know better, I'd think you ran into some problems with the powers that be." He sat down on the bed and eyed him closely. "Have you heard Winfried is missing?"

Ambrose looked away, his dark eyes narrow, and his knuckles white.

"Don't worry about him," Albrecht said. "It's no loss to any of us. Probably drunk in a ditch, people will think. Drunk on his own self-righteousness, that is. But you probably best keep out of sight for a while. You know, so you don't frighten the children. Besides, you're supposed to still be in Walders searching for Silas. That's a long trip, I hear.

Especially not knowing where that crazy Englishman is liable to be."

"Well, thank you, Doctor."

Albrecht lifted a bushy brow. "For what? You're the one doing me the favor by going on that trip you're still on. I'll just be sure to tell everyone you're still there. Now I have some things for you." He rummaged in his bag. Bottles clinked and tinked, lost in the darkness. "Ah, here we go." He held a yellow, milky mixture. "Arnica in warm sweet milk, boiled with frankincense. Make a compress and put it everywhere it hurts. Change it every three hours. It's sticky, but it'll clear a bruise quick. And at the very least you'll smell a little better." The bottle thumped on the desk and he reached back in. "Ah! And best of all, laudanum for the pain. And senna, to keep from you getting costive. But"—he wagged a finger—"keep a bed pan near. I'll not be responsible for any messes."

"I'll put it to good use. Thank you." Ambrose shook the bottle and held it to the light.

"Yes of course. The dosage is on the bottle. Mind you follow it closely or you might die."

Frowning, Ambrose set the bottle aside. "Duly noted."

"Yes, well, I thought, with your condition, you could do with a little relief."

"Doctor," Ambrose said, "why did you want to see me? I know it wasn't just to give me drugs."

"Ah…" Albrecht groaned and hung his head. "It's happening again. It slowed for a time. But now it's started. Nobody's died yet, but they're sick. It seems to be in a circle around the Voss house; Jacob and his wife and Genovefa and Virgil Heitzman next door. Although you'd never guess. They mostly closed themselves off years ago. Which actually makes it all the stranger. Why would they get sick?"

"You said it can't be poison," Ambrose said.

"I don't see how it could be. There's no evidence of it. And who or why? Are you sure you didn't learn anything else from Silas? Nothing you can remember?"

Ambrose shook his head. "Sorry."

Albrecht threw up his hands. "It figures."

Steps echoed on the stairs and in the hallway, and the two men grew still, staring at the door with held breath. A key jangled and turned in a nearby room before the door clicked shut. Ambrose breathed deeply and shook his head, holding up the tiny laudanum bottle. "Two teaspoons a day? I hope this is good for nerves." But Albrecht stared at the floor, unanswering.

"Doctor," Ambrose said suddenly. "Is there any medical cause or rationale for an inanimate body becoming animate again?"

"What?" Albrecht asked, brows raised in puzzlement. "Do you mean the dead coming back to life? You're a priest. That's God's provenance alone."

"I don't mean a dead body," Ambrose explained. "Not totally. I mean, mostly dead. Can a partial, deathlike state create a derangement of the nerves and sensorium in one who might come back?"

"Ha! Winfried and Florian must have hit you harder than I thought. Have you had headaches? I worry you have water on the brain."

Ambrose stared at Albrecht and the doctor shifted uncomfortably.

"Well, I should think so!" Albrecht finally said. "Anyone coming back from the dead is bound to be addled in the mind. Of course, those coming back…those only mostly dead…will be coming back in a pine box six feet underground. So who's to know if they're addled or not? Although I've heard at times they dig the bodies back up if they need to examine them for whatever reason, and sometimes there's scratches on the inside. They weren't dead when they were buried. Godawful thing. Worst thing really."

"But no one really comes back?" Ambrose pressed. "There's nothing in the far-flung corners of the world to cause such a thing?"

The doctor squinted at him, perplexed. "Dead is dead." He shook his head. "Why do you ask?"

"Just something I saw at the graveyard. Some wine left at a fresh grave. Clearly intended for the deceased. Or not quite deceased."

"Some folk here are from the East: Bohemia and Moravia," Albrecht said. "There are some unusual customs in the Old World. Not all holy or to be taken seriously."

Ambrose thought for a moment. "I suppose. Thought I'd at least ask. Well, turning to the matter at hand, what do you think is making people sick?"

"Miasma, if I had to guess," Albrecht said. "Some foul air. It's later than usual, though, and worse, but foul gasses seep from the grounds, especially the lowlands."

"Silas said there are caves in the earth," Ambrose mused. "They stretch underground. He said the Cinderella Rock is named after the evil spirits that live underground."

"Spirits. Miasma. I don't really care what you call it, so long as we find an answer."

✠

CHAPTER 24

The Trials of Poor Killian

November 22, 1859

K illian trudged, head bowed. The eastern road rose slightly to a hill in the distance. At its top, a meadow overlooked the town, pale in the light of early winter. The road was an old Indian trail that ran to Manitowoc, on the shores of the great lake Michigami. It was sparsely traveled. A lone merchant or traveler passed him on his way to Altona or Kiel, and he pulled his coarse hat over his eyes, mumbling "Hello" as he looked away.

A weight hung over him, following him through the tiny town and into the pasture and forest beyond. He hurried to flee the pressure of unseen eyes upon him, but the feeling in his mind lingered. Finally he slowed, wandering the forest road in a depressed gloom. Black sin stained his soul, forever dampening the light of his heart; he feared the hand of judgement upon him. The world was drained of color, now so much duller and dark, the vital breath of life itself bled from it. He walked the cold and barren wastes of his spirit, wandering in purgatory and waiting but to fall into the seething, eternal fires below. The faces of his family rose in his mind and he wept.

The wood was silent but for the crunch of leaves and the whistle of the wind through the trees, gathering from the open marsh and pasture to the west. Great clouds roiled and billowed in the steely sky above, blocking the sun here and there. In awe and fear, Killian stared up into their threatening darkness; there weren't such clouds back home.

Maple leaves, brilliant red, floated and drifted, settling all around him. "A bright and late drop is a long and cold winter," the old ones said around their morning coffee. How long had he been here? An entire season had slowly passed, and he found himself no closer to leaving. His adventure in the New World had grown savage and dark, and he longed to be home: to hide in the parish church of his boyhood, under the warm reds of stained glass and the shiny wood of the pews, worn smooth from so many hands. He long to be safe again: to wander carefree the green hills and pastures of youth, now forever a lifetime apart.

His feet slowly climbed the hill as the road rose. White stones, old and moss covered, marked a small trail that branched and wound through the trees, running north. He had never noticed it before, and he found himself wandering amongst the twisting, turning bends, stepping over gnarled roots and fallen logs, eventually coming to the bright meadow seen from below. Tufts of coarse, tall grass mingled with stands of red sumac, their feathery heads blowing in the breeze, and here and there, blackened stumps rose from the dead meadow, the remnants of a fire long ago. Old char, crackled and broken, lay scattered. Tall trees surrounded and concealed from the world outside, and an odd calm lay on the land.

A giant lump caught his eye. A boulder stood in the center: white limestone, weathered and crumbling. Pits and pocks opened randomly across its surface, gouged by long years of ice and wind. Deep fissures had split the rock in two, and in its center, a thick post of old graying pine stood wedged in the largest crack. The bare wood rose into the air, split and holed from woodpeckers, and at its top a large branch had been nailed and lashed to form a cross.

"It's peaceful up here," a voice said.

Killian whirled in panic. Piercing blue eyes met his own, vivid and gleaming, and a tangle of wild hair fell over a plain brown robe. Father Valentine watched him with a faint smile, approaching silently.

"I'm drawn to this place too. When I need time to think. When I need to be reminded of my mission," he said, in his voice a touch of nostalgia. "This was where I saw the white calf, you know?"

Killian fidgeted nervously, desperately wishing to leave.

"Have you not heard that story? Come, sit." He motioned to the rock. "I bought this land, sight unseen, on behalf of the Association—that is, our Association of Christian Brotherhood—where we are to live the ideals of poverty, community, and prayer, like Saint Gregory of Nazianzus before. You see, I was chased out of Germany—my congregation and I—for wanting to return to simpler ways." The man stared, his gaze fixed and piercing, as Killian squirmed.

"I thought you were threatened with excommunication, for calling for the death of the pope?" Killian said, instantly regretting it.

"Well, that would indeed make things simpler." Valentine smiled and leaned against the rock, his face serene. "Power is complicating. And corrupting. In any case, I bought this land in Milwaukee, having never seen it. I had no idea if it was fertile, or waste. Much land here is gravel underneath. But I trusted in God that he would not lead us astray. When we arrived, I had no idea where we would build the town. The land was thick and overgrown with forest"— he waved his arm—"as you can see."

"Always are the true children of God challenged to trust and have faith. So I prayed, a day and a night. And that's when I spied a white calf. A calf the color of freshly fallen snow, where it had no right being. It was a sign. We followed it to this very place. It led us to this hill overlooking where the town is now. And then it disappeared. That's why we chose to settle here."

"It's a beautiful spot," Killian said doubtfully, as he gazed at the charred wood jutting from the brown grass.

"Where is Tobias?" asked Valentine, his eyes far off and wistful. "I miss him. I hope he hasn't left early without saying goodbye."

"He went to Walders with Ambrose," Killian nervously lied. "They hoped to find some explanation for the recent deaths. There's a doctor there."

"Oh… People always die, you know?" Valentine winked at Killian. "I thought he might stay for good. You might stay too, if you'd like. This is a good place. A good place to get to know yourself."

Valentine gazed at the town below, stroking his beard with coarse fingers as he sat, lost in thought.

"Forgive me," Killian ventured. "But do you know what it's like here when you're gone? Do you know what your priests do in your absence?"

"Oh, you speak of Anselm. It's true—he has a strictness about him. Some might call him harsh or claim to suffer at his hands. But you do know he is part of my design?"

Killian shook his head.

"I used to be like him. I had the same chasm in my heart, forever separating me from knowing God's true love. Anselm has his place and his purpose, and maybe his potential."

"What *is* his purpose?" Killian asked.

Valentine grew silent, seeming not to hear. Killian shifted uncomfortably in the stillness, eyeing the path and desperately wishing he could leave.

"Do you know what suffering is?" Valentine asked suddenly. "It is proof of man's original sin—that sin that separates man from God in his own heart. Suffering is but the evidence of that. But in an act of mercy, the Lord has made it such that this suffering is its own redemption. This sin of separation is only burned away and made pure in the very suffering of that separation itself. That people suffer is proof of their separation and further proof that they need to suffer more, for it is also proof of God's love."

Killian cowered at Valentine's blasphemous words. He tried to look away, but the wild man seemed to grow before him, holding him in his gaze. He felt suddenly naked, as if every thought were laid bare.

"How do I know, you may ask?" Valentine continued. "I know because I have transcended my own suffering."

He held up his wrists for Killian to see. The pale bulging flesh of an old scar lay gnarled and rough on his palms, round and ragged at the center. He turned them over. The same scar bulged from the back.

"I was nailed to the cross, like Christ," he said. "I willed it. I wanted to know his heart. I had nails pounded through my flesh and I was hoisted up. For three days in the sun, the dark, the wind and the rain. And what did I see? On the last day, he appeared before me. Transfigured and in all his glory. Christ came to me and I understood." He tapped his heart. "And all my pain fell away."

He grasped Killian by the shoulder and drew his face so close that his wind-blown hair tickled Killian's cheek.

"Do you understand? God does not come to you in times of joy. One only meets God in the poverty of the spirit. That is what it is to be an empty vessel. *Let us cleanse ourselves from everything that can defile our body and spirit. And let us work toward complete holiness because we fear God.* But what you don't know is that emptying the vessel isn't enough. You must throw the vessel away. That's why I allow Anselm to be strict in his ways. People come for love but stay out of fear. Yet I haven't the temperament for fear anymore. Think on it. See if you understand."

Killian stared in silence, afraid to speak. Valentine's amber eyes seemed to glow of their own accord, and in the gray and clouded light, the burned meadow appeared as a ghastly netherworld and Valentine the demon within. When he thought he could take it no more, leaves rustled in the distance, and a white head of thinning hair broke the treeline.

"Speak of the Devil. Here he comes now," Valentine said.

Anselm approached, hands hitching his robe as he stepped gingerly over the lumps and hollows. As he approached, he glared at Killian, but Valentine only laughed to see him stumbling. "He spends too much time indoors," he said softly.

"Father," Anselm said, his voice dripping with disapproval. "I hate to remind you, but you've promised to tend to the sick and dying. A crowd is now gathered at the church for some time. Some ill, many more worried. Will you be coming to minister to your flock?"

"You see," Valentine whispered, "he has his uses."

The wild priest stood, and a strange and distant expression passed over his face: a sudden mood like shadow on a sunny day. "Like I said"—he turned to Killian—"people are always dying."

Valentine stepped lightly over the rough ground. Quick steps hopped across the hollows and fallen logs and past the ash and char. Anselm turned to follow, but Valentine waved him away. The wild priest disappeared, swallowed into the woods, his long hair blowing wildly in the breeze.

Anselm turned and glowered, his face red at such dismissal. He narrowed his eyes and scowled at Killian, wrinkles spreading across his pale cheeks and brow. Killian held his breath, looking here and there. The deep wood surrounded, with no exit.

"I know about Winfried," Anselm said.

Killian froze, his blood ice cold. "What…what do you mean? What do you know? Is he all right? Did he come back?"

"I know he is missing," Anselm hissed. "I know he is not all right. And I know he is not coming back."

"I'm sorry to hear that."

"I know you have something to do with it. And I'll find out what. I also know about Ambrose. Florian told me that much. Where is he? Should he suddenly reappear, while Winfried remains missing, well, that confirms foul deeds have transpired."

"There may be many foul deeds," Killian said, his voice shaking. "Perhaps we should speak to Father Valentine about this."

Anselm's thin lips curved into a cruel smile. "Do you fear me?" He laughed. "I assure you, the wrath of man is the least of your worries. You are only tolerated by Valentine's good graces. But he will not shield you forever. Oh, such things may happen to you under the cover of night, when your soul shrinks and your heart grows faint."

He paused, letting his words sink in.

"I know you have seen the bishop's room," he continued. "You think you are clever. You think you are so sly to have snuck in and out. But the watcher told me. You will never find Stephan. He is never coming back."

"But why?" Killian pleaded. "Why is Valentine keeping him? Just let him go. No matter what he's seen, Europe is too far away to police the Americas. Have the decency to not make him suffer!"

"How little you know," he scoffed. "You will learn in time that all must play their part. As for Valentine, do you think he's the only one with designs? He is manic and deluded. He has deceived himself into thinking he has seen the face of God and he dwells in that happy lie. He is an old fool grown soft in the mind, given to the sloth and indolence of his idle imaginings. He presumes the Lord is knowable through love, that he alone may understand that love, and that one need only let go of themself to find the Kingdom of Heaven within. Would the forgiveness of original sin were so easy, any whore would find the way unbarred. Even Eve."

"But the people follow *him,* not you," Killian said.

"Of course they follow. They fall in love. But they aren't molded. Not made pure. He understood this once. But no longer. So let him play his games. He doesn't possess the power he thinks."

Killian tried to stand, but his knees were weak. If he ran, he might be able to make it. He and Tobias—and Ambrose, if he could be convinced—would have to leave for Walders, maybe even on foot, but they would still leave. The edge of the wood was near, past the charred stumps and scatterings of limestone rock. Yet something kept him from running; something drained his will.

"Do you know what is love?" Anselm continued. "It is suffering, which you will learn much of. Suffering is that which redeems us in the eyes of the Lord. It washes away sin and makes us pure. But what is it if only I suffer? What of the salvation of others? To redeem my fellow man through cleansing suffering is a true act of love, even if I must forego my own redemption. Do you not see my sacrifice?"

Anslem stepped forward, his voice tense and urgent as a menacing look passed over his eyes, like hunger. Killian backed away in alarm.

"But does this choice not further deny God?" Anselm pressed. "Do I not then suffer all the greater for my sacrifice? To willfully stand apart from God, that others may stand together? Like the Fallen One himself? Our work is a necessary evil. And we shall be redeemed. Redeemed as he is and our redemption shall be that much the sweeter. You look on in horror. But for this, I will gladly play the role of the Devil."

Killian stumbled and Anselm caught his arm, pulling him close, cold eyes boring into his.

"Now repent!" he commanded. "It is only through repentance that one is transformed, for repentance forsakes the duplicitous heart. Repent now and confess your sins, child!"

Dizziness swept over Killian. He swayed, held fast in the old priest's grip. The sickening burden of his secret weighed heavy upon his heart, searing and scaring, until he could bear it no longer. He wished to say. To speak. To tell the truth in the light of day. Some force compelled him. He struggled as a violent shaking swept his being and opened his mouth.

"I…I have nothing to confess," he said.

Anselm cast him to the ground in disgust. "It doesn't matter," he spat. "Your soul will be cleansed all the same. You will suffer in good time. And I will know your heart and all of your sins. Now go. Go back to the other sinners."

Killian crawled on shaky legs, desperate to run. "Why are you telling me this?" he cried.

"Why?" Anselm laughed cruelly. "Because, boy, you don't matter."

Soft browns swirled, blurring as Ambrose stared at the ceiling. The blink and flitter of heavy lids brought the old boards into focus—the rough gouge of chisel and draw knife—only to fade in a haze of melting lines, once again. A curious lightness spread through his body, as if his veins were filled with air, and his dizzy head floated far above. The pain melted away, still there but somehow unimportant.

The dusty cobwebs of last year fluttered in an unseen draft, its cold creeping over his face and prickling his skin. How long had he lain here, staring at the ceiling? Days? Or was it weeks? He knew every inch, even with his blurred vision.

His skin flushed, hot and itchy and trembling, yet he felt clammy and freezing. A chilly sweat clung to his brow and dripped down his neck, cold on the damp pillow. The thump of his heart grew slow. *Too slow. I should worry.* But he didn't. His breath grew long and deep, yet somehow not enough. Two spoons? He looked at the vial to be sure.

A soft tap came at the door.

Albrecht again. What does he want?

Ambrose ignored and stared at the ceiling, fading in and out. The tap came again, quick and urgent but still soft. He sighed. The room swirled as he slowly sat up, the pain in his ribs screaming through a distant and foggy haze. With a grunt, he pushed it out of his mind.

The knock came again and light steps shuffled outside.

"Hold on," he coughed. The handle was out of reach, so far away.

The door opened, creaking, and the cold hall drafted on his bare feet. A porcelain face smiled nervously at him. Raven hair fell softly upon a slender dress, dancing upon the swell of her breasts as her hazel eyes looked on him with concern.

"Annaliese?"

"Oh, my God!" she exclaimed.

He winced as she touched the swollen bruises of his face, yellowing at the edges. "What happened?"

"I really shouldn't say," he muttered. "Only…avoid Anselm and Florian."

"Oh." She smiled sadly. "I know that already."

The bed creaked as he sat down hard, his head falling heavily against the plaster wall. Annaliese held out her arms to steady, gently shaking him. "Ambrose, are you all right?"

He held up the vial and shook. Liquid splashed within. "I don't think I trust the doctor."

"Oh. Laudanum." She sighed. "My father was on that when he was sick with fever of the brain. He only got better when he stopped taking it. My mother threw the bottle away and threatened the doctor. Then everyone said he got better by the will of God."

"It doesn't help and it doesn't hurt," he mumbled. "Well…maybe it hurts. Something's not right."

"Don't take it with whiskey!" she cautioned.

"Duly noted." He fell against her, sapped of all strength. "I couldn't even imagine it. It seems to have taken my taste for it away at the moment, anyway."

"What have you gotten yourself mixed up in?" She held his head, lest it fall back against the wall, and he blushed at her touch. The faint smell of lilac enveloped, bringing back hazy memories: summers on the lake, the warm sun on his young face. Annaliese's black hair tickled his cheek. But his mother's was brown. He shook his head, confused. The dim room came back into focus, its dark corners in gloom.

"Why are you here?" he asked. His bare legs poked from under a nightgown, threadbare and much too short, and he quickly covered himself in embarrassment.

Annaliese's cheeks turned rosy as she pulled back, her hands shaking slightly. "Maybe I shouldn't have come."

"No." He touched her arm as she turned to leave. "I'm glad you did."

She smiled, glancing at the room and back at him. Bottles lay about on the floor and lined the sill, yellow sun sparkling in green and brown glass. Scraps of paper sat in piles, scribbles of hastily written notes drawn to the very edges. A pool of black ink blotted the desk, a dingy rag beside it, half-heartedly used to wipe and now dried beside the spilled inkwell. It had the look of a man given up or gone mad.

"What is all this?" she ventured, tracing the mess of the fevered notes from the night before.

"Gruesome stories to frighten children. Tobias and Killian found this in Abbey." He fumbled with the book from the desk. "Spirits and demons and undead things."

The old paper was grimy and oily between her fingers. Jotted notes of several different hands filled the pages in the corners and edges and spare sheets stuck out from within, covered in hastily written scribbles and sketches.

"I don't read French," she said. "What is a grimoire?"

"A book of magic. For whatever that's worth." Ambrose glanced away, dismissively. "Pages and pages of nonsense."

"Why wouldn't you think it's real? People in the West always scoff at such things. Is it because it's not fashionable?

"It's not rational." He turned and the room swirled in fuzziness around her, gold and brown dancing, his head floating somewhere above. *Neither am I.*

"Humph, well, I think rational is just what's fashionable," she said matter-of-factly. "We had stories back home, you know. People locked their doors, even in the deep forest."

"Oh." Ambrose frowned. "Well, what would cause something like these deaths back home?"

Annaliese let out a light sigh. "You'd probably think me foolish and uncultured."

"Please," he said. "Culture doesn't seem to be getting me anywhere."

She glanced away, hesitant at first. "The dead talk to one another in their graves, you know? That's why some aren't buried in the graveyard. They don't want them to corrupt the others. But sometimes an ill-hearted *černokněžník*, a sorcerer, will come through the village and stir them up. And well, some things have an appetite no matter what, even after death. I don't know what you call them in German."

"Do you mean the *nachzehrer?*" He thought of the passage in the book. "Why?"

"Tragedy." She sighed again. "Someone driven mad by pain and loss becomes senseless in death, but…they're always still searching, desperately… Back home, when so many pass so quickly, we think it must have a beginning." Her eyes watered and it seemed she whispered to herself. "So who here died a tragic death? she said nervously. Well, anyway," she said nervously. "I know that flies against modern sensibilities. Now you must really think I'm crazy."

"Well, as a man of the cloth—"

"I don't think of you as a priest. I think of you as a friend," she chastised. "Anyway, Killian told me where to find you. He said you'd had it…rough."

"I have." He nodded. "Like I said, avoid Anselm and Florian. Winfried…you probably don't need to worry about him."

"I'm not worried about Winfried." She squeezed his hand. "I'm worried about *you*. Ambrose, are you all right? Someone came at you and did these things! Anselm and Florian and Winfried, I should guess." She scowled, eyes narrowing in anger.

"But *why* are you worried about me? It would be so much easier for you not to."

"You really cared about Issa," she said. "After she died, most people wanted to forget. That's how it always is. I had to care in my own way. Alone. I couldn't breathe a word to anyone. And, well"—she glanced at the empty bottles and plates—"you don't look like you're doing well."

"I'm sorry," Ambrose said. "I'm sorry I couldn't do more."

"They're trying to make you not care," she said suddenly. "Do you know what I mean? I remember what it was like to first come here. I was still just a girl. I didn't want to leave, but I was still bright and full of optimism. Anything could happen in this New World. But day by day it's chipped away until there's nothing left. When you came, I remembered something. Something I was starting to forget." She reached out and touched his hand. "I don't want you to forget."

He nodded and the room spun around him. Bits of memory flickered, bright and fleeting: the sunny summer day at Le Havre, boarding the ship; the cry of the gulls and the laughter of children in the market; the bright expanse of ocean and the first glimpses of distant land. All fell away to a brooding heaviness, a resignation where brightness had once been.

"I don't know what I'm doing here anymore," he said. "I cannot see the way. I don't know what God is calling me to do. But I know I must do something. Maybe we can help to remind each other?"

Annaliese squeezed his hand, lightly, her cheeks turning red. Ambrose looked down in shame, suddenly self-conscious of the squalor of his room, the filth in the corners.

"Do you think there is a basic goodness in people?" he said. "I always felt that as a child. Even in the meanness and drunkenness of the streets and bars, the brothels and factories. I always felt people were just confused. But there was still goodness there, underneath it all. It was just momentarily covered up, like clouds against the sun. My mother never went to church after my father died. When I was sent to the Catholic Boys' Home I'd never really heard of sin.

"Well, they were sure to teach me all about it." He laughed bitterly. "But I always thought the church still mirrored a basic goodness, a basic godliness, even despite its human flaws. But sometimes it seems the flaws are all there is…"

His eyes watered and his throat grew tight. But try as he might, he couldn't swallow it away. "I'm sorry! I'm so sorry. This isn't how a priest should act."

She brushed his cheek with a soft hand. Ambrose blushed at her touch but didn't pull away. She smiled nervously as the warm light fell through the grimy window, painting her in yellows and golds, and in his laudanum stupor she appeared as an angel.

"I think I was right about you," she said. "The spirits talk about you. They've seen you in the woods. They whisper in the glens and glades. I can't understand them, but they say your name. They don't talk about just anyone, you know. Few see or hear them. And sometimes people see them and forget."

"I don't know. I haven't heard or seen anything…" Ambrose's head swirled with confusion. She grew fuzzy as his eyes lost focus: a blur of gold and white against the darkness behind. He wrinkled his brow, trying to understand. *What is she saying? Is this all a trick of the mind? Is the laudanum clouding my senses and conjuring false spirits and imaginings?* Her hand felt real in his; he squeezed to be sure.

"No one else in this town sees." She heaved a sigh. "Only an old woman, grown cold and bitter. The town gossip. My aunt, Gilli Platten. They said she was beautiful once, with light that shone from her eyes and brightened all those around her. But she was told long ago her light wasn't holy and the voices in her head weren't His voice. Now she's wretched."

"I've met her." Ambrose nodded. "In the post."

"I never want to become that! I'll leave before I ever do." She squeezed his hand. Her face hard and defiant.

"But…where will you go?"

"I can't go home. I haven't the money. And there is no home to return to. The farm is gone and the woods are cut down by now," she said. "So I think I would go west."

"I've heard of the West," Ambrose said. "I've heard it's wild! If it's anything like Walders, I can't imagine… What of your family?"

"They'll do fine without me. Sometimes, I think it would be easier on them. I'm something strange to them." She looked down, her eyes sad. "I remind them of my grandmother. I barely knew her, but I've heard the stories. She lived in the woods too. She had her herbs and her secret ways. Secrets her grandmother taught her long before. But she was an embarrassment to the family. The village priest spoke against her. Then my father came. A German Catholic from the West. When my parents married, he made my mother disown my grandmother and never see her again. He said anyone who left offerings to *Mesyats* couldn't be trusted."

"What is *Mesyats?*"

"The moon. She finds her lover in the summer but leaves him in the winter. Then returns to him again in the spring. My father thought this was a bad influence."

"Well," Ambrose said, "it is pagan."

"That doesn't mean it's not true!" she said, her eyes flashing. "Well, at least she has the *Leši.*"

A wave of sadness swept over Ambrose in the dim gloom. He grabbed Annaliese's hand as if she would run away that instant. "If you leave. I would worry about you," he whispered.

She looked at him, her eyes suddenly fierce. "I'm stronger than I look."

✠

CHAPTER 25

Of Funerals and Black Magic

November 27, 1859

Heavy silence shrouded the wood. A chill rose from the marsh and gullies below, and Killian pulled his collar tight against the damp and seeping cold. The wood was silent but for the rustle of his feet, and a loneliness hung on that bitter November night. The pale light of the slivered moon cast the forest floor in long shadow; its thin crescent moon above was crossed in twigs, skeletal and bare, and he shuddered just to look at them.

He kept his head down, the dim yellow of the lantern bathing the ground in soft light. Ahead, the giant trunk of an old willow rose black in the moonlight, its thick roots gnarled and tangled in the darkness below; the same roots he and Tobias and Ambrose had hidden among weeks before. He felt the rough bark, hard and ridged beneath his hand, and he slowed. His heart grew heavier the closer he got to the body, and his hand tightened on the lantern to firm his resolve. It was just ahead now.

His foot caught a tangled root and he tumbled, crashing to the ground in a rustle and snap of leaves and twigs. Night vapors washed over, cold and damp and musty, as Killian lay sprawled, face against the earth. The tiny light flickered and died, and the darkness rushed over him. His heart raced as he looked about in a panic; shadows behind the trees seemed to shift and stare. With shaky fingers, he hastily lit the lamp then peered into the darkness. All was still, yet his skin was prickled with goose bumps. Winfried was near. What would he find in the darkness?

Killian crept forward, breath shallow and quick. The ground sloped down to the gully, and his feet easily fell forward, faster than his heart willed. Too soon, the lump of leaves lay before him, and he stared, frozen, unable to move but unwilling to leave. The memory of that night rose, even as he fought to push it away: the shouts and cries, the cold fear and hot anger. And finally the dead silence. A lump balled in his throat, and his chest ached as his hands slowly brushed the leaves away from the dead man. He knew he shouldn't. His mind screamed for him to stop, but he needed to see.

Winfried stared back, preserved in the late-autumn chill, his open eyes dull and unseeing. Pale light cast his face in ghastly white, forever cold. No more warmth would ever flow in those veins. Killian's breath caught in his throat, and his hand shook, the tiny flame dancing. The body was hideous in the pale light, its countenance a contorted and frozen gasp. It was no longer Winfried at all. In one moment he had made sure of that. The haunting visage stared accusingly; he had stolen the life from him, and with it, any chance for Winfred's salvation. Killian looked now at the body and saw on that ashen face a reflection of his own heart, and he knew he was damned, as well. He would forever walk apart, separated from the Lord's light he once knew. All that awaited was damnation; a blight on his soul that would never be removed.

The preparations didn't take long: a candle at the head and foot and sides, in the shape of a cross; a white sheet, folded nearby, to cover. He knew what he must do, yet he stood still, staring at those dead eyes, unable to look away. Long moments passed and the moon slowly crossed the black sky as night deepened.

"Why did you do it?" he said finally. His eyes watered, and he didn't know if he was asking Winfried or himself.

"Please forgive me," he continued. "As I forgive you. And maybe the Lord will forgive us both… Though I know I don't deserve it."

With the rest of the body bare of leaves, he sprinkled it with holy water and covered it with the sheet. He had never performed a funeral before. His first one would be for the man he himself had killed.

"The Lord said, 'I am the resurrection and the life. He who believes in me will live, even though they die, and whoever lives by believing in me will never die.'" Killian made the sign of the cross. "'Because we know that the one who raised the Lord Jesus from the dead will also raise us with Jesus and present us with you to himself… So we fix our eyes not on what is seen, but on what is unseen, since what is seen is temporary, but what is unseen is eternal.'"

He covered the body again with wet leaves and dead twigs. The white sheet was hidden under black and brown, and everything looked again as forest floor.

"This body is committed to you, oh, Lord. By the power of your word, you calmed the seas at Galilee. Please calm the turbulent seas of this one's heart. And mine…" His words faltered and his voice grew shaky. It seemed a paltry service against the weight of such suffering. "I'm sorry Winfried," he said. "I don't know what else to say."

Slowly Killian walked along the southern road. The dark night held the wood in still quiet, and the forest seemed like an empty waste of lost souls and he was lost among them. Was this purgatory? Had he died? The bare trees of winter stood like sentinels in this twilight land, neither living nor dead, and long shadows stretched as the night grew old. Yet still he tarried, the thought of returning to his tiny room too much to bear.

The sound of hooves came from the distance. A deer crossing in the night? But it grew louder. It wasn't a deer— it was a horse and cart! Killian dashed into the wood and hid in the shadows of the trees, his heart racing—who would be traveling at night and why?

The cart drew to a stop almost at his feet, and he froze, deathly still. The dark horse snorted impatiently and stomped, gumming at the bit. Its large black eyes gleamed in the moonlight and stared directly at him.

"You did a poor job packing the wagon!" It was Florian's voice, dark and thin. "Be quick and fetch it. Pack it up right this time!"

A shadow jumped from the side and stooped, hefting and grunting. Something had fallen from the wagon, and the figure strained to heave it back in again.

"When you see him, say not a word. Only speak when spoken to and avert your gaze," Florian directed, as the second figure climbed back into the wagon. "And remember, if you can't follow something as simple as that, there are other, less pleasant uses for you."

He cracked the whip and the wagon jolted, clopping out of sight. Killian gasped, his lungs filling with the cold night air. Long seconds passed in the dark as his heart raced.

A soft rap came at the door. Ambrose looked up from his desk, which was strewn with papers. *It can't be Albrecht*

again. The door creaked open, and Killian peered back nervously from the hall, glancing to make sure no one was watching.

Ambrose waved. "Come in! Come in!"

Killian glanced about the room, relieved to see it tidier now. Dust had been swept from the corners, and the bottles and plates had been cleared. The only clutter now were papers still stacked here and there—obviously notes from the book. Ambrose seemed more himself; his bruises, yellowed and faded, were mostly gone. His eyes even seemed sober.

"You look better… Clear," Killian said.

"I am," Ambrose said. "I threw that damn medicine away. I'm feeling more myself."

"And what about the alcohol? Did you throw that away, too?"

Ambrose scowled, hurt at the insinuation. Similar things had been said to his father. "I'm fine! I mean, yes…mostly. What about you? I'm sorry, with everything that happened, I wasn't in my right mind to say this before, but thank you for saving me."

"I'm fine," Killian looked away dismissively.

Ambrose paused. Was that a flash of anger in the young priest's eyes? He had every right – more than every right. Yet it was strange to see him thus. Ambrose wished he could comfort him, but could think of no words to say and let it go. "Killian, I've been meaning to ask… Did you tell Annaliese I was here?"

Killian shuffled nervously. "I did. Did she come to see you?"

Ambrose frowned, as if struggling to remember. "I…don't know."

Awkward silence fell on the dark room, and Killian looked away uncomfortably. "Here." He handed him a burlap bag. "Here is that…*thing* you wanted."

Ambrose took it, holding it awkwardly. He opened his mouth to speak but thought better.

"Why do you want *that?*" Killian asked, shaking his head. "I'm really starting to worry about you."

"Don't. I'm fine. Just…don't tell Tobias."

"I can't stand this anymore, Ambrose," Killian said. "I don't know what's real or not, and the longer I'm here, the further I stray. I need to go home."

"I know. And I'm sorry." Ambrose sighed. "It won't be much longer."

"I overheard Florian and another on the trail last night. They were taking a cart to see someone—someone they didn't want anyone else to know about," Killian said and sighed. "I don't think you'll rest until this is done."

He opened the door to leave.

"Killian," Ambrose called out. "Don't tell Tobias!"

The door closed and he was alone. The world around him lay in dark silence. Only the yellow lamp flickered, the black smoke of kerosene thick and pungent. Ambrose reached into the rough burlap, his fingers squeamishly searching until he found the soft smoothness of feathers. He placed the dead raven on the desk.

A tiny black eye stared at him accusingly. In the dark, it seemed to move and follow, and he thought he saw the tiny beat of a heart. *No, it's cold and still. Dead for days.* He turned the wick high, and the room brightened as he drew the mortician's blade. Grimacing, he set to work.

The blade cut cleanly in old flesh. The slime of oil coated Ambrose's fingers, but the blood had gone hard some time ago. Tiny bones cracked as he wrenched the blade forward, while all the while the eye still stared. He shuddered and closed it. Soon the heart lay cold and hard on the desk, placed next to a pile of thorns from a hawthorn tree.

The gaping hole stared at him, and in a wave of nausea he tossed the raven out the window in disgust. He wiped his hands to be rid of the feel, but the oil wouldn't come off. Gritting his teeth, Ambrose opened the book and suddenly understood why it was so grimy.

He took a thorn. It was thin and hard in his hand as he leaned forward, staring. *Lord, what am I doing? How is this God's work?* He desperately hoped the purity of his purpose outweighed the sin of the method, and he hesitated. There would be no turning back from black magic. His soul would be as forfeit as those witches burned in the fires. Surely the Lord would understand? He began, softly, to chant.

"*Adibaga, Sabbaoth, Adonay...*" He pierced the heart with the thorn.

"*Qui sussum mediator...*" Another thorn.

"*Landa zazar valoi...*" Another.

After seven he stood, hands outstretched. "The person whose black magic and evil have tormented this town, I call their name to be revealed. Is it Valentine or Anselm who holds Bishop Stephan hostage?"

The heart sizzled and sputtered in the flame as he held it to the lamp. Fat dripped, crackling on the wick and dropping, slick, onto the table. He held it above a chamber pot of water, letting the gamey oil pool on the water's surface as the book instructed. Thick smoke filled the room, bringing the smell of burned and rotten flesh. Gagging, Ambrose opened the window, but the smell lingered, hanging on his clothes. Still he held it to the flame. The heart grew charred, and white ash fell to the table until finally nothing was left.

As the dawn broke and dim light crested the horizon, Ambrose swept the ash into the chamber pot filled with the water and the drops of thick oil, stirring it all together.

"Ravens are the keepers of secrets," he intoned. "Show me your secret. Who has taken Stephan?"

He dipped clean paper into the water and watched as the ash and oil soaked, spreading across its white surface. He whisked it in and out and held it to dry. The ash and oil traced the page in squiggles and lines. But there was no name. *There is no name!*

"Damn it!" he cried. There was no name. The book had lied. He collapsed into the chair.

Cold raven fat stuck tacky to his hands, rank and rancid, and the air was thick with the smell of charred, rotten flesh. He was exhausted. And still there was no name. He hung his aching head in frustration. Nearby, the floors creaked and dressers banged in neighboring rooms as other guests dressed for the day. A door squeaked open in the hall, and heavy steps stopped short. "Jesus, what is that smell?

November 27, 1859

Your Eminence Cardinal Eberhard,

Please forgive yet another report. Surely this shall reach you when we are already long underway and the danger has passed. Yet it is in all of our best interests to keep you fully apprised of the situation, in light of Fr. Ambrose's assignment to the new parish upon our return.

I fear this delay has worked ill upon him. The backward beliefs of this town eat at his wits, and I fear our prolonged delay may very well have a lasting impact. This is to be pondered over, as a fitting station must be found when he returns.

Our dear Father is given to long days on end remaining sequestered in his room, refusing both food and drink. It does not help that the doctor has clouded his mind with laudanum and who knows what else. It should be a wonder that he doesn't develop a habit for it and become as one of those wretched and infirm souls, languishing in a torpid haze, their strength of will and character fading as the body weakens.

But what is worse is that he pours what little strength he does have into unholy books most foul and filled with dark arts. It is not bad enough that he is consumed by the questionable stories of Brother Clement, but I am quite convinced there is more—handwritten notes tucked within those pages, filled with spells and incantations and various occult and forbidden practices.

It is true, this town—this land—mirrors a certain darkness. The doubts one brings seem to grow, and a meanness enters the heart where it was unknown before. Yet Ambrose seeks it out as well. This has always been his nature, it seems. He seeks to bring such darkness into light, yet I fear it shall do naught but drag him to the darkness instead—a darkness of doubt.

St. Gregory reveals a temperament heretofore unacknowledged, least of all by Father Ambrose. There is a dark and morbid fascination, justified by a certain holy righteousness, yet at its heart driven by a curiosity far different. I fear it will take but a nudge to waken that which has been long buried. And then we may lose him. Until such day arrives, or until the day of our long-awaited departure, I shall watch him keenly and beckon him from that ledge.

Yours in Christ,

Father Tobias Schenk

"Are your bags packed?" Tobias asked Killian. Thick fingers parted the drab yellowed curtain as he stared suspiciously out the window.

"They were packed a week ago."

Clothes lay folded on the patchwork quilt of Ambrose's bed. Books and pens and notes were stacked neatly on the desk, along with an old Bible and, on top, the book.

Tobias eyed Ambrose. "You're looking patched up and there's not much hint of bruising. I doubt anyone in town would even notice. And it seems you can walk finally."

"Sore still," Ambrose said. "But travel will do me good. I just have scraps of paper for the fire and then all is taken care of." As he sifted through odds and ends in his bag, his hand fell to the giant feather, caressing its smoothness.

Tobias frowned. "It'll be good to leave."

"I wish I had figured it out," said Ambrose. "There's so much that's not right."

"Be happy you get to leave at all!" Tobias chided. "Remember, others haven't. You could be in a shallow grave in the woods instead of Winfried, and then something most definitely wouldn't be right. Not right at all! Don't press your luck where you're not wanted."

"You don't feel like we've left things undone?" asked Ambrose. "We were supposed to find Stephan."

"We know he's still here," Tobias reminded him. "And you'll alert the authorities in Milwaukee. You haven't given up. But you must be smart, not foolhardy. This town is getting the best of you, and Killian can endure no more. He may never forgive himself."

"I feel—" Ambrose started.

"I will leave you here if you are not on the wagon to Kiel in the morning!" Tobias yelled, his eyes glaring.

"All right." Ambrose sighed. "Let me attend to some things."

Tobias nodded. "I'll get the tickets."

The hall felt strange and unfamiliar. Yellow sun lit the floor at the bottom of the stairs in waves of worn, brown grain—more sun than Ambrose had seen in weeks. The large hall was empty, the morning travelers having long since departed, though the sweet smell of bacon and biscuits still permeated the air. Harold Fessler stood tallying at the bar, a nub of pencil in hand. The room was silent but for the scratch of quick figures on rough paper. Ambrose took a breath. The floor creaked as he stepped into the dining hall for the first time in a month.

"Father." The man glanced from the bar, an eye raised over his thick mustache. "I didn't hear you come in last night. I see you're back from Walders. Good. I was about to rent out your room. I thought you might have skipped town."

"Without giving you your fine clothes back?" Ambrose laughed scornfully. "I would never!"

"Ah, haven't lost your wit, I see." Mr. Fessler turned back to his numbers. "I reckon you bought those clothes by now. You already paid more for them than what they cost new."

"Then I should expect you owe me," Ambrose said.

"Hm," he grunted, tugging at the end of his mustache with thick fingers. "I'll be sure to take it out of your bill."

"I'm sure you will. Tally that bill up today, if you don't mind. I'll be leaving in the morning."

"So soon?" he said, not bothering to look up. "Well, I should miss your pleasant company."

Ambrose sighed, ignoring him. He tossed the ragged stack of papers on the bar. "Kindling for the stove."

"Hm?" Mr. Fessler glanced up and squinted. The ashy, oily paper of the spell lay on top, squiggled lines tracing in odd patterns. He picked it up and held it to the light. "Doodling maps now?"

Ambrose's brow pinched. "What?"

"This map of Chilton," he said. "It's not terrible. But you certainly didn't miss your calling. Stay a priest; you're likely better at it."

"Chilton?"

"Well, you drew it!" Mr. Fessler scowled. "Don't get huffy with me. I'm just telling you what I see. It's certainly not Walders."

"Right." Ambrose paused, and took the map back, holding it carefully in his hands. "Thanks for reminding me! Please excuse me. I've forgotten I've some place to be!"

Ambrose burst into the street, the door rattling as it slammed shut. Behind, Harold Fessler shook his head. A piercing wind woke Ambrose and painted his cheeks rosy red and he felt more alive than he had in weeks.

The spell worked! The dark arts were real. He didn't know how he had gotten the spell wrong and why it had given him a map and not a name. But it had worked nonetheless. And if this spell worked, so would others. He knew where Bishop Stephan was being held. What was more, he was beginning to understand the cause of the town's sickness.

✠

CHAPTER 26

The Nachzehrer

November 28, 1859

"What do you mean you're going to find Issa?" Tobias peered from behind the post office, checking the street. After Winfred's death, it was best not to be seen too often, especially with Ambrose acting so unpredictably. Out of sight was out of mind, and they hoped to remain so, until they could finally leave. Cold drizzle clung to the few remaining hairs on his head and muddied the ground, as the last of the autumn leaves swirled in gusts, rustling about the corners of old crates and barrels, left to rot. The clomp of hooves echoed off the rough walls, mingling with shouts and calls for lunch. He shook his head. "Issa's dead."

"I know," said Ambrose. "But it's the only thing that makes sense. I can't rightly explain it. If I try, you'll think I'm crazy. We should just go and see."

"If you can't explain it, maybe you are crazy and maybe it only sounds like a good idea in your head." Scowling, Tobias crossed his arms. "Maybe it's not worth doing."

"I know. I thought so too. But now I'm not so sure…" Ambrose's eyes were distant, and his voice trailed off. A dark shadow passed over Tobias; he had seen this look before, mostly when Tobias scolded underlings. He never expected to be on the receiving end of it.

Killian opened his mouth, anxious to break the tension, but closed it again and looked away. Uncertain and uncomfortable, he was for the moment forgotten.

"Nothing makes sense," Ambrose continued. "There's a sickness, but it doesn't have a name. It doesn't have the manner of any other known illness. It spreads but only to some. It's not the cold, damp miasma. If it were, everyone would have it. It occurs in families—Bernd and Claudia, for example—but not strictly so. It took the miller and the carpenter. If this sickness spread by breathing the same air, half the town would have it, but certainly not these four. The only relation they all had to one another is a close relation to tragedy—whether Issa's actual death or proximity to her home."

Tobias sighed. "So what?"

"So what sickness spreads like a curse? In our enlightened time, I can think of none."

"You're not a doctor."

"There are stories," Ambrose continued, "from the East: Bohemia, Moravia, Silesia. Stories of souls not at rest. I can't believe I'm even saying this, but nothing else makes sense. And"—he glanced away—"it's written about in the book."

"That damn book!" Tobias howled. He kicked the ground hard, and dirt knocked and sprayed on the old boards of the building.

"I know!" Ambrose pleaded. "But there must be something to it. I didn't believe it either, but I did a spell to find the one responsible. There was nothing else I could do—"

"You did a spell?" Tobias's eyes grew wide. "You're performing dark arts now? I'm sorry Ambrose, I cannot keep this from Cardinal Eberhard. I must recommend—no, I insist—that you undergo conversion and intervention at the abbey back home. I'll recommend to the cardinal that you be remitted to St. Peter auf dem Schwarzwald."

"But it worked!" Ambrose said. "Here is the map!"

"Those are just random squiggles!" Tobias crumpled the paper and threw it back.

"Listen!" Ambrose shouted. "The notes said, 'Coming from the pagan East, devouring after death, haunting the churchyard, villages plagued by mysterious deaths that look like a sickness but aren't, beginning in tragedy or violence.' All these deaths began after Issa's suicide. There's some evil magic at work. 'Haunting the darkened churchyard.' Isn't that the strange bowl of wine at Otto's grave? I think someone is trying to make all this come to pass."

"I won't entertain your wild delusions!" Tobias seethed, his black robes flapping as he shook his fist in the air. "Killian and I will tie you up to bring you back if we have to. It's not just Stephan. It's not just saving this town. Your very soul is at stake."

"What do we risk if I'm wrong?" Ambrose said. "We leave as planned and I forever look the fool. Probably I'll be assigned to a backwoods parish where I'll be promptly forgotten about. But what if I'm right?"

"Why?" Tobias roared, his crimson face inches from Ambrose. "Why would someone do this, even if it were possible and not monumental superstitious nonsense?"

"Mortification," Killian said softly.

"What?" Tobias said.

"Something Anselm said… I didn't want to tell you. He said the Association's work is a necessary evil—suffering to purify the soul, to hasten the coming of the Kingdom. He said, *We must through many tribulations enter the Kingdom of God.*" Killian made a disgusted face and looked away. The dong of the bell tolled the noonday Mass, solemn and sad in the distance, and the street beyond quickly grew silent and empty, as white flakes fell, swirling in gusts.

"I hate this place," Tobias said, pointing a finger at Ambrose. "And soon you'll be as crazy as them. So you'll dig up the body of that poor girl and what? Drive a stake through her heart?"

Ambrose buried his hands into his pockets. "I don't know."

"And what of disturbing the dead?" asked Tobias.

"She wasn't given a Christian burial, no matter what Valentine said. If we exhume her, we can rebury her properly."

"She is a suicide," Tobias said. "Her soul is unfit."

Ambrose threw his hands up. "Then what do you care?"

"My God!" Tobias fumed, spraying spittle. "Fine, we'll do this just to show you what a fool you've become. And after, it's St. Peter's for you or, even better, an asylum!"

Thin snow lay in patches on the forest floor. White flakes floated and danced on the light breeze, settling in the nooks of branches and frilly tufts of grass. Ambrose walked the western road alone. Tobias and Killian had left in anger, storming off to the hotel and leaving him to his troubled thoughts. He longed to be away, and his heart led him farther from town, into the quiet of the wilds.

The road became a muddy trail as it dove into the thick woods, and dried stalks of dock and goldenrod gave way to crowded underbrush. The forest held a brooding silence; the woodland creatures had bedded down, hiding from the steely skies of a coming storm.

With bowed head and sullen heart, Ambrose walked. As the weeks had turned into months, he recognized himself less and less. He struggled to remember, lines creasing his brow at distant memories of home, now faded and blurred: his mother in the kitchen, the nutty smell of bread wafting in the morning breeze; Monika dancing in the park, the summer sun bouncing off her golden hair. He fought to grasp it, but the image slipped through his fingers. He couldn't picture her face.

The abbey at Karlsruhe was a world away: its arched halls and stained glass; soaring voices and the organ filling those stone walls. Ambrose thought of the fond farewells and smiles of his brothers, now so long ago. *Am I lost?* He was entirely alone. He longed to be home, yet his heart lingered in this dreary place, and he felt a man apart and outside of everything he had once known. *Can I ever return?*

What was happening to him? Peculiar memories rose inside: feelings and impressions, somehow familiar. An odd nostalgia beckoned in the shadows of his mind, calling. It was a feeling he had not felt since he was a boy, wandering in the hills and forests. When did it awaken? With the spell? Or the ungodly nature of the town? Conviction had always driven him on, seeking ever the good and just, yet in his heart he could no longer tell what was light and what was dark. Had he ever really known?

The clop of a horse broke the silence, gray ears poking above the hilly trail. Ambrose quickly stepped behind an old oak, his back firm against the rough bark. Images of Florian and Winfried rose in his mind, and he held his breath as the *clip-clop* grew closer then suddenly stopped. A rider dismounted.

"That's a dreadful hiding spot."

He jumped as a finger poked his ribs. Annaliese stood giggling at him, cheeks red from the cold as she stood bundled in a blue felt coat.

"Oh, thank God." Ambrose sighed. "You almost gave me a heart attack!"

"I could never do such a thing." She laughed. "Still, it's good to keep a man on his toes." She smirked and Ambrose looked away, his face hot. *Why does she fluster me so?*

"Well, you look better," she said. "You actually have color."

"I took your advice. I threw the laudanum away."

Annaliese nodded. "Good. So who were you hoping not to come across in the woods just now?"

"Hopefully no one real. I've had strange thoughts in my mind lately. You're not afraid to be alone in the woods with so many recent deaths?"

"This is not the place I am afraid of." Her eyes were suddenly fierce, surrounded by hair blown wild in the gusty wind. But the next moment she softened and was a young woman again. Was it a trick in Ambrose's mind? She seemed both here and not, and he blinked, fearing she might disappear. He longed to touch her, to be sure, but instead he turned away.

"I have to leave," he said, his throat tight. "In the morning. To Milwaukee or Fond du Lac. Although Tobias may insist I leave this country entirely."

"Oh. I see." She looked away.

"I don't want to. I don't think my job is finished here. But Tobias insists. He worries I've fallen into un-Christlike ways. I'm sure to face harsh discipline when I return home. It will be worse if I fight it."

"You have to follow your heart." Annaliese sighed. "At least do that."

A flurry of snow danced in gusts, falling on her black hair and about her neck. Ambrose's thoughts drifted again to longings and imaginings of a life that might have been. His chest grew tight as they stood in silence.

"I want to solve this," he said finally. "What would your grandmother say about sorcerers? The *černokněžník?* How does one become one?" He flushed, embarrassed at the foolish sound of his words.

"By making a pact. An evil one."

"And what could a *černokněžník* do? Could it raise the dead?"

"He can do whatever the demon can."

"And have you seen one?" he pressed.

"You don't see the *černokněžník*. You only see what it does," she said. "Why?"

"There's something I need to do tonight."

"If you're hunting a *černokněžník*"— her eyes narrowed—"be careful."

Annaliese grew quiet. The coming winter storm stirred the branches above, whistling, as the wind blew cold on Ambrose's cheeks.

"So this is the last I will see you…" She reached behind her neck and untied the leather cord of an amulet—a green cloth bag, no bigger than a coin. It was old and worn and embroidered with stitching in the design of a knotted star with flames behind and, below, a coiled snake. "This was my grandmother's," she said, tying it around his neck. "To keep you safe."

Ambrose hesitated, not wanting to take such a precious memory, but knew he could not refuse such a gift.

"What will you do?" he asked.

"I will leave. I'll pack tonight. You reminded me of something. Something I don't want to forget. I'll always be thankful for that. I'll go wherever the line takes me."

"But—"

She kissed him softly, warm and moist lips on his cheek. "I'm stronger than I look."

Tobias and Killian and Ambrose found themselves in the cold dark forest, the wind howling and shrieking above. Their lanterns flickered yellow in the blustery gusts, threatening to go out, and heavy flakes of wet snow fell on their coats and about their necks. Cold water soaked their boots, where the heavy snow had melted on the sloshy ground, and their hands, wrapped fast around shovels and lanterns, ached against the bitter, damp chill.

"This is wonderful night to get sick," Tobias grumbled. "With any luck, we'll die on Christmas."

Killian buttoned his coat tightly and sniffed, the slush soaking the hem of his robes and creeping up his legs.

"See? The boy's gone and caught a cold already," he said. "Bishop Plank will bury you in your own shallow grave when his favorite nephew dies. Which is maybe better for you. You can avoid St. Peter's altogether."

"The boy's fine," Ambrose growled. "You can gloat about my suspension when I'm proven wrong."

"Humph. Won't take long, I imagine."

The trees thickened on the southern trail. The wood lay in darkness as black clouds hid the moon above; the pale sliver poked through the heavens, faint upon the fallen snow, only to hide again. Silently they walked, heavy feet squishing and stomping in the mud. Tobias slid on the slick trail, stopping to scrape the thick clay from his boots and cursing under his breath.

As they neared the Abbey of the Holy Ghost, the bare trees fell away and the trail opened on the meadow and graveyard. White snow fell on winter's dead grass that rustled and swayed in the wind. In the distance, the dark steeple gleamed in the pale light and a tiny flame flickered: a candle in the abbey, a brother at his nightly prayers. The crosses and stones of the nearby cemetery were decked in crowns of soft white. Ambrose's heart pounded and he looked away, memories of the fateful night of his attack still fresh in his mind.

"I wouldn't have thought you'd be so eager to walk this path at night after what happened last time," Tobias said. "You know, after you almost died."

"Killian, are you all right?" Ambrose said, ignoring the older priest. But Killian was silent.

"Issa's not buried in the graveyard," Tobias said. "So where are we going?"

"In a glade, to the south. Not far," Ambrose explained. "It was as close as they could get."

"How do you know that?"

"Albrecht told me."

"Now why would he ever do that?" Tobias shook his head. "You know, I think you encourage each other."

A deer trail, barely visible, ran south of the graveyard, deep into the woods. Brambles and prickly ash guarded the entrance, tearing at their robes and cutting at their flesh. Tobias leaned against an ash tree, arms crossed, while Ambrose hacked with a shovel. He paused and looked up, sweaty and tired.

"Oh, no." Tobias shook his head. "This is your adventure. You clear the way."

The path finally opened, and Ambrose stood, cold and wet on the other side. "There," he said. "It's just ahead."

"You know, vampires can't be killed at night." Tobias sneered, sarcastically. "You have to hunt them during the day."

"What? Are you serious?"

"How the hell should I know?" Tobias scowled. "You'll find out, I guess."

"What is your plan, Ambrose?" asked Killian. "What are we doing here?"

"We're trying to lay a soul to rest and stop the suffering of others," Ambrose said, shaking his head. "Has Tobias gotten to you too?"

"I just want to go home," he muttered.

"And what if it is some undead thing? Then what are you supposed to do?" Tobias said.

"The book"—Ambrose scowled as Tobias rolled his eyes—"The book says to place a coin in the mouth, a *viaticum,* to remind it that it's dead. Then it will stop."

"Ohhh. Does it have to be a gold coin? Or can it be silver? Copper? How about a wooden-nickel beer token? How much is the entry fee at the Pearly Gates these days?"

Tobias heaved a sigh. "A child could see this makes not an ounce of sense. You've gone soft in the mind. I think Winfried must have knocked a little water onto your brain."

"You know, I don't know that I'm right, and I don't want to be. I want to be sure," Ambrose said. "Anyway, we're here."

The dark wood opened onto a small glade, gently rolling. The dappled sun in soft green leaves would have been cheerful in the summer. Ambrose could picture Issa and Augustin, happy in the grass, staring at the blue sky. But the cold, dim light of winter's moon cast a macabre pall on the land.

A solitary mound rose in the middle, covered in soft white, a wooden cross, poor and bare of any name, stood above. The clouds parted slightly to bathe the land in ghostly light, and a heavy sadness fell upon them. The three priests approached in silence. Odd tracks crossed the snowy ground, and they saw the mound lay collapsed and broken open, dirt spilling all around.

"They couldn't even bury her deep." Tobias shook his head. "Now the scavengers have gotten her. What a heinous desecration, even for a suicide. They must not have even put her in a box. How else could anything have gotten to her? What an awful end to a short and tragic life."

Ambrose gazed into the hole, but only darkness stared back at him. His breath deepened as he breathed a sigh of relief. "Well, at least it's not what I thought." He turned. "I'm sorry. I'm sorry to both of you. Maybe you're right. Maybe my judgment is sorely clouded. Maybe this place is turning me into something I don't want to be." He took hold of Tobias's shoulder and looked him in the eye. "I'll go to St. Peter's. I'll ask for it myself."

Tobias nodded and smiled in pity. "We'll get you back. You're not so far gone."

Suddenly, leaves rustled in the distance and a branch cracked. They turned in alarm but saw nothing.

"I think maybe the scavengers are back," Tobias said. "There's nothing we can do. No point to rebury someone without a casket. Probably not much left anyway. Say a prayer if you like. But I think we've done all we can."

Ambrose stepped forward, hat in hand.

Just then, a growl rose in the darkness, throaty and hoarse, and the snap of twigs drew closer.

"Say it quick and let's go!" Tobias whispered.

A black shape darted in the dark. They whirled. The growl now came from the other side, a hoarse groan.

"What is that?" Killian cried.

"It's the Lord telling us to leave!" Tobias said. "We've overstayed our welcome. This isn't a fit place for people anymore. Leave it to the wolves and bears. Let's go!"

As they hurried to the trail, a blur of black flashed behind, knocking Ambrose down before darting away. Cold snow and mud soaked his robes, clinging as he sprang back up.

"What is that? It's not a wolf!"

"If it's a bear, we're not long for this world!" Tobias cried. "Damn your adventures, Ambrose!"

A shadow leapt again from the trees. This time Tobias tumbled to the ground, flailing as the dark shape pounced on top, clawing with gaunt limbs.

"Hey!" they cried, beating the thing with their hands. Ambrose's bloodied fists struck about its bony head. It paused and turned, staring. A thin face met his; dead eyes stared at him blankly. Withered, dry skin stretched tightly across skeletal cheeks while flaxen hair hung caked in grime. His heart dropping in fear, he stumbled as a hiss and groan rose from its black mouth, rank and rotten, and it swiped with a clawed hand across his cheek.

Tobias finally threw the thing off and struggled to his feet. "What is that?" he cried. But Ambrose could only stare, his face an unearthly shade of white.

They circled, backs together, staring into the darkness and inching toward the head of the trail. Burning pain traced Ambrose's jaw as hot blood dripped from his cheek down his neck. For the moment, all was still. Only the wind whistled in the trees.

"It's gone! Let's run!" Tobias cried.

They crashed toward the trail, fleeing the darkened glade. Thick trees loomed near, growing closer. They were almost there when a shape leapt from the shadows. Tobias stumbled, midstride, the monstrous thing on his back. Ambrose froze as the creature stared at him; pale light gleamed gray from sightless eyes. The thing seemed to laugh as its black mouth opened and lunged, and a howl of pain filled the glade as it bit into the old priest's neck.

Ambrose and Killian charged, beating the creature with sticks and rocks. Branches cracked across its back, and in a bloodcurdling cry that split the night, it leapt into the darkness and was gone.

Tobias lay still. His glassy eyes stared at the sky, unblinking as hot blood steamed in the snow. "Tobias!" They shook him. "Tobias!"

"Is he...?" Killian said.

"Dead..." Ambrose whispered. "He's dead..."

They stared, blinking. The storm wailed and shrieked around them, white snow blinding against the black night. Branches cracked and shook above, yet they couldn't move and the passing moments seemed to last forever.

As they stood in silence, a cry of rage rose in the dark.

"Ambrose!?" Killian cried. "Ambrose, let's go!"

They turned to run, but the figure stood blocking the trail. They could finally see her now, in the moonlight. A summer dress hung loosely on her bony frame, torn as if gnawed at the edges, with large patches missing.

"Oh my God! It's Issa!" Killian cried.

Ambrose dug into his pack, frantically searching, his hands finally touching metal. He drew the mortician's blade.

Fear dragged him to the ground, shaking his knees. A verse rose in his mind. His voice shook as he cried, *"Et ipsi vicerunt illum propter sanguinem agni et propter verbum testimonii sui et non dilexerunt animam suam usque ad mortem! They overcame by the blood of the lamb and by the word! Ecce Crucem Domini! Behold the cross of the Lord!"*

A garbled sound rose, like a laugh. Issa dropped to all fours, foaming and snarling as she made ready to charge. A flash streaked forward. Pale eyes raced toward Ambrose, dead and empty. His hand shook, holding fast the blade, and his heart pounded in his chest. She was almost on him. Darkness flashed and his mind reeled. He reached for the cross around his neck, but to his surprise, he didn't find the cold metal of the crucifix. Instead, his hand clutched the warm soft fabric of Annaliese's amulet. A strange feeling welled inside him. It was not faith but rather a moment of courage and anger, where before there had been only fear.

He stood his ground as she leapt. The blade pierced deep. A gurgled cry rose, pained and awful and the creature fell to the ground kicking. It bared its fangs and, sneering, raced into the cover of darkness. Ambrose looked at his hand. Fresh blood covered the blade. Fresh blood from this dead thing.

Ambrose and Killian ran into the night as fast as they could. Branches slapped and tore but they didn't feel them. The pale meadow opened, the lumps of graves in the distance swallowed under a flurry of snow. Finally they cast themselves behind the headstones, huffing and gasping, wide eyes peering fearfully toward the dark wood. Long minutes passed as their hearts pounded in their chests. Killian lay frozen in fear and trembling.

"Hey!" Ambrose shook him. "Are you all right?"

"What was that?" he cried.

"A *nachzehrer*. I don't think it's following us. I stabbed it with the knife."

"That was Issa!"

"It was. But it's not anymore."

"You knew!"

"I only read the book," Ambrose said. "I tried to tell you."

"Tobias is dead!" Killian shouted. "We should have just left!"

Ambrose hung his head as hot tears burned his cheek. His chest ached, as if cold hands squeezed his heart. Tobias was dead because of him. "I have to go back."

"What? No!"

"I have to make sure."

"Ambrose, don't leave me!" Killian screamed. His face was ashen, and in the dark he looked like a specter.

"Go back!" Ambrose said. "Run back to the hotel as fast as you can! When you get there, lock the door! If I'm not back in the morning, board a train for Boston or New York, whichever is cheaper. Don't stop in Toledo. Don't take a boat. There's money enough for fare in my room. In Tobias's there's sure to be more. Don't wait! Head east. Write the cardinal if you have to. Stay at abbeys and inns where you can, but get out!"

"Ambrose, don't leave!" Killian called out. But his black robe already had faded, lost in the darkness.

As Ambrose neared the glade, he slowed, listening for the crunch of snow or snap of twigs. He crouched, waiting, searching in the night, but there was nothing. An age passed in silence. Finally he crept forward, inch by inch. Cold fingers of wind caressed his neck, searching for his warm heart, but he didn't notice.

In the darkness, doubt entered his mind. He couldn't possibly move Tobias's heavy body. And he had nothing with which to perform a service or to bury him. The shovels were long lost in the darkness. Yet his chest ached to see him one last time. *To do what?*

He stepped into the glade as the light of the morning poked over the eastern horizon, pale white in the empty branches and sparkling on the new snow. White powder hid all the night's tracks. It covered the grave and its hole. It covered the red blood, spilled on the ground. The thing was gone. Ambrose turned, looking here and there, running and whirling round and round. There was no body!

PART III
Wasuskeqsinoh

☩

CHAPTER 27

Love and Loss

December 1, 1859

Ambrose sat in the dark of the fading afternoon. Sleet pattered softly against the window of his room, splattering in slushy drops on the open sill, while tattered curtains blew in the wind. He stared into the heavy clouds of the steely sky. Winter's chill crept across his bare skin and icy sleet fell wet on his bare feet, but he didn't notice.

Why didn't I leave?

A lump balled in his throat that he couldn't cough out, and he tried to swallow it with whiskey. It burned his throat and he coughed, the bottle sloshing in his hand and spilling in his lap. Though he vowed to give it up after that horrid night in the graveyard and his descent into laudanum stupor, he found himself drawn to the numbing comfort once more. *I am not so different from my father, after all.* He had tried to talk to Killian, to make him understand. But the young priest's eyes had flashed betrayal. Grief stricken, he had run away, disappearing into the wet, cold white of the storm.

We will never be the same.

Hot tears rolled down his cheeks. Tobias was dead, his body gone, taken and desecrated by some infernal thing. Eaten. There would be no funeral. What could he possibly tell them back home? They were meant to watch over one another and he had failed.

He scribbled feverishly. The metal nib of his pen scratched across the rough paper, shaky and unsteady, as hasty words poured into his report: a confession. Black ink flowed, blotted and splotchy from tears on the page.

Evil isn't created. It follows.

The book hadn't prepared him. He hadn't believed, not really. Even after the *inaemehkiwak*. Even after the spell. Not until he had seen Issa's dead eyes, searching and hungry. What a fool he had been.

How could God allow this?

The pen clattered to the desk, falling from his hand, and he sat back as the room spun. Someone had caused this. Through dark arts, someone had brought this thing into being. A man of the cloth. *How can this be?* A darkness crept into his heart, even as he fought to push it away: doubt.

A knock came at the door.

Ambrose shrank from the sound, desperate to flee and hide, and he gripped the arms of the chair, knuckles white, as the room grew tight and narrow.

"Ambrose?" the voice whispered.

He stumbled to the door, his legs threatening to give out with each wobbly step. Finally he gripped the cold knob tight and, holding his breath, cracked the door open. Annaliese stood before him, pale against the gloom. Her hazel eyes met his and she blushed as she glanced nervously down the hall. Her eyes grew wide as she took in the room, dark in the gray of the storm. The biting smell of whiskey was everywhere, and on the desk, a half-empty bottle sat beside the scribbles of an open journal. Cold sleet fell on the floor in slushy drops and pools. Annaliese entered and closed the window, pretending not to notice.

"How is it you always find me like this? You're the only one…" Ambrose started, embarrassed. "I thought you were leaving this place?"

"Mr. Baumgartner declined to sell me a ticket on account of my upbringing and my parents' good name." She rolled her eyes. "I saw Killian… Oh, Ambrose, I'm so sorry!"

"What did he tell you?"

"He…only told me Tobias died."

"Did he tell you I killed him?" he asked her. "I wouldn't leave and I wouldn't let them go. Now my friend is dead." He sat on the bed, his head in his hands. His lips trembled and he looked away, lest he break down in front of her. "I thought I knew. I thought together we could… I thought goodness would prevail."

"But it's not your fault!"

"How could God let such things be?" His chest grew tight as anguish washed over him. The world was empty and cold, and he was lost in the middle, his vows and faith hollow and meaningless. The room spun, and he fell against her, sobbing, forgetting all shame.

Annaliese squeezed his hand and smiled sadly. There was nothing she could say. No words would ease the pain or make sense of it. She stroked his hair and sang in a gentle voice, soft and sweet. It was a tongue he didn't know— perhaps a lullaby or an old folk song—strange yet comforting. In her soft embrace, he felt the blessing of sweet forgiveness.

> *Snívaj sa ti sníčok, ach snívaj,*
> *keď vstaneš, sníčoku vieru daj,*
> *že ťa ja milujem,*
> *srdečko svoje ti darujem.*

He sank into her lap, smelling her warmth, feeling the rise and fall of her breath, the gentle rhythm and flow. Annaliese drifted in and out of focus as her soft voice soothed. As she held him in her eyes, the pain in his heart was forgotten. He felt a saving grace in her warmth where there had been only misery before.

He reached to touch her face, his hand rising to her meet her soft lips. Her breath quickened, but she didn't pull away. Her skin was soft beneath his hands. He had never touched a woman before. Not like this.

With a trembling hand, she undid the ties of her blouse and her breasts fell free. His fingers felt their supple smoothness and he paused, afraid and uncertain. She squeezed his hand to her chest and his heart fluttered—he lost himself in her, and in that moment felt whole again. They fell back upon the bed, his arms firm around her and lost in a tangle of soft hair.

In the early morning, Killian stood outside Ambrose's door. Something made him pause—a feeling. Something was off. He opened the door a crack and peered cautiously into the room. The old hinges squeaked as the door opened to the sunny floor, filled with morning light. The room was a mess of crumpled papers and bottles, overturned and rolled against the walls and in the corners, and clothes lay strewn about. The stale smell of liquor wrinkled his nose. He saw Ambrose's bags weren't packed. His cassock lay in a wrinkled pile and, beside it, a fabric of soft pale blue with an edge of white lace.

He stared, confused. Where had he seen that fabric before? That was…

The sheets stirred. Ambrose turned in his sleep, the blanket falling to his side. A hand lay on his chest, small and delicate. Killian stepped back. This was the right room. But…

"Ambrose?" he whispered.

The hand stirred, pulling the blanket back. Wavy black hair spilled out in a tumble as Annaliese opened her sleepy eyes. Ambrose snored, naked beside her.

"Ambrose!" he cried.

Ambrose startled awake. The room blurred, unrecognizable. Killian stood in the doorway, eyes wide in shock. The warm comfort of black sleep broke in the cruel light of morning. Images flooded back. His heart sank with the memory of the past days. His head ached, and he tasted the sick sweetness of whiskey, tacky in his mouth. Piercing pain stabbed and twisted, clawing at his eyes, sharp reminders of the night before. He glanced at Killian, dizzy and confused. The young priest could only point.

Annaliese gathered the blankets around her, hiding under the old and worn, rag patches. Ambrose felt her body, hot against his side.

"Oh no!" He leapt from the bed. "Oh, no! No! No!"

"Ambrose?" Killian cried.

"No! This can't be! We can't have done this!"

Annaliese stared back, hurt. Red lips trembled as her eyes watered.

"Ambrose?" he said again.

"Get out of here, Killian!" Ambrose shouted. "Get out of here now!"

Soft sobs rose from under the covers. Small fists balled the sheets around Annaliese's head.

"Annaliese," Ambrose said. "We can't have done this. We can't!" He drew the sheets away and gently shook her. "Tell me we didn't!"

The blanket thumped as she threw it on the floor. Her small hands struck his chest, forcing him away as she stood naked before him. He looked away, but she grasped his chin, hard, and forced his eyes back, her porcelain skin flushed as she glared.

"Is this all I am to you?" she said. "A night's comfort?"

"I'm sorry," he stammered. "This can't be. I have vows!"

"To what?" she cried. "Where were those vows last night, when you needed them?"

"Was this your plan," Ambrose wailed, "when you said to look for a tragic death? Was this what you wanted all along? To make me lose my way?" His head reeled in hurt and anger, yet knew he was in the wrong and he regretted saying it.

The color drained from Annaliese's face and she grew deathly white. Her jaw clenched, cold and hard, and her hazel eyes bore into him, stabbing at his heart. Ambrose stepped back, suddenly afraid.

He heard it before he felt it. A crack like a gunshot popped in his ear. The room was still, frozen. Then the pain exploded across his cheek, red and scalding, as she smacked him as hard as she could. He fell to the floor naked, eyes tearing; he stumbled as he tried to stand. His ears rang and the room spun.

"I'm sorry!" he said.

"No!" she cried. "You don't get to look at me!"

She pushed him hard to the ground and he crashed into a pile of bottles that clinked and tinged, surely waking the whole floor. Annaliese hastily fumbled with her buttons before the door banged against the wall and she fled down the hall.

In the morning light, his room was painfully clear. It was filthy from the night before and he took in the mess of it all. His cheek burned and he closed his eyes in shame, wishing he could be away, far away, anywhere but here.

A floorboard creaked as Killian peered in. "Ambrose, what did you do?"

"I don't know."

"What do you mean?" Killian cried.

"I had a moment of weakness!"

"A moment of weakness!" Killian picked up Ambrose's crumpled robe and threw it at him. "A moment of weakness! Tobias is dead and you had a moment of weakness? Was this all for nothing? Was this terrible journey just for you to forsake all your vows? Does Tobias's death mean nothing to you?" He kicked a bottle hard against the wall. "Did he die for this?"

Killian's eyes flashed in anger; Ambrose had never seen him like this before. He fumbled with his robe. Why couldn't he get it on? His clumsy hands struggled blindly, trying to remember.

"What of Annaliese?" Killian pressed. "What of her reputation? What of her family? Do you care nothing of the consequences to her?"

"Stop," Ambrose pleaded. "Please stop!"

"We need to leave! Now! Before you ruin anyone else."

"Please…" Ambrose said. "Please Killian."

"The coach to Kiel leaves at noon," he said. "I won't endure another day in this place. I'm leaving. I expect you to leave with me."

Harold Fessler chewed the edge of his pencil absentmindedly. The slick ends of his oiled mustache wagged as he added figures. "Checking in September fourth. Checking out December first. $0.44 a day. Forty-eight days. $21.12. Thirty percent discount for the long stay brings it to $14.78."

"That's forty-seven days," Ambrose corrected. "But I'm not staying tonight. So that would make it forty-six."

"Humph." He scowled, scribbling. "Forty-six then would be…$20.24. Less thirty 30 percent is $14.17. Plus clothing rental for twelve and a half days at $0.05 per day is exactly $0.61, which would put it at… Oh, look at that…$14.78. And we shall all be ever so sad to see you leave." He handed him the receipt, a sneer raising the corners of his mouth.

Ambrose sighed, digging into his bag.

"What happened to your face?" Mr. Fessler said, looking at Ambrose's swollen cheek. "Never mind. I don't care."

"Five cents a day is criminal. I took you to be an upstanding gentleman not a gouger."

"Yes, it's such a shame that Mr. Gatterman was pigeon eyed and took forever to mend your robe. But I, as well, took you to be a priest, not a floater and a Johnnie," he said, scowling. "The whole hall smells of coffin varnish. Which you didn't have the decency to buy from me, mind you. And don't think I haven't heard what goes on in your room. What of her? What's she to do when you're gone? I've a daughter here too, you know. I'll be damn pleased to see you leave. You and your Willie-Boy companion."

Ambrose flushed, his ears bright red, as he dropped coins, clinking, on the old bar. The din of the kitchen was strangely quiet. Amalia's blond head spied from behind the door, eyes giggling. He couldn't see her, but he could feel her. He set the old clothes on the bar and shouldered his bag.

"Keep them." The barman tossed them back. "You've earned 'em."

Ambrose slowly walked the frozen street. He should have hurried, but his heart held him back. Harold Fessler was right. For all his good intentions, he had caused nothing but pain. How many more lives must he ruin? Tobias was dead. Annaliese was forever shamed. St. Gregory was still beset by death and disease. Stephan was still lost or imprisoned, and it was clear now a black sacrilege was at the heart of it all. *I failed. In everything I set out to do, I failed.* He knew if he boarded that coach, nothing would change; nothing would be redeemed. Stephan likely would die, if he hadn't already, and Annaliese would be forever outcast. Valentine and Anselm would have won, the town still under his sway. *Was it all for nothing?*

The church bell tolled solemnly. It was already noon. He spotted Killian pacing, some twenty yards away as the coachman in his weathered gray jacket stared at his pocket watch. The man glanced up, clicking it shut and tapping an old pipe against the worn sideboards. He was tall and thin, and maybe in his fifties; his oily brown hair was streaked gray, and even at such a distance, Ambrose could see he was missing several teeth and the rest were stained yellow. The brown morgan beside him snorted impatiently, anxious to stretch its legs; a moment later, it plopped hot dung, steaming in the frosty air.

"Right. All set then?" the coachman said. "I've places to be, when not shuttling around you *fainéants.*"

"I've already said goodbye to Meinhard," Killian said, placing Ambrose's bags in the wagon. "He's bound and determined to find you and have some kind of send-off. We have to leave now or we'll never be rid of here! I haven't spoken to Valentine; I don't want to see him. What would I say when he asks after Tobias? Let's just go. I have the tickets. The only thing for us to do is head to Kiel."

Ambrose stared at the ground, his heart heavy. "Killian, I'm not going to Kiel. I'm going to Chilton."

"What?" Killian threw up his hands.

"You were right. This can't be for nothing."

"Ambrose, please!"

"I'm sorry." He looked away. "I can't leave. Not yet."

The coachman cleared his throat, and the sideboards squeaked where he shook them in annoyance. "Listen, you two called a wagon. I'm taking you somewhere. Hurry up and figure it out so we can be on our way."

"Just take him," Ambrose said.

The man crossed his arms. "I was told there would be two fares."

"Fine! I'll pay you mine too, but just make sure he gets to Kiel."

"Ambrose, no!" Killian cried. "You're coming with me!"

"Listen," Ambrose said. "I failed. I failed everyone. I've lost my way… I can't go back like this."

"Damn it, Ambrose!"

"Go home, Killian. Get on the wagon and leave this all behind."

Killian turned to gaze at the winter sky. A lone crow circled above. It seemed always a crow was watching. What was it about this place that they could never leave? "What's the fare to Chilton?" he finally asked the coachman.

"Same distance. Same fare. Better for me, as it's closer to home."

"Then we'd better go."

"Killian, no! You're going home!" Ambrose said.

"Someone has to keep you alive." The young priest sighed. "Or I will have failed too."

"Killian, you should—"

"We're going to Chilton, goddamn it!"

✠

CHAPTER 28

The Road to Chilton

December 1, 1859

T he ancient woods rose all around them. Broad maples and towering elms spread their bare branches to the winter sky, and the barreled trunks and knotted arms grew ever thicker as they lost themselves in ancient forest. Silence blanketed the land, broken only by the clop of the horse and the creak of the wagon. Far from town, the dirt road narrowed to scarcely a trail, winding through the low marshlands. A bed of leaves lay so thick that Ambrose barely could tell where they were going or where they had been, and all about was an endless sea of brown that stretched in all directions.

Deep grooves and ruts cut the mud from travelers before. Frozen and hard, they struck the wooden wheels and the wagon jostled and lurched. The morgan snorted and grunted, pulling hard against the broken earth, and Ambrose and Killian cursed as they were tossed about. Ambrose held fast against the splintery wood, his knees and elbows banging against the sides, while the coachman bounced merrily in the spring seat, ignoring the cries and groans behind.

The sky grew dark and heavy flakes floated here and there, when finally the road rose and left the ruts and furrows of the frozen marsh below. He packed his pipe, and soon white smoke swirled in citrusy notes and hung about his weathered face, while a jaunty tune rose from his lips, falling in fits and starts with the lurch of the wagon.

"Sir," Ambrose said, clearing his throat, "How far is it to Chilton?"

"We take the Tote Road across the Kilnsnake Road to the Old Winnebago Trail. Should arrive nightfall." The old pipe clicked in his teeth and he scowled. "But you should know, the proper name for Chilton is Stantonville, not what some would-be English land baron would have you believe. You have not been here overlong, so I'll pardon your not knowing."

Ambrose raised a brow. "Would-be English land baron?"

"John Marygold. *Connard!* Thinks he can buy up the town and walk himself right in. Write himself into history. Erase the Stantons. Chilton"—he spat—*"nom très bête!* You know, he changed the name to honor his childhood home, Chilington. Couldn't even get the name right."

"Pardon me, but what is *your* name?" asked Ambrose. "Where are you from? I have not heard a French accent like that before."

"That's because I am not French," he said, laughing. "You don't know this country very well yet. I am Jean-Émile. My family is Porlier, from Montreal. But I was born in La Baie Verte."

"Oh, you mean Green Bay?"

"Ah…once the British took over," the coachman said, shaking his head. "At one time, things might have gone differently."

"Things always could have gone differently," Ambrose said, and stared miserably into the endless woods stretching into the distance.

"Who are the Stantons?" asked Killian.

"Eh? I might have forgot you were there, as quiet as you've been," said Jean-Émile . "Moses and Catherine. You cannot find a better man in all of Calumet County. Generous. God-fearing. A preacher even. And Catherine is a strong one. As clever as they come. Moses built the mill with his own hands. First negro in the county. First civilized man in the county, in fact. I don't know if he escaped or was emancipated. I don't rightly care. He built the mill and everyone else came."

They fell quiet again. The dense forest gave way to marshland, and a flurry of white flakes whirled all about them. The cattails and old grasses whispered in the wind, heavy under the weight of wet snow, and the clop of hooves echoed on the old bridge as they crossed a lazy creek. Ambrose's heart stopped; it was the same creek he and Silas had followed on their hunt of the Steinthal monster. It seemed a lifetime ago but was not more than a month and a half.

"Jean-Émile," he said suddenly, "has anything weird happened in the area lately?"

"Eh? You don't know the history here, do you? You'll have to be more specific."

"Well…anything that seems not quite right? Anything… not explainable?"

"You ask some odd questions," Jean-Émile said. "Plenty not right around here. But all explainable. I don't quite get what you're driving at. If you're after New World oddities, the Menomenee told of a giant winged monster in the area. I saw it once, years ago!" He turned and winked. "Some miles out west of the Kilnsnake. A great black monstrous thing with red eyes! It flew off with a yearling doe. Lucky it didn't have a taste for grown man, though I would be too stringy. But they do say it takes children that wander out. Moses and Catherine lost their young daughter not more than four years ago. Men from all around—Stantonville, Brothertown, Stockbridge—searched for days. But they never found the poor thing.

"Strange men and strange beasts and even stranger spirits find their way here. Some folk have seen even spirits or specters or revenants or the like. They say there's an old man in robes in the forest. An old man or a ghost. He walks the woods at night. No one knows why."

Ambrose leaned closer. "What else do they say?"

"Hm," Jean-Émile said, shaking his head. "There is always a quarrel with Gravesville. That's the town just across the river. It is the same town, almost. Ah, so sad. Leroy Graves is a pigheaded man but decent by most accounts. Still, the townsfolk were up in arms when they lost the county seat last year. I think the people have gone mad on both sides. Crops failed this year and livestock have fallen over dead. The Gravesvilleites say Stantonville salted their fields in the middle of the night and poisoned their cattle. And Stantonville says they burned down the church and the mill and some hay barns."

"That's awful" Ambrose said.

"Ah, it is. And you know, the weirdest thing, the food from the land seems not as good now. It's bland, doesn't have life anymore. Even the beer has gone sour. I don't know what it is, but joy has left. No one smiles. But I suppose with so many sick that is to be expected."

"What are they sick with?" asked Ambrose. He looked urgently to Killian, who scowled and looked away.

"Who is to say? The young and old alike, they are simply enfeebled." The coachman cracked the reins as they rounded a bend and started up a small hill. "But you know what is worse? There are prowlers in the night who take advantage, robbing the very graves of those just dead. I tell you true, that ground is disturbed and bodies dug out. Ah, what a world. Can you fix such people? I think even priests like you cannot. *Pisser dans un violon!* So they say. A waste of time."

He lit his pipe again and gummed it in thoughtful silence. The sweet smell of tobacco wreathed and wafted around his old felt hat, warm and comforting in the cold air.

As dusk rose, yellow lights twinkled in the distance, lamps and fires flickering in the town's windows. The forest fell away, opening to a bare field of stumps and brush. The thumps of axes echoed in the distance as trees fell and crashed. A great fire rose, crackling, high into the darkening sky. Men surrounded, throwing in branches and boughs as smoke wove through the air.

"What a brutal sight!" said Killian. "Do they need to tear it up so? It reminds me of home. All the trees are cut down in Heitersheim. Such a shame."

"Yes, they are always clearing the forest here," Jean-Émile said. "Soon there will be none left. Like so much that is now gone. Not just trees, the old ways, too. They say they are an industrious people and their labor is a heavenly virtue, but in truth they only live for today."

The town rose up around, out of the fallow fields of winter. The foundry roared and clanged, filling the air with the din of metal and black coal smoke, acrid and heavy. The *ting-ting* of a bell rang in the distance, calling for dinner and men closed their doors and locked up for the day. Ambrose marveled at the size of the town as he looked at the shops; Anton Bell ~ Wagon Maker; E. Nellessen & Sons, Blacksmithing, etc.; E. Guck Beer Saloon. The street stretched on, dimly lit by the lamplighter making his rounds, as men in wool suits and hats strolled the evening, their wives holding fast their arms.

"The Westen House is just ahead," Jean-Émile said. "It is a stagecoach stop, but also a hotel. You can eat there, too, but the food down the street at Gutheil's Saloon is much better. The Westen House is for lovers of kraut and caraway. You'll not likely wish to share a room after."

The wagon slowed as it neared the hotel. The giant wooden doors of the stable hung open and old straw spilled into the street, the smell of manure rolling out to greet them. A young man leaned against the door, cigarette in hand. He squinted and rubbed his stubbly face as the cart drew close.

"Francis will tan your hide, he catches you smoking in the barn!" Jean-Émile yelled.

"Ach!" the man spat. "Piss off, ya old Canuck. What do you know anyway?"

"Jiri Neidl, you put that out now!"

"Ya? And what will ya do if I don't?"

Jean-Émile's face turned red and he hopped from the carriage. A long stride took him to within inches of Jiri's face. The young man sniffed and spat, puffing out his chest. Jean-Émile glared and feigned a strike to the left. The man dodged, but a giant calloused right hand boxed him hard in the ear.

"Ay!" Jiri cried, tumbling and bleeding as the cigarette fell, red-embered into the straw.

Jean's gristled hand yanked him up and threw him against the door, grabbing the cigarette from the shit and piss of the ground.

"Oh, ho ho! Not so tough, ah?" Jean-Émile stubbed the glowing end out on Jiri's forehead. Bright bits of ember fell in the young man's eye and spilled down his face. "Ah, you fucking whelp! *Bébé triste! Pathétique!* Go home to your mother. I catch you here again, Franz will do you worse."

Jiri cried out and held his head, stumbling as Jean-Émile dropped him to the floor. He scurried as the coachman kicked his backside hard, and the three men watched as he ran down the street.

"Ah, what can I say?" Jean-Émile shrugged. "These children, they think they are men."

"Only a fool smokes in a barn," Ambrose said.

"A fool indeed."

They grabbed their bags and looked up. Yellow moonlight illuminated the window; the words WESTEN HOUSE glinted, etched in leaded glass. "Here we are." Ambrose said.

"Would you like to buy a paper, sir?" a voice said.

Ambrose turned. A girl, not more than seven, stared back at him, newspaper in hand. Her curly red hair poked from beneath a ratted bonnet, and she smiled, a newspaper in her dirty hands: the Chilton Times-Journal. He glanced briefly: "Bray Warns of Depression in '57."

"No, child," he said. "Your newspaper is two years old! But here, take this." He dropped a half cent into her hand.

She reached out to touch his robe, pawing and grasping. "Black is my favorite color," she remarked, her eyes growing wide. Her face became a ghastly smile, and Ambrose stepped back, alarmed at the change.

"You are not the Ambrose I remember," she murmured. "You are a demon wearing his skin."

"How do you know my name?" Ambrose recoiled. "Who are you?"

"My name is Consequence." She turned, giggling. Her pigtails whirled in a flash, and she skipped down the street.

"What is with that child?" Ambrose cried. "She is as if possessed!"

"Eh?" Jean-Émile turned. "Her? Who knows? The children today, they are all terrible. I do not even listen anymore."

Ambrose and Killian looked to each other eyes wide in alarm. The girl was gone, but a strange feeling lingered in the air.

"Very well, here you are." Jean-Émile tipped his hat. "I bid you adieu."

Their bags secure in their room, they wandered the bustling streets. Men in top hats walked arm in arm with women in frilled dresses and mink hand warmers. Steel-tipped canes click-clicked on the brick streets, and men tipped their hats. "Good evening, Fathers."

A carriage passed. The sleek brown horse clopped, snorting as it pranced merrily in the night, and the driver clucked as he gummed a cigar, filling the air with the white smoke of sweet tobacco.

"This is nothing like Gregorstadt!" Killian exclaimed. "This is what I had thought to see in the New World."

"Fortune seems to have skipped that town completely," Ambrose said. "This is a totally new world. It has some Old World culture but not the heavy depression or troubles of our time. I'd almost forgotten they called this the land of opportunity. This downtown seems like some of the older towns of the East, even."

The sweet smell of a dining hall wafted toward them: succulent meats and the cinnamon and spice of some rich dessert. Gutheil's Saloon lay ahead, bright light dancing in the leaded glass as the clatter of plates and laughter spilled into the street. The glimmer of white china shone through the glass, among the reds and blues of opulent dresses, and a man on the stoop checked the time, pausing to squint at Ambrose's ratty, mended robes.

Killian shook his head, confused. "This doesn't look like a saloon."

"No, it doesn't," Ambrose said. "It looks expensive. I don't think we can afford this! Not after being gouged at the ST. GREGOR."

"It figures. Our only trip to the New World takes us to that place," Killian said. "Why couldn't Stephan have gotten lost here?"

"Maybe he did," Ambrose said. "We have the map, after all. And you heard Jean-Émile. There's a man wandering the woods. Maybe more than one. Maybe Valentine is watching over him. Do you agree with me now?"

"Tobias is still dead!" Killian said. "Do you agree we should have left while we had the chance?"

Ambrose looked away. They walked in silence, leaving the bright lights behind. Narrow streets opened to the side, businesses dimly lit: Schlichting Pharmacist, Lovett Boots & Shoes. The door to a tavern banged open, and two men shoved each other in the doorway. A piano played a lively tune: a bawdy American song. It spilled from the open door into the street and above, the shingle swayed: the DOWNTOWNER.

"What do we do now?" Killian said. "How do we find Stephan, even if he is here? How will you stop Valentine or Anselm if you find them? Are you going to kill Valentine, Ambrose?"

"What? I don't know… There has to be some way to stop this."

"Is it possible you're making this all up? Imagining this?"

"You saw her!" Ambrose said. "You saw Issa!"

Killian shook his head. That night seemed so long ago. The shock had made Tobias's death unreal, and he scarcely remembered what had happened. "Maybe she wasn't dead," he said. "Maybe she had the canine madness."

"Now you're doubting? What of Stephan's room? What of that thing you saw, watching you?"

"I don't know, Ambrose!" Killian cried. "I think this place is making me crazy. I think you're making me crazy. Now that I'm away from St. Gregory, this is all too much to believe."

Ambrose scowled, his jaw trembling in anger. If Killian didn't believe even now, no one would believe him back home. "I'm going in that tavern," he growled. "You do what you want."

✛

CHAPTER 29

What Are You Doing Here?

December 1, 1859

The door opened and Ambrose blinked against the smell of stale beer and old smoke. Gruff faces turned to stare, eyebrows raised, and the tavern fell dead quiet. Only the piano still hummed slightly. The man before it stared at them over an odd sign: THIS PIANO IS THE HARDEST WORKER HERE. PLEASE DON'T SHOOT IT. SHOOT THE PLAYER INSTEAD. A woman, her hand on her hip, eyed them suggestively from the bannister, *a soiled dove,* as they were called in the West. Ambrose looked away uncomfortably.

The barman set a glass down with a clack, breaking the silence, and everyone burst into laughter. A man in middrink sprayed foam across a table, beer dripping from his ragged mustache, and men threw their cards down and shook their heads.

"What are you doing here, Fathers?" the barman said in English. "Come to save us?"

"I just want a meal," Ambrose said.

"We don't give a church discount."

"I wouldn't have it anyway. I'd just like a meal and a place to sit."

"Make 'em do a ride with Evie," a voice yelled, "otherwise they ain't welcome."

"No church discount there either, fathers," the woman said, smirking.

"I don't understand what they're saying! They're drunk and slurring," Killian whispered.

"Ambrose! What the hell are you doing here?" A thick hand slapped his back. "I swear, wherever you are, there's always trouble!"

Ambrose turned, surprised to see Silas behind him. The man bowed, hat in hand, as a toothy grin spread across his bright red face.

"Mr. Messam!" Ambrose said.

"Come now, it's Silas! We're friends. "Henry, get a round for my fellows here, and we'll take a room in the back.

"Ambrose, what's going on?" Killian hissed.

"What are you doing here?" Ambrose asked Silas.

The man smiled and pulled him close, liquor thick on his breath, as he whispered in his ear. "I have a wagon for old Franz Guthiel. Some might say I pinched it and road off in the night. This isn't some cheap swill, mind you. It's imported! French brandy! Don't ask where or how! And keep it to yourself!" He winked. *"Sei ruhig, ja!"*

"Cheers, lads!" They clinked glasses in a back room. Beer splashed on the table, running down Ambrose's arm and soaking the sleeve of his robe.

"Forgive me, I'm jolly!" Silas said. "I'm flush at the moment. A little hard work is finally paying off. Even if it's under the table. You two, though, seem a bit worse for the wear."

"To your health." Ambrose raised his glass. "I'm sorry. I'm afraid we're not the best company at the moment."

"I should say not," Silas said. "In fact you look rather dour. But I suppose I've never seen you to look otherwise. So, perhaps this is your native condition. Well, they say a man must be his own best company, so, I shall endeavor to make merry on my own!"

They sipped in awkward silence. The yellow flame of the lamp flickered on the wall in an unseen draft, black smoke sharp in Ambrose's nose, and the thick smell of fried pork crept from the kitchen. A girl peeked into the room and plopped a bowl of hot cracklings on the table, oil popping. Ambrose's stomach growled and tightened, and he realized he didn't know the last time he had eaten. The crackling crunched oddly as he bit down, and gamy fat coated his tongue and the roof of his mouth. A wave of nausea swept over him and he set it down in disgust.

Suddenly shouts rose from the dining hall. Chairs screeched, scraping across the floor. "You son of a bitch!" someone yelled. "You calling me a cheat?" yelled another. A glass shattered on the floor. "Hey! Hey!" The barman banged. "Take it outside!"

"Getting lively out there!" Silas said, pushing the backroom shut. "Thursdays are like that. I don't know why."

"Ambrose, damn it! What's going on?" Killian said, slamming the table.

"I'm sorry," Ambrose said. "Silas, this is Father Killian. He's one of the members of the commission I came with. Unfortunately his English is poor.

"Ahhh." Silas nodded. *"Französisch?"*

"How's your French, Killian?" Ambrose asked.

"Worse," Killian muttered. "It's not English I don't understand. It's drunk English."

"Well, this is an English establishment," Silas said, careful to be slow and clear. "So, you'll likely hear a lot of English here. And while I can endeavor not to speak English, I must point out that this is a tavern, so I can't endeavor not to be drunk.

Killian rolled his eyes, "English is fine."

Silas chuckled to himself and downed his beer. The piano took up a lively tune, keys banging and smacking, loud even through the walls of the back room where they sat. "Is he trying to break it?" Killian said. The click and stomp of heels hit the floor as Evie and another girl danced around the tables in peels of giggling laughter. A drunken chorus rose from the hall next door.

Oh, my name it is Sam Hall, Sam Hall.
My name it is Sam Hall, Sam Hall.
My name is Sam Hall and I've cheated great and
small,
one step above the law.
Fuck you all!

Well I killed a man they said, so they said.
Well I killed a man they said, so they said.
He had it in his head,
to turn me in, instead.
So I shot him good and dead. Fuck you all!

"Tell me, Silas," Ambrose said, raising his voice above the noise, "if you're selling to Franz Guthiel, why are you at an…establishment such as this? Why are you not at Gutheil's Saloon? Did he not care to offer a meal and a drink for your trouble?"

"There's that sense of humor!" Silas laughed. "Can you imagine a more awful place to spend an evening? A bunch of foppish dandies. Not quite my company."

"It did look expensive." Ambrose sighed as he stared at the cold, greasy cracklings in disgust.

In the room beside, the song roared away, boisterous and out of key. Harsh bellows shook the whole building and rattled the windows as all the drunk men took up the tune.

They'll hang me up so high, so high
They'll hang me up so high, so high
They'll hang me up so high, and I'll dangle in the
sky
But I ain't told no lie
Fuck you all!

And the preacher man has cause, he has cause
And the preacher man has cause, he has cause
The preacher man has cause,
To tell me of God's laws
Well he can suck my cock and balls, Fuck you all!

The walls hummed and Ambrose couldn't help but smile and shake his head, relieved to forget the awful guilt of Tobias, if only for a moment. Killian, though, only glowered and shook his head.

"Wait," Silas said. "Weren't there three of you? Where's the other?"

"Dead," Ambrose said and stared at his hands. The moment was broken.

"Oh, I'm sorry. What happened?" asked Silas. "Does this have anything to do with that problem you had?

"Yes, what happened, Ambrose?" Killian scowled across the table, his eyes flashing. Ambrose looked away; nothing he could say would ever change what had happened.

It was strangely still, and they couldn't remember when the music had stopped. Suddenly the piano keys in the hall crashed with an angry bang. "Quit playing that same goddamn song!" a voice boomed. Chairs clattered and a man yelped, thumping to the floor. "You want to play?" the piano player yelled. "Have at it, you son of a bitch!"

Bang! A shot cleared the air.

"How many times do I have to tell you it's not the piano's fault?" the barman yelled. "You keep banging it and this next shot is going to remind you right quick! Damn thing is already out of tune."

They heard the men in the hall outside grumble as they resumed their game of cards. Killian turned back to the table, his fingers clicking against the worn wood as he glared at Ambrose.

"Let's all just relax and have a drink, shall we?" Silas said, raising his hands. "No need to get tense."

"It was that sickness," Ambrose said. "But it wasn't a sickness at all, like you said. It was some *thing*. A horrid creature, created or transformed. A mockery of life. A girl cut short in the promise of youth, brought back as a hideous dead thing. A *nachzehrer,* according to that damn book. You knew enough that it wasn't an ordinary sickness. I swear, if you had an idea of what it really was, you damn well should have told me!"

Silas sat in silence for some time, stroking his beard. The hall outside was boisterous; strange against the brooding quiet of their little room. Ambrose knew there must have been a time, once, when he didn't feel such anger and sadness, but he couldn't remember when it was. The days had all bled one into another, and it seemed it had always been this way. What could Silas say now that would make any difference?

"These things follow from the Old World," Silas said finally. "Some are here, of course. Native but with different names. The *inamekwak,* which you might call a *nachtkrapp* in the Old World. But some things are peculiar. They follow in the minds of those who come—not only in the minds, mind you. They're not made up. But there is a power in belief, you know. A communion. It opens doors. Anyway…how do you know for sure?"

"I saw the damn thing!" Ambrose exclaimed. He downed his beer and slammed the glass on the table in anger. "I saw it bury its face into Tobias's neck and leave him dead on the frozen ground!"

"If it even is this thing." Killian scowled. "In the light of day, I think was just be a sick girl, rabid and taken to madness."

Silas shook his head. "You should know better than that. You're young. Your generation is turning away from good sense, ignoring what lies right in front of you, for the thoughts in your own head. It's clear that you're in shock from the whole affair. But still, you should know better."

"It is hard to believe," he said, turning to Ambrose. "The *nachzehrer* doesn't leave its grave. It drains life while it's still in the ground, always hungry, always feeding, until it consumes even itself. But it never leaves. Are you sure of what you saw? There are other creatures, you know."

"Nothing else matches. If that book is to be believed," Ambrose said. "The first did die, drained and consumed, like you said. Her parents wasted away, taken by a fever that gave way to delirium. It's only when I had my suspicions and sought to put an end to it that it showed itself by the grave at night."

"At night?" Silas said. "You should never conduct such business at night. Ah…I thought such things were well-known. What do they teach you, anyway? Weddings and funerals only, it seems. Still, it's strange behavior. Something's not right. This isn't an ordinary turning."

"Ha! Ordinary!" Killian said. "I need another drink." He stormed out of the room, slamming the door.

"He's not doing very well, is he?"

"Neither am I," Ambrose said.

"I'm sorry. Entering this world isn't easy. It never is. There is always sacrifice."

The door squeaked open, and Killian sat down in a huff, glass foamy and spilling. He scowled as he stared at the cobwebbed corner, ignoring them.

"So what's causing this?" Silas stroked his beard and leaned back. "Something with that town, it would seem."

Ambrose sighed. "I thought of what Eloi said. 'Evil follows.'"

"Indeed. So what is it following?"

"There's only one possibility, really. But I needed to be sure," Ambrose said. "I did one of the spells in the book to give me a name, but it didn't work." He unfolded the map on the table. "It gave me this."

"And what's this?" — Silas grimaced at the oily paper in his hands — "It smells terrible."

"I believe it's a map of Chilton and the surrounding area. It seems to lead us to that X in the middle. I think those are the caves Eloi mentioned. The ones called *Wasuskeqsinoh*. I don't know why it gave me a map and not a name. I went through the whole damn ritual, even with that foul raven heart."

"Heart?" Silas said. "I've heard you're supposed to use the tongue. The tongue is what tells you. But I can't say for certain. I've never done this spell before. I guess it will have to do. Who is it leading to?"

Ambrose shrugged. "I don't know. Valentine, I should expect. Or one of his followers, maybe Anselm or Florian. Hopefully we'll find Stephan there as well."

"Who?"

"The bishop we were sent to find," Ambrose said. "Stephan von Draheim. Though if he ever escapes captivity, he might well go by his Polish name, Szczepan Drahim. Anyway, they must be keeping someone, or something, where that X is. Killian witnessed a cart bound there from the abbey, filled with supplies, but also—"

"A body," Killian interjected.

"Strange…" Silas stroked his beard. "Very strange. And how is it you're always in the middle of this, Ambrose? I'd say you have strange connections to this man. Or it would seem fate is trying to be rid of you."

"He was my father's friend," Ambrose said. He shook his head as old memories flooded back: Stephan and his father drinking wine late into the night; his mother singing as Monika danced by the fire. He would sit on the man's knees as he told him of his wild travels across the East and his childhood in Polish Prussia. It had been years since he had seen him and his heart ached with guilt.

"He's a good man, according to my uncle," Killian said. "Very rational and grounded in the sciences. He took a keen interest in the plight of the poor, even protesting internal church politics. He wasn't well liked for that."

Ambrose nodded. "It's true. Stephan was a sympathizer of Johannes Ronge, although I don't believe they ever met. This was before Ronge was so radicalized and forced to flee after the failed revolution in 1848. Together they opposed the pilgrimage to the Holy Coat of Trier."

"I must say I have no idea what you are talking about," said Silas. "His kidnapping would seem politically motivated, but I don't quite see how it relates."

"Nor do I, really," Ambrose said. "At the time, the church was hoping to shore up its power against government encroachment. But Stephan saw it as an abuse of the superstitions and poor education of the impoverished and naïve lower class. He felt they weren't uplifted by their betters in true faith, but rather mired in superstition and heretical ideas. He would have none of it."

"Valentine named Ronge the antichrist once," Killian said. "Or at least one of them—I think he named several. I thought Stephan was even on that list at one point."

"It would seem your poor bishop so angered that crazed priest that he wasn't content to simply let him return home, but felt he had to make an example out of him," Silas said. "He must have had quite the vendetta. Now he's immersing himself in the black arts, besides. It pains me to say, but some rituals call for sacrifice: the blood of a holy man. Be prepared for what you might find."

"That's something I simply can't allow myself to think," Ambrose said.

The table grew still. Outside, the world carried on, oblivious. Men shouted and glasses spilled. The piano played in fits and starts. Evie's voice rose in shrill laughter, her hard shoes clicking as she ran up the stairs just over their head. To Ambrose, the whole thing seemed grotesque and absurd, and he understood Annaliese's disgust at the mention of this town.

"You know," Silas said. "An odd sickness recently fell on Chilton too. People wasting away. They say strange folk have been seen, prowling about at night, but no one knows who. And there's fresh graves disturbed come morning. Some even dug up. They say there's a depraved sort running around, most likely some feeble mind or pervert. But now I'm not so sure. This is too much of a coincidence. Of course, we can't know until we see the graves. There are signs, you know? Ways to tell. We'd have to go at night. It won't do to linger in the cemetery during the day for all to see."

Just then, the outside door banged open. "They're at it!" a man cried. "They're at it again! Damn Gravesvilles! Someone tried to break into Minnie Bircher's house! Some fool tapping on the upstairs window, spying on her daughter. A few men chased him off, but the barn lit up as if on its own. Must have been more than one. The horses are dead and the barn's in cinders!"

"Damn Graves!" Voices shouted and the room exploded, chairs clattering against the floor. "Get your guns and get after them!" someone yelled. "Out! everyone out!" the barman hollered. "Tavern's closed! Free drinks tomorrow to whoever nails the bastards!"

"Well, we're not going tonight!" Silas said. "The whole town will be up in arms. We'll be lucky to see no one shot or hanged and none of the town burned down come morning. This is mob justice till first light. Meet me here tomorrow at dusk, assuming everything blows over. I suggest you head back to the hotel quick as you can and lay low. And try not to get shot!"

Ambrose and Killian stumbled through dark alleys, hiding behind old crates and piles of filth. Shouts rose in the street, angry voices yelling and cursing, and the thump of boots raced across the brick streets in the dark, growing near and passing in quick shadow. The howls of dogs rose in the distance as shots rang out into the night: first left, then right, then front and back. The whole town erupted in gunfire, echoes ringing in the alley, and Ambrose's heart pounded as he led Killian on. "We need to keep off the main street!"

Torches flickered, racing toward them, yellow light wavering on the alley walls.

"Fuck!" Ambrose said. He looked around for a place to hide, but everywhere was bare and open.

"Ay! Who's that?" Four men stopped short, gripping pistols and rifles.

"Just priests!" Ambrose cried. "Trying to get back to the hotel!"

"What's yer names? And where ya from?" The tall man said, eyeing them with suspicion.

"Ambrose and Killian, from St. Gregory. Just arrived and staying at the Westen. Just visiting a friend!"

"Couple of priests in an alley?" A stocky man glared. "Something ain't right! You from Gravesville?"

"We've never heard of it before tonight! We were just at the Downtowner. You can ask the barman."

"Shit, two priests at the Downtowner?" He rubbed his square face. "That definitely ain't right. Just shoot 'em Ed."

Damn it! How does this madness follow me? Ambrose looked desperately down the alley, gauging if they could outrun them. If they couldn't, it would be the last thing they ever did.

"I ain't shootin' one priest, let alone two!" Ed said.

"Ed, we gotta go!" the scruffy man urged. He looked anxiously down the alley, his beady eyes darting nervously.

"Just leave the bastards. You'll hang, you listen to idiot Dobbin here."

Bells clamored above the chaos, a frantic *dong-dong* from the church. "Shit!" Ed yelped. "Shit! Shit! We gotta go!" He waved them on. "Let's go!"

Dobbin tapped the barrel of his pistol against his head. "You're lucky."

As soon as they came, the men left, their shadowed backs racing toward the river and disappearing in the click of fleeing boots.

"Fuck!" Ambrose said, collapsing, his hands on his knees.

"God damn it! Why are we here?" Killian cried.

"Come on!" Ambrose pulled him forward and they raced into the night.

Light shone ahead—torches and lamps, where the alley spilled into the main street. The sharp smell of gun smoke bit their nose. A throng marched past on its way to the bridge. Men yelled as pitchforks shook in the air, beside rifles and muskets, "Burn 'em! Burn 'em down! Get the cocksuckers!"

Ambrose and Killian stopped short, hugging the alley wall as they passed. The Westen House was on the other side of the street and the mob was in their way. A man stopped suddenly, staring at them in suspicion. He pointed his six shooter at Ambrose's head and cocked the hammer, "Who are y—"

"Burn 'em!" Ambrose shouted. "Burn 'em all!"

"Ay! Burn 'em!" The men yelled back and shot in the air. The crowd pressed forward.

"We need to get away from this madness!" Ambrose said.

He grabbed Killian and pulled him forward. They wove into the crowd, pushing and forcing their way across the street. The Westen House neared, red lettering painted large on the window. The shingle approached and was gone, passing overhead. Caught in the rush, the angry mob swept them forward.

Bells tolled in Gravesville as the town across the river woke up. Dark figures ran and gathered in the night, massing on the far shore. Tiny flashes lit the bank as they fired warning shots into the air. A lone figure, bent under a heavy load, dashed across the bridge. He stopped in the middle and left a crate before racing back, a spool unwinding in his hand. The mob pressed on, pouring onto the bridge, Ambrose and Killian stuck in the middle.

Boom! A burst of light and heat rocked them backward. Flames erupted as the bridge exploded, collapsing in a fire of roaring timber, steam hissing and popping in the river below. Ambrose hit the ground, gasping amid a cloud of black smoke.

Moments passed in a daze. Men struggled to stand, swaying and dizzy, brushing ash and dust from their hair and face. A deafening ringing filled the air, blocking out all else. Ambrose whirled. Mouths opened and moved, but no sound came out. He shouted to Killian, but his voice was only a hum and Killian stared blankly, unhearing.

Broken beams and bent metal stood where the bridge had been, the Manitowoc River flowing swiftly below. A crowd stood on the far bank, rifles and muskets in hand, their faces silhouetted by the yellow of torch and lantern. Shocked by the blast, the mob stared in a daze at the gaping hole.

Before long, a great thunder of hooves clattered on the street, growing louder and louder. Police rode on horseback, the sheriff in blue at the lead, followed by a dozen deputies and volunteers, pistols drawn and shouting. The last of the mob cleared the streets, darting into the shadows of the alleys and the trees at the riverbank.

"Run!" Ambrose yelled.

Cold wind burned their lungs, their throats hoarse and aching as they raced into the night. Voices shouted everywhere and hooves echoed in the alleys all around until they no longer could tell if they were coming or going.

"There!"

They ducked into a dark alley and cowered behind crates and boxes as the city raged.

"What the hell!" Killian exclaimed, panting. Their hearts drummed in their ears as the night grew quiet again. Several long minutes passed as the shouts grew fewer and more distant and the random pop of gunfire finally stopped.

"You know, this is just like back home." Ambrose shook his head. "Do you remember the revolutions?" He paused, then added, "You may have been too young."

"No, and I'm not sad I missed them."

"So much for adventure."

"I didn't know this is what adventure was," Killian said, scowling, "Anyway, let's get back to the hotel and get off the street!"

They crouched behind corners and barrels, waiting, darting into alleys and passages, then waiting again, careful to stay in the dark and away from the few large streets that were lit with streetlamps. Shadows stretched and moved, grown long in the swinging lamplight, as the police made their rounds down dark streets.

The black windows of the hotel lay just ahead. Ambrose and Killian crouched and ran, the wooden stoop squeaking underfoot. A yellow light crept closer—a police lantern, hidden by the corner of an alley.

Ambrose grasped the cold knob in his hand. "It's locked!" he hissed. "They must have locked it because of the mob!"

"Hey, you!" the deputy yelled and drew his gun. His finger was twitchy and the panicked look in his eyes warned he would rather shoot than talk. "What are you doing? Get over here!" He raised his gun, level with their heads, and pulled the trigger. It popped in a haze of smoke and the brick wall beside their heads burst in a shower of sharp crumbles and dust. The two priests took one look and bolted, running with all their might.

Quick footsteps followed close behind. "Get back here, thief!"

One road led to another: left, right, alleys, and main streets. The footsteps grew softer, sometimes stopping, confused, looking where they might have gone. On they ran, lungs burning, when suddenly the alley spilled onto a darkened park by the river, sloping down to the riverbank. The black shadows of trees drew near. No one followed but still they ran before finally crashing through the underbrush and collapsing in a pile of dead leaves, hidden behind the thick tree trunks all around. They lay on their backs, panting and gasping.

Moments passed—minutes or hours, they couldn't tell. The night was quiet, with only the rushing river splashing beside them, bubbling in the rocks and roots. No voices shouted in anger. No gunfire broke the night. Ambrose's heart slowed. The cold, wet December air crept off the water, seeping into their robes and coats, and he shivered as icy beads of sweat rolled off his forehead, chilling him as they traced his neck.

"I think we have to wait until morning. I don't want to risk going back to the Westen with these crazed police and vigilantes on the streets." he said. "It's lucky that officer was old…"

"I should have listened to you." Killian shook his head bitterly. "I should have just left you here and gone home alone."

☩

CHAPTER 30

Graverobbers

December 2, 1859

As the sun rose, the empty streets were still, and the few folk about spoke in hushed tones. A shock lay on the town, the night before shameful in the light of day. The older folk shook their heads while the younger looked away, embarrassed, their faces pink as they pulled their hats over their eyes. A grizzled man swept the cobblestone, broken glass tinkling in the light as he brushed it into the morning paper. Stark letters read, "A Night of Chaos, State St. Bridge Exploded, 20 Jailed."

Ambrose sat in Guthiel's Saloon, gazing out the window. Hot coffee steamed in his hand, chasing away the chill of the night, as he rubbed his aching muscles. "I'm wiped out," he said.

"It's a good thing I found you," Silas said. "I can't believe the Westen isn't open yet, and we have to eat here. Shouldn't have been locked to begin with. Franz is a bit paranoid. It's probably not the best line of work for him honestly."

Ambrose looked around at the warm space filled with chattering townsfolk, and his face softened. It seemed a proper establishment; bright sun gleamed off polished wood and twinkled in the crystal and silver. They did look out of place against so many well-dressed townsfolk. Their dirty and ratty cassocks—and Silas's deerskin jacket and pants—didn't blend in well. The barman wiped the glasses behind an oak bar, eyeing them curiously. "Well, this café is fine with me!"

The kitchen door creaked open, and a dapper man bustled out with steaming plates of eggs and ham and toast. Savory-sweet filled the air as dishes clattered on the table.

"Oh, Lord be praised!" Killian rubbed his empty stomach. "I've never been so hungry. Of all the ways I imagined Ambrose might get me killed, I didn't think starvation was one of them. I haven't eaten for days!"

"It's true," Ambrose said between a mouthful. "I can't remember the last time. Was it two days ago? All I've had is beer."

"You're both just lucky you didn't get shot," Silas said.

The fire in the hearth crackled and popped, warmth filling the cozy hall. Whispered voices from the tables nearby lulled in gentle hum, and Ambrose yawned as a wave of tiredness washed over him.

"What happened last night anyway?" asked Killian.

"Ah, people are crazy," Silas waved his hand. "There's no accounting for them. But I do think they've grown crazier of late. There was always a friendly rivalry between the Stantonville and Gravesville, but the last several years it's been something more. A lot of rumors lately…and suspicion. But no one can really say from where. It only took a little spark to blow the whole thing up. Literally."

"But what actually happened?" he pressed.

"Well," Silas said. "It appears folk were prowling about, spying where they shouldn't have been. They were chased off. No one actually caught a good glimpse of them. Then several barns lit up and all the livestock in them, right at the same time. That pretty much set the town off. Of course, they thought it was Gravesville. It didn't take much to point the

folks of Chilton in that direction, just hearsay and assumption. Then Gravesville woke up and blew up the bridge. But you saw that yourselves. Probably blew your ears out!"

"But was it Gravesville?" Ambrose said.

"Before you showed up again, I would have said sure and not thought much about it," Silas said. "But maybe someone has been stoking the fire a bit, now that I think about it. But who and why? I suppose it could be this Valentine of yours, bent on purifying the world. Sounds like he'd find that appealing."

Ambrose sat back and sighed. "I'm confused. How would he go about doing it? He has his followers—Florian and Anselm—but what about Issa? How does a man bring that into being?"

"These things aren't created. They're *corrupted,*" Silas explained sipping his coffee. "Some people are easily confused—both the living and the dead people. Usually from fear or false promises, but really anything could do it. Bad stories are what they all are in the end. But no, they're not created—no one has that power. They're corrupted."

"Oh." Ambrose paused for a long moment. "Can they be uncorrupted?"

"Jesus, Ambrose, isn't that your job?" Silas laughed.

Ambrose frowned and Killian looked away, uncomfortably.

"So what of these disturbed graves?" asked Ambrose. "How does that figure in to this mess? Is that Issa?"

"No. I don't know what it is. We'll need to actually see the site and examine the ground. Maybe we'll be able to tell. But it's not Issa…or what was Issa. A *nachzehrer* feeds on the living. Some monsters feed on the living, some on the dead, some on both. But it's never straightforward. Some dead are actually living. And some of the living are actually dead. You can see it in their eyes."

"What?" Ambrose said. "That makes no sense."

"Not everything is explainable," Silas said. "Some things you have to get a feel for."

Ambrose studied the room. The rich, polished walnut of the smooth, wooden walls matched the warm gleam of the tables, and the velvet wallpaper of the half wall was a soft and deep burgundy. A fire crackled in the fireplace at the far end, flames bouncing off the green tile of the raised hearth. Women chatted, cheeks red with blush, and lace embellishing their collars in delicate white, while their husbands nodded to one another, pulling at their styled and tapered beards and speaking in hushed tones of the night before. Were they alive? Or were they dead? And did they know it? It all seemed unbelievable. "How do you know so much?"

"I told you," said Silas. "I've been around. I've seen things. Dabbled. I have books of my own, you know? I told you when we first met, but you didn't want to believe me."

The table fell to silence. Silas sighed, stroking his beard as Ambrose stared at the hot mug in his hand. The bright morning seemed surreal after so many dark, twisted nights. Steam whirled as he blew, rich oils swirling in the black cup and shimmering in the winter light. Men in wool suits and pipes chatted at nearby tables about places like New York and London, oblivious to their conversation. The woodsy scent of tobacco filled the room, everything oddly normal.

"What about possession?" Killian asked. "Is Issa possessed? If she's not just sick and mad, that is."

Silas took a long draw of his coffee. "The church makes a big deal out of that. But I've honestly never really seen it. That, I think, falls under the category of believing a bad story."

"Jesus cast seven demons out of Mary Magdalene," Killian said.

"That's a metaphor for the seven deadly sins," Silas replied, then turned to Ambrose, puzzled. "Why is youth so literal?"

Killian folded his arms, scowling, and looked to Ambrose in protest. The sweat and grime of the night before traced his young face in dark wrinkles, black rings below the eyes, and he looked a good twenty years older than his age. A horrid thought passed Ambrose's mind, and he could not stanch the bitter welling of remorse. *Maybe that is who he is now.*

The young priest stood abruptly, bumping the table and spilling coffee on the white linens as his chaired thumped loudly. The room turned to stare with grunts of disapproval at the disheveled figure in his wrinkled and soiled cassock. But Killian ignored and turned his back, staring out the window at the wreckage of the bridge nearby. Ambrose and Silas waited in silence, exchanging worried glances. Finally, he sat down in cold silence, glaring at no place in particular.

"Look," Silas said after some time. "I don't mean the issue of possession is a bad story. I mean a bad story lets it happen. It's not how you think. Well, it is *how* you think, actually. A strong mind and a strong heart guard the doors, so to speak. It's the confusion that'll get you"—he tapped his temple with his finger—"that constant gnawing doubt way back in your skull. And how does that start? A bad story. One we're told or tell ourselves, it doesn't matter. And believe it or not, one of your favorite institutions, which shall remain nameless, does a fair job of sowing those very seeds of doubt. Fear lets the Devil in a lot easier than a little laissez faire free spiritedness. Somewhat ironic, wouldn't you say?"

"I don't quite like what you're implying." Killian frowned. "Anyway, are there demons or not?"

"Why not?" Silas said. "But the stories you've been taught only tell a small part. So don't think you've got everything figured out. I've seen way too much to believe that."

Killian struck the table. "That's blasphemy!"

"That's reality!"

The café suddenly went silent. Startled faces turned, staring at them. A man pulled at the edge of his mustache, disapprovingly, and pages shuffled and rustled as he snorted before turning back to his paper.

"I don't know," Ambrose said. "If it's all stories, how does anything actually happen in the real world? And how could you possibly do anything about it?"

"It's communion," Silas said. "Rituals, spells, prayer—they're all communion. There are many ways to commune. And many things to commune with."

"I've heard enough." Killian threw up his hands. "I can't believe any of this."

"Doesn't matter," Silas said. "Will your belief change things? Did your belief stop the *nachzehrer* and keep it from killing Tobias? Did his?"

"That's for God to decide," Killian said, glaring. "That's God's power. That's my belief."

"Great!" Silas said. "So please stay out of the way and try not to let your belief get you killed."

"Ambrose, how can you listen to this?" Killian implored.

"Well, if your seminary taught you anything useful, now would be the time to speak up," Silas said. "Listen, we won't know—and you won't believe—until we actually see it. And the first thing we need to do is snoop around that cemetery... but we can only do that at night. So I suggest you eat up, and rest up, and keep your righteous indignation to yourself."

That night, against Killian's will, they walked the fallow fields to the cemetery. The bright light of the waxing moon lit the ground in stark white, and dried wheat stalks crunched and split underfoot. Eerie calls rose in the distance, the haunting cries of an owl, the cackle of coyotes. The dark shadow of a homestead loomed, roof gray in the light as the bitter smell of ash and char crept across the blackened fields to meet them.

"I suggest we don't use lanterns," Silas whispered. "The fields are too open. The people are on edge enough as it is. Last thing we need is to explain what we're doing in a cemetery at night. These are Minnie Bircher's fields. She's the one was being spied on last night. The cemetery is just on the other side of her land."

"Maybe something came to her house because the cemetery is so close?" Ambrose said.

"That could very well be. Look…" Silas pointed at charred rubble. "Her barn that was burned."

"What'll they do if they catch us out here?" Killian said, flustered.

"Nothing good."

A tangled hedge took shape in the distance. Thorny hawthorn walled the cemetery in places, growing in a rough but broken line, while brambles and thorns wove dense and impassable patches. An old rail fence lay fallen in many places, its rotted wood split and cracked. Bare swaths of ground shone in the moonlight, the grass around eaten back. Ambrose's foot felt a familiar squish as he slid in the dirt: fresh manure.

"Ack," he spat, rubbing his boot in the grass. "Is this a pasture?"

Silas nodded. "Yep. Mr. Breed doesn't keep up the place or mend the fences, I'm told. The whole cemetery is a cow pasture now. At least they keep the grass short over the graves. Should be easier to find what we're looking for. The new graves are in the back, I think."

Quietly they approached. An old iron gate hung broken on the hinges, half buried in the dirt, its dark posts tilting. Rust covered an old plaque, flaking and falling, the words barely readable: BREED CEMETERY. Faint moonlight lit the old gravestones in the distance, casting long shadows on the ground, and a chill wind rustled the grasses forlornly.

"There," said Killian. "What's that?"

A hill of dirt was mounded beside a wooden cross. Fresh chunks of frozen ground lay in clumps, the soft earth below cast about, as of something furiously digging. Ambrose and Killian stood behind Silas, peering cautiously at the black hole that tunneled into the earth.

"What do we have here?" Silas said. Fresh dirt crumbled in his hands, the musty smell of cold earth rising to meet them, heavy in the damp air. "Ground is still loose, not yet frozen. This couldn't have been long. Let's risk a little light. Keep an eye out, though." He reached into his burlap bag and drew a revolver, which he stuffed into his belt. "Did you at least pack some protection?"

As Ambrose drew the thin mortician's blade, its edge gleamed in the moonlight. Killian stared at Silas, wide-eyed and empty-handed.

"You should be better prepared, Father Plank," said Silas. "Here, take this." He drew a long knife and handed it to the young priest.

Killian held the heavy blade awkwardly in his hand, as if afraid he might cut himself. He was unused to the severity of its size; the only knives he had ever wielded were those at the dinner table, and holding it now, the evening took on a deathly serious air.

Silas lit his lantern and squatted, peering into the hole and examining the dirt. "Don't get too close!" He waved. "We don't want to mess up any tracks."

He stared for some time, peering this way and that, crouching on all fours and sniffing the earth. The wind whispered eerily in the trees, and Ambrose looked over his shoulder, the feeling of eyes upon him.

"You're lucky," Silas said. "The hole doesn't go all the way down. Something wasn't digging its way out. Something was trying to get in. But by the look of it, we interrupted it. Or it ran off. Seems it can't dig deep enough to get to the grave before the morning light. That, at least, means there aren't more monsters about."

Ambrose leaned forward. "But what was it?"

"Look at this."—Silas pointed—"A print. Not an animal's."

At his feet, the ground was pressed in. Soft earth smooshed, unmistakable. A hand. More handprints spread out, everywhere, as if the person had been on all fours.

"It's a man's hand," Silas noted. "It's a big print. There are no shovel marks. No boot prints either. Someone was digging by hand. And look at this. This mark here…" He pointed to a number of scratches across the frozen ground. "Claw marks. It takes a lot of strength to dig through frozen ground with your bare hands. Whatever this is, it's not a man anymore."

Killian shuddered. The grave looked like Issa's, dirt strewn all about. Memories of Tobias flashed in their minds. Ambrose turned, looking round and round, his blade clenched and held high, as Killian backed away, his own blade trembling.

"I think it's gone. Whatever it was," Silas said softly. "But we should leave, just the same. Sooner the better."

A branch cracked in the brush. They spun. A dark figure stood at the gate. Silas drew the revolver. Another shape appeared. And another.

"Hey! What are you doing!" the shape yelled. "We got 'em, boys! We got the fuckers!"

A shot rang out, flame blasting from the shadowed man's barrel, and the black shapes ran toward them.

"Shit! Run!" Silas hissed. The flame whirled as he threw the lantern at the men. Silas turned, pushing the other two on, and they ran as fast as they could, diving through the brush and bramble, scraping their arms and faces, hot blood flowing in the cold night. Cries and shouts rose behind them as their pursuers ran the long way around the thicket.

Their legs pumped and lungs burned as shots echoed behind, amid hollers and the thump of their feet growing closer. The fields opened wide before them, bright in the moonlight, and Ambrose silently cursed the men who had cut down all the trees.

"There!" Silas wheezed. The dark shape of a barn grew near, its long shadow stretching. "We'll be trapped in there, but I can't run anymore!"

The old door squeaked open, and the warm scent of hay and manure wafted around them. Pigs snorted, asleep in the pen below, and grunted as they woke to the sounds of footsteps above. The three men scrambled, aching arms pulled themselves up piles of hay that slid underneath. Grassy dust puffed in their faces and stuck to their sweaty skin. Finally, their hands touched wood and they yanked themselves up into the rafters as pigeons cooed and flapped around them, startled from their sleep.

Silas peered down at the door below, panting and clutching the shit covered beam precariously. "This always happens with you, Ambrose. I'm beginning to think you're bad luck."

"We know you're in there!" a man shouted. "We'll burn you out! I don't care if we lose another barn!"

Lamps flickered in the gaps of the plank siding. Men gathered below, their shadows milling about, two, then four, then six.

"We got 'em trapped now!"

"Are they really going to burn the barn down?" Killian hissed.

Dogs bayed in the distance: hounds.

"They've got our scent!" Silas said. "We have to run. No matter what. No matter how tired you are or how much your lungs ache. Manitowoc River is half a mile away. If we're lucky, we can make it. Now go!"

They scrambled to the back, hands clambering across rafters, thick with years of dried and chalky pigeon droppings. The open end of the loft neared. Below: a pile of manure.

"Nothing for it!" Silas jumped. Ambrose followed. Then Killian.

Soft hay and shit broke their fall, ice cracking as they sank, squishing into cold and wet filth. As soon as they hit the ground, they were off, their feet pounding the ground. The barn grew small behind as the hounds' bays neared.

"Aye, they must have gone out the back!" a voice shouted.

"Do you see them? Do you see them anywhere?"

"No! But the dogs'll get 'em!"

The howls were on their heels as hooves thundered across the field. Still, they ran, on and on. Ambrose's legs burned and his chest ached. Every step felt weaker than the last. His mind reeled in panic. The river was near—but was it near enough? Dark elms rose, and the bank snaked just ahead, gurgling and splashing.

"To the other side!" Silas bellowed. "Don't think. Just do it!"

Ambrose crashed through thin ice, plunging into frigid water. Cold gripped him and froze his muscles, pulling him down, clamping like a vise. He struggled against the current, his arms slow and heavy. His head bobbed as icy water crashed in his ears and nose and filled his lungs. The current rushed them downstream as they struggled to stay above, and he felt his body slowing, not responding. His mind grew dull as the world sped by. *Is this how I die?*

Suddenly a thick branch poked his side, hard at the ribs, scraping and tearing as the current swept him past it. He desperately reached, numb in the cold, unsure if grasped it, or not. He yanked himself from the rapids and felt solid ground beneath his feet.

Killian swept by and he caught his cassock. With one hand on the branch and one on Killian's robes, Ambrose pulled with all his might, but the current was too strong and sucked them into the black. Just as his strength gave out, a hand reached out from the darkness and grasped his collar. They struggled and strained against the pulling water, inching slowly, slowly toward the shore. Finally all three men collapsed on the bank, shivering and wet and freezing.

☩

CHAPTER 31

Faites de beaux rêves!

December 3, 1859

The bitter cold of pre-dawn morning found them in Jean-Émile's cramped, dirty one-room cabin. Pale moonlight barely shone through the tiny and grimy windows set in the rough walls of stripped pine log. Old guns and traps hung from rusted nails pounded into the wall, and clay chinking lay in piles where it had fallen. In the middle of the cramped room was a rickety table, sticky from old oil and spilled food, and in the corner next to the fireplace was an unmade bed on rough wood planks. At its foot, an old brown goat lay in a bed of straw, lazily chewing its cud, its yellow, goat-eyes studying them suspiciously, as it periodically bleated and grunted.

They sat by the fieldstone hearth, teeth chattering under scratchy woolen blankets as their clothes hung on the mantel to dry. Ambrose peered nervously out the window as the tiny flames of lanterns passed in the distant black fields. Heated voices yelled, far off yet far too close.

"Thank God we came out of the river where we did," Silas said. "Any farther downstream and we would have frozen. Any closer to town and we would have hanged. It's good your cabin is tucked in the woods and hard to spot.

Who would have thought we'd be bunking together again? It's just like old times!"

"All of Stantonville has gone crazy and you come banging on my door in the middle of the night? And now you say you are why it is. I don't know how to thank you." Jean-Émile said, sarcastically.

"This mush'll do just fine." Silas frowned, stirring a bowl of bland cornmeal. Steam rose in the cold, a chilly draft blowing in from dark corners.

"Ah, you damn English. You be thankful you get anything at all," Jean-Émile muttered. "And you, priests, back in St Gregory, I should have trusted my gut and just driven away."

Silas winked at Ambrose and Killian. "He's always been like this—moody—long as I've known him. Don't pay him any mind. He'll warm up to you." He turned to Jean-Émile. "And besides, there's no need to be mad at the English. After all, you know you're not French, you bloody dolt?"

The old goat stood and stretched, shaking off bits of straw and dirt that fell around. Its stiff legs thumped over to the table, where it nudged its oily head against Killian, gently headbutting and chewing on his robes.

"Well, we're very thankful you didn't drive away," Killian's face was an uncomfortable red as he tried, unsuccessfully, to push the goat away. "And if you hadn't let us in, I'm sure we would have frozen to death."

"Oh, see?" Jean-Émile motioned to Silas. "That's how you be polite. Maybe you could learn from this man?"

"How do you know each other?" Ambrose asked.

Silas chuckled. "I've known this fool for years."

"Seems like you know everybody."

Silas shook his head. "No. Not everybody. Just the interesting ones. But this one, always going on about his parentage. Porlier this. Porlier that. I swear, he thinks it's important. But it's unfortunately not interesting at all."

"Eh." Jean-Émile rolled his eyes. "I at least know my line. Not like you, *paysan.*"

"Your grandfather was little more than a *paysan* when he left France a decade after *La Révolution,* and you want to talk titles?" Silas said.

Maaa, the goat bleated, annoyed at being woken, its floppy ears flapping as it shook its head at Silas. The boards thumped under its hooves as it snorted. Jean-Émile tossed it a crust of bread and it sauntered over to nuzzle the man's calloused and dry hand.

"Are we safe here?" Ambrose interrupted. The cries in the fields grew closer, and he eyed the rough walls as if they might suddenly collapse. His heart hammered at every cry, and he imagined the old pine door bursting and glass shattering.

"No lights," Jean-Émile said. "We'll keep the fire low and wait the few hours for morning. I hope the floor is comfortable for you, because that's where you'll be once your clothes are dry. I have just these blankets, and one of them I'll be using. So you can get some straw from the barn, bundle up, and decide who's in the middle."

Ambrose eyed the floor and sighed. White trails of frost crept from the door across the rough wood and grew in tiny crystals on the edges of the window. A chill draft inched its icy claws through his blanket, even as he sat by the glowing fire.

"We'll have to stay holed up here for a couple of days," Silas said. "We should take this chance to keep our heads low. This fool town is on edge. I don't think anyone saw enough to know it was us, but I'd rather not take that chance on a foolhardy jaunt through the streets. Jean-Émile, can you check on King Henry? He's at the Westen's stables. Bring him back if you can. And smell out the mood on the street?"

"Of course. Why not?" he scowled. "The whole town on the lookout. But why not just stroll down the street and inquire after your horse? What's suspicious about that?"

"And this"—Silas crossed his arms—"after what happened in Sheboygan?"

"Ah, I never should have asked your help. I never hear the end. How could I know it was the mayor's niece?"

Silas laughed and shook his head. But Ambrose and Killian glanced up in quick surprise, a look of doubt in their eyes. Jean-Émile tossed his hands in the air in exasperation. "I was a young and pretty man once!" The man's unkempt and greasy hair, fell across a wrinkled brow and he smiled a toothless smile, amidst months' old stubble. Ambrose nodded, politely. But for the life of him he could not imagine Jean-Émile as either young or pretty.

They stared at the worn table, cracked and sticky with bits of old grease, as they listened for the searchers outside. The old goat nudged Killian once more, putting his hooves on the man's knee and standing up to sniff his face.

Killian turned his head away, twisting back and forth in exasperation. "Is no one going to explain this goat?"

"Eh? That is *mon Bébé!*" Jean-Émile said, surprised. "You treat her well!"

Killian sighed as the goat clamored over him, eventually forcing him to sit on the cold floor, as it stood on the chair and looked down to sniff his hair with its hot breath.

The room grew still as the last cries and shouts of the townsfolk died out. Hot embers hissed and glowed in the darkness as Jean absently poked at the ash and char, his face lit in the dying light.

"I think they are gone," he said. "And now, I think we turn in." He tossed them their cloths, hot from the fire. "Sleep tight," he said. "Don't let the bedbugs bite. *Faites de beaux rêves!*"

The next day dawned bright, but they dared not leave the cabin. At first light, Jean-Émile headed to town, leaving the three weary travelers to spend the day in cold shadow. The hours passed slowly. A yellow square of sun inched across the floor, dim through the grimy windowpane. They ate cold mush and bacon in silence, and Ambrose shivered in his robe and blanket. Even by the fire, the cold damp of the nearby river soaked into his bones, tightening and aching. *It's like an ice chest in here!* They were altogether miserable. Silas and Ambrose had it in mind to nose about to pass the time, but Killian protested. Finally, they sat back down and stared at the table in glum boredom. There was nothing at all in the room to nose about in, anyway.

Silas lit a pipe and leaned back, stroking his beard and lost in thought. Sweet smoke, blue and white, rolled and turning lazily in the small ray of the sun. "Want some?"

"Will it warm us up?" Ambrose asked, teeth chattering.

"It couldn't hurt."

He tore thin strips from an old *Chilton Times-Journal* and filled them with tobacco. Carefully he rolled it, his practiced fingers nimble despite their weathering and thick callouses. Bébé wandered the room, hooves clicking as it eyed the rolled cigarettes. Sniffing, it snuck up behind Silas and stole one from the table, gumming and chewing.

"God damn goat!" Silas grumbled as he rolled another. "It's a right bloody barn in here."

Soon Ambrose and Killian sat at the rickety kitchen table, puffing white smoke, rings rising around them. The acrid taste was sharp in Ambrose's mouth and his head grew light, but he did feel warmer. Killian, meanwhile, hacked and coughed, his throat burning and his eyes watering.

"Why are you helping us?" the young priest said, still gasping and panting.

"Lord, how should I know? Ever since Ambrose stumbled upon me in the forest, three-quarters dead, it's been my fate to keep him alive for some reason," Silas said. "I'd feel terribly bad if he died at this point. All my effort so far would have been for nothing."

"Well, thanks, I suppose," Ambrose said.

"Just put in a good word for me at those Pearly Gates, if that ends up being a real thing. Lord knows I've been surprised in the past," said Silas. "But I have to admit it's harder to move around in town with everyone eyeing each other. It's not good for my line of work. The sooner it clears up, the better."

"And what exactly is your line of work?" Killian said.

Silas winked. "Whatever needs doing."

The shadows grew longer, the winter light fading as the sun fell in the West. It had been quiet, but they were still on edge, listening for sounds of the angry town at the door. The stoop creaked and the door cracked slightly open. Ambrose's heart raced. *They* found *us!* Silas grabbed his gun and Killian hid under the table just as a head poked in through the door, peering at them in the darkness.

"Ha! I got you!" Jean-Émile cackled, pointing.

"Damn it!" Silas snapped. "You God damn Canuck! You were supposed to give a knock!"

"No! No! So much better this way!" He held his belly, laughing. "Your faces!"

Ambrose slumped against the wall. He cursed silently as his heart slowed. Killian stood and paced nervously beside him. Only Bébé was exited, and pranced over to greet Jean-Émile, bleating and baaing.

"Can we get out of this cabin then?" Ambrose said.

"Hm, I wouldn't recommend it," Jean-Émile said. "Not unless you want the town on you. I'd say you have another night at least. The Sheriff is edgy and everyone is looking over their shoulder, thinking maybe the next man is the man to turn in. The jail is full of supposed ne'er-do-wells that were in the wrong place at the wrong time. Drunks mostly."

They groaned and sat down, dejected.

"Oh, you don't like my company now?" Jean-Émile laughed. "Maybe you want to try your luck on your own? That's no problem. I don't know if I like your company either. But if you leave, you'll miss dinner."

Silas made a face. "What? More mush?"

"Oh, you silly man," said Jean-Émile said. "No, we will have a proper dinner. Something hot. And a little bread and beer. It's good." He clapped Silas's shoulder. "I know you will pay me back, eh? Rumor has it you have a score from old Franz Guthiel."

The coachman reached into his bag and set a loaf of bread and a jug of beer on the table with a thump. Soon, the fire crackled, merry and bright, and a hearty stew bubbled on the pot above.

"What about King Henry?" Silas asked.

"Eh, I'm sure he's safe in the stable and he'll remain that way…if you get back to him. "The town is too riled up. I won't go asking now. Better for me and better for you, too."

Irritated, Silas frowned and muttered to himself.

The stew roiled, thick steam carrying the scents of peppered squirrel and bits of old bacon. When it was finally ready, they ate in happy silence. Ambrose felt warm for the first time in days as he finally pushed the bowl away and leaned back, sipping his beer and staring at the hearth's bright embers.

"Tell me about this Valentine," Jean-Émile said. "He seems like quite the fellow."

"Well," Ambrose said. "I'll tell you the little I know."

They talked long into the night. Ambrose told of Valentine's personal war with the church, the flight of his congregation to the New World, the founding of St. Gregory around his "vision," and Stephan's quest to bring him back to the fold. Jean-Émile nodded as Ambrose told of the bishop going missing and all the things they had seen in the town: Father Valentine's grip on the people, Anselm's iron hand, the unholy room that had been the bishop's prison at the Abbey of the Holy Ghost.

"There were two brothers in brown robes from the abbey who were sometimes on the roads at night," Jean-Émile said. "I think no one else saw them, but I'm not so close to town, so I'd spy them at night at times. I think they're this Valentine's obedient dogs. They might get in the way of you finding your bishop. There were two. One skinny, wispy, like a strong wind would blow him over, though he seemed clever. The other was a bulk of man. Slow on the uptake. I haven't seen that one for some time."

"He's dead," said Killian. "I killed him." Ambrose looked up, surprised by the bluntness of his honesty and dismayed by the bitter look in his eye. He opened his mouth to speak but thought of Tobias. The old man's death was on his hands; a sin he could never wash clean. A sickening regret washed over him, and he looked at Killian in sadness. *We are the same, you and I.*

"Ah, well there you go," the coachman said. "I would not have guessed you had it in you."

Killian looked away, his face red.

"It is just fine!" Jean-Émile clapped his back. "*C'est la vie!* Besides, what do they say? Wrong place, wrong time, eh? I did not like him anyway." He took a swig of beer and turned back to Ambrose and Silas. "But tell me, where will you find these people?"

"Here, I think." Ambrose drew the map from his bag and unfolded it on the table.

"And what is this? Ah, a map! Someone has been doing spells. But not very well, it seems. This X is where it all leads to. That is the caves, of course. The old Indian caves. *Wasuskeqsinoh,* they call them."

"Eloi said that," Ambrose replied. "But how would Valentine or Anselm even know where they are?"

"People like that are drawn to those places," Silas explained. "You know the people I mean. Eloi could say more, but the little I know is that the caves hold burial chambers of the ones who lived here once. Not the Indians now but the ones who were here long, long ago. Eloi said his people never go there. It is where they would bury their medicine men and shamans, deep in the earth so they would not roam after death if they were corrupted. There's a power to those places. Your black priest finds it like flies to shit."

"And you have to find it too," Jean-Émile said.

"Are you going to help?" asked Silas.

"Ha! I'll take you there, but I'll be damned if I'm going in with you! Call me what you will, but this is not my concern. No one is paying me to be on a Catholic commission and no priest stumbled upon me in the woods. I have no call to risk my neck here."

"Figures." Silas shook his head. "After all we've been through."

"Ha! By now, I've learned your crazy adventures are your own, my friend." Jean-Émile laughed and scratched Bébé's rump. The old goat rubbed its head against the wall in pleasure. "What is digging up these grave anyway? Is it the same as is lighting the fires?"

"I'd say not," said Silas. "Something is digging in, not out. We have that going for us, at least. There aren't more undead rising. But the prints were from a man's hands—or what used to be a man. Not the *nachzehrer's*, if Issa is the only one. And a *nachzehrer* doesn't feed on the dead anyway. I'd wager it's a scavenger. Possibly unintended. But no scavenger has the faculty or call to light a fire. They'd sooner flee it. So I think these are two different things."

Killian scowled and shook his head at such talk. He muttered and looked away, his brow creased with wrinkles.

"It seems the shock has gotten to our young priest here and he clings to only what he can see in front of him. It seems he does not believe," said Jean-Émile. "He will."

The next day drew on like the last, filled with long waiting. The sky clouded and the sparse light was dim and gray, the cabin still oozing a damp chill the fire couldn't chase away. They sat shivering and miserable, picking at cold leftovers from the night before. Ambrose stared out the window at the white and brown of fallow fields and stretching forest. His stomach was a twist of knots. Even Bébé lay curled by the fire in a bed of warm straw, utterly uninterested in them.

Killian sighed. "This is intolerable."

"It's not the cold," said Silas, though he gathered his coat about himself. "It's the waiting. The waiting is the worst part."

Snow fell, tiny flakes swirling outside the window. Silas puffed on his pipe and shuffled cards, the old stiff paper thwapping the table. His gray hair stood on end as he scratched and pulled, studying the deck through a haze of white smoke, as if reading tarot.

"You have to get your weapons ready," he said casually. "Killian, I don't trust you with a gun. You're liable to shoot yourself or, worse, me. That knife will have to do. But you have to learn how to use it. I don't have time to teach you, so take it to heart when I tell you the most important thing is not to drop it. Seems simple, but you'd be surprised what happens in the heat of the moment."

Killian opened his mouth to speak but closed it again. He crossed his arms and glared at Ambrose. "I thought we were going to be home for Christmas."

"Take the knife out," Silas said, ignoring him. "Feel it. Feel the weight. Get used to it. Don't hold it like that, like it's some dumb thing in your hand. Hold it like it's a part of you."

Killian grasped the knife. It was heavier than he remembered. Heavy and cold. The blade started thick and drew to a long vicious point. It was more like a small sword than a knife: bigger and clumsier than a knife for fighting, not that he had any experience with that.

"Ambrose, you have that mortician's blade," Silas said. "It's not the best to walk into a fight with, but it's oddly appropriate, all things considered—a mortician's blade to hunt the undead. But it's better if you rack your brain for any of your priest knowledge. Valentine will try to confuse and addle the brain—best to keep the ole' mind clear and sharp."

"What priest knowledge do you mean?" asked Ambrose.

"You tell me! It's not my calling. But words have power. Even the ones from bad stories." He winked at Killian. "So see if you can't figure it out." He turned back to his cards, shuffling and drawing. He tossed a two of spades on the table and frowned. "Not what I wanted. Not a good omen."

"What about Issa?" Ambrose said.

"It's not Issa! It's a *nachzehrer,*" Silas said. "I guess we'll find out when we get there. Can Valentine or Anselm control it or just summon it? That's an important question."

"How do you kill it? Assuming it's real," Ambrose said. "With silver, like the stories?"

"Silver is just for werewolves." Killian said.

"Not according to the book. It seems to work on anything unholy, to a greater or lesser degree."

"Ha! Good luck with silver," Silas scoffed. "Have you ever tried to use a silver weapon? Even opening your mail with a silver letter opener, the thing is liable to bend. Imagine trying to stab an undead. The blade would blunt and turn off a rib or even a hand. Then you're rightly screwed. And don't think of using silver bullets either. That's an old foolish French bedtime story. Use a silver bullet and you'll never hit a damn thing. It'll shoot wide every time."

"Then why is it in all the stories?" Killian protested.

"Judas was paid thirty pieces of silver for betraying Jesus," Ambrose said. "Silver is the mark of betrayal for the unholy. At least that's what I've heard."

"Who knows?" Silas said. "If it works, it works. It does burn them. But try fashioning a weapon out of it and you'll soon learn it doesn't make the slightest bit of difference, as using it will just get you killed. Far better to have a steel blade and hack as hard as you can."

"I don't know if I can do that," Killian said, holding the blade doubtfully.

"You'll find out soon enough." Silas pointed to the setting sun. "It'll be dark in an hour. We'll leave then. You'd better hope the *nachzehrer* isn't prowling tonight, especially if you can't handle yourself. You'll drop the blade and piss your britches, and that'll be the end of you."

✠

CHAPTER 32

Oily Goat and Black Mud

December 3, 1859

The storm howled, blinding white and hiding the path. Jean-Émile led them south on foot through the dales and glens, careful to avoid the road and neighboring farms. "It is shit weather," he remarked. "But it is good for you at least. No one will be out today. Not unless some foolish sheep has broken the fence and gotten lost."

Deer trails ran, crossing the forest in every direction. Jean-Émile chose the ones leading south, but they twisted and turned and doubled back, taking them astray, and they were forced to stop and curse and walk back and forth to find new ones. The darkness made for slow going. Their lanterns cast only faint yellow against the snow-filled black, and they snagged their boots on stray roots and stumps, cursing as the snowy branches slapped them in the dark. The night wore on and still the storm howled. Their humor waned as they trudged in silence, sloshy flakes falling about them and soaking into their coats and pants. Their feet splashed in puddles, and they were soon numb from cold. Ambrose couldn't begin to guess how far they'd walked. Miles and miles, he thought bitterly. What would he find at the end of it all? Would he find forgiveness?

The trail suddenly split. "No! Why? Why?" Jean-Émile threw his arms up. "Stupid deer! Why this way?" He cursed, looking back and forth at the map and the dark night beyond. They waited in miserable silence as he scratched his head and shook wet flakes off the crumpled paper.

"Do you know where you're going?" Silas asked, annoyed.

"Eh? Piss off. You think you know better?"

Silas grabbed the map, pointing in the dim moonlight. Jean-Émile nodded the other way; they stood arguing, arms crossed.

"It is this snow!" Jean-Émile said. "It is washing away all the lines."

Silas pointed to the left, but Jean-Émile shook his head. The wind roared above, muffling their voices as the coachman stomped his feet.

"Fine!" Silas growled. "We'll go your way. Let's just go."

They hadn't stepped more than a foot when thunder cracked in the distance, rolling across the dark sky. The woods shook from the mighty boom and they jumped in their boots.

"Did you hear that?" Jean-Émile's jumped in surprise. "Thunder! In a winter storm! Who has heard of such a thing? I don't like it. I don't like it at all! Let's go!"

They hurried on, the trail leading them deeper into the dark wood, dipping into the hollows and around the old cedars of an unknown marsh. All the while, the wind hissed in the trees like fell voices.

Killian froze in place and put a hand to his ear. "Do you hear that?"

"It is the old spirits of this place," Jean-Émile said. "They don't like us here."

"I don't like us here either!" Killian said.

Lightning illuminated the sky, and dead marsh trees flashed white like old bones. Another peel of thunder split the air, echoing and rumbling off the rocky bluffs in the distance, and they winced at the crack and boom.

"Are you *sure* you know where you're going?" asked Silas.

"I will leave you here if you don't shut your stupid face," Jean-Émile said, scowling in the yellow light of the lantern. Their heated voices rose again as they stared at the map, pointing and yelling.

"Oh, will this never end?" Killian said, shivering. "I suppose there's no hope of a fire at this rate!"

Ambrose huddled in the poor shelter of a cedar, his feet soaked and freezing. *Why this night, of all nights? What I wouldn't give to be in a warm bed!* His thoughts drifted to crackling fires and dry clothes.

"How close do you think we are?" Silas said. "Let's get up in those rocks and out of this wind."

"Close, sure!" Jean-Émile said. "The bluff is near and there we may be at least out of the wind. But for the love of Christ, shut up and stop complaining, or we'll never get there!"

Silas and Jean poked the earth with sticks, testing, but even so, the soft ground often gave way and they sank into the cold muck. Ambrose's hands splashed into water as he tripped and fell, Killian beside him. Soon they were covered in cold, black muck, struggling under the weight of so much mud.

They inched forward as the storm wailed, growing fierce. Cracks and booms peeled and echoed against the stone bluff, while lightning burst in flashes of eerie white. In the light, they saw the old bluff was split in fissures and grooves; deep cracks stretched up to the top, now hidden in the darkness, and holes pocked the side, etched by eons of wind and rain. When their hands finally touched the crumbling limestone, they were too tired and cold and wet to even curse.

"Many caves here," Jean-Émile said. "We need to find the right one. But first let us leave this awful wind and wet. I spy a place ahead.

Deep hollows and caves opened as they passed, the floors submerged. Many were small and narrow, yet a few stretched far back, awash in dark eeriness, their ends unfathomable. Cold drafts gusted within and Ambrose hurried past, imagining hidden eyes staring at him in the dark.

Finally they stumbled upon a path that wound up among the fallen rocks and rotted logs. Whether it was natural or carved long ago, they couldn't say.

The way grew steep and Ambrose hugged the side as rocks skittered and clattered underfoot, falling over the edge. Mercifully the wind grew less severe as they climbed. It howled over the ridge but hadn't the strength to find them in the rocks. They couldn't have been very high up, certainly not as high as the foothills of St. Gallen, where he wandered as a boy. But in the darkness Ambrose's mind played tricks on him, and he imagined an endless chasm far below. *Look at me, frightened by a molehill!*

Strange shapes took form in the light as his nose was pressed to the rock: ancient shells and the swirling forms of sea creatures from long ago. They sparkled in the light, dusted with tiny crystals of calcite and quartz. He brushed his hand across their rough surface in wonderment at some forgotten past. Another time, he would have stopped and studied them. But in the cold, wet darkness, he could only press on.

The path eventually opened on a small ledge and, at its back, the shallow cave they had seen below.

"Ha! Get you gone! Get out, you!" Silas waved the revolver and stepped into the dark. The tiny lantern wavered, casting its yellow flame against the back wall. "All clear!"

The cave was shallow but deep enough to shelter them. Killian and Ambrose huddled against the back wall as the wind raged at the mouth. Silas and Jean-Émile cursed, bent over a pile of bark and sticks and branches, somehow scattered at the entrance.

"Did somebody leave those?" Ambrose asked. "Do you think they'll come back?"

"Don't know and I don't care." Silas bent before the tinder, sheltering with his hand as he grumbled. "Damn wind!"

"Maybe it is too wet for fire," Jean-Émile said, "Maybe we make do with blankets. Maybe it is better no one sees our light. We are now very close."

"To hell with that!" Silas protested. "I'd rather die warm and seen than cold and miserable and hidden."

Finally a spark took. It smoldered, and the oily smell of birch filled the cave, warm and comforting, growing in yellow tongues that licked at the branches and sticks, cracking and hissing. Ambrose's heart leapt for joy as he stretched his hands to the fire. *Thank you, God!*

"Dry off as you can. The wood won't last long," Silas said. "Dry your socks and boots too!"

"Ah, look." Jean-Émile held up the charred end of a branch. "Someone was here before us. And what is that? Someone left us wood!"

There, in a corner of the cave, lay a stack of firewood. "Oh, what good luck have we! Ho ho ho!" Jean-Émile exclaimed. "Or…maybe it is bad? Maybe someone comes to use this cave often? That would be bad indeed."

"Not tonight, I'll wager," Silas said. "Let's warm up and have another look at that map."

"If only the snow had not washed so much away. I cannot say for certain what I see," Jean-Émile said. "So many caves here. But which one? Probably they are all the same and lead to the same place. But will you take the risk? I think not. Maybe we should wait until light."

"What if he knows we're coming?" asked Ambrose.

"Ah, that is a good question," Jean-Émile said, frowning. "Then you are not so good, I think."

"That's not very reassuring."

Long hours passed as the wind and snow swirled in the marsh below. They sat huddled against the back of the hollow, sharing the thin blanket. Red embers glowed, warming the rock and casting their faces in yellows and golds, their eyes twinkling in the night.

Killian dozed in fits, while Silas and Jean-Émile snored quietly. Ambrose nodded off, tired but unable to sleep. The storm slowly waned, but the occasional crack of distant thunder and flash of lightening made him jump.

A movement caught his eye, a black shape skulking between the trees.

"What was that?" he cried. The others stirred, peering into the darkness.

"What was what?" asked Killian, shaking.

Another flash lit the marsh and it was gone.

Thin rays of morning light broke through the clouds and lit the land in pale white. Heavy snow covered the earth, hanging from sagging branches and falling in clumps in the warming air, the white ground broken occasionally by pools of black water. The marsh woke with the call of chickadees—*chick-a-dee-dee-dee*—echoing off the rocks. A cardinal flittered in the trees—a flash of red—and was gone. Ambrose peered over the ledge at the ground below. Whatever creature had stirred the night before had long vanished, its tracks now hidden.

The men stretched, stiff and sore, and Ambrose, weary from his sleepless night, rubbed his head and neck. The fire was cold and dead, and they ate their meager breakfast in silence, gnawing on hard crusts of bread and strips of dried goat, its cold fat thick and gamy. Ambrose's stomach turned. *Worse than balten brei!* Only Jean-Émile enjoyed it, licking the oily grease from his fingers.

Killian pointed. "Are those cart tracks?"

Snaking through the soft ground, around the stagnant pools and cedars, two tracks ran side by side, covered in snow, their furrows barely noticeable. The snaking line twisted and turned around the rocks and trees, following the higher ground before finally ending behind an outcropping in the distance.

"Good eye, Killian! Those look like cart tracks to me." Silas peered from the ledge. "With any luck, they'll lead us right to the cavern. I can't imagine any other reason someone would be out here. Must be from the abbey."

"Well, we found it." Killian sighed miserably. "Guess we'll be on our way then."

Walking the marsh should have been easier in the light of day, but the storm hid the softer patches of ground in white. The swampy earth squished and oozed beneath their feet, its brackish water soaking into their boots, only to suddenly give way as their legs sank up to their knees. They gripped and yanked and struggled, pulling one another and collapsing, exhausted, upon the solid ground, only to take another step and sink again.

"Fucking mud!" Silas snarled.

The trail was farther away than it seemed, and the sun was high overhead before the outcropping grew near. Its rough walls were cracked and fissured, and black holes hissed cold air from deep in the earth.

They walked in wretched silence, sinking and splashing in the cold muck, when finally the ground rose slowly above the water and the dense cedars gave way to thickets of white birch. Their legs sank less often and less deep, until at last, at midday, they found themselves on solid ground again. Ambrose stared back in disbelief; they couldn't have gone more than a quarter of a mile.

"Merde!" Jean-Émile panted, hands on his knees. "Why do I do what I do?"

As far as they could tell, the trail led to the rock wall, where it stopped abruptly. No shelter stood nearby. Only a small turnaround for the cart showed any evidence of people.

"Look!" Silas pointed. A narrow path wound its way up the side of the rock, barely noticeable. It looked recently used. Chipped stone and snapped branches showed where someone, or several someones, had dragged something large and heavy. But the night's snow was as yet undisturbed. No one had come this way today.

"No one is out and about yet. That is good," Jean-Émile said. "But when they see your tracks, they'll know you are."

"Ever the optimist." Silas frowned. "Well, nothing for it."

Up and up, they climbed, the path winding past weathered stone and dead and fallen trees. Ambrose's skin crawled as if touched by the ghosts of those ancient ones before. He looked around, ill at ease, feeling as a trespasser. Soon they spotted a great split in the wall ahead. The path ended before a dark crack as wide as a man. They stood silently at the sides, unwilling to stand before that blackness.

Silas struck a match and puffed on his pipe. White smoke wreathed around them, filling the air with a woodsy smell, comforting against the chill. "I think we need a break," he said, passing the pipe.

Ambrose peered into the darkness. The cold draft struck his face and sent a chill through his body. His hair stood on end, and he felt it again; they were being watched.

"Do you feel that?" he said. "Like something doesn't want us here?"

"That's maybe a good thing, in this case," Silas said. He puffed and stroked his beard in thought, and the wooden pipe clicked against his teeth. Finally he sighed and shook his head. "Are you coming?" he asked Jean-Émile.

The coachman shook his head. "Ha-ha, no," Jean said. "You are on your own. But bring me back something nice, eh?"

"That's too bad. I didn't take you for a lily-livered coward."

"Eh? Fuck you! *Fils de pute!*"

"All right." Silas waved his hand. "Guess we're on our own."

"I will wait here until just before sunset with a big fire…if I can get one started," Jean-Émile said. "If you are not back by then, you are on your own, my friends."

"That's all I could ask for," Silas said. He grasped Jean's shoulder and looked him in the eye. "Well, I guess this is goodbye." He turned to the priests. "All right you two, remember what I told you. And Killian, quit moping. Stiff upper lip now!"

With that, they plunged into the darkness.

☩

CHAPTER 33

A Dark Betrayal

December 3, 1859

The narrow crack extended deep into the rock, and the wind at the mouth grew slowly quiet. The only sound was their breath and the hard scrabble beneath their feet, as they traversed the narrow passage. Bat guano lay thick on the ground at the entrance, frozen and at least a foot thick. It must have been revolting in the summer. But the bats were all gone for the winter and no other life stirred within. Thankfully, there were no sleeping bears or cougars, and soon they left the guano behind, stepping on the cold rock that stretched ever onward into the dark.

Silas led them deeper, carefully winding and twisting around the jagged rock that split and spilled in the path. Yellow light illuminated the walls beside them, tiny flames shaking, but the darkness in front stretched on, unbroken. Silas gritted his teeth, lantern in one hand, revolver in the other, while Ambrose felt his own hand drawn to the cold handle of his blade.

"Ambrose, I'm scared," Killian whispered.

"Maybe we should have left Killian with Jean-Émile?" Silas said.

"Maybe we should have gotten on a train and left for Chicago!" said Killian. "I've made my choice."

"Suit yourself," Silas said.

The cold wind picked up. The dim light shining through slivers in the rock above showed glimpses of gray sky beyond, the cold air rushing up to greet it. Soon they left even that light behind and trudged farther into darkness. After some time, the tunnel opened, giving way to a vast cavern. The *plink-plink* of drops in hidden pools echoed in the tomblike silence and, far ahead, they heard the rush of water gushing and spilling in unseen darkness. The paltry light of their tiny lamps scarcely lit the way, and in the dark, unearthly shapes took form, wonderous and awful. Pillars of stone reached down from the ceiling and up from the floor, dusted in calcite and aragonite, that shimmered and flashed in yellow flame. Pools of black water extended into the distance, lost in the unseen vastness, their surfaces still and cold as death. Here and there, domes of limestone rose from the ground, smooth and wet and glistening, like puffballs littering a forest floor, while veins of shimmering crystal glittered, stretching through the rock wall like spiderwebs.

Ambrose held his lantern to the wall. Ancient shapes danced across the smooth rock. Figures of red and white, frozen in the timeless darkness, ran across the primordial walls. Men with bows and spears chased the mighty game of forgotten times across the ancient, painted stone: giant deer and hulking, horned beasts, and bizarre creatures with impossibly long snouts, and many more that he could not fathom. Here and there he spied strange symbols: odd shapes, sharp and angled, in obvious pattern; triangles lay one upon another, ascending and descending; zigzags, like lightening, crossed concentric circles; and stylized figures held fierce bows and spears. He gazed in wonder. "What is all this?"

"Ancient tales of the old ones here long ago," Silas said. "Their hunts. Their movements and wanderings. Their symbols and magic that none can now read. These places have power still, even if the ones who made them are forgotten. That's what called Valentine and Anselm. But let's not tarry here!"

Silas marched on ahead, but Ambrose gave one last look at the ancient paintings. His hand touched the rough stone, involuntarily, and he shivered with goosebumps at the thought of a primordial past stretching back farther than he could imagine. He looked in fear at the lanterns of the other two, now far ahead, and hurried to catch. *I hope those spirits aren't still down here after all these years!*

The path led on: the smooth stone floor marked by piles of rock on either side. The piles were different than the weathered rock of water and time. They were broken and jagged. Someone had placed these piles here, perhaps long ago, to mark the way. Had it not been for these guide stones, they would have quickly lost their bearings. Even so, Silas made note of the features around them. "Remember that one. The one that looks like a horse."—He pointed—"And this boulder by the stream."

On they traveled, through the long cavern. It narrowed at the far end, and now, so far away from the surface, the cold damp seeped into their very bones. The air held hints of wet stone: an earthy, but clean smell. It was surprisingly light and easy to breath, as if it had not touched any other creature's lungs in all eternity. The path slowly rose up and narrowed, heading to a ledge above, when suddenly, a rough-hewn stair emerged from the slick stone. Ambrose's heart quickened at the signs of chisel on the rock. Seeing the evidence of men broke all sense of wonder, and with a sense of foreboding, he finally came to the top and saw a dreadful sight. All around him were stacked rows of piled stone: rectangular mounds of rock in ordered file and, in the center, a ring of scorched rock, blackened from ancient fires.

Ambrose stopped and stared. *This is familiar. This is...* He turned round and round. "These look like..."

"Cairns," Silas said. "Underground cairns. This must be where the long-forgotten tribe buried their dead. We're surrounded by them. I hadn't imagined seeing so many."

"I hadn't imagined on seeing any at all!" Killian said, shaking. "Oh, what rotten luck."

Here and there the old stones lay fallen before them, rolled off their piles to expose the bones beneath—gray bits of arm and leg bones and the sharp end of ribs. The heads of stone axes and hammers lay at their sides, and the dull green of copper lay about their necks and brows.

"Don't touch them!" Silas cautioned. "Best not to disturb the dead."

Killian took a step back. "Why would I ever touch them?"

"Just don't get curious!"

They quickly hurried on. A natural stair led still higher, leading to a second ledge above. They climbed, anxious to leave the cairns below, yet as they went, they spied round shapes that lined the path, oddly stacked, and too round and uniform to be stone. Ambrose held his lantern high. But he knew what it was before he looked: rows and rows of skulls, their black eyesockets staring at him as they smiled in the darkness.

"Well, it wasn't you, Killian. But someone got curious, it would seem!" Silas said. "Curious enough to line them all up. Was that Valentine? Or was this some peculiar custom from ages ago?"

"I don't care," Ambrose said. "Let's hurry!"

Again, the feeling of eyes was upon him. He tried to ignore it, but something didn't want him here. He couldn't help but think of malevolent spirits gazing angrily from the shadows, disturbed by his passing. He rushed on, into the small chamber beyond, as Silas and Killian followed after. But this room was even more terrible! A foul musk hung in the frigid air: the smell of old death. He knew it from his father's clinic, just as he knew it from the cemetery vaults and mortuaries. Ambrose stopped short at white bundles at his feet. They could only be one thing: bodies.

His heart sank as Killian trembled beside him. Were they just stumbling blindly from one horrid place to the next? How would they ever make it back? Or, would the spirits of the dead, or worse, transpire to block their way and seal them forever in this tomb?

"This just gets worse and worse!" Killian cried. "How is this possible?"

"Anything is possible. Accept that and life will go a lot easier for you," Silas said. "But these here are not old! It seems your friends have been active. They have a collection going."

"For what?" Ambrose grimaced.

"Necromancy, it would seem," Silas said, matter-of-factly.

"How do you know so much, and by what unearthly power are you so calm?" Ambrose asked. "Have you been drinking?"

"I hardly see what difference that makes," Silas said. "Now's not the time for judgment. By all rights, we are on a holy quest! If the crusades, and your Catholic faith, have taught us anything, it's that those on a holy quest can do no wrong."

Ambrose rolled his eyes. "I'll pretend not to hear your mocking tone. But I'm not judging—I'm jealous!"

"Well, my dear father," Silas said, "this is not my first time falling afoul of the dark arts and sorcery. Although it is my first time encountering a deranged priest. So I suspect this shall prove interesting. And what is interesting is exciting!"

"Dear God, where did you find this man?" Killian said, wailing in despair.

"Come now, don't take the Lord's name in vain. Isn't that what you folk always say? Now buck up! We've a stretch to go and an ending unclear. Now's not the time to be dour."

He led them on, yet despite his cheerful mood, Ambrose couldn't shake the feeling of dread. He reached for his cross for comfort and safety, bringing it to his mouth to kiss it, but as it touched his lips, he realized it was not his cross, at all, but was Annaliese's amulet. Somehow it felt more real in his hands, and though he felt he shouldn't, he clung to it, his cross forgotten.

The cavern narrowed to a tunnel, leading deeper into the heart of the earth, and they left the smell of death behind. Yet, all too soon another smell filled the air: the acrid scent of kerosene, faint and far away. *We must be getting close!* The tunnel twisted, growing narrower still, and the smell grew stronger in the tight space. Soon they reached a bend, beyond which a red light glowed. They slowed, careful of the skitter of rock underfoot, and with each step, Ambrose's breath caught in his chest.

Silas pulled them close. "Remember," he whispered, "keep your mind clear. If I know anything about this sort of thing, I know this: no matter what happens, don't lose your wits! I don't know what we're walking into. Nor do I know if it's just one or whether there are others. And where is that *nachzehrer?* I swear, the closer we get, the more foolhardy the whole idea seems. But that's just the fear talking—the trickery of the mind. This quest may be foolhardy, but it's not foolish!"

"What will you do when you find Valentine?" Ambrose asked.

"What will *I* do?" Silas lifted a brow. "I was meant to believe this was *your* little holy quest, Ambrose! I have plenty else I could do with my time. The question is, what will *you* do?"

"I'm not sure." Ambrose frowned. "I didn't think we'd actually get to this part. I guess I never thought about it."

"Well, you'd best start and be quick, because like it or not, we're at this part now!"

"I need to find Stephan," he said. "And I need to stop this madness. If I can talk to Valentine, maybe I can reason with him. Maybe he and Anselm can be saved."

"It figures I'd be destined to be the savior of such a bleeding heart." Silas shook his head. "I hope your misplaced faith doesn't get us all killed. But whatever faith they taught you, or you found, or you were born with, use it. But also use your blade. Remember, Valentine's just a man. And the *nachzehrer* is just a body. As long as there's a body, there's something to work with. If your heart wavers, think on your verses and prayers…or a girl back home. Or fella. Whatever keeps your head straight. Just be prepared to use your knife—the both of you—should it come to it."

"But what if there's things with no bodies?" Killian said.

"Oh, you and your demons." Silas sighed. "In that case, we're rightly screwed. Just remember"—he grabbed Killian by his cassock and looked sternly into his eyes—"don't drop your blade! Right, on we go."

They crept through the tunnel, careful in the dark, but the red light approached before any of them wished. Soon the narrow passage opened into another cavern, this time lit by iron lanterns that hung from the wall. The room was awash in their fiery glow, and the flames flickered red on the wall like one pictures of the bowels of hell. Before them, the path led down in narrow and twisting steps, leading into a wide basin filled with stalagmites and cold and dark pools that flickered, like scarlet pools of blood, in the light. Steep rock encircled, but to the left the wall suddenly gave way to a deep chasm, its deathly fall lost to the darkness. Far below, the rush and churn of water crashed against the rocks, filling the cavern with a dull roar.

From the tunnel, they saw the path climb the far side up to a wide ledge that overlooked the basin. Candles and lanterns wavered and flickered, illuminating what must have been an arcane study, and here and there, tucked in the natural holes and pockets of the rock, were old books and scrolls and vials. Dried herbs hung alongside burlap sacks stuffed with feathers and branches and odd bones, and everywhere on the walls were symbols and writings in red or black, but whether they were of blood or paint or ink, Ambrose couldn't tell.

"What is this place?" Killian whispered.

"Some kind of dark sanctorum," Silas said. "Be on your guard!

As they descended, a heavy dread swallowed them. Strange noises played tricks on their ears—echoing like the familiar voices of those long gone—and shadows flitted just out of their vision. Water rushed softly in the depths, growling like a beast hidden in the blackness below, and the plink of drops in cold pools stood their hair on end. Their eyes darted at imagined sounds and footsteps following.

"Do you hear that?" Killian said softly. "Someone's calling me. You don't hear her voice in the distance?" He peered fearfully into the dark, his hands trembling.

"Keep your wits, boy," Silas said, but he stopped and stared too, listening to voices of his own.

The air grew heavy and clinging, thick and oily, and they struggled to lift their feet against the awful feeling. Finally they stopped, exhausted. Ambrose opened his mouth to speak but closed it again, fearful to break the silence. Nothing stirred in the darkness, yet the cavern was frightfully alive. He imagined black shapes all around, watching and hungry, surrounding and circling. Even Silas kept looking over his shoulder.

"Ambrose," a voice hissed.

He looked about, but there was no one. Was it just the wind?

"Ambrose," it hissed again. "What are you looking for?"

Ambrose spun. No ghastly shapes appeared in the gloom, yet something felt close, watching. His heart stopped and his blood ran cold. No matter where he turned, eyes followed—eyes he could not see. Silas circled, revolver drawn, while Killian cowered behind. They had heard it too.

"Who are you?" Ambrose said.

"You know who I am. I am the one you seek. The one you've sacrificed so much to find. What will you do now that you've found me?"

His heart leapt in his throat. "Stephan!"

"Of course." A gray-haired man appeared suddenly above, where no one had been just moments before. He stood gaunt and withered, with a light in his eyes that filled them with fear. Tight skin stretched across his hollow face and his eyes flashed a ghastly light of their own, as if possessed. His red robes fluttered in an unseen wind, and in his bony hand a sword gleamed, bound in stalks of witch hazel. But it was Stephan! It was his father's dear friend, the same man he had known and loved as a child, yet now changed. Where Ambrose remembered his warm smile and tender heart, there was now a cold and malicious sneer. This was not the man he had known!

"You are changed!" Ambrose cried. "What has Valentine done to you? How are you imprisoned here?"

"Imprisoned?" Stephan laughed viciously. "Who do you think leads these people? Who do you think works tirelessly from the shadows? Do you honestly believe Valentine possesses the power to raise Issa from death?"

"No…" Ambrose said. "What are you saying? I cannot believe any of this! Your captivity has made you confused!"

"Don't be so dull witted," Stephan sneered. "Everything is according to design, I assure you."

"It was never Valentine, at all, was it?" Ambrose cried. "It was you! Tobias died because of you!"

Ambrose's head grew light. The room spun in a blur of reds and browns, and he stumbled, his feet splashing in the blood red pools.

"Tobias played his small part and fulfilled his middling capacity. But Valentine"—he laughed again—"Valentine is manic and deluded. He has deceived himself into thinking he has seen the face of God, and he dwells in that happy lie. He is an old fool grown soft in the mind. He has been tempted by false teachings and fallen astray, given to the sloth and the indolence of his idle imaginings! In his arrogance, he thinks Christ came to him, when he strung himself up on his own cross. He presumes to know Christ's love. But he will pay for turning his back on the Lord."

"Why?" Ambrose cried. "Why have you led these people down such dark and false paths? Why are you hiding here amongst the dead? You're given to madness, Stephan. You have lost your way!"

Stephen thrust his arms into the air. He seemed to grow before them, the cavern filling with a terrible presence that forced them back. The sword in his hand gleamed as he held it aloft.

"You will address me as 'Your Eminence'!" he cried, his booming voice filling the chamber. "Who are you to talk about ways, when you have so completely lost your own?"

"You've corrupted..." Ambrose stuttered. "You've turned men upon each other. You twisted people and made them unnatural and unholy!"

A smile grew on his devilish face as Stephen looked down in vicious glee, the sight of them cowering before him filling him with laughter. "Have I now? Is it not you who defiled the dead with your spell to find me? And in what unholy book did you find that spell? Are you sure it is not you who is deceived? Poor Issa. Augustin too. They were alive before you came. There was a natural order. Death arrived with *you,* Ambrose."

Ambrose's head grew light, and the cavern swirled, shadow and blackness fading into one. Only Stephan's face was clear before him. He reached to steady himself but found nothing to grasp. He struggled to cry out, but the words were stuck.

"You are a heretic!" he finally managed. "You betrayed your faith!"

A ghoulish smile spread on Stephan's withered face as he stared from the rocks above. In laughter, he pointed at Ambrose with the tip of his sword. "Have I know? And what is that talisman around your neck? You speak of faith, yet your own choice is clear." He shook his head in mock pity. "And how many people have you betrayed? How many have you abandoned? Your mother? Your sister? They sold themselves for you. How do you think they spent their nights when you were in seminary? Of course you know. You hear those whispers in the dark corners of your mind. So many sacrifices for you and how have you repaid them? Wasting time chasing idle imaginings on the other side of the earth, fallen into drunkenness and womanizing. What of Annaliese? She was always so innocent, but fearless. I can see how you would fall for her. What is her life now, when she's been spoiled by you? How many people will you ruin? I am a heretic? So are you! There is no difference."

Hot tears rolled down Ambrose's cheeks and his heart ached. Shame washed over him and his mind clouded. He turned and, in that moment, thought only to cast himself into the depths of the watery chasm below, to be free from all memory. He had never felt so exposed; the eyes of judgment—those of Killian and Silas and yes, God—were upon him. He longed to hide but couldn't look away. In a haze, he saw the blur of Stephan staring down. And beside was a figure, shrouded in black shadow, its red eyes glowing.

"You are in league with devils!" Ambrose cried.

"Who are you to come before me? You who have forsaken all vows?" Stephan roared. "You have betrayed both of your fathers. Your mortal father lies rotten in the ground, his miserable life wasted on you. Your vows to the Father above are broken, fallen before your self-pity and weak resolve. You took whatever holiness you had and spilled it inside some poor girl. So who are you, Ambrose, to condemn me? Pass judgment not on me but yourself!"

Darkness clouded Ambrose's mind, and he cowered in fear, too overcome to move.

"But we're all sinners here." Stephan smiled gently. "We're all drinkers of lust and revelers in filth. And I'm no different. We stand apart so others may stand closer. That is our fate, to not meet God until the very end. We stoke the purifying fires. You don't know this yet, but it is true. You stand beside me in that fire, even now. Can you not feel its warmth, the anguish in your heart? Can you feel it burn away your sin? Burn away your heartache and confusion? Your loss and fear? Do you see? It is your salvation. Come with me and I will show you the way. Trust me, and look on me with love, as you once did."

"Don't listen, Ambrose!" Silas shook him. "Don't let him into your mind!"

Ambrose blinked, his mind clouded and dark. Stephan towered above, and somewhere, far away, Silas's voice called to him.

"Quomodo cecidisti de caelo Lucifer!" Ambrose gasped. *"Ad infernum detraheris in profundum laci!"*

"Fool!" Stephan sneered. "Hell is not so deep as you think. And not so hard to leave."

Stephan turned to Silas and Ambrose fell to his knees, cold sweat upon his brow, as the bitter fog of the spell faded.

"Oh Silvanus, ever the man apart," he went on, "doomed to wander the wastes alone, unloved and unwanted. What a life is yours? Empty days and bitter nights, waiting for your pitiful end. What sorry comfort do you take in those desperate, black hours, only to wander in the judging light of day, yet again?"

"So says the man hiding in the shadows, creeping amongst the dead," Silas sneered.

Stephan laughed, cruel and mocking. "I feel no shame."

Their eyes met and Silas swayed suddenly. He clenched his jaw and grimaced, cold beads of sweat glistening as Stephan's eyes bore into him.

"Ethan would be a man now," Stephan said. "A man, grown and strong, with a family of his own. That is, if he hadn't slipped through your fingers. Do you think of him still? Do you even remember his face? Or the look in his eyes as he was swallowed by those salty waves, his small warm body food for cold fish?"

Silas gave a cry and fell, staggering.

"And your wife, your lovely wife Hannah, who doted over you so, who waited ever for your return as you lost yourself to drink and loathing. Do you think of her, who died lonely and brokenhearted, languishing in the squalor of the factory houses? There is no redemption for you!" Stephan said. "You are damned like the rest. How many years before the blackness takes you, waiting and waiting, every day as miserable as the last?"

Silas dropped the lantern. It fell, clattering on its side and hissing as the cold water snuffed its tiny flame. He raised his hands to his sobbing face, the cylinder of the revolver pressed against his cheek as waves of tremor washed over him. He grew ghastly white and a wail rose from deep within his anguished chest. He wept, fallen in despair at Stephan's words.

"You could end it," Stephan said. "You could make it all go away. No one would fault you. A simple click and nothing more. No more pain. Pull the trigger."

Silas trembled and his eyes rolled as if in a dream. Slowly he lifted the gun, the polished barrel turning toward his temple. He shook, fighting and shaking, as his finger grew white around the trigger. Ambrose screamed, but there was no sound. Some force froze him to the ground and stole his voice. He could only watch in horror as Silas turned the gun on himself, and in his mind he saw the man's head explode like Goodie Gudmund's that fateful night.

Silas closed his eyes, pressing the tears down his cheeks, and sighed. His chest fell and he squeezed.

Pop!

His hand jumped as red flame shot from the barrel. With his last ounce of strength, he turned the gun on the bishop. Rocks exploded in a cloud of dust and gravel, the boom echoing in the chasm below and rushing up to meet them again and again. The spell was shattered, and Ambrose let out a cry, grabbing Silas and pulling him to the ground, while Stephan clasped his hands and cackled.

Killian pointed. "Can you not see the demon behind you?" he shrieked.

Swirls of smoke faded into the darkness as they looked, blending with the shadow. "Fool!" Stephan said. "Who serves who? *Occurrent daemonia onocentauris et pilosus clamabit alter ad alterum. And the demons and foul and unholy creatures of the earth and the hells shall meet and the wild goats and beasts shall cry out to one another!"*

Stephan now turned his gaze to Killian, and the young priest stepped back in fear as the man's cold eyes pierced him. "We are all demons here, boy! Death is on your hands. Never forget that. You gave yourself to wrath, blood boiling in your veins and a club in your hand. You crushed his skull. You stared into lifeless eyes in the cold light of the moon." He smiled, cruel and mocking. "That sad funeral wasn't for Winfried—it was for you. Did you think it absolved you? Your faith is a lie. What would your uncle Walter think of you? May your robes strangle you in your sleep, their weave so much stronger than your weak heart!"

Killian struggled to look away but couldn't. His heart sank, twisted in guilt and shame, and he longed only to die. Stephan smiled down in cold satisfaction as his poisoned words wormed their way into their hearts.

Black vapors like smoke swirled and wreathed his bony frame as the shadowy figure beside whispered in his ear and the stone trembled at its fell voice, as if groaning from deep and fiery depths.

Although Ambrose couldn't hear the words, the sound filled him with terror, sapping his strength. "How have you become this evil thing?" he cried.

Stephan laughed. "Your life is tempered with sorrow and doubt and loss. One could say you are branded with a certain mark. You are a man of your time. Of the three, I thought at least you had potential. You are ripe for the wisdom I have to share. If you would only give in.

"I was there when Pius fled Rome. When the revolutionaries fired their cannons upon the Quirinal. Did you not know? Of course not! You were hiding in Konstanz. I saw him flee—our pope—disguised and under the cover of darkness. In that moment I saw how weak faith is. And when the cannonballs crashed against those stone walls and the doors splintered open, I stood with my brothers of the cloth in line before that angry mob. They vowed to kill us all! Imagine my shame to see those priests grovel and beg, forsaking their faith and pleading for their worthless lives. Not one stood up to those devils, broken into that holy city.

"In that moment I knew! My eyes were opened and my fear fell away. I knew it was the Devil that furthers God's plan. Not those sycophants. The weak of faith were to be culled and cast away in this glorious moment of truth. The Lord was served by these Devils and I would make myself one of them!

"I grabbed the blade from the executioner's hand and drew it across the neck of the nearest priest myself. I felt his hot blood on my hands. All perished, yet I survived, because I made myself a devil—a devil to do the Lord's work. To cleanse the world of weakness and sin."

Lines of sadness spread across his withered face and he frowned. "I am done with all of you. Should any of you have such strength as may serve the Lord, I will guide you. If not, let the dead take you."

He stepped back, red robes melting into the shadow beyond and, with him, the demon. Ambrose blinked as wisps and swirls of thick smoke faded, leaving only bare wall behind. They stood slowly, waking from the god-awful dream of Stephan's spell. Ambrose strained but couldn't remember what had happened, his memory dim and hazy. Silas checked the cylinder and frowned in confusion; only five bullets.

"Did I fire?" he said. "I remember firing."

"Where's Stephan?" Ambrose said. "Where did he go?"

Rocks clattered above and the trio whirled. Shadows danced like hidden figures, darting behind the rocks. The hair stood on the back of Ambrose's neck and he drew his blade. Something splashed, close, but hidden and confused by echoes and the rush of water below.

"Something's here!" Silas exclaimed.

A wail rose, dry and wretched. They turned, but too late, as a black shape leapt from the darkness. Silas shrieked as it fell upon him, while Ambrose flailed at the man's side, grasping and pulling at the thing as his companion thrashed and fought.

Hands and limbs struck in a flurry of blows. Ambrose fell, grasping and pulling as Silas swung round. A claw swiped in the darkness, and sharp pain seared Ambrose's arm. Hot blood ran freely and he fell to the ground in a cry, scraps of gray fabric in his hands.

"Get this thing off me!" Silas cried.

The dark figure writhed and squirmed, its limbs wriggling as its mouth snapped, teeth sharp and long. Silas pushed with all his might against the beast as it clawed into his flesh, dragging his neck closer. Ambrose struck at the creature as Silas staggered. The blade met hard skin, like leather, before piercing deeper. The monster screamed, and a blur flashed as searing pain tore through Ambrose's cheek.

Silas grabbed the thing by scraps of tattered dress and cast it against the wall. It turned on all fours, biting and snapping. Snarls of ratted yellow hair fell across its withered face, hiding its dead eyes, and a soiled dress hung from its skeletal frame.

"Shoot it!" Killian cried.

"That won't work!" Silas said.

"Shoot it in the head!"

"It's dead. It doesn't have a mind anymore!"

"Then why did you bring the gun?" Ambrose said.

"For you, if you can't figure this out!" Silas cried. "There's two of you. One of you be a goddamn priest!"

"How?"

"Say a fucking prayer, Ambrose!" Silas commanded. "Say anything!"

The *nachzehrer* crouched, ready to spring, and Silas circled, gleaming blade in hand. Killian dropped to his knees, and the knife clattered on the floor as he grasped the cross at his neck. Ambrose dragged the young priest away, crying out, "Help us, Lord, in our hour of need!" But the creature only laughed.

It pounced again, a flash of black shadow falling upon Silas. Cold steel glinted, whistling through the air. Vicious teeth snapped, its hissing breath fetid and rotten, like death itself. Silas wheezed and fell, the *nachzehrer* leaping from his chest as claws whirled through the icy air.

Killian hit the ground hard as the thing fell upon him, tearing and ripping. A shriek of pain pierced the air as the *nachzehrer's* desiccated hand touched the cross at his neck, and with a wraithlike howl, it leapt and was gone, hidden in the rocks, the smell of burned and rotten flesh suffusing the air around them.

"Don't lose it!" Silas screamed. "Don't lose it in the dark!"

They circled, back-to-back, eyes darting at every shadow or flicker of light.

"How do we kill it?" Ambrose asked Silas. "And don't tell me by being a priest!"

"Stab it in the heart, while I try to cut its head off!" Silas said. "Just hack at the goddamn thing! Keep it away from your neck! And Killian, goddamn it, I told you not to drop your blade!"

Killian hurriedly grabbed the blade from the ground and held it awkwardly in front of him, as the scrape of claws skittered around them, scurrying and hiding among the rocks. A face peered from behind, dead eyes dull and gray, staring at them, unseeing. Ratted hair, thick with old blood and filth, fell upon gaunt cheeks that stretched as the hideous mouth opened, black and cavernous, a stiff tongue extending. One hand inched forward, then another. The skulking form grew close, sniffing, licking its lips at the iron in the air. Blood dripped everywhere, turning cold as it ran down Ambrose's arm and cheek and soaking and glistening in Killian's robes. Silas panted, exhausted, his face and neck a hatchwork of tears and gashes. The revenant crouched, dead muscles quivering as they tensed and gathered. Silas raised his blade.

Ambrose's hands trembled as he reached for the cross at his neck yet again.

"Whatever you say," Silas said, "you have to believe!"

Ambrose's finger felt the soft cloth of the talisman. It wasn't what he sought, but in that moment, a strange courage welled in him. He held his blade aloft as the thing pounced.

"Sub tuum praesidium confugimus, Sancta Dei Genitrix!" Ambrose cried.

The *nachzehrer* staggered in mid jump, falling to the ground in a daze. Silas swung. His bright blade plunged into its chest as blood flowed from the wound. The creature glared, shaking its head as if dazed, before crouching again, ready to spring.

"Nostras deprecationes ne despicias in necessitatibus nostris, sed a periculis cunctis libera nos semper!"

The creature stumbled again. Silas hacked as feeble arms rose, batting and clawing. It wailed a bloodcurdling scream that echoed in the cavern, piercing the men's ears. Silas struck again as it lunged, its teeth sinking and tearing into the man's arm as he shrieked in pain.

"Virgo gloriosa et benedicta!"

Silas swung the blade, heaving and gasping, cutting deeply and hacking again and again, in desperate swings as the *nachzehrer* hissed and clawed. Finally it sank to the ground and did not rise again.

They collapsed. The *nachzehrer's* head lay on the ground before them, its brittle yellow hair tangled between Silas's fingers.

"Jesus Christ!" Ambrose cried.

"Do you have a coin?" Silas asked. "It doesn't have to be much. A half cent will do."

Ambrose handed him a half penny from the folds of his robe. Silas opened the monster's leathery mouth and placed it on its gray tongue, then carefully closed it again.

"Can't forget that. That's the most important part." Silas nodded. "Charon's obol. To pay the ferryman of the dead. Of course, she's already dead; in this case, it just keeps her that way. You only have a little time before she'll come back to life. Now let's push the body over the chasm."

"Will that work?" asked Ambrose.

"I have no idea," Silas replied. "Now give me a hand. Killian, stop staring at your navel; get up and help." But the young priest hugged his knees and shook against the rock, refusing to move.

Silas and Ambrose grabbed the body. Its leathery skin was tough in their hands, and blood trailed along the rocks as they dragged the corpse to the side of the chasm.

"One, two, three, heave!"

The body plunged into the darkness below, its dress fluttering as it fell. They listened, ears to the edge, but no splash or thump came from below.

"Well, that's the end of that." Silas dusted off his hat and wiped the blood from his face.

The cavern was still. Where Stephan had gone, they could not say. The red flames of the lanterns flickered against the rock, but no other creatures stirred, and Ambrose grew suddenly aware of the pain of his wounds. The gash in his arm burned like fire, and sticky blood grew dry in his fingers. His cheek throbbed, hot and fevered. Silas and Killian looked no better.

Ambrose knelt. "Killian, are you all right?"

They examined the young priest, peeling back the shreds of his cassock to reveal the cuts and gashes across his chest and arms.

"Doesn't look too deep," Silas said. "You'll live. But best clean the wound. Wounds from the dead are liable to make you mighty sick." He reached into his bag and pulled out a bottle. "Killian, look at that!"

The young priest turned quickly and Silas doused his chest in whiskey.

"Damn it!" he cried.

"There," Silas said. "All better. All right, Ambrose, you're next."

Their wounds burned like fire from the liquor, and the two priests winced and cursed.

"Your plan didn't work, Ambrose," Silas said.

"How could it be Stephan?" Ambrose said. "My father's friend. The man I *loved* like a father?" He hung his head in anguish. His childhood memories were poisoned, those moments of joy now painful. The man who had inspired him in faith and brought him to the priesthood had betrayed them all. A bitter doubt grew in his heart. How could the bishop have fallen so far? Had it all been a lie?

"What about the demon?" asked Killian. "I can barely remember what happened, but I'm left with an awful feeling. And I know what I saw!"

"I'd wager it all was a trick of the mind," Silas said. "That forgetfulness is a hallmark of such things."

"But I saw it!" Killian protested.

Silas gave him a knowing look. "We all did. That's the trick. But to hell with this bishop. He can wait until I've had a smoke."

Soon puffs of white filled the air. Silas passed the pipe around, and Ambrose breathed the hot smoke into his lungs, chasing away the cold dampness. They stared at the ground for many long moments. Ambrose ached, his body torn and utterly fatigued. In the darkness, the strength of his spirit was gone, his faith finally spent. There was nothing more to hold on to. Silas and Killian whispered to each other; Silas doing his best to fill the young priest with courage. They left Ambrose alone; something in his eyes warned them to stay away. But as Ambrose stared into the black nothingness, a hot anger welled inside—a feeling he'd never felt before. His veins coursed with a fire as something awoke.

He stared at the mortician's blade. It was sharp—beyond sharp. He didn't know why, but he drew it across his arm, watching the blood well from his skin and drip onto the cold floor, as Silas and Killian watched in horror.

"I'm ready," he said.

✠

CHAPTER 34

My Will Is Not My Own

December 2, 1859

A narrow path led to the ledge above, twisting around the rocks and stalagmites. Killian stayed below, petrified and refusing to move, his white face buried in his knees. Ambrose and Silas ascended the rocky stairs. White crystal shone in mineral pools, eons of drops dripping from above. They slipped on the slick rock, falling occasionally and splashing in shallow water. Cold sweat swept over him in waves and his sight grew dizzy. "Focus on your breath." Silas grabbed his shoulders and shook him. "Don't let your mind wander to dark places. Say a prayer. Or keep hold of your cross. Whatever you need to do, do it."

Ambrose seethed in silence. It was all Stephen: the man who had been as close as a father. It was Stephan all along. It was Stephan who had tormented the town and twisted their faith with false teachings, worming his way into the minds of Anselm and Florian and Winfried. It was Stephan who had drawn the vile *inaemehkiwak*—and who knows what else—towards him. It was Stephan who raised Issa from the dead. It was Stephan who killed Tobias. *How could any of this be?* A blind rage passed over Ambrose. God had given his power through that black magic. What kind of God would desire a servant so evil?

The ledge opened before them. They could see now the old books in holes and pockets in the stone, their dark covers etched and drawn in strange symbols and words. Below they spied a desk littered with odd bottles and vials, along with herbs and many-colored stones.

"Wait!" Silas grabbed Ambrose's arm. On the floor were rings drawn in fine powder and candles had been set to form the points of a star.

"What is that?" Ambrose asked.

Silas held the powder to his tongue. "Salt and ash. A summoning circle!" I've read of this but never seen it. But where is the summoner? And more important, where is the summoned?"

They looked around in the dim light. Bare rock stretched as far as the ledge, leaving no other way up or down. They turned about, but nothing stirred in the darkness.

"There's no way out," Silas said.

Killian looked up from below, still cowering and hugging his knees. "Is it over?" he called.

"Is it over?" a voice hissed. "It has only just begun!"

As if from nowhere, sulphury smoke billowed and wreathed in the circle. A brazier of flame atop a goat skin appeared where none had been before. Stephan emerged from the shadows, his red robes taking shape before their eyes. He stood before the brazier, and in his right hand was his sword bound with hazel.

Roiling wisps of shadow swirled beside him, smoky and inky as they took the vague form of a man or demon. Two glowing embers were set in a face of smoke, roiling and twisting. Its mouth opened to blackness and its cruel laugh filled the cavern with the stench of brimstone.

"You killed my *nachzehrer,*" Stephan snarled. "Now you will take its place! But first you will die, consumed by wrathful appetite. Let the fires of hell purify your wretched and petty souls. There shall be no mercy for the damned. Now let us pray." He pointed to Silas. "Come to me, my child."

Silas's face twisted and strained as a hidden force compelled him. His feet stepped forward against his will, inching toward the circle. Panic lit his wide eyes and sweat beaded off his brow. "Ambrose!" he shouted.

"Stephan, let this evil go!" Ambrose cried. "Renounce this madness! Renounce it all! Come back with me! Let us leave this place! If you loved my father, leave now!"

"It is the simplest lesson, yet you will not learn," Stephan said. "Your self-righteousness is sickening. *As a dog returneth to its vomit, so a fool to his folly*. And so you shall perish in the flame, your sin consumed in hellish fire. But despair not, for when the flames lick your heart and burn your soul, know you shall be reborn as something pure. Watch now, the cleansing of such sin in this one you would call a friend."

Stephan struck the roiling smoke with his sword. Metal flashed and gleamed and flame and spark erupted, singeing the ends of hazel in red ember. Hideous howls of pain filled the cavern from the gaping maw of smoke.

"Bind him!" Stephan commanded. "Bind him and burn him! *Coniuro vos daemon Flauros! Relige et incende!*"

The cavern rumbled. Stone shook and trembled as the demon strode across the stone, hooves of smoke striking the floor. Its ember-red eyes burned in hunger, and it raised a clawed hand, beckoning to Silas. It opened its smoky mouth and a tongue of red flame flicked, as it hissed in an ancient tongue, *"Lisróf!"*

Silas groaned in sudden pain and his face grew tight in panic. The smell of burning hair wove through the air as the ends of his long hair and beard smoked white before breaking into bursts of yellow flame. The man's skin turned red as fire popped around him, singeing hat and jacket.

"Ambrose!" he screamed. "I hope you've thought of something useful from that good book of yours! It would be nice to hear from your God sometime soon!"

"Sile!" Stephan cried. He cackled, clasping his hands in glee as Silas's mouth clamped shut. Smoke billowed from his nose and the man's eyes pleaded as the flames burned in his hair and took to his clothes.

Ambrose's heart thrummed wildly and the room blurred. The rank smell of sulfur and burned hair and flesh filled the air, acrid and sick in his nose, and he stumbled back, trying to right himself. In a blur, the demon took form in his mind, a black shape, muscled and thick, amidst a haze of smoke, its red eyes piercing and boring into him. He couldn't look away; the eyes were so familiar. *How do I know this thing?* An intention took form that was not his own. Words rang in his mind, a voice, clear like rolling thunder: the demon's voice. *Do it!* He looked up to see Stephan smiling in sick laughter, fuzzy in the distance and unaware. *Do it!* The demon commanded again.

His feet stepped forward, of their own accord, the voice willing them on. Ambrose knew it wasn't his will, but he didn't resist. In his anger, his will and the demon's were aligned. He began to run, faster and faster. Hard stone gritted and scraped as he passed the circle below, his boots scattering the ash and salt. The demon turned in wicked smile as fear suddenly spread across the bishop's face.

"No!" Stephan cried. "Stop him!"

The demon turned to give chase but was too slow.

"What are you doing? Stop him! Why don't you hurry?"

It was too late. Ambrose crashed into Stephan, throwing the bony man to the floor. In an instant, the brazier was snuffed out and the horrid sounds of demonic laughter filled the cavern. Silas fell to the floor, and the flames were extinguished in puffs of smoke as he was released from its grasp.

Desperately Stephan clawed his way back to the goat skin, but it was too late. The demon whirled in smoke before him as panic set on his face and he raised his arms, shrieking, "Stop! Stop! I command you! Return to the hell from which you came!" He swung his sword, but the blade passed through the smoke with ease and the demon laughed in mockery. "Stop! Stop!"

"Ite in pace! Ite in pace!" Stephan cried. *"Asyel, Castiel, Lamsiyel, Rabam, Erlain, Elam, Betlam, ego vos coniuro! In nomine Patris, et Filii at Spiritus Sancti!"* He swung again but struck nothing.

The demon drew near to whisper in his ear, and it's flaming tongue hissed, "They do not care."

The hideous form billowed, dissolving before them. Stephan shrank, his arms outstretched as the blackness entered him, seeping into his body. Hideous expressions moved across his features like a legion of faces beneath his own. Moaning and fighting, he struggled to stand. Suddenly light lit his eyes in infernal fire and his flesh turned red as if burning.

"Stephan!" Ambrose cried. "Out! Out! I cast thee out, demon! In the name of Jesus Christ, our Lord and God, Mary and Michael, I cast thee out!"

Stephan turned, his gaunt face red and glowing; his robes smoldered as he rose. But it was no longer Stephan. Possessed eyes stared out at Ambrose, malevolent and otherworldly, a twisted smile on his face.

Before he could think, Silas knocked Ambrose out of the way. He charged, grabbing Stephan's robes in fury and dragging with all his might. Black smoke rose around him as he pulled, and Stephan grasped and struggled as the demon fought to control its new body. The ledge neared and Silas braced and hurled him with all his might. Darkness swallowed as Stephan plummeted into the depths, two points of light staring back from the darkness. Haunting laughter mixed with the roar of the water below then was gone.

Silas and the two priests burst out of the cave into the cold winter dusk. The setting sun lit their faces, warm and cheery after so much darkness, and the dim light was dazzling as they stood blinking. The warm smell of smoke rose to greet them, and below, a roaring fire of old logs danced merrily amidst the lengthening shadows of the cedars. Tears of joy streamed down Ambrose's cheeks, and his heart ached as if it might burst. Silas panted behind, dragging Killian with him.

"You've still got your strength, boy. Now shake yourself off and use it. I can't carry you through these woods all the way back to town." He leaned Killian against the rock wall and breathed the cold air. The chill breeze on his bare and blistered head made him smile, and Ambrose saw that all that was left of his hair were tufts of singed stubble sticking out here and there, and his leather coat hung cracked and charred, ash falling as he moved.

"Are you all right?" asked Ambrose.

"Fine." He spat blood. "Never better. Why?"

"It's just…" Ambrose shook his head. "No reason…"

"Did you grab those books from the cavern?" Silas asked. "Tell me you didn't leave them in there."

"They're here." He opened his bag, showing the black bindings and tattered edges, stuffed among his few possessions. "But I don't know why you want them."

"They're not for me. They're for you. If I'm not mistaken, you'll be needing them."

Ambrose looked at him, brow pinched, but before he could speak, a voice called from below.

"Ho! You return after all! I was just about to leave! And here I thought King Henry would have a new owner. But alas, I have to endure your pleasant company for some time more, eh? But tell me, what did you bring me?"

"Shut up and get the dynamite!" Silas said.

"Oh, you are an awful man!" the coachman said, laughing. "No appreciation."

They stuck the red sticks in the walls and cracks. The fuses hissed and crackled, fire racing as Jean-Émile and Silas leapt, running down the path to the marsh below.

"I don't know what else is in there," Silas called. "And I don't want to find out! Cross your fingers we can close this hole!"

The bluff side burst in a great crack of sound, dust and stone showering the ground around them. Split rock crashed upon itself, filling the hole in a pile of rubble, the boom echoing off the bluff and extending into the distance.

"Well, that's that!" Silas said as the last pebbles bounced at their feet. "That was unexpected!"

Killian whirled suddenly, eyes fierce with anger. "I thought you said there was no such thing as demons!"

"I said there was no such thing as possession!" Silas said, "But it's true. I didn't expect this. I'm sorry, Killian. I don't always get it right. But listen,"—he patted the young priest on the shoulder—"You're alive! You made it! Who else can say they faced a demon and walked away. You didn't even piss your pants!"

Killian scowled and turned. "Let's just go."

"Yes. I think that is not such a bad idea. Your tales will have to wait," Jean-Émile said. "Night is coming quick and we have a walk ahead of us, unless you prefer the comfort of this beautiful swamp. Lucky, though, the way back should prove quicker."

"Right, let's buck up. And thank our lucky stars!" Silas grinned. "Somewhere ahead, there's a hot meal and warm bed waiting for each of us."

CHAPTER 35

Wherever the Line Takes Us

December 4, 1859

T he next morning found them at the Westen House. The early sun streamed through leaded windows, hopeful and bright, falling on the polished oak table in squares of yellow. Steam rose off hot plates, the air rich with the nutty sweetness of griddle cakes and bacon. Hot tea steeped in a giant pot, toasty brown in white cups. They were sore and bruised but laughed in good humor. Killian wore his spare traveling clothes, his cassock rent and torn beyond use, while Ambrose sat in the giant shirt and pants bought from Mr. Fessler. Only Jean-Émile looked even remotely respectable in his old trousers and coachmen's jacket. Silas gingerly touched his burned head, wincing. Spying eyes watched from nearby tables, and hushed whispers passed around them as children pointed. But the four of them could only laugh.

Ambrose stared into his tea. "Do you think he's dead?"

Silas shrugged "How could a man survive a fall like that?"

"I suppose the demon took him, in the end anyway," Ambrose said.

"What now?" asked Killian.

"Well, now I suppose you go home," Silas said.

Killian frowned. Lines of sadness passed his face, grooves and wrinkles where there had been none just months before. Ambrose looked at him in pity and remorse.

"What?" Silas said. "Aren't you excited?"

Killian nodded. "I am. I'm excited to go back home, to the things I know. I don't understand it here and I don't think I ever will. But I can't help but return with a feeling of shame. I feel like I've done both nothing and terrible things at the same time. I wasn't any help. I doubted the entire time. And I have Winfried's blood on my hands."

"Well, you don't doubt anymore," Silas said. "And as for Winfried, we all have blood on our hands. That's just something you learn to live with."

"I'm not sure I can."

"Well, I hate to say it, but you have an entire lifetime to figure it out, my boy."

"So that's it then?" Killian said. "We just learn to live with it?"

"That's it."

"Well, then I guess there's nothing more to do than move on."

"If you hurry, you can catch the train to Fond du Lac and from there, Chicago," Jean-Émile said. "It leaves in half an hour, if it's on time."

"Well, I suppose now is as good a time as ever," said Killian. "Ambrose, are you ready?"

Ambrose sighed. His decision broke his heart, but he knew he had no choice. "I'm not going with you, Killian."

"What do you mean?" the young priest cried. "You did what you set out to do. What more is there? The *nachzehrer* is ended. Stephan is dead. You knocked him out of the circle yourself. You brought an end to all this. You freed St. Gregory, even if no one will ever know. Don't you deserve to come back?"

"It wasn't me." Ambrose shook his head. "It wasn't my power that pushed Stephan in the end. But it wasn't God working through me, either. I'm not the man who left La Havre only a half year ago. I don't know what I am anymore. I can't go back. There's nothing for me to go back to. My mother and sister would never recognize me. I would only bring them pain. Here is my report." He handed Killian the bound ledger from his bag. "The last pages are blank. Fill them in with whatever you need to. Tell them what happened. But tell them I died."

"No, Ambrose!" Killian slammed his fist on the table. The china shook and rattled and the Friday morning crowd stared at him, annoyed and alarmed. "After all that's happened? You must come back! What about your faith?"

"I'm sorry," he said. "I don't know if I can find it any anymore."

Killian looked down, his eyes blurred with tears. "So I've lost everyone."

"You best hurry, my boy," Jean-Émile said. "Or you will miss your train. Then you'll lose yourself too. Don't stay where you don't belong."

Killian rose and embraced Ambrose one last time. "I will pray for you," he said.

The sun set on the Hotel St. Gregor, shadows growing long in the streets of St. Gregory. Ambrose rapped softly on the door, standing in the dark hall. The old floor creaked in the room beyond. A yellow lantern flickered beneath the door as soft footsteps approached. There was a moment of hesitation before the handle slowly turned. His heart skipped, quick and anxious, and he suddenly longed to leave. What right did he have to stand before her now?

The door opened a crack, and a pale face of porcelain-white stared back, hazel eyes glittering in the light. Annaliese looked away in disdain.

"I didn't know where I'd find you." Ambrose's voice shook. "I thought maybe you were here… I mean, I hoped not… But I didn't know where else to look."

"Where else would I be?" she scoffed. "There's no home in this town for a girl who lays down with a priest."

"I'm sorry," he said.

"I made my choice. Don't concern yourself with me. Anyway, did you do what you needed to do?"

"Yes," he said. "I think I finally did."

"Then where are your robes?"

"I…can't wear them anymore," he said. "I can't go back."

"What are you talking about Ambrose? What about your devotion and faith?"

"There's nothing outside of this room that can save me," he said. "I cannot ask you to forgive me. But if I am not with you, I will wander this world forever lost."

Annaliese's eyes widened and her arms fell to her side, hesitating. She turned, raven hair whirling, staring out the window into the night. Moments passed in heavy silence, the only movement the soft rise and fall of her breath. Ambrose stared after her, his chest tight and aching, desperate for the right words to say, but he knew there were none. There was only bitter silence.

"Where will we go?" she said finally.

He reached out to her. Her skin was soft beneath his hand and he held her close, his head buried against her neck. A wave of tiredness swept over him, such as he had never felt.

"Wherever the line takes us," he whispered.

Ψ

CHAPTER 36

Revelations

December 4, 1859

Anselm sat in the dim light of the moon. The small cell in the attic of the abbey was filled with the musty smell of old and forgotten books, hidden away in the shelves of the secret room—their most precious collection. They must remain hidden and kept safe for the bishop, as they would not last the cold damp of the caves. He ran his hands across the old vellum of a nearby tome. What a shame it would have been to lose such a book. And lose it, they would have, had it been in the caves. He urgently needed to speak to Stephan. They had suffered a great loss at the hands of Ambrose.

He waited long into the night, impatient as the sliver of moon passed the window in its nightly arc. Finally he lit a lantern. The match burst in a flame of sulphury white and the wick took, crackling and sputtering as it grew. The yellow flame chased away the shadows, barely extending beyond the table, yet in the darkness it illuminated a shape in the corner.

"I hadn't heard you come in!" Anselm said. "How long have you been here?"

"Long enough," the voice said. "I like to watch…"

"There is much we need to do. Winfried is dead, as you know. They destroyed our sanctum. How will we bring the Lord's vision into being now?"

"Winfried has risen," it said. "Nothing is lost."

"But they destroyed our sanctum. That wicked Ambrose. We are weakened. After the commission, it will take but a single wrong remark to rouse Valentine's suspicion. Then we will be for naught."

"Have you so little faith?" it said. "Everything is proceeding according to plan."

"How can you say that?" asked Anselm. "We are nearly exposed."

He paused. Something wasn't right. He studied the man in the corner, bringing his lamp closer.

"You are not Stephan!" he said.

The man looked like Stephan, but he was not. His eyes glowed with a light all their own, lit with an infernal fire, and his skin smoldered red, as if burning.

"The plans do not change," it said. "The trap is set."

"The plans?"

"My plans," it said. "For my plans are different than yours."

"What are you?" Anselm cried.

"Do you not know?" it said. "I am what you prayed for."

Anselm recoiled, stepping back.

"Are you afraid?" it said curiously. It rose and stood before him, letting its robes fall to the floor. Anselm could see the fire burning within, and he shuddered and shrank.

"Look on me!" it cried. *"For I am fearfully and wonderfully made."*

Thus Ends
Book One of the
St Gregory Archives

For book two updates,
short stories and special content,
join the newsletter.

Explore the world of St Gregory:
charlesharlanboehler.com

Please leave a review!

Charles Harlan Boehler

Irving and Poe taught me to read. Father Gilsdorf taught me to write. At least he tried - I wasn't the best student. I'd like to think I'm well-rounded. I've had a lot of character building experiences in life, and I've always taken great pains to make sure those experiences have never made any money; after all being poor is character building, and I am nothing if not committed. I grew up subsistence farming in the savage wilds of the American Heartland, pre-internet. As a toddler I lived in a haunted Catholic Preparatory school and am likely haunted myself. I have a degree in German Historical Linguistics, that I am not putting to any sort of good use. I lived in a monastery as a Zen Buddhist monk for several years. I've gotten sick in third-world countries and robbed in first-world ones. I was propositioned to smuggle hash from Nepal into Germany by a Nepalese "movie star" who owned a gem shop in Kathmandu (I declined). I maintained a malaria mosquito colony (for research) and refilled ATM machines, plainclothes, with a duffle bag stuffed with $60k in twenty-note bills in downtown Los Angeles. I was locked into the Père Lachaise Cemetery overnight in Paris looking for Oscar Wilde's grave (I didn't find it). I've studied eclectic and traditional systems of medicine and almost killed myself several times. I've done some stuff I shouldn't write about, but I've never been to jail, thankfully. Much of this time, I was a drunk. I'm not proud or embarrassed by any of this. There's a line from a song by The Brian Jonestown Massacre, "I know myself. I feel no shame. No shame at all."